The Tapes
of Wrath

Barry Cain

Published 2018 by Hornet Books
Text © Barry Cain 2018
This work © Hornet Books Ltd
ISBN 978-0-9957658-3-2

Cover illustration: Mark Manning aka Zodiac Mindwarp
Cover design: Neil MacKenzie Matthews, Pat Gibbon
and David Roberts
Proof reader: Suzannah Young

'Storm in a Teacup', words and music by writers
Lynsey De Paul and Ron Roker ©
Reproduced by permission of Sony/ATV Music (UK) Publishing
Limited, London, W1F 9LD.
Special thanks to Danny Rubin for granting permission to use his
words from the screenplay of *Groundhog Day*.
Also, special thanks to Ernest Thompson for granting permission to
use his words from the screenplay of *On Golden Pond*.
All reasonable effort has been made to trace the copyright owners
of any and all of the material in this book. In the event of an
omission, many apologies, and if you are the copyright owner,
please get in touch.

Printed by CPI Group (UK) Ltd, Croydon CR0 4YY

Hornet Books
www.hornetbooks.com
info@hornetbooks.com

Follow us on Facebook
www.Facebook.com/HornetBooksPublishing/

DEDICATION

This book is dedicated to my parents, Pat and Betty, who passed away within a few days of each other in 2012, a year after they celebrated their diamond wedding anniversary and received a telegram from the Queen.

It's also dedicated to the love of my life–Dina–and my three sons, Paul, Andrew and Elliot, who mean the world to me.

I wrote this while I watched my parents wither and die. The last time I saw them together was at the undertaker's–their coffins were side by side and open. Alone, I touched both their faces at the same time and wept like a child.

Never got over that one.

Although *The Tapes Of Wrath* is fiction, I wanted to stamp the fabrications that lie herein with a seal of authenticity by writing about things I've experienced first-hand and then twisting them to fit–I am an only child, I did work for *The Citizen* in Gloucester, I have written about music and travel, I do live in North London. And *Amadeus* is, indeed, my favourite film. Oh, and I did once meet a brunette in The Unicorn in Stepney Green when I was twenty. I often wonder what happened to her.

But I can assure you I've never smeared coke on my knob, I've never been unfaithful, I don't smoke industrial amounts of skunk–have you seen the price of an ounce?–and I don't suffer from premature ejac...

Prologue

Detective Constable Tom Evans liked his new job.

He liked the fact he could wear jeans to work and didn't have to shave every morning. He liked the fact that his days of chasing drunk drivers down dark country lanes across North Wales were over.

He liked the fact he was in London, patrolling the streets in unmarked cars and hunting villains of every race, creed and colour. Okay, so he'd only been in town for less than a week and hadn't yet left his desk, but Tom liked the fact that adventure lay just around the corner.

He also liked the fact that it was Friday night and he'd been given the weekend off. He had a dinner date with a bunch of old buddies who'd similarly swapped the bright lights of Rhyl and Bangor for the big city after university. They were celebrating his first week as a Londoner and it was his firm intention to get hammered.

It was 6.15pm when he started to tidy his desk.

'DC Evans?'

Tom turned around and was confronted by a tall, thickset man, aged about 45. He had a shock of black hair, flecked with grey, and a short, sharp moustache–and when he smiled his cheeks swelled like a hamster with a hoard. He looked like the dictator of a junta on the other side of the world.

He sat on the edge of Tom's desk.

'Yes?'

'I'm Detective Superintendent Choudhury. How they treating you?'

'I've only been here a week, sir. It's pretty good, so far.'

'Wait until next week. A little birdie tells me you have a first in English Literature from St. Andrews.'

'Your little birdie is correct.'

'Wow, a Welshman studying English at a Scottish university.'

'And my mother's from Belfast.'

'You really are a true Brit.'

DS Choudhury's accent was Hackney, but his words were Hampstead, the perfect combination for success in the modern-day police force.

'What can I do for you, sir?'

'That same birdie also told me you're a free man over the weekend.'

'That's a pretty good informant you have there. Any chance I could have access?'

DS Choudhury ignored the question. 'I'd appreciate it if you utilised that time by wrapping your critical faculties around this for me.'

He placed a USB stick into Tom's hand.

'What is it?'

'A book of around 80,000 words. I'm sure a man with your education can manage that.'

'Depends on what sort of book.'

'Seems to be a novel of some kind. It was found on the body of a shooting victim at a house in Highbury. There were two other bodies at the scene. All were white males and it appears they were related.

'One was aged around thirty, one was in his late fifties and the other was knocking a hundred with a hole in his face the size of a melon. It was like a scene from a Coen Brothers movie. The middle guy had the USB stick in the small front pocket of his jeans. His name was Adam Tate. The old man was probably his father, Bobby, and the younger guy probably his son, Ben.'

'Weird.'

'You said it. Weirder still, it looks like Adam shot the other two before turning the gun on himself.'

'His father *and* his son?' Tom was shocked.

'Appears so.'

'Some kind of family feud?'

'Well it certainly wasn't some kind of *Family*-fucking-*Fortunes*. I thought you were supposed to be clever. Anyway, I want you to read it, pronto, and see if it throws any light on the case. I haven't the time and I don't know a living soul who could read 800 words over a weekend, let alone 80,000.

'Here's my card. Ring me on Monday with your thoughts. There's only one file, *Sheds4*. Shouldn't be too difficult to find for a scholar like your good self.'

'I'm betting you're a bit of a scholar yourself, sir.'

'A first in Chemistry from Imperial.'

'And *you* became a copper?'

'And you became a copper?'

'Yes, but, Chemistry?'

'Yes, but, English Literature?

'Yes, but, Chemistry?'

'I'll tell you about it someday. Let's just say I was the world's first test tube bobby. Now, if you don't mind, I've a hot date with a chicken vindaloo and a weekend of golf beckons. Oh, and don't get too pissed tonight.'

'I see the walls have ears.'

'Well, this is a police station. Goodnight, DC Evans. Sweet dreams.'

Tom slipped the memory stick into the small front pocket of his jeans before hitting the town and getting lagged-up on Hoegaarden and JD and Coke.

The next afternoon, at his newly-rented flat, he opened the file on his laptop.

He liked the oddness of the title and recognised the quote at the beginning. And something about the author's name rang a bell.

That's it! Adam Tate. He wrote *Like Clockwork*, that Tom read when he was 13. He remembered it had had a profound effect on him for a week or two.

He started to read…

FUCK THE SHEDS

A Gangster's Revenge

By Adam Tate

PART ONE

Happy the man, and happy he alone,
He who can call today his own:
He who, secure within, can say,
Tomorrow do thy worst, for I have lived today.
Be fair or foul or rain or shine,
The joys I have possessed, in spite of fate, are mine.
Not Heaven itself upon the past has power,
But what has been has been, and I have had my hour.
(Horace, from *Odes.*
Translation by Dryden)

CHAPTER 1

Tate & Lyle

He had an itch inside.
Deep inside.

And it was getting deeper every day.

He couldn't get her out of his head. He saw her face everywhere, even in the fleeting blankness of a blink. He was greedy for sleep because she'd be there waiting for him and when he awoke each morning he didn't want to open his eyes because she lit up the swirling darkness where all dreams end.

For the second time in his life, Adam Tate was in love so deep and so wide and so crazy, it took his breath away. He wanted to feel her sweet, sweet tongue in his mouth again, coiling itself around him like a snake on heat and pulling them both down through that swirling darkness into a world of light where he would dance with her in eternity.

And that was just the first kiss.

He hadn't felt this way about a woman since he met Laura–and they'd been married over 35 years. Like a screwed-up Indiana Jones, Adam unearthed an emotion long buried by the debris of time, and it was a doozie.

He'd never once been unfaithful in body or mind. Even the odd wank under the bedclothes in the morning, on the rare occasions he woke up with a hard-on, would always end with his wife in his head. He'd tried to imagine other women from movie stars to neighbours, but it was no good. He could only come with his wife when it came to self-abuse.

Until now.

Adam first met Kate at a reception thrown by a cruise company to celebrate the release of a new brochure. He was there in his guise as freelance travel writer and she ran a small PR firm that specialised in hotels, cruise lines and ski resorts.

When he discovered her surname was Lyle, he pointed out that if she went out with him they'd make a sweet couple. She laughed, and Adam hoped to God that it wasn't a sympathy laugh, because she was cute and blonde and young and the proud owner of a rapier-like wit that chilled him to the bones, already shivering under a layer of shit coke and dead skin.

He, on the other hand, was 56 with a headful of grey and a faint dusting of psoriasis scales caressing the shoulders of his black jacket. He wondered if she was just appeasing that gulf of years that separated them. Adam hadn't cared much about his appearance for a long time and it was a little uncomfortable.

They exchanged cards and moved on. He thought about her for a few days and then she was put out with the rest of the garbage in the giant wheelie bin that got him through this passionless play.

Adam Tate was getting old and he knew it.

At first it was the little things. He'd complain about lost TV remotes until he realised the guy who left the control in the bathroom was him. He'd often say, 'Eh?', not because he was deaf but because it bought him time to make sense of the words he'd just heard. It took an eternity to pee. Booze-ups now consisted of three pints of San Miguel shandy and a pub quiz once a week. And then he'd be up four times in the night pissing. Eternally.

Then it was the bigger things like his life, his wife, his kids, his career, sex, haemorrhoids. How would he die? When would he die?

Then it was the biggest things, money and drugs–he was running out of the former and the latter didn't seem to help much anymore. He needed to smoke and snort more these days and it wasn't cheap, hence the dearth of dosh.

Worries come hard in the sad, sweet fifties.

He met Kate again three months later at another cruise reception.

Her hair was longer, her smile was wider, and her eyes made you listen when she spoke.

'Hey, Adam, I've a bone to pick with you. Last time we met, you never told me you wrote *Like Clockwork*.'

'I seem to recall I was too busy making inane jokes about surnames.'

'And as for your name being Tate. I can't believe it never clicked. I read *Clockwork* about 15 years ago when I was 16 and absolutely loved it. But why don't you mention the book on your card?"

'To be honest, it wouldn't mean a thing to most people. I wrote it over a quarter of a century ago.' So, she's 31, he thought.

'But didn't it become a film or something?'

'Kinda. Channel 4 picked it up and ran it over three hour-long episodes, considered shocking at the time.'

'Did you write the script?'

'Kinda. Well, I started to, but couldn't get the hang of it. They sacked me after a week.'

'Still. Make you rich?'

'At that time, kinda, but not mortgage-free rich.'

She was asking all the questions and that was so, so cool.

He could count on the fingers of one hand the number of people he'd met over the last ten years who remembered *Like Clockwork* and certainly nobody as young as Kate.

'Didn't you write any more books?'

Those fingers on that one hand had all asked the same question.

'Two, actually–*Up in the Dumps*?'

Adam waited for a flicker of recognition, but none was forthcoming. He felt like Salieri playing his tunes to the bemused priest in the lunatic asylum at the beginning of *Amadeus*.

'It was about a guy who bets his life savings of a hundred grand on the royal family being ousted within six months. He loses but becomes a celebrity with his own chat show.'

'Can't say I know it.'

Why should she?

Dumps went down in flames, but it was nothing compared to the unmitigated disaster of the next book.

'Then I wrote *Big Boys Don't Cry*, about a guy who reaches seventy and then starts to grow younger by the day.'

'Oh, like *The Curious Case of Benjamin Button*?'

Why don't you just say Mozart and be done with it?

'Yeah. Bad timing. Nobody knew about the F. Scott Fitzgerald short story. Or rather, I didn't know.'

'How did your "about a guy" books do?'

Sharp. Oh, so sharp.

'First one shit, the second one, shittier.'

'Oh well, you've done something most people would give their right arm for.'

'What, have two conversations with you?'

'That goes without saying. No, having your books published and being out there and meeting someone at a party in St. James who read one of them and who happens to think it's all very cool. God, you must be fifty. It never occurred to me.'

'More than that, I'm afraid.' He wished he hadn't said that.

'Sixty? Seventy?'

'Piss off.'

She looked shocked and then laughed that sexy, cloggy laugh of the smoker that Adam, who was partial to the odd cigarette, always found so attractive.

'Do you smoke?' he asked, knowing the answer.

'Yes. Do you fancy one?'

'Absolutely. But what about a fag first?'

It was a *Carry On* line that took him over the edge. As he followed her sexycloggy body out into that misty, autumnal night, Adam Tate kinda knew things would never be the same again...

CHAPTER 2

With a Song in My Heart

The next morning, he found an email from Kate on his laptop.

Good morning, Adam. Lovely to see you again. I'm up for a third conversation if you ever fancy it.

Kx

He didn't know how to approach this. There's no way it could be a come on. She was gorgeous and he was 56, she was sharp and he was 56, she was a woman and he was 56. Married. Two kids. Career in tatters. Both parents still alive and totally dependent on him. Fifty-six.

But Kate read his book when she was sweet 16. Something he wrote when he was 34 and she was ten and she loved it. The age difference was still the same, still vast, but not vast enough to prevent the early stages of a hard-on stalking his M&S boxers.

No, she was just being a friendly PR, that's all. It was her job to be nice. She probably hadn't even read his book. She was after something that definitely didn't involve sex, but what on earth was it?

His contacts? Kate knew ten times more people in the business than he did.

His opinion? He had no opinions about the travel industry. All he ever wanted was the occasional break from his family and a bunch of free meals.

His fashion-sense? Last night he wore a black suit he'd had for eight years, bought from a Greek Cypriot wholesaler in Tottenham for 85 quid. His fake white Versace shirt came courtesy of a fake

Versace shop he found in Kusadasi when the cruise ship he was reviewing was in port.

The Who's 'Substitute' sprang to mind.

Fuck it.

Adam pushed the reply button.

Hi Kate

And it was lovely to see you to. I agree, a third conversation would be good. Obviously, my clock works.

Adam x

As he pushed the send button he noticed the 'to' in the first line without a second 'o'.

She'll think he's a moron.

And what about that stupid last sentence? She wouldn't get it.

He couldn't have written a worse email. What a klutz.

He'd ruined the chance of an assignation with a gorgeous young woman because of a missing 'o' and a lame joke.

She didn't reply.

A few weeks passed. Adam was sitting in front of his laptop playing Hearts on Pogo Games.

Click.

His inbox popped up to 442 virtual sheets of shit that stretched back a year. He checked the sender's address–kate.lyle.lyleassociates@aol.com

Hi Adam

Sorry for not replying earlier. Yes, your clock does work well, for an old geezer. Hey, I've moved into a new flat and I'm back in my beloved Islington. Why don't you bring me a bottle or two of something nice and a few glasses too (notice the extra 'o'?). I only have shitty small ones and I love big ones! That one's for you as I know you like your smut, à la Carry On.

Say next Tuesday? 7?
Kxx

Two kisses.

Hey there, lonely girl
am or pm?
A x

Shit, was that a bit forward?
Click.

7pm, dickhead. And don't forget the something nice with a big one.
Kx

Just the one kiss this time.

Hi Kate
The something nice you already have in abundance. And the only big thing I could bring along would be my unbridled excitement at the prospect of seeing you again.
Come on, ten out of ten for a pair of mature Gorgonzola lines. Or do I really mean it, in which case I'll come empty handed? You'll have to wait and see.
The plot thickens…
Adam

He felt uncomfortable signing off with another x Click.

Yeah, the plot thickens into sickening cheese. I won't let you through the door if you have the unbridled audacity to turn up without a bagful of booze, some fucking big glasses and a song in your heart.
Kate

CHAPTER 3

First impressions

At 7pm on the evening of their third conversation, Adam Tate stood outside a house in Barnsbury Road holding a carrier bag containing two lukewarm bottles of Lanson and another bag with six large glasses and a couple of champagne flutes. He was smoking a joint and wondering what the hell he was doing there. It was insane.

But insanity turned to intrigue as the smoke began to take effect and the night had a thousand eyes...

The entrance to her basement flat was down the side of the house and the pathway lit up in front of him as he set off the security lamp. He felt like an escaping prisoner caught in the spotlight as he walked to the end of the path where the front door was located. By the time she opened the door, he'd been once again engulfed by the November darkness made heavy by the smoke of a million fireworks.

'Hello, gorgeous.' And she is, he thought. My God, she is.

'Hello, celebrated author.'

Adam kissed her on each cheek. Her smell was intoxicating. 'Well, more inebriated than celebrated.'

'Step this way, Mr Tate.'

She wore blue jeans and a white tee shirt blasting RELAX with an eighties bullet and when she laughed her face shone like, well, like a crazy diamond.

He handed her the bag with the champagne. 'Here's the bagful of booze.' Then he handed her the other. 'Here are some "fucking big glasses"–with a bonus. And the song in my heart is 'Can't Take My Eyes Off You'.'

She peered into the first bag. 'Lanson, huh. Very nice. But I was expecting Cristal, at least.'

Kate Lyle was a piece of work, no mistake.

A real piece of work. He kept repeating it. A piece of work. It made him feel safe.

He followed her down the hall, past a lounge on the left and two bedrooms and a bathroom on the right, to the kitchen at the far end. She pointed to a pine chair at a pine table next to the fridge. The room was long and narrow and a little scruffier than he'd expected. There were a few unwashed dishes in the sink and a couple of dirty mugs on the draining board. She was a busy girl and always looked rushed off her feet on the two previous occasions they'd met.

He removed copies of *Vogue*, *Horse & Hound* and *Mojo* from the chair she indicated, placed them on the floor under the table and sat down.

'I'll put the champagne on ice. In the meantime, white or red, Adam?'

He loved the way she said 'Adam' because that 'Adam' was an 'Adam' with potential, an 'Adam' of mystery, indeed, an 'Adam' who'd written a book which she absolutely loved when she was 16. In fact, he was an Adam who could be any 'Adam' he wanted to be, tonight.

It certainly wasn't the multitude of Adams seen by his wife over the last thirty years. The Adam of the smelly socks and psoriasis. The Adam that sat in front of the TV watching movies for hours without a word in his head, living life vicariously through every classic celluloid moment.

The Adam who lost sight of his family while he locked himself away to write books that were never published. The Adam he sometimes hated more than life itself.

'Whatever you're having is fine by me.' He hoped she'd say red.

'White it is then.'

It was an omen. He loathed white wine. The evening would be a disaster. A profound disaster. It felt like he was already cheating on his wife, the woman who cooked him ten thousand meals and bore his children...

'Shit!'

'What's wrong?'

'I'm all out of white. But I've plenty of red, if that's okay?'

...before going on to bore him.

'That'll be fine, Kate.'

She opened the bag with the glasses, filled two of them to the brim with a foxy little lightly-chilled Rioja and brought them to the table. She sat down on the other pine chair. Before Adam could say anything, she jumped up.

'Oh, I forgot the music.'

Kate went down to the other end of the room where she slid her iPhone 4S into a dock of the bay. 'Wondrous Stories' by Yes stunk the place out.

This really was an omen.

Adam loathed Yes. He could never spend an evening with someone who liked Yes. His wife hated Yes. And she was a virgin when they married. She shared his life, his dreams, his failures, his desperation. And he loved her. Always...

'Shit,' said Kate, a look of mild terror taking the sun out of her eyes for a moment, but then she laughed that sexycloggy laugh and she was back in the groove. 'How did that get on there?' She went back and touched the screen on her iPhone. Grace Jones started to sing 'I've Seen That Face Before'.

...but always is a long time...

'Do you fancy a line?'

...a long, long time.

The scene was set. Who was this 'Adam'? Who was this 'Kate'?

'So, Kate,' said Adam, still rubbing a few powdery remains of coke onto his gums. 'I guess you know a little bit more about me than I do about you. I suggest you fill me in.'

'Ooh, 'ark at 'im,' she said, sounding uncannily like Barbara Windsor.

'You learn quickly. Am I that obvious?'

'Far from it. So, what do you want to know?'

'Where were you born?'

'In a village called Highnam which is just outside...'

'Gloucester.'

'My God! How did you know that? Nobody outside of Highnam has ever heard of it. Shit, even I used to forget it sometimes.'

'I once dated a girl from Highnam. This is incredible.'

'Now this is getting seriously weird. What was her name?'

'Diane. Diane Smalling.'

'Doesn't ring any bells. Different generation, I guess. That's incredible. How come?'

'I was a trainee reporter on *The Citizen* and lived in Gloucester for nearly three years back in the platform soul era of the seventies.'

'Really? A *Citizen* reporter, huh? Where did you live?'

'In a converted barn near Painswick, a place called Bulls Cross.'

'The Woolpack! My favourite pub on the planet. Laurie Lee territory. This is unbelievable. Cheers.'

Kate raised her glass and took a long draught before topping her glass up.

'Anyway,' he said. 'Forget that for now. I want to hear about you. I've heard about me from these lips of mine once too often and I'm hungry for someone else's life.'

'Hungry, like the wolf?'

'Durannie, eh?'

'I beg your pardon? I was still crawling on all fours in their heyday.

'So, where to begin... My dad was the chief executive of a large engineering firm, my mother was, is, a GP. I have two older brothers, one is a barrister based in Lincoln's Inn, the other a doctor who specialises in nephrology and has a private practice in Harley Street. My dad died when he was fifty. I loved him to pieces.'

Adam wondered how many times she'd repeated those words to people she hardly knew. Was she going through the motions?

'How did he die?'

'A coronary in the middle of the night, out of nowhere. Both my brothers were living in London, it was just mother and me. She tried so hard to revive him, so hard.'

'How old were you?'

'Sixteen.' She lit a cigarette. Adam bummed one. It felt decadent to smoke in someone's kitchen.

'His death hurt me a lot and I went off the rails a little. I used to do a load of smoke and ecstasy. Don't get me wrong, I had a wonderful time and wouldn't change it for the world, but my mother used to get on my back and I couldn't stand living with her. Poor woman, she never did get over my dad. They were so in love.

'My only way out was university. I passed my A levels, I was always good at exams, and landed a place at Liverpool reading English Lit. Had a ball. I seldom returned home during the holidays, though when I did, I noticed mother was a lot mellower. It suited us being apart and we've since become good friends.'

'Are you sure it was your dad's death that sent you over to the dark side?' asked Adam. 'I guess it couldn't have anything to do with reading *Like Clockwork*.'

'So, you're the bastard that put me on this road to depravity. You deserve a drink.' She topped up his glass.

'So where did you spend your holidays while you were neglecting your mum? That's a lot of time.'

'In London, and I didn't neglect her. I just didn't want to see her and that's a mightily different proposition. A Greek girl on my course, Lenya, became my best friend and it turned out her dad was a shipping magnate who owned a huge house in Belgravia. So, I'd roll up there and it was heaven. We used to go clubbing five nights a week and Lenya paid for everything with a bottomless piece of platinum plastic.'

'So, what happened after uni?'

'Well, believe it or not, I got a first. I didn't have a clue what I wanted to do and then a friend of Lenya's who owned one of the clubs we used to go to mentioned he was looking for a manager and he thought I'd fit the bill.'

'Manager? But you had no experience.'

'Which is what I told him, but he assured me it didn't matter. Basically, the bugger wanted an attractive young girl fronting the place. He thought it would be a good image. He was right.'

'What, you actually took the job?'

'Too true. What with a salary here, a few notes there, I was clearing over £600 a week. It was a doddle. I met so many people who've helped me since then. I also discovered I had a flair for promotion. I began organising events at the club, mainly for private companies, but it soon became obvious that you could fill the club two, three times over for each gig.

'I stayed for 18 months and then started my own events company.'

'So, you were what, 22, 23?'

'Twenty-two, and never been kissed.'

'That's pretty young to start a company.'

'It's a young business. Oh, I know back in your Victorian days that would've been unheard of, but things are a little different now, old man. Women do have the vote, y'know. Surely you must've been around when that law was passed.'

'I voted for it. At least, I think I did. It's hard to remember these days. I knew I couldn't carry on this sham forever. I'm too old for you, girl, our love could never last.'

'Cheers.' She laughed and they clinked glasses.

'So, you started this events' company...'

'Yes, and it did really well. But the better it became, the harder it got, if you get my drift. You can only do that for so long.'

'Do what?'

'Party, basically. That's what you do. I was snorting and drinking all the time, yet still having to keep my shit together. It was killing me.'

She suddenly sounded like Amy Winehouse.

My God, this woman was an impressionist too. Was there no end to her talents?

'Amy Winehouse?'

'Correct. Well spotted for someone of such senior years. Anyway, to cut a long story short, I was offered a job in a PR company as MD.'

'MD? But you had no experience.'

'Which is what I told them, but they wouldn't take "no" for an answer and made me an offer I couldn't refuse. And at least I knew they weren't after an attractive girl fronting the place.'

'So how old are we talking now–24? 25?'

'Twenty-five, unfortunately. That's why I omitted the "young" from the middle of "attractive girl" in my last sentence. Did the job well too, or was it too well? The company specialised in the travel sector and I made it my business to get to know everyone I needed to know before leaving three years later to open my own agency, Lyle Associates, specialising in the travel sector, naturally.'

'So, you were 28?'

'What is this age business with you? Why do you want to know all the time?'

'It's an old man's thing. I never used to be remotely interested in people's ages but the older I get, the more interested I've become. It's like being a kid all over again when ages were constantly fascinating and nine-and-a-half seemed so much more than nine.'

'So, it's an old man's thing–shrivelled and senile with a headful of age. Or is it rage? How old are you, Adam?'

'I said interested in people's ages, not mine. Let's just say I'm old enough. More importantly, how old are you?'

'Thirty-one. I told you that the first time we met. And you're mid-fifties. I knew that all along.'

'So, what do you actually do?' asked Adam. He was straying into 'mind the gap' territory and afraid he might get lost.

'Now? I'm an attractive girl fronting the place. I bring in new custom and make sure I have enough people to deal with that custom to give me time to bring in more custom and so it goes on and you get bigger.'

'How big are you?'

'How big are you, Adam?'

'Mae West.'

'That's right! Thought I'd throw one in for your age group. But, in answer to your question, I have six people working for me, so not big.'

It seemed like a lot of people to Adam. This was one successful woman. The flat alone must be worth a mill. And so young. So young.

'So, Kate, what do you do when you're not working and clubbing?'

'Well...'

'Let me try and guess, if that's okay.'

'By all means.'

'Let's see, you like clubbing but not just for the social side. You actually adore music and it has a kinda spiritual effect upon you which has helped you through some sticky times.'

'Go on.'

'You're into fashion and are thinking of moving into that market.'

'Continue.'

'You're a horsey girl. Bet you had one called Rebecca or something. And I also reckon you were pretty involved in the equestrian world when you were an events organiser.'

'Anything else?'

He could only do one impression, but it was a belter.

'You like boats, but not the ocean. You go to a lake in the summer with your family, up in the mountains. There's a long, wooden dock and a boathouse with boards missing from the roof and a place you used to crawl underneath to be alone.

'You're a sucker for French poetry and rhinestones. You're very generous, you're kind to strangers and children and when you stand in the snow, you look like an angel.'

'Oh my God, Adam! Bill Murray, or should I say Phil Connors, in the most romantic movie ever made. Wait, wait... How are you doing this? I thought you were supposed to disappear, or I was, or something.'

'Andie McDowell! You're so right—*Groundhog Day* is the most romantic movie ever made. Kate, you're a dream.' Oops.

'Okay, okay, and that was a scream,' she didn't seem to notice. 'But seriously, you were spot on about me, Mr Moonlight. How on earth could you know? I don't recall telling you any of that.'

Mr Moonlight. She remembered the name from *Like Clockwork*. 'Elementary, my dear Lyle.

'To begin with, I moved three magazines from this chair—*Mojo*, *Vogue* and *Horse & Hound*.

'I saw how your face lit up when Grace Jones started to sing, like it touched something inside that doesn't get touched that often. Ooh, missus. Music is special to you and I know its healing powers. Plus, you read about it at the kitchen table.

'On the first two occasions we met you were easily the best-dressed girl in the joint. Fashion is obviously important in your life and you're bound to know enough people in that world to help an ambitious gal like you spread her wings. Plus, you read about it at the kitchen table.

'And *Horse & Hound* and Highnam go together like love and marriage. Remember, I knew the Highnam girls and a lot of them had their own horses. Again, you'd have contacts in that world and someone like you would've taken advantage of that. Plus, you read about it at the kitchen table.'

'Someone like me, eh?'

'Yes. Someone ruthless and calculating and utterly devoid of emotion. It doesn't take a Sherlock Holmes.'

'No, but it takes someone with imagination and nous. You're a clever chap, Mr Tate. Would you like to dance? Wait, let's have another line first.'

And the line hit his brain like a train as she grabbed his arm.

'Wait,' she said. 'Why don't you open the champagne?'

Always changing her mind. Madcap and menacing.

There were two empty bottles of Rioja on the table. They'd consumed them like wildfire. Shit, he'd had, what, a toke, some coke, and four cigarettes all washed down with a bottle of red. And now he was opening a bottle of champagne.

It all seemed very dangerous.

Really, what was he doing?

As the cork exploded, Michael McDonald's version of 'You're All I Need To Get By' glided out of the speaker like a honey-drenched Cadillac.

He was doing well.

Kate led him by the hand down the hall and into the lounge. The oak-floored room was long and wide and dominated by a huge, Georgian marble fire-surround. The only light was provided by the four spots in the garden through the French windows and there were two more speakers that piped the music into the room.

They held each other tight. Tight enough for Adam to feel the music flowing through her body.

'I've always fantasised about dancing with the man who wrote *Like Clockwork*,' she joked. Adam may have heard sweeter words, but he couldn't remember when.

'Mr Moonlight, huh? You have a good memory considering you haven't read it for 15 years. And what was a 16-year-old from Highnam doing with a book like that?'

'It was so powerful and, believe it or not, I could identify with a lot of it.'

'Oh, right,' said Adam sarcastically. 'Especially the bit about the acid-ravaged gang on the London council estate.'

'Duh, obviously not. But it was the way you wrote about how it felt being a teenager. You really got it right–for me, anyway.

'You shouldn't have written any more books, then *Like Clockwork* could've been your *Catcher In The Rye* or *To Kill A Mockingbird* and

I'd be dancing with a legend now instead of an occasional travel writer. My life is full of disappointment.'

'Kate Winslet. Brilliant.'

'How the hell did you get that? Very impressive, Mr Tate.'

'Thank you, Miss Lyle. Stick with me and it'll be sugar for my honey.' Jeez, did he just say that?

His leg slid between hers, but he managed to avoid a hard-on. It didn't seem polite.

Is this how it feels to be unfaithful? Like, good? Where was the guilt, the recrimination? If he was cheating he should be unhappy, surely. That's how he always expected it would be and that's why he didn't screw around because he couldn't take any more unhappiness.

Adam wasn't a man for dalliances. It would have to be true, deep, unswerving love, the kind he found with his wife, and that just wasn't possible. And even if it was, he couldn't bear the pain of losing one of them. It simply wasn't worth it. As Adam grew older he came to realise that sadness wormed its way into everything eventually, like a virus.

But, at 56, he'd never experienced real grief. Nobody close to him had died. Even his parents were still alive–his father was 95 and his mother 79–and they relied on him to keep it that way. No wonder he felt old, he'd been surrounded by it for years.

Then Stevie Wonder sang 'Lately' and Adam crawled out of that parent trap and melted into her arms.

This wasn't being unfaithful, this was dancing in the moonlight with a beautiful woman who was a piece of work. A real piece of work.

His lips brushed her neck and she sighed as he kissed her cheek. He stopped, pulled away slightly and looked straight into her eyes, and she stared straight back. He nearly said, 'Kiss me, Kate,' but thought better of it. His mouth searched for hers, gently, so gently, and, as their lips blended, their tongues reached out to each other. He gave up everything he was and ever would be at that moment.

No-one had ever kissed him like that. No-one.

He realised he hadn't kissed anybody in 28 years. His wife hated it, or she hated the way he kissed. She put up with his 'sloppy' tongue for a while and then declared her mouth a one-tongue zone, her own. He hadn't tasted her saliva since 1984. For over a quarter of a century Adam had gone through life truly believing he was a shit kisser.

But either he was wrong or Kate was good enough for both of them. Earth Wind & Fire's 'That's The Way Of The World' caressed the room.

They danced to slow Motown, slow soul, slow reggae, slow jazz, slow Joni Mitchell, and as the cool, cool notes cascaded over them, they kissed and held each other like it was the end of the world.

She rested her head on his shoulder and he suddenly remembered the time. He looked at his watch. Shit! 2am.

'Kate, I'm so sorry. I didn't realise, it's late and you have to be up early tomorrow. I must go.'

'Good idea.' Adam noticed she looked a little relieved. Was he still a shit kisser?

'I had a wonderful time and wouldn't change it for the world,' he said. 'I've never known seven hours pass by so quickly. I'm so glad we met, Kate. So glad. But tell me something.'

'Yes.'

'Would it be rude to ask for one last kiss?'

He was begging. He was desperate. He might never kiss anyone ever again and this was his last chance.

'No.'

'What, no, I don't want you to kiss me or no, it wouldn't be rude to ask?'

'Er, the latter, I think. I'm definitely for turning.'

'Maggie Thatcher. You should do this for a living.'

'You're sharp, Adam, I'll give you that.'

In other words, he may be sharp, but he was still a shit kisser.

'I've always wondered what it would be like to snog a former prime minister.'

'Good job I didn't impersonate Gordon Brown.'

And they kissed, and he wanted it to last an eternity because that seemed longer than always and forever put together.

But it was late. He had to go.

CHAPTER 4

Tyrone Power
with Bollocks

As you've probably observed, Adam Tate was not someone you would readily describe as a happy man. The sadness that permeated his life was the kind that inevitably follows a bitterness borne of frustration.

He was forced to live with the fact that he had once tasted a success he couldn't sustain. He was a one-book wonder and might as well have used the pseudonym Edison Lighthouse. The ultimate low came when he was dropped by his publisher after *Big Boys Don't Cry* sold zilch and he discovered there wasn't another publisher in the land remotely interested in Adam Tate. The dream was over. His mojo had flown.

He was forty then and Laura was pregnant with their second son, unplanned. She considered an abortion but they both knew that was out of the question. They were told it was a boy from the scan and had already decided on a name–Jack. The first boy, Ben, was 14. The money Adam made from *Like Clockwork*, including the Channel 4 deal, and non-returnable advances for the two subsequent books, left him with about eighty grand clear plus around five grand a year in royalties, but he'd been living off that for eight years by then.

Thankfully, Laura had worked for a London council ever since they were married. She ran the translation unit and was responsible for sending freelance interpreters into the local community where over 120 languages were spoken.

Adam remained at home while Laura returned to the council at the end of maternity leave and, for the next ten years, he never noticed his sons growing up because he was far too busy smoking dope and writing novels that would never be published and watching his money slowly burn in a smouldering fire of direct debits and standing orders.

Then, an old journalist friend of Adam's who worked on *The Independent* persuaded him to write a travel feature on Malta and organised a hotel in Valetta for a week. Adam hadn't been on a foreign trip involving work since the early eighties and welcomed the opportunity of getting out of the house where money burned.

He discovered a flair for travel writing and trains and boats and planes became a way of life for a few years. Jack was 15 in a blink, Ben had moved out, married and made a shedload of money in hedge funds and Laura still worked at the council.

To make any kind of money out of travel writing you have to do a lot of travelling and a lot of writing, a lifestyle which Adam warmly embraced at the beginning. He was making about twenty grand a year reviewing week-long cruises from large balcony staterooms for a variety of consumer and trade publications. It wasn't enough, but it helped.

Laura bought all the groceries and paid for both Ben and Jack's private lessons after school plus put Ben through university. She also covered the major outlays like a new kitchen. Adam sorted the mortgage and all the bills. Laura always assumed that *Like Clockwork* still managed to rack up royalties and Adam never encouraged her to think otherwise. She had no idea he was raiding borrowed money with fierce regularity.

Adam had re-mortgaged the house twice without her knowledge– it had always been in his name–and was spending a small fortune on skunk and coke.

For the past few years, Adam's parents' health had been deteriorating. Adam, an only child, did all their shopping, cleaning, laundry, the works. It left little time for anything else. He couldn't leave his parents for more than a day and a cruise was a week minimum, so he was forced to decline press trips and though he still tried to keep his hand in with the odd cruise industry interview for a trade mag, he knew he was already stuck in an out-of-sight-out-of-mind quagmire.

The invitations to classy joints for brochure launches dried up. The *Clockwork* money dried up. The freelance income dried up. He reckoned he could last another six months, tops, before he'd be dried up. He'd have to go cap in hand to Laura and that would be a nightmare as it would confirm her worst fears.

Besides, Laura's job was now in jeopardy. Swingeing cuts meant the translation unit was a luxury the council couldn't afford anymore, and her job was on the line. Sure, she'd get a decent redundancy and pension package, but she had a teenage son, a re-mortgaged house and a husband with the earning power of a two-toed sloth.

Whatever the pension was, it wouldn't be nearly enough.

He was now waiting on a tumour.

A rodent cancer was burrowing into his dad's head like a fat, pink snail leaving the shreds of his senses in its slimy wake and Adam was waiting for it to finally reach his dad's brain and nail him. Then he'd find his dad's stash–he was convinced there was one hidden in the house–pay off his debts, and float down the river for the rest of his days.

Adam loved his wife and she still turned him on, but the absence of both kissing *and* blowjobs took its toll and they made love only about ten times a year–birthdays, Christmas, St Valentine's Day, the usual. He hated watching her grow old, it was too close for comfort. She was a constant reminder of his mortality–every line told a story, every story told a lie. She was nearly sixty for Chrissake! And so was he. Shit.

Because they had sex so infrequently, Adam found it difficult to last long but fortunately, Laura came pretty damn quick, too. He consoled himself with the thought that at least, when it mattered, they were sexually compatible.

In fact, Laura Tate hadn't had an orgasm in 15 years, around the time Jack was born and when she first started thinking her husband was an intense disappointment. He'd made so many promises, painting a future of glitter and glory, a wonderland where they would live forever. She loved his depth, his enthusiasm, his determination. But since the failure of his writing career, Adam became a shadow of the man she knew and admired. His soul was diseased. He didn't care about her, the boys, any kind of family life. Laura couldn't remember the last holiday they all spent together.

She was glad Adam suffered from premature ejaculation because she wouldn't have to think of England for more than ninety seconds, two minutes top whack, and as he came she'd make the appropriate noises. Although she loved Adam more than any other man she'd ever met, she always knew she could never match the passion that bordered on adoration he harboured in those early years of their marriage. She also knew that passion would burn itself out sooner rather than later. But being adored was sexy and back then she couldn't have been happier.

When they met, she was 22 and he was 19. It was in The Unicorn pub in Stepney Green and her long, straight, black-as-night hair almost touched the hem of her mini skirt. He couldn't take his eyes off her and she was flattered. Adam was never one to chat up girls, but he somehow felt compelled to go over and introduce himself and let her know he was in the world.

Big, bad Barry White burst through the pub speakers as he walked towards her. She stood with three other girls and they were laughing. She was the most beautiful woman he'd ever clapped eyes on.

'Haven't I seen you somewhere before?' The classic, cliché-joke approach.

'No. I think you're wrong there, I'm afraid.' London accent but not harsh. This one would never drop her aitches for anyone. She was the first girl Adam had met who kept hold of his reflection in her eyes and he wanted those eyes to be his reflection's home for all time. He'd been carrying mirrors with him all his life. It was the only way through.

'Are you absolutely sure? Do you know you are the most attractive woman in this room–and I'm a connoisseur.' Bit more sophisticated.

'I think you must have left your glasses at home.'

'I can assure you, I don't wear them, well, that is, I do wear them, for watching TV or taking driving lessons.' The lost, innocent line.

'Well, you should.'

'Should what?'

'Wear glasses.'

This girl was tricky. The intellectual? The poet? The villain? The guy with a secret? The guy in love? The good guy? The bad guy? For someone who rarely chatted up girls, Adam knew a lot of moves. He'd picked them up from books and movies and he'd never used them before. He was out of his depth.

Which card to deal? He was losing it, losing it so bad he almost failed to hear what she said next.

'Because I think you might look cute in glasses.'

He'd cracked it. Sold himself. At least he was trying to be original and that always did it for Laura. Soft, tall, small-breasted Laura, named after the Gene Tierney movie and the haunting theme song that enraptured her mum in the dark at the local picture palace.

When he found out she was three years older than him, the moment seemed even more exciting. She gave him her phone number and they went out a week later. He proposed on the sixth date and they married when he was 22. Laura was already working for the council when they met, and Adam was in his first year as a trainee reporter for *The Citizen* in Gloucester and visiting his mum and dad in Islington for a few days.

She lived with her parents in Walthamstow and, for the next two years, Adam came to London every weekend. He completed his indentures when he was 21 and landed a job on a paper in south-east London. He moved back in with his parents and, within a year, with a little help from their friends, they saved enough for a deposit on a house.

Adam's dad, Bobby, was the main 'friend'. He gave them ten grand to put down on a house in Muswell Hill. 'Nice place, Muswell Hill,' he told Adam. 'Always fancied living there myself.' He stipulated that he'd give them the money on condition the house was put in Adam's name only and Laura went along with it.

Bobby Tate was a 61-year-old, semi-retired gangster when Adam married. The working bit usually involved cigarette machines and sharp suits, but he was slowly walking out of the shade and onto the sunny side of the street and the legit way was less hassle.

Bobby's face had been slashed by a cut-throat razor when he was 19 during a gang fight and he had a scar that ran from his temple to the bottom of his chin. He wore it like a medal and was clean-shaven every single day of his life. He'd been a handsome man–like Tyrone Power with bollocks–but never once cheated on his wife, highly unusual for someone in his line of business.

Coral Tate hated her name because it sounded like someone old. Bobby called her 'Cor,' which, co-incidentally, was the first word he uttered when he saw her in The Pat's, a pub off Chapel Market, in Islington. Coral was a cracker all right, twenty, brunette and as sexy as they came back in 1951.

Bobby was knocking 36 and thought he would stay single all his life. He never wanted family responsibility because his life was dangerous and deceitful and it wouldn't be fair. But all that went out of the window when he clapped eyes on Coral.

The pianist in the saloon bar was playing 'Ain't Misbehavin'' when Bobby bowled over to her.

'Darlin', you are without doubt, *the* most beautiful girl I've seen in a long, long time. And that includes all the movies I've seen too. What's your name?'

'Coral. Like the sea.' She sounded cocky. Bobby liked that.

'Coral, eh? I've never met another Coral in all my life. Coral. I don't think I've ever said the word before. C-o-r-a-l. Who you here with, Coral?'

'Some of my cousins and a few friends.'

'Let me get you all a drink, Coral. I like saying it now. Coral.'

'No, no, there's too many of us.'

'Coral, don't be silly. You go and sit back down with them and I'll get someone to send them over. I had a good win at the dogs tonight and your money is no good here.'

Bobby kept them in drinks all night, which impressed Coral. She lived with her mum, dad, three sisters and four brothers on the top two floors of a rat-infested tenement block off Pentonville Road. She wanted out, big time.

Coral acquired a taste for the good life after spending almost the entire war in an Oxford mansion when she was evacuated in 1939. The elderly couple who owned it lost their only son, a colonel killed at Dunkirk, while she was living with them and they treated her like a daughter during the four years she stayed there. She went to the local village school and even had her own horse. After the war, she continued to visit and stay but the couple died within six months of each other in 1947. They left her a hundred pounds and she was a little disappointed.

As a result of that wartime sojourn, Coral was educated, discreet and fiercely independent. Bobby adored her and they were married within a year of meeting. After two miscarriages, Adam turned up four years later.

Bobby gave her the lifestyle she wanted. He became a gangster because all his mates were, because he wanted the best, because he adored cheating the law. But mainly because he was a hard bastard who could handle himself.

He adored Coral. Her Oxford education, coupled with sublime good looks, set her apart from the crowd, like 'Billie' Dawn in the second half of *Born Yesterday*.

Bobby found the whole package completely irresistible and Coral knew that from day one. Everything she ever dreamed of wanting, she got. Everything she never dreamed of wanting, she got. But it wasn't enough. She never loved him, how could she? He was an uncouth villain with a disfigurement who had never read a book in his life. But he always had money when nobody else did. He provided.

So what if he was stupid? Sex wouldn't last forever. As Bobby grew older, he began to disgust her even more. His tongue disgusted her, his mouth disgusted her, his tobacco stained saliva disgusted her. Neither of them knew much about cunnilingus–tongues and vaginas were incompatible in those monastic, post-war days. And the thought of sliding Bobby's penis into her mouth was inconceivable. Bobby had never been a ladies' man. Straight fucking was all he knew and straight fucking was all he got.

Coral stayed around for the money.

And now they were both old and frail and ill, but they still stayed around.

For the money.

CHAPTER 5

Sizzling Lamb Chops

*H*i Kate
*Thank you for such a lovely evening. I had a ball, I think. I'm so
sorry I outstayed my welcome. I guess there's no more in the tank for a
fourth conversation now.*
A x

Adam waited all day for a reply, but none was forthcoming. He
waited all the next day. Nothing. He was distraught and that scared
him. He'd only met this woman three times and here he was,
distressed because she hadn't sent him an email. What on earth was
happening to him?

Five days went by. Still no reply. She obviously had no intention
of seeing him again. He'd made a fool of himself. What was he
thinking, dancing and snorting and boozing and snogging at his age?
Kate was a vivacious, alluring woman, 25 years his junior. How could
he ever believe that she would be interested in such a grey-haired
monstrosity?

But they kissed. And it was sublime.

Yes, for him. It was obviously less embarrassing kissing him than
pulling away. Plus, she was pissed and coked-up to the eyeballs. She
obviously didn't know what she was doing. It was all so obvious now.

What a cliché. What a pathetic, insignificant cliché of a man he
was.

Plus, it also confirmed once and for all that he was a shit kisser.
Laura was right. Laura was right about everything. He was lucky to
have her. She was a wonderful mother. He wouldn't know how to
exist without her. She was the light of his life...

Click.

Hey Author
I'm having a dinner party with a few special friends next Thursday and I'd love it if you could come. Free?
Kxx

...but light grows dark, eventually.

Hi Kate
As a bird.
A xx

Click.

Great! 7–pm–my place. You're not a veggie, are you?
Kx

No. I like my meat, as the actress said to the bishop.
A x

Click.

Ah, that's a shame because I am and so are the other dinner guests. So, it's veggie pickings I'm afraid. Hope that doesn't put you off.
Kxx

Adam laughed out loud. He couldn't remember the last time he felt so elated. Yes, he could–when he was with her.

Kate, you bitch! What a con artist. I'll bring along my mate Big Mac if that's ok.
See you at 7...pm. Your place. I'll follow the aroma of sizzling lamb chops wafting out your kitchen window.
A xx

Click.

*And if you bring Big Mac round, your bollocks will be sizzling along
with the lamb chops.*
Kx

I get the picture. It's a godawful small affair.
A x
Click.

When you've got mousey hair. I ain't just a pretty face, Moonlight.
Sweet dreams.
Kxx

Adam figured sweet dreams meant end of correspondence, so he
didn't reply. But he would've said, *'"pretty" doesn't begin to describe
your face'.*

CHAPTER 6

Last of the Monochrome Mohicans

For the past twelve years, Bobby Tate's head was slowly collapsing under the weight of a massive rodent cancer spawned in his ear that slowly travelled down the side of his face, eating everything in sight. He looked like a First World War victim of scalding shrapnel, his cheek blasted off, leaving a crater full of muscles and bones visible to the naked eye. Unfortunately, it wasn't the half with the scar.

He managed.

In its infancy, the cancer was operable, but Bobby refused all surgery. His sister had died under anaesthetic during minor surgery, so he told them to stick their operation up their arse.

He managed.

Once, a fly stole into his open wound, laid eggs, and flew out again. Within days his face was infected by maggots. He was like a living corpse and they had to operate to remove every single one by hand.

He managed.

The pain was unbearable and, in the early stages of his illness, Bobby took prescribed morphine in tablet and patch form. But they kept upping the dosage until he didn't know shit from a tree and started having conversations with his dead mother. He refused to take another dose and instead took about 2500mgs of soluble Paracetamol a day for the next ten years. He'd recently gone back onto the morphine because nothing else worked anymore.

He managed.

When he was 89, Bobby fell over in the street and snapped his femur in half. They had to insert iron rods into his leg during, ironically, a major four-and-a-half-hour operation.

He managed.

He'd also managed to look after Coral for many years.

She was diagnosed with mitral stenosis and atrial fibrillation when she was 42. Bobby spent a lot of time caring for her and she saw another side to him which surprised her. She didn't fall in love with him, she fell in friendship. They'd never been so close.

But, despite her constant illnesses, Coral managed because Bobby was strong enough for both of them. At Coral's insistence, he kept Adam away from the wild side, and she heaved a sigh of relief when her son finally went off to Gloucester to pursue his dream of being a journalist. She knew Adam wasn't cut out for a life of villainy, even though she made it her business never to find out exactly how Bobby made his money. No, he was more like her—softer, receptive, bright. Let him find his own way.

During the periods Coral managed to cope with her ill-health, Bobby would whisk her away on cruises, sometimes three or four times a year. She always looked good and Bobby loved showing her off. It was the gangster in him.

He gave up crime on his 65th birthday when Coral's health started to deteriorate, and they'd been living off the proceeds ever since. He had a few fingers in a few pies and he used to hint that he had a lot of money stashed somewhere in the three-bedroom ex-council house in Highbury. Bobby bought it for a knock-down price through the 'Right to Buy' scheme after unfailingly paying rent to Islington council for fifty years.

And that was Adam's legacy—a mortgage-free property in Islington worth about half a million plus the distinct likelihood of a substantial amount of cash. Not a bad haul.

He had it all figured out, that's why it was worth giving up the day job because his dad was almost there and his mum wouldn't be able to live in the house alone. She'd have to go into care and what would she do with all that cash?

Adam was trying to arrange for his parents to have a tenants-in-common agreement on their house, but his dad was proving to be obdurate. The agreement would mean that each of them would own fifty per cent and when one of them died Adam would receive his, or her, share, worth around a quarter of a million, so avoiding inheritance tax. And as it was more than likely to be his dad, he'd then arrange to have power of attorney over his mum's financial affairs and sell the house, pocket the money and pay the other half into his mum's bank account. That money should see her out comfortably plus the leftovers would be his, again free of any inheritance tax.

Adam knew there was no way Coral would live at his house. He also knew there was no way Laura would live with Coral. They hated the sight of each other.

Coral blamed her daughter-in-law for ruining her son's career. He married far too young, and to a woman older than him, a woman who couldn't encourage him, nurture him and love him as much as she could. She knew her son better than anyone and it hurt her to see him make such a big mistake.

And she'd been telling Adam this, relentlessly, for a long time.

Laura knew Coral felt like that because Adam spilled the beans during a particularly mean row while she was pregnant with Jack. He couldn't help himself. She kept up appearances for a while, as did Coral, but, like Adam's kisses, she decided enough was enough and they hadn't set eyes on each other for ten years. Adam took Jack round to visit occasionally when he was growing up, but that fizzled out. Ben hadn't seen them since Bobby gave him 21 quid on his 21st. And Bobby thought he was being generous.

Bobby couldn't give a toss about his son's wife and kids. He never took to the girl or her family who he thought were a bunch of wankers from Walthamstow. And she gave Adam a pair of wankers for sons. Her mum and dad were dead now and fucking good riddance.

These days, he was far too busy revisiting his past, walking through that poverty-stricken nurseryland sandwiched between the wars. He grew up on the mean streets that ducked and dived between King's Cross and The Angel, scratching for money on building sites and street markets before deciding that the crooked way made more sense.

He spent the entire war in London after failing the army medical because he had flat feet, and he watched the city lose its virginity to the thousands of GIs that poured in, providing Bobby and his crew with an endless stream of money through prostitution, gambling and the occasional murder.

Before the war, London was a city of islands, people weren't so mobile and many worked locally. The Yanks and the bombs opened it up and a combination of war-induced technology and large-scale immigration rammed it home.

He fiddled while London became a city, *the* city, full of Eastern promise and Turkish delight, princes and thieves, Rastas and rebels, mice and men. He hated it and spent much of the flim-flam fifties and bouncy-tit, MFI sixties inflicting horrendous injuries on Maltese ponces, Cypriot spivs and West Indian desperados.

Bobby, who had only seen black faces in *Tarzan* movies and *Gone With The Wind* until the Yanks came to town, was horrified by this mighty influx of people. London was spiralling out of his control. For a man like him, growing old in his city had become increasingly bizarre, threatening and beyond all reason.

And now, here he was, the last of the monochrome Mohicans, raised in an austere Pleasantville and opposed to colour of any kind. He lost his smile years ago, when the cancer devastated his face. He wanted nothing more to do with life outside a few hundred metres' radius of his home. It was Bobby's Last Stand.

Adam loved his parents but watching them slowly disintegrate in that mortgage-free house in Islington was the most depressing thing he'd ever experienced. He was an only child; life without his mum and dad was unthinkable. A mother's love beats them all, hands down.

Adam had planned on having them around forever. How could he want the only people who ever brought him an egg and bacon sandwich and a cup of tea in bed to pack up their molecules in an old kit bag and take the last train to Clarksville?

It was all too absurd.

But he concluded it was for the best if they did pass away. It'd be a blessing for them and he'd end up being minted. Drinks all round.

His dad, once so tall and strong and Godlike, could hardly walk or talk now and it was pitiful watching him struggle to eat the mashed-up special-menu goo for the man with the cancer face that Meals on Wheels dished up every day.

But he managed because he was big, bad, Bobby Tate and they could never take that away from him, no matter how hard they tried. His wrath kept him alive. It was an old man's acrimony–colostomy bags bulging with self-reproach and disappointment hurled like Molotov cocktails into a mob of rampaging years.

CHAPTER 7

Waltzing Through Life

'Where are you going tonight?' Laura and Adam were having their daily phone conversation. She at work, he at home.

'I told you,' said Adam. 'It's a reception for a cruise company.'

'That's good. You haven't been to one of those in ages. You might get some work out of it.'

'That's why I'm going.'

'When do you leave the house?'

Always the same questions.

'Around six.'

'Oh, so you'll be able to give Jack something to eat before you leave?'

'I guess.'

'There are pizzas and some fresh ham and cheese in the fridge. There's no bread, so could you get some?'

Always the same questions.

'I guess.'

'We need milk as well, don't we?'

'I guess.'

'I love your enthusiasm.'

'Highlight of my day, nipping down to the shops and buying bread and milk followed by the sanguine delights of either sandwich-making or pizza-baking.'

'And whose fault is that?'

'Yours and mine, honey. Yours and mine.'

'I can't talk to you when you're like this. I hope you haven't been smoking dope in the house. Have you?'

The same questions.

'Yeah, sweetheart. And I've also been chasing the dragon, shooting smack and snorting inordinate amounts of ketamine. I need them to go down the shops and turn on the oven.'

'Dope ruined you. It took the wind out of your sails and now you can't function without it. How many times do I have to keep telling you?'

'About a million.'

'Where have all the dreams and schemes gone, Adam? You've waltzed through life without a partner and you'll regret it one day.'

'Nice lines, Laura, "dreams and schemes, waltzed through life without a partner". See, living with me has its advantages. You've developed a neat turn of phrase under my tutelage.'

'I'd rather have developed a life without having to go to work every day and then come home and cook and clean and do the washing and ironing and then get up early the next morning to do it all over again like some unbearable *Groundhog Day*. You had the chance to develop my life, Adam, and yours, but you decided taking drugs was more important. That's the only reason why your last two books didn't sell. You were too screwed up to write.'

The mere mention of *Groundhog Day* conjured up visions of Kate. Laura's words drifted into that swirling darkness.

Aah, Kate.

He felt like Homer Simpson with a donut on his mind. Laura was nearly sixty. Kate was 31. Kate kissed him. Kate loved his book. Kate wanted him to meet her special friends. Kate was the dog's bollocks. Kate was cooking him a vegetarian meal tonight.

And Laura will never know.

That made him feel good.

Aah, Kate.

D'oh!

CHAPTER 8

I Said, Goddamn!

At 7pm, Adam Tate stood outside a house in Barnsbury Road holding a carrier bag containing two bottles of Cristal and a box of handmade Belgian chocolates. He was smoking a joint and wondering what the hell he was doing there. It was insane.

But insanity turned to intrigue as the smoke began to take effect and the night had a thousand eyes...

'Hello, gorgeous.'

And she is, he thought. My God, she is.

'Hello, celebrated author.'

Adam kissed her on each cheek. Her smell was intoxicating. 'Kate, I have an uncanny feeling of déjà vu.'

'Ah but Adam, this is Groundhog Day with a couple of knobs on– literally.'

She wore a black number to die for, a black number that cried out to be paired with achingly beautiful blonde hair, a black number made for a 31-year-old woman who loved his book. And when she laughed, crazy diamond.

He handed her the bag with the champagne. 'Here's another bagful of booze.'

'Cristal, huh. I expected nothing less. Ooh, and chocolates. You're a doll.' It was the first time in his life that anyone had called him a doll.

'Your wish is my command.' What was he doing, buying champagne he couldn't possibly afford?

'Actually, what you should've said is, "Face it, girl, I'm older and I have more insurance."'

'Kathy Bates.'

'Movie?'

'Er, *Fried Green Tomatoes*...'

'Nearly.'

'*At The Whistle Stop Cafe.*'

'Yes, Mr Tate. I'm impressed, yet again. I think you'll enjoy our game tonight.'

'What game?'

'You have to name the movie as well as the actor, with a bonus for the character name. It's my little party piece. Now, my other dinner guests have heard some of them before, so we'll leave those to you, but I've thrown in a few new ones for everyone to guess. I warn you, you're up against movie buffs. Oh, and the winner gets a prize.'

'What is it? Another conversation with you?'

'Nothing that special, I'm afraid. You'll have to wait and see. Step this way, Mr Tate.'

He followed her into the lounge where their tongues had entwined. Tina Turner's version of 'Let's Stay Together' eased through the speakers.

The pine breakfast table from the kitchen was now a pine dining table positioned close to the French windows. Adam noticed there were four place settings and was a little surprised; he thought there'd be more. The room was illuminated by the flames of a hundred candles augmented by those garden spotlights, witnesses to his shit kissing.

'Hannah, this is Adam.' They cheek-pecked.

'Hullo, Adam, I was a huge fan of *Like Clockwork*.'

Hannah had taken a moment to clamber out of the deep blue sea of a leather sofa. She was fat, fab and forty. It was all about the smile and the ping in the voice and the unwavering eyes and the bounce in the step as she breezed up to him, all indicating utter contentment and an unassailable generosity of heart. In other words, he liked her. He told himself it had nothing to do with the fact she was a "huge fan" of his book; but for someone who Googled his own name every day, it sure helped.

'Thank you.'

'Hi, I'm Joel, as in Billy, and I'm afraid I haven't read your book. I'm not a novel man.'

'In every sense of the word, unfortunately,' said Hannah.

'Incidentally, when Hannah said she was a huge fan, she was alluding to her size.'

They shook hands and Joel had one helluva grip.

He was probably about 45 but looked ten years younger–a lean, six-three with big, laughing blue eyes, thick, wavy black hair, possibly dyed, and an accent that revealed public schoolboy roots. This guy was a dreamboat and Adam's arse dropped about an inch. Luckily, he was wearing boxers.

Was Joel competition for Kate's heart?

'Oh, ignore him, Adam,' said Hannah. Adam could see the words in comic book speech bubbles when she spoke. She was just that kinda gal. 'Joel's an upper-class prick with a privileged lifestyle.'

Rich too. At this rate he'd been scraping his arse off the floor by the end of the night.

'Did you know Hannah here is thinking of writing a book in the style of Lynne Truss's *Eats, Shoots And Leaves*?,' said Joel. 'She wants to call it *Eats, Drinks And Smokes* but I think a more apt title would be, *Eats Like A Horse, Drinks Like A Fish And Smokes Like A Fucking Chimney*.'

Adam always thought a well-spoken 'fuck' sounded so much more effective. When an oik swears it's because he can't think of another word to use. When someone like Joel swears it's because he's thought of a hundred other words but 'fuck' would seem to be the most appropriate.

This bloke had everything going for him. Adam wondered what he did for a living.

'Adam here has brought some Cristal,' said Kate. 'Isn't he a sweetie?'

'Very nice, Adam,' said Hannah. 'Makes my Liebfraumilch look a bit lame. And it doesn't say much for your Bollinger, Joel.'

'Vintage Bollinger, honey. Keep your eyes on her, Adam. If you're not careful, she'll drink the lot.'

'Very droll, Joel,' said Hannah. 'And that takes some saying when you're pissed.'

'Would you like some Bollinger, Adam, as it's nice and chilled?' Kate asked.

'Love some.'

Kate went into the kitchen.

'Cigarette, Adam?' asked Hannah.

Wow! Smoking in the lounge. More decadent than the kitchen. He lit up with Hannah.

'I don't smoke tobacco,' said Joel. 'I'm strictly a skunk man.'

'Well you occasionally smell like one, that's for sure,' said Hannah.

'Are you two together?' Adam asked.

'Good heavens, no!' said Hannah who started to laugh. 'What on earth would I see in that long streak of piss? No, we're just good friends.'

'Well, if he's a good friend, I'd hate to see how you speak to your enemies.'

'Exactly, Adam,' said Joel. 'You see what I have to put up with. My wife won't have her in the house, but that's mainly because she's too wide to get through the front door.'

So, he was married.

Adam felt a sense of relief, until he realised that he was married too.

'Boom, bloody boom,' said Hannah. 'Like I haven't heard that before. I warn you, now, Adam, Joel's a bit of a boring old bastard. You know what these public-school tossers are like.'

'Well,' said Joel, 'this public-school tosser is about to roll a spliff. Do you indulge, Adam?'

'It has been known–and it is nearly Christmas.'

Joel was a big joint man. He started to create one the size of a small cigar but without a hint of tobacco.

Adam looked on, fascinated as Kate placed a glass of champagne into his hand.

'That's a big one, Joel,' said Adam.

'Well, I definitely know you're not talking about his penis,' said Kate, and even Joel had to laugh.

'Stop it, Kate,' he said, 'or you'll make me drop this glorious ganja. You're sounding more like Hannah every day. What did I do to deserve friends like these, Adam? You're a man of the world. Tell me.'

Was 'man of the world' a euphemism for, 'You're an old bloke'? He could smell the unlit skunk from ten feet away. Was Joel a dealer?

'Seems to me, Joel, there aren't many people in the world lucky enough to have friends like these. So, in answer to your question, you must have done something pretty wonderful.' He'd already had a smoke tonight. He could say anything.

'Where did you find this man, Kate?' asked Hannah. 'He's adorable.'

'At a car boot sale. He only cost three quid.'

'Well, you certainly had a bargain there.'

'I reckon I could've got them down to two if I'd haggled more. At least.'

'Ignore her, Adam, and get some of this down you.' Joel handed him the joint and a lighter. 'Here, you launch her.'

'Adam stubbed his cigarette out in an ashtray. 'I christen this joint "The Tree of Knowledge". God bless all who smoke her,' he said.

'Very clever,' said Joel. 'Didn't Adam pluck the forbidden fruit from the Tree of Knowledge in the Garden of Eden?'

'That was Eve, actually,' said Kate.

'So, it *was* a woman who brought sin into the world,' said Joel. 'I might have guessed. You two have a lot to answer for.'

Adam couldn't listen. Bells were ringing in his head and his heart was pounding. He'd taken three tokes before handing it to Kate. This was serious shit. Great.

Kate took one puff, she preferred a line to a smoke.

Hannah had a couple of hits and Joel and Adam finished it off.

'We're having Indian vegetarian tonight, so I thought I'd put everything out at once,' said Kate. 'Saves me from getting up all the time. It'll be like *Come Dine With Me* on speed.'

'Good idea,' said Hannah. 'I'll come and help you serve up. Boys, go and sit down and be prepared to be waited on by two beautiful, voluptuous women. Well, one beautiful, voluptuous woman and Kate.'

Left alone with Joel, Adam slid into his usual stoned-interview mode. It helped break the ice and meant he didn't have to talk about himself.

If the person he was with was a dullard, Adam would merely switch off, nod occasionally and think about his parents, his wife, his wealthy son, his desire to be respected, his mortality, Arsenal.

There was only one phrase that would anchor his drifting mind– 'Don't you think so?' It was guaranteed to prompt him to respond immediately with, 'Difficult to know,' swiftly followed by another question. He wouldn't be drifting tonight.

'So, Joel–incidentally, you're the first Joel, the angels did say...'

'Was to certain poor shepherds in fields where they lay,' continued Joel. They both roared with laughter.

'So, Joel, you're the first Joel I've ever encountered.'

'And I'm the only Joel I've ever encountered. It's a rare old moniker. Bet you can't name more than three famous people whose name begins with Joel. Actually, if you get three I'll be impressed.'

'I guess Billy Joel doesn't count?'

'You guessed right.'

'Joel Grey, the *Cabaret* man. Er, oh the racing driver Joel Schumacher. Joel, Joel...'

'See, told you.'

'Hold on, isn't one of the Coen brothers a Joel?'

'He is. Well done. Get a fourth and I'll pour you a glass of champagne.'

'Got it! The old Hollywood actor Joel McCrea.'

'Excellent.' He topped up Adam's glass.

'Okay, Joel, let's see if you can name say, five famous Adams. There's another glass of champagne in it.'

'Well, for starters there's the Hollywood triumvirate of Adams– Sandler, Goldberg and Baldwin plus the *Chicago Hope* son of Alan, Adam Arkin.'

'Sorry, did I say five? I actually meant six.' Joel was hot. 'I didn't realise you were a movie whiz.'

'No sweat, what about the rock triumvirate of Clayton, Counting Crows front man Duritz and Ant?'

'But Adam Ant's not his real name.'

'I wouldn't let Stuart Goddard hear you say that. Then there's Adam Faith, TV *Batman* Adam West, and let's not forget Adam Rickitt, an earlier version of Nick Tilsley in *Corrie*...'

'Enough. I bow down to your superior knowledge of Adams. Even I wouldn't have got some of those.

'Are you in the business?' he continued.

'Kind of. I source music for films, TV ad campaigns, documentaries, you name it. They tell me the mood they want to invoke, and I come up with an appropriate song or piece of music. I deal directly with the publishers and agree the fee, including my cut.'

'Wow, that's amazing!' A stalwart drug expression. 'What have you done that I'd know?'

'The Suzuki car ad campaign...'

'What, the "If you Suzuki, like I Suzuki, oh, oh, oh what a car. There's none so classy as that fair chassis" one?'

'Certainly did. Sales shot up and I received a nice bonus. I do the odd film, usually pretty obscure, but one of my claims to fame was helping out with selecting the music for *Groundhog Day*–in my humble opinion, the most romantic movie ever made.'

Adam was impressed. 'Wow! That's incredible. What music did you end up selecting?'

'Actually, none of my suggestions were used, but it was an honour to be involved in the whole process.'

'It's funny, Kate said the other night it was the most romantic movie ever made, too. I never knew anyone else thought that but me.'

'Ah, kindred souls, tonight, Adam. That's Kate's speciality. She has a knack of mixing and matching.'

'How long have you known her?'

'Years. We first met when she was 21 and managing a nightclub in the West End. Can you imagine? 21! She was holding an event for a drinks company and asked me to provide the music–I used to do a bit of corporate DJ-ing back then. We clicked and worked a few times together. We've never shagged, I'm afraid, though before I met my wife I would've loved to. Isn't she gorgeous?'

'Is she seeing anyone now?' Adam immediately regretted asking that question. In fact, he couldn't believe he didn't already know. It was usually one of the first questions he asked. But not Kate. He couldn't bear to think of another man holding her tight as they danced.

'Not that I know of. She lived with a guy for a few years who turned out to be a complete bastard. He was an alcoholic junkie but very clever and very wealthy. I was so relieved when it ended. Kate deserves so much more, she has a heart of gold.'

'What's that about gold?' Hannah was carrying four plates and Kate brought up the rear with another four. The dishes were overflowing with pakoras and piazis, poppadums and chutneys, bhindi bhajis and saag paneers.

Adam had a feeling this was going to be one of the great nights.

'So, Hannah, what do you do?'

He was sitting next to her and facing Kate. The food was divine.

'I was a prostitute, high class naturally. I only worked the five-star hotels. I was choosy and very expensive.'

'No? I mean...' Adam stumbled.

'I made enough money to eat what the hell I liked. Oh, there were still a few chubby chasers but by then I decided to quit and go legit, as it were. I now own a small chain of sex-shops and have a burgeoning mail-order business. It pays the rent.'

This was either true or a Joe Pesci 'I amuse you?' moment from *Goodfellas*. Shit, what does he say? 'Get the fuck out of here?'

Joel to the rescue. 'High-class whore? You would've struggled in Wormwood Scrubs, my luscious.'

Joe Pesci. Brilliant.

'Hannah acts for a living, Adam,' said Kate. 'You might even recognise her–she's been in everything from *Poirot* to *Midsomer Murders* via *The Bill* and *Pride & Prejudice*.

He'd never seen any of them. Cop shows bored him, and he'd rather read the classic than look at someone else's interpretation of it.

'The TV work bumps up the income,' said Hannah, 'but my real love is the stage.'

'Hannah regularly appears in West End plays,' said Joel. 'You name it–*The Woman In Black*, *The Mousetrap*, *Blood Brothers*.

Adam never went to the theatre. He preferred movies, even though the last film he saw at the cinema was *Superman Returns* when Jack was ten.

He didn't recognise her, but who cared? Adam had never eaten an Indian vegetarian with an actor before, and a successful one at that. He wondered if she usually played a fat, fab and forty character. That would help. Immensely. He laughed out loud.

'Sorry, it's the dope. I can't believe Joel worked on *Groundhog Day*. How cool is that?' 'Cool' was an okay word for a fifty-odd-year-old bloke to use. Wasn't it?

'You found out a lot in five minutes, Adam,' said Kate.

'It's the journo in me, I'm afraid. Can't resist it. But seriously, how cool is that? It's one of the finest movies ever made. Did you meet any of the stars, Joel?'

'I once bumped into Bill Murray in a lift at the film studios when they were shooting the movie. He was still wearing the weatherman suit from the opening scene. A make-up artist was dabbing a spot on his nose with a small brush.

'"I hope she nose what she's doing," he said. It was surreal.'

'It's such a romantic movie,' said Hannah, 'and I agree with you Adam, it is one of the finest movies ever made.'

'Absolutely,' said Joel.

Joel's 'kindred souls' remark reared up and roared.

These people did think like him and Kate did categorise and introduce like-minded people to each other. He wondered how many other categories there were. He wondered which category Kate would rather be in. He wondered if it was this one–after all, she did say 'special friends'. But then she probably said that to all the boys and girls.

He grew weary of that seesaw ride. A dinner party cliché was required. 'What's your all-time favourite film, Hannah?' he asked.

'Joel and Kate know the answer to this. I have a great passion for Milos Forman's *Amadeus*.

'No! That's my favourite film.' It was. That had never happened before. It was uncanny.

'Really?' said Hannah. 'Kate, how on earth do you do this?' She looked at Adam. 'I treat myself to a viewing once a year, speakers full pelt.'

'Does the family watch it with you?' Adam inquired.

'I live with a cat called Sugar and that's more than enough for me.'

'You never married?'

'No. Nearly did once, but he couldn't cope with my working hours and weeks away filming. Basically, he couldn't cope with my career.'

'What did he do?'

'He was an estate agent; cue the inevitable jokes, Joel?'

'Never, my sweet. But you must admit, you were once two up and now you're two down and in need of total refurbishment.'

Hannah ignored him completely. 'Jeremy was rich...'

'All Jeremys are rich, my dear,' said Joel. 'It's in their DNA to be rich.'

'I was going to say, before that misogynist stuck his rather large hook nose into my words, Jeremy was rich but a veritable peasant when it came to matters of the arts. Whereas, I'm penniless but a connoisseur. However, Adam, you must stop hogging the questions, so unusual for a man. Let me ask you a few.'

'Fire away.'

'Let's open the Cristal first,' said Kate. 'Anyone fancy a line while I'm up.'

'Up as in physically or mentally?' asked Joel.

'Both. Well?'

'I thought you'd never ask,' said Hannah.

'Love one,' said Adam.

'Not for me,' said Joel.

'He'd love one really, but he has difficulties snorting up through that u-bend of a nose,' said Hannah. 'Cristal and coke, I've died and gone to heaven. Kate, you know how to throw a dinner party and, if this was *Come Dine With Me*, I'd give you ten out of ten in the cab home afterwards because I'd be stoned and pissed.'

'And not because of the food, eh? Bit of a backhanded compliment, Hannah,' said Kate.

'The food was sublime, darling,' said Hannah. 'As always.'

'As always'? So, Hannah's been here for dinner before, almost certainly with Joel. Was there another man sitting in this chair whose favourite movie was *Amadeus*? Another man who kissed Kate at midnight as they danced to Earth, Wind & Fire? Another man with two bottles of Cristal and a plaintive smile?

'So, Adam,' said Hannah as Kate left the room. 'Are you married?'

'Yes, for nearly 35 supremely happy years, give or take 25 or so. Two boys, Ben and Jack aged 29 and 15. When we found out that's what happens when you have sex, we stopped having sex. Then we forgot and had sex again and Jack came along.'

Joel laughed. 'You're very funny, Adam. Dry as a bone.'

Dry didn't begin to describe it.

'I read your book about twenty years ago,' said Hannah. 'I thought it was powerful. How come you haven't written any others?'

By the time he'd finished describing his Quixotic literary career, Kate appeared with an ice bucket containing the two bottles of Cristal and a small silver platter with three lengthy lines of coke.

As Adam opened a bottle, Kate snorted a line.

'I said, goddamn!'

'Uma Thurman as Mia Wallace snorting coke in Jackrabbit Slim's toilet in *Pulp Fiction*,' said Adam, immediately.

'Correct, with a couple of bonuses. That was one of those for you alone.'

'I didn't get it first time round,' said Hannah.

'I did,' said Joel. 'But you have to be on your toes with Kate. She sneaks them in. That's what makes it such fun. You're a good sport, Adam, and please pay no heed to the insults. I love Hannah to death. It's just a thing we do, we've always done.'

'Only difference is, I really mean what I say,' said Hannah. 'You are a wanker, Joel.'

For a moment, Adam felt uncomfortable.

And then Joel laughed. And they all laughed.

'Fasten your seatbelts, it's going to be a bumpy ride,' said Kate. She smiled, and Adam wanted to freeze time like Samantha in *Bewitched* so he could reach across and kiss those remarkable lips repeatedly and they'd always be smiling because he could kiss after all.

'Bette Davis,' said Joel. 'The movie was *All About Eve* and her character name was, it was...'

'Have to hurry you Joel.'

'It was....'

'Sorry. Time's up, anyone else?'

'Was it, "Margaret Benning?" asked Hannah.

'No, but close.'

Adam fell back down to earth.

'Margo Channing.'

'Of course!' yelled Joel.

'Nice one, Adam,' said Hannah.

'See, told you he was sharp. As sharp as they come is Mr Adam Tate. But we'll get you yet.'

Marvin Gaye was getting it on and Adam was in heaven.

He had the girl of his dreams in front of him, a delightful wind-up of an actress seated next to him and the most fascinating man he'd met in a long time was pouring him a glass of champagne. He had chemical overload of the bloodstream, his heart was beating fast and all his senses were working overtime

There was a full pack of Marlboro Light on the table next to three more lines of coke. The Stereo MCs were connecting, and the conversations snapped, crackled and popped. And it was only 9.30!

If he was the last to leave he would kiss her again and she'd respond like before and then he'd know. Tonight only confirmed what he realised since that second meeting–he adored her and he was sure she felt the same way about him.

His mobile phone rang and 'Dad' flashed up on the screen. Adam thought about switching it off, but anything could've happened.

'Excuse me everyone, I need to take this. No questions without me, now.'

He stepped out into the hall.

'Adam, it's mum. You'd better come quick.'

'What's wrong?'

'Your dad's gone berserk. He's called me everything, went for me, smashed plates, I don't know what to do.' Coral started to cry.

No. Not this. Not now.

'Please Adam, I need you here. I don't know what to do.'

'Okay, okay. I'll come.'

'Please hurry.'

Adam went back into the lounge. 'Apologies, my dad's been taken ill and I have to go.'

'Oh, I am sorry Adam,' said Hannah. 'This was turning into such a lovely evening.'

'As am I, Adam, as am I,' said Joel. 'Are you sure this is not a ruse to avoid helping with the washing-up?'

'That's a mite insensitive even for you, Joel,' said Kate.

'Only trying to lighten the load, as it were. Sorry, Adam, I didn't...'

'Don't be silly, Joel, no offence. My dad's 95 and mum's 79. They're both house-bound and live in Highbury. I'm an only child and for the last few years I've done everything for them and I admit, it is a major bind at times. In fact, do you know the numbers of any discreet hit men?'

They all laughed but Adam was crippled inside. He might not see her again for months, even years, yet there was so much he wanted to tell her, so much he wanted to share.

'Kate, have you the number of a local cab firm?'

Five minutes later, the cab arrived. Kate walked him to the door.

'Oh, it's such a shame you have to go. The evening was just beginning.'

'Look,' he said, aching for her mouth. 'I know this sounds lame, but would it be possible to kiss you, just once? For luck, y'know?'

'Just once?'

Did that mean she wanted more than one? Or was she reiterating what he'd said?

'Just once,' he replied.

'Okay. Just once.'

And they plunged again through that swirling darkness towards the light.

Just once.

And, in the back of the cab, Adam Tate plunged into despair.

CHAPTER 9

Half a Man

C oral opened the door.

'You don't know what I've been through here. I can't put up with it anymore.'

Coincidentally, that's precisely what Adam was thinking.

'Where's dad?'

'He's sitting down now, but you should've seen him earlier. He was out of control. I've never seen him like that before. Never.'

'You mean he's okay now?'

'Only just this minute. I swear, I thought he was going to kill me.'

'He's not going to kill anyone, mum. He can barely stand up.'

Neither could she, these days. But Coral looked good for a woman knocking eighty.

She wore a touch of make-up, even though she never set foot out of the door, and every time she looked in the mirror she saw a twenty-year-old woman who could still make heads turn.

'You never saw him. You can't leave me here like this, not tonight. Can't you stay, Adam? You go in and see him and I'll put the kettle on.'

The air was hot and rancid. Bobby felt the cold and had the central heating running full blast from morning 'til night. He turned the gas hobs on first thing for an hour and the electric fire in the living room was never off, even in the summer. His wound emitted an aromatic cocktail of rotting flesh and perfume from the 99p shop that would creep around in all that heat and leave its mark in every corner like a cat.

Bobby was sitting in his usual armchair. The hole in his face was covered by a dressing that had to be replaced every day by a district nurse from the local clinic.

'All right, son? What are you doing here?' he spoke in half words, his mouth collapsed on the bad side of his face like a stroke victim.

'Mum rang me. She said you were ranting and raving, out of control.'

'What?'

Adam was talking in the direction of the non-existent ear and he moved to the sofa.

'Mum rang me. She said you were ranting and raving, out of control.'

'Fuck off! She's talking out of her arse. What do you fucking take me for, a 22-carat cunt?'

'Nah, 24-carat more like. And don't use that word, dad. You know how mum and me always hated it.'

'What, carat?'

Adam was convinced he saw a half-smile play across that half-mouth.

Bobby Tate was half the man he used to be. He once weighed 14 stone, now he was seven. He once had two ears, now he had one. He once had a fist as big as his foot, now it was as big as his flaccid cock which hadn't seen an erection since Frankie said 'Relax'.

Adam could deal with half a man a lot better than he could a whole one. For the first time in his life, he felt older than his once-intimidating father who had dominated everyone and everything. He was no longer Bobby Tate, underworld legend. He was Bobby Tate, frail old man with a disease that made him look like the Phantom of the Opera.

He'd outlived all his former cronies who inevitably died in their sixties, the victims of hard-drinking, chain-smoking lives infested with the relentless fucking of perilous members of both sexes.

Bobby gave up smoking fifty years ago when the dangers first became public knowledge. He was never much of a drinker–three gin and tonics was his maximum. As for women, there'd been a few before Coral but none since. Such perspicacity served him well–

he was, after all, 95 years-old. But his head was full of fractured memories and paranoia and pain and Adam decided he didn't want any part of that. He'd rather drink, smoke, have a bit of relentless fucking and perish in his sixties.

'So, are you okay now?'

'Of course I'm fucking okay. Why wouldn't I be? Your mother's losing her fucking mind. She needs to go to the pot house.'

'There's only one lunatic in this place and it certainly isn't me,' said Coral as she walked in carrying two cups of tea.

Bobby looked at her with such hatred it was terrifying. It only lasted a moment, but it was clear the cancer had eaten clean through to his soul.

'And how would you cope if they put me away?' asked Coral.

'I can look after myself.'

'You can hardly stand, let alone walk.'

'I was dancing round the fucking kitchen this morning.'

'And then you woke up. I can't put up with him anymore, Adam. I can't. He needs looking after and I can't do it. I'm too ill myself.'

Coral hardly sounded like a woman who, ten minutes previously, had been in fear for her life. Adam couldn't believe he'd been dragged from paradise to this putrid hell hole just to watch his parents argue, like they always did.

He desperately wanted to go straight back to Kate's but, apart from smacking of desperation, it would be presumptuous to assume Hannah and Joel were still there. No, it was out of the question. Stupidly, he never put her number on his mobile. He couldn't contact her until he reached home.

'Adam's going to stay tonight,' said Coral.

'I didn't say that, mum.'

'Please. You can sleep in my bed.' For many years Coral and Bobby slept in separate rooms. The thought of sleeping in an old woman's bed made Adam feel nauseous, mum or not.

'Is he? Oh, good,' said Bobby. 'Live football's on.'

'Dad, it's 11.30 at night. There's no live football.'

'Yes, there fucking is. Arsenal are playing Spurs, live. What do you fucking take me for, a 22-carat cunt?'

Adam wept without shedding a tear.

He rang Laura and told her what had happened. It then occurred to him that he could use that excuse in the future. Laura would understand and she'd never ring his parents' landline. Such breath-taking indifference made the perfect cover.

If only he hadn't messed it up with Kate. Ruining her evening, begging for a kiss. One kiss...

He slept on the sofa, or tried to. It was too short for him to stretch out and the coke still kept a light on because this darkness disturbed him.

It was about 3am when he first saw the mouse. It darted out from under an armchair and crossed the room in the blink of an eye. It stopped on a mat by the sofa for a moment and then ran back behind the armchair.

A few minutes later, it did the same thing. Adam picked up his shoe and waited. Sure enough, the confident mouse again emerged from beneath the armchair and ran, a little slower this time, to the mat where it sat up on its haunches and started to wash itself. Adam brought the shoe firmly down on the freshly-cleaned rodent and splattered it across the mat.

Before he knew it, Adam had smashed that shattered carcass with his shoe at least twenty times, accompanying each whack with a 'Fuck!' Its flesh and bones were ingrained in the mat and still he whacked and still he screamed, 'Fuck!'

Above him, old snores, inside him old sores that never healed, beyond him, old scores to settle. And still he whacked and still he screamed, 'Fuck!'

He stopped when Kate wrapped her arms around him and whispered, 'Everything's gonna be all right, Adam. Everything.' He sat back in the sofa in that hothouse, cradling his mouse-stained shoe like a new-born baby.

And then he wept.

CHAPTER 10

No Next Time

*H*i Kate
I am so sorry about last night. My mum went into panic mode about my dad and I'm all they have. False alarm, really, but I thought it was too late to head back to yours and I don't have your number on my phone. I ended up staying the night around their place. I hope I didn't spoil the party which, incidentally, was great. Hannah and Joel were a joy and it broke my heart to go. I did give you ten out of ten in the back of the cab, though. I liked your food so much more than Hannah's and Joel's and I thought their cooking was spectacular. Whenever you want me to come dine with you, I'm your man.
A xx

He prayed she wouldn't take her customary eternity to reply.
Click.

Hey Adam
We were all sorry you had to go, and I'm glad your parents are ok. Shame, you could easily have come back. Hannah and Joel stayed until 3am and we had a great time. Better luck next time.
Kx

3am? He was murdering a mouse at 3am. With his shoe.
But he was consoled by the fact that there would be a next time.

Hi Kate
That was a ferociously quick reply, for you. So, what 'next' time do you fancy?
A x

She didn't reply. Was he too quick or did the inverted commas create a verbal contraceptive, lessening the sensitivity?

Two weeks went by.

There would be no next time. He realised that now. And it broke his heart.

Adam was sitting in front of his laptop playing Hearts on Pogo Games. He did that in between daily visits to his parents who persisted with life. His dad was 95. He'd won. He'd crossed the finishing line years back but kept on running like a decrepit Forrest Gump. He knew he shouldn't think like that, but after two solid years of fetching and carrying, Adam had really had enough.

Bobby refused all offers of help from the council because he didn't want any care workers wandering around the house. Consequently, he and Coral relied completely on Adam, who knew the layouts of every Sainsbury's, Tesco's, Morrison's, 99p Shop, M&S, Waitrose and Budgens in the area. This was the price he paid for a tantalising legacy and he was beginning to wonder if it was worth it.

He wanted out, but he needed the money and he knew that if he stopped helping, Bobby would make sure his son didn't get a single penny.

He'd rather burn the house down with the money still inside. He was old, he was senescent, he was occasionally incontinent, but he was still a vindictive bastard.

Adam was falling into that parent trap more and more every day.

And still she never said what 'next'.

Click.

Hi Adam

Sorry no communication. Been on a couple of press trips to Dubai and Geneva and snowed under with work. All good. I need to unwind, Mr Moonlight. I need to kick out the jams, and we're not talking strawberry or raspberry here.

So, my place, next Thursday. 7pm. Come armed.
And dangerous.
Kx

Was that a come on? Did she mean sex? Did 'armed' mean Durex? And what was 'dangerous' all about? Was she going to seduce him? Was he going to seduce her? What if his shagging was worse than his kissing? What if he came at the drop of a hat?

Adam had no idea about the mating habits of young women. Did they take the pill? Did they have drawers full of contraceptives? Did they wear coils? Did they take the morning after thing? Did they give a fuck?

Or was Kate just being Kate?

His whole body started to tremble.

But you're only old once.

Hi Kate
Glad to hear you're thriving. Then again, I could never imagine you doing anything else but thrive. Dangerous thriving, they can nick you for that.
You're lucky, I'm free that night. What is it about 7pm with you?
A x

His hands were shaking as he typed. But it was kinda marvellous. Click.

Didn't you know? 7 is my lucky number. And luck had nothing to do with you being free. Am I right or am I right?
Look forward to it. I won't be cooking by the way. Just thought I'd mention it.
Kxx

It was another two kisses moment.

He'd stumbled across the most incredible woman alive and she wanted him to come armed and dangerous.

He'd never felt so happy.

CHAPTER 11

Coke Cock-Up

'**A**dam, we have to talk.'

It sounded serious. The last time Laura said that, she was pregnant with Jack.

It was the night before he was due to see Kate and they were sitting at the kitchen table eating an M&S-three-course-meal-for-two-with-bottle-of-wine-ten-quid-special that Adam spotted while getting some ready meals and a sherry trifle for his parents. Jack was upstairs in his room playing *Call of Duty* with half the world.

They still lived in the same house that Bobby had contributed to when they married. It was in a leafy part of North London, home to chic Edwardiana, elegant diffidence and a smattering of actors from *Eastenders*.

Laura wanted children from the moment they moved in and took full advantage of overcoming Adam's inveterate ambivalence on the fifth Friday night after a Chinese takeaway, two bottles of ice cold Beaujolais nouveau and the removal of some sexy underwear from M&S that she had never worn before or since.

As Ben grew, Adam gradually began to convince himself that his son stole his love affair. He was greedy for his wife, but she was greedy for Ben. Laura came from a big family and liked a noisy house. Families made Adam nervous. That's why it took him 22 years to get married and another 34 wishing he hadn't.

'Talk? Talk about what?'

'About Ben.'

'What about Ben? He's all right, isn't he? He's not ill?'

'No, nothing like that. He and Julia are splitting up.'

'What, like a trial separation?'

'No, it's a divorce.'

'A divorce? How come nobody told me? This must've been going on for some time.'

'I only found out a few days ago.'

'But Amy's only two. What's wrong with them? Are there other people involved?'

'I don't know any details. Ben wouldn't tell me over the phone. The thing is, I've said he can come and stay with us for a while, 'til this mess is sorted out.'

'With us? Why? I'm sure he'd prefer to rent something. After all, he can afford it.'

'Ben needs our support, Adam. He needs his family. This is a traumatic time for him and I couldn't bear to think of him sitting alone, night after night.'

'So, when is he moving back?'

'Tomorrow.'

'Tomorrow?' Laura nodded. 'Jesus, you don't mess around. By the way, you do know I'm out at a cruise reception tomorrow evening?'

'I forgot. Another reception?'

'What do you mean, "Another reception"? The last one I went to was weeks ago.'

'Five weeks.'

'You keep count? I won't be late. It starts at seven. So, I guess he'll be taking his old room, y'know, the one I use as my office.'

'Your office? Don't make me laugh. It's a place where you sit in front of the computer and play cards ALL DAY.'

She emphasised the last two words with hands as far apart as a fraudulent fisherman. That was how it was with Laura, exaggeration–'EVERYONE thinks you're a bastard'. 'You'd be the LAST person I'd marry if I could do it all again'. 'It was the BIGGEST mistake of my life, marrying you'. At least, that's how it sounded to Adam. And how did she know he played Pogo Hearts?

Yet, sitting round the kitchen table–enjoying the food, enjoying her looks, enjoying her familiarity–Adam began to wonder where it had all gone wrong. Sure, she drove a steamroller over his dreams, but didn't he lie down in front of it?

Was she really that bad? Was he really that good?

'Not all day, just ten hours of it.'

Laura couldn't help laughing. She never could. There was nothing mealy-mouthed about Laura's laughter. It was true and proper and always lit up her face and he'd see, for a moment, that look that made him believe he was the most wonderful man in the world. That look full of, expectancy.

But she gave up on him when he failed to lead her into the Promised Land and when he finally started to realise he'd let her down—many years after she'd realised it—the marriage was kaput. No good times, no bad times.

But was he really that bad? Was she really that good?

Laura wasn't wearing any make-up but tonight she looked like a woman half her age. The only feature that told a different tale was her eyes. Those once fat, fruity, Walthamstow balls of fire now looked spent, burnt out, a couple of gravestones in an overgrown cemetery. That was why the marriage hadn't worked out—he wasn't into necrophilia.

But on this night, she seemed a little different. A little more *alive*. It was probably because she was excited at the prospect of Ben coming back home and being a mother to him all over again.

Or did she simply seem more alive to him because he'd scored a gram of coke and he wanted to smear half of it on his erect penis and test drive it on her because he remembered someone saying once that coke on the cock makes you last for hours? Just in case. Plus, if he did have sex tonight, that would make him less sensitive tomorrow. Just in case.

'Don't go to the reception, Adam. You should be here when Ben arrives.'

'I can't. It's important.'

'No, it's not. You won't get any work out of it.'

'Thanks for the vote of confidence.'

'You can't leave your parents for more than a few days, you know that. I don't know why you delude yourself. You can't go on a cruise.'

'What do you care? You haven't seen them in years. I thought you might have made an effort, seeing as both your parents are dead.'

'I can't be with people I don't like.'

'You don't like me.'

'That's completely different. I've no choice, unless, of course, you walk out. But why would you do that when the cooking and washing and ironing is all done for you?'

'Ah, but I still like you.'

'No, you don't, Adam. Your head is shoved too far up your arse to like anyone apart from yourself. And the tragedy is, you don't even like yourself. A self-hater with his head up his arse is going nowhere.

'That's you in a nutshell–Nowhere Man.'

Kate called him Mr Moonlight. She knew him and Laura didn't and that was perilously close to 'my wife doesn't understand me' territory.

Rusting platitudes were corroding his spirit.

Nowhere Man was a dandy.

She still had the magic touch.

But she didn't know, she really didn't know.

He was in possession of the ultimate secret, a carnal secret, a seven-magpie secret.

'If I'm a Nowhere Man, lover, it was you who led me there.' He could hear the disdain in his voice, but he couldn't help it. He knew sex was out of the question now.

'I've never had time to lead you anywhere,' she said, out-disdaining his disdain by a country mile. 'I was too busy bringing up those boys while holding down a full-time job. If you'd have been sensible and listened to me, you would have invested that *Clockwork* money in property. Think what you would have got for a hundred grand 25 years ago. The rent would've achieved a far greater return than leaving it in the bank and the asset would now be worth ten or more times the initial outlay. We could've sold it now and retired early and in comfort. You were an absolute fool.'

Adam could see where Ben got his business brain. She was right, of course. But back then he thought he'd get 100k for every book he wrote. His confidence knew no bounds after the success of *Like Clockwork*. The world was at his feet. 100k for every book? Shit, make that 200k.

It took a while, but he'd finally come to terms with being a failure, so why did she have to keep reminding him of it? Kate didn't know he was a failure. And if she did, she didn't care. To her, he was an author she always wanted to dance with at midnight. And that was enough for any man.

'Frankly, my dear, I don't give a damn.' A lame retort, but understandable, in the circumstances.

'You really are a complete tosser.'

'Fuck off.' Adam didn't want to swear, it was a kneejerk reaction to being called a tosser.

'Why do you ALWAYS do this?'

'Me? Hold on, who was just called an "absolute fool", a "Nowhere Man", oh yeah, and a "complete tosser"?'

'Enough. Eat your food, go in the other room and watch TV 'til three in the morning, like you normally do. I want to tidy up and go to bed.'

Why didn't she say, 'I want to tidy up and go to bed and make love to you and hold you in my arms through the darkness and tell you how much you mean to me.'?

Why didn't she say, 'I want to tidy up and go to bed but before I do, I'd love so much to suck your big, hard, coke-covered cock.'?

Or why didn't she even say, 'I want to tidy up and go to bed. Give me a goodnight kiss.'?

She didn't say anything.

Kate wouldn't be like that.

She was unfettered; a free spirit who kissed like an angel. She knew what men wanted. It was instinctive.

'Sweet dreams, Laura. I'm sure I'll figure in them somewhere.'

He stood up and turned with a flourish. He hadn't done that in an ETERNITY.

At the very least.

CHAPTER 12

What Kate Did

At 7pm the following evening, Adam Tate stood outside a house in Barnsbury Road holding a carrier bag containing two bottles of chilled Chablis. He was smoking a joint and wondering what the hell he was doing there. It was insane.

But insanity turned to intrigue as the smoke began to take effect and the night had a thousand eyes…

He could feel the wrapper of coke move in the top pocket of his shirt as he walked down the floodlit pathway. It made him feel safe.

'Hello, gorgeous.'

And she is, he thought. My God, she is.

'Hello, celebrated author.'

Adam kissed her on each cheek. Her smell intoxicated him. 'Kate, I have an uncanny feeling of déjà vu.'

'Ah, but Adam, this is Groundhog Day. Is there anything I can do for you today?'

Close your eyes and it was Andie McDowell.

'I'm sure I can think of something,' said Adam in his best Bill Murray as he handed her the bag.

She wore blue jeans and a baggy black tee shirt with a multi-coloured, bead-embroidered tiger emblazoned across the front. That blonde/black combo was a scorcher and, as he followed her down the hall, he was mesmerised by her tight body weaving in time to Lauryn Hill's version of 'Can't Take My Eyes Off You' that was drifting out of the lounge and filling the whole flat.

'Thought you might appreciate the song, Adam. Have you heard the Muse version?'

'No.' He'd never even heard of Muse. Pop music, once such an all-consuming passion, was now inconsequential, another cog in the endlessly-spinning wheel of consumerism, to be lumped in with all the other gratifications–Facebook, TV, Twitter, football, YouTube, movies, wars. The world was now full of celebrities and soon they'd outnumber everyone else. He'd had his 15 minutes of fame. He'd wanted at least a few hours–and that was the hard part.

Adam had lived the last quarter of a century believing he had unfinished business and that was no life at all. It was a feeling far worse than bitterness where everybody is to blame but you. With unfinished business, you can only blame yourself for not finishing it and self-blame is the worst blame in the world.

'Chablis. Lovely jubbly. I'll put them in the fridge. Meanwhile, here's one I made earlier.' She poured him a large glass of ice cold Sauternes and he sat at the pine table. He'd developed a taste for white wine. 'Cheers, Adam. It's lovely to see you.'

'And it's even lovelier to see you. Love the tee shirt.'

'It's supposed to be a Bengal tiger. I bought it on a beach in Goa and it's been like a good luck charm.'

'So, did you wear it tonight because you think your luck's in?' He could feel that wrapper rubbing against his breast again. It emboldened him.

'My luck's always in. The question is, do you feel lucky?'

'Clint, eh?' said Adam. 'That's your first male impression. Is there no end to your talents?'

'Now you come to think of it, probably not. But there is an end to yours.'

'And where do my talents end, Kate?' He felt a little agitated.

'At the Ring of Confidence, Adam. I think you've given up believing in yourself.'

'Is it that obvious?' She'd never spoken to him like that before, and he was only two sips into the evening.

'Elementary, my dear Tate. You haven't had a book published in years.'

'That's because they're crap.'

'So, why are you writing crap? You're obviously capable of better things. I believe you're wasting your talent because you have absolutely no faith in your abilities. I would kill to write like you. You had a few knockbacks and you've come up smelling of shit. It's pretty pathetic.

'And now you say you can't do any travel writing because of your parents. I've never heard such a load of bollocks. You're using them as an excuse. You're scared, Adam.'

'Scared?' he laughed but he was as nervous as a bridegroom at a shotgun wedding. 'Scared of what?'

'I don't know. Everything? You're married. You have two sons. If you were away and anything happened to your parents, you'd have back-up.'

It was the first time Kate had mentioned his family. A gloom immediately descended on the evening.

'They hate each other. It goes way back.'

'Why do they hate each other?'

'For starters, my dad doesn't like or trust anyone. See, he used to be a gangster.'

'Really? What like Al Capone or the Krays?'

'Not quite. He was a straight gangster, if you get my drift. He treated crime like a 9-to-5 job–it was a way to earn money. His family were important to him and he'd always come home after 'work' while his cronies went out drinking and whoring. That's why he was never caught and that's why he's still alive. He's seen out everyone he knew–and for what? A life of pain and hate? Growing old is, I can assure you, Kate, undeniably bad.'

'Better than dying young.'

'True. But growing old with the shadow of death a constant companion ain't a barrel of laughs. I'm starting to feel the pangs of mortality and it's already worse than piles.'

'What about your mother? Where's the hatred there?'

'My mum could never get over the fact that my wife was older than me. She thought I was far too young to get married and she blamed Laura for ruining my career.'

'Is that all?'

It was the first time he'd mentioned Laura's name. This was turning into a night of firsts. He wasn't sure if the first he really wanted would happen now, in light of this conversation.

'It's enough.'

'So, what about your boys? How old are they?'

'Ben is 29, married with a two-year-old daughter and lives out in the wilds of Surrey. Jack is 15 and too wrapped up in *Call of Duty* and 15-year-old girls to give a toss about grandparents that his mother never mentions. I'm all alone, Kate.'

Shit, that last sentence did sound pathetic. This was all going badly wrong. Where were the laughs, the moves, the tongues?

'Do you know something? The Adam Tate who wrote *Like Clockwork* wouldn't talk or think like you do now, and he definitely wouldn't have accepted the kind of life you seem to be living.'

'Hello, that was another person, another planet. Failure humbles a man. It rips his roots from the earth and leaves him a prisoner of a capricious wind that blows him to kingdom come. A combination of mirrors, photos, bathroom scales and rejection slips have done for me, Kate. Well and truly.' Dope talk.

'You had me at "Hello".' Kate liked dope talk.

'Renée Zellweger as Dorothy Boyd in *Jerry Maguire*. You had me when you said, "My name's Kate Lyle." Let's have another drink.'

Kate poured the wine. 'I want to show you something. I won't be a moment.'

Adam wondered if she'd gone to fetch some coke or was slipping into some sexy underwear like Sienna Miller in *Layer Cake*. Or, preferably, both.

She came back holding a dog-eared paperback copy of *Like Clockwork*.

'I turned the place upside down because I knew I had it somewhere.'

She thrust the book into his hands.

Adam hadn't seen it for several years. He wondered how they managed to get away with the blatant rip-off picture of a skinhead brandishing a cut-throat razor on the cover with the lurid blurb– 'Being the adventures of a young man whose principal interests are LSD, rape, murder and The Beatles'.

He flicked through it and saw that someone had written comments in the margins on nearly every page.

'Did you write these?'

'I do that a lot with books I like,' said Kate. 'Just ideas that come to me when I read something inspiring or thought-provoking.'

'Well, it looks like you used to get inspired and provoked a lot when you were 16.'

Kate laughed, and Adam closed his eyes for a moment so he could hear.

'Adam, would you do me a small favour?'

'Your wish is my command.'

'Would you read that first chapter to me?'

'You're joking, right?'

'Never been more serious. In fact, if you don't, "you can get out of here before I throw you out, wretched slummy bedbug."'

'Miriam Karlin, the Cat Lady in A Clockwork Orange.'

'Knew you'd get that one. Come on, Adam, it'll be like my own personal reading.'

'How can I refuse?'

He glanced at his mugshot inside the book–bearded, youthful, full of misplaced confidence.

He turned to page one and stepped back into the past and it was some kind of wonderful.

It's raining outside.

What else?

Pitter-patter, pitter-patter, pitter-patter, pitter-patter.

'I tell you something, that's the best start to a pop song I've ever heard.'

We're discussing The Fortunes. Frank doesn't get my drift.

'What, you mean 'You've Got Your Troubles'?

'No Frank. The follow up, 'Storm In A Teacup'. The one that begins, sublimely, 'One drop of rain on your window pane…'

Paul picks it up immediately, 'Doesn't mean to say there's a thunderstorm coming…'

Frank smiles and sings in his best Otis Redding, 'Rain may pour for an hour or more…'

George sounds like Steve Ellis from Love Affair… 'But it doesn't matter, you know it doesn't matter.'

I'm on again and go straight to the third verse, 'One little word that you may have overheard…'

Frank–'Doesn't mean to say that my love for you is dying…'

Paul–'Don't start crying over second-hand lying….'

George–'It doesn't matter, you know it doesn't matter…'

Everyone in the cinema foyer–'It's a storm in a teacup, brewing up double all those tiny little troubles. It's a storm in a teacup, it really doesn't matter if it pitter-pitter-patters all the day…

Pitter-patter pitter-patter ….'

'That's poetry, Mr Moonlight. Poetry in motion.'

And we laugh as Frank trips over and George dances round him, aping the kickingshit Alex pounding the fuck out of F. Alexander in A Clockwork Orange.

The film we've just seen.

The film we've just seen.

'George, you sound just like Steve Ellis,' says Paul.

'I know,' says George. 'The Love Affair guy.'

'But why do you sound like him?'

'Because I am him. I've always been him, like I've always been all of you.'

George usually glides the God surf when the acid starts to kick in. If he doesn't, it's shit acid. George knows his stuff. He knows more about acid than stolen car stereo cartridges, and George knows a fucking lot about stolen car stereo cartridges.

'The universe rocks, man. Truly rocks.'

I don't know who said that. My head's full of Orange going tick-tock tick-tock. Boom!

This is the strongest yet. Where does George find it?

'That was some film,' Frank never stuttered when he was on acid. He lost control and the click click click on his scratched record became immersed in the grooves. We called him Mr Moonlight after The Beatles song 'cos he sang it every day.

'Some film. Some fuckaluck film. Some cool fuckaluck film.'

'This is strong acid, Paul,' says George, something he's never said before. George was the one who coped when it all got out of hand. Who's gonna cope now?

'That was some film,' Moonlight repeats like a mantra. He's still lying on the floor with George bent over him.

'Paul, this acid is fucking perpendicularly strong,' George reiterates, the calm slowly being squeezed from his eyes by the pressure of his ever-expanding brain.

And then I see Moonlight's snarling eyes and I know, I just know. I'm pregnant with know, I brought know up. I nurtured it, loved it. I fucking know.

'You know something?' It's all I can say. My heart isn't in the rest. Moonlight stands up. He clearly isn't impressed with landing the F. Alexander role.

'Are you a cunt or something?' asks Moonlight.

Nobody could talk to George like that but Moonlight. Nobody.

'What, like you, Moonlight? The stuttering shitfuck.'

Nobody could talk to Moonlight like that but George. And I mean nobody.

They always laughed. Always. But not tonight.

Pitter-patter, pitter-patter. Pitter-patter…

'You read so well, Adam. It's like you actually wrote it or something.' She smiled. 'Let me top you up with some Chablis before you continue. This is turning into some night.'

He hoped she'd say that.

On the way home, I watch the rain that dances in the street lights twist and turn into my mother and then watch her crawl inside me. I manage to shit out her smoking corpse as we approach the estate. The pavement is strewn with hot death, strands of scalding steam rising like fingers that squeeze the juice from the fat, wet moon. I look at the others. Nowhere men in the midst of insanity. It wasn't where we're going, it was why the fuck bother coming back? That kind of thinking used to scare the shit out of me. But not tonight. Not this fingermoon fuckaluck night.

I turn and there's Paul standing in the middle of the road like an angel in a cardboard birthday heart singing 'Tonight' from West Side Story. He could've been Romeo or Juliet and I feel a pang in my cock and a bang in my soul and the heavens look good tonight.

When I turn back I see the fiery doors that lead into our palace and I run towards the blaze.

Hold it.

This is heavy-duty acid.

I'm okay.

I've been taking it long enough to know I'm okay.

And those doors reignite and I'm back floating downstream into the golden furnace and it's a long way down and I hear screams behind me and my body is swelling at an alarming rate and I'm fucked. Well and truly.

'Are you all right, love?'

It's Mrs Gatsby, Gordon's mum. Everyone knows Gordon Gatsby.

'Er, yeah'.

'So why are you lying on the grass in the rain? Why are all of you lying on the grass?

'Yeah, we're all right Mrs Gatsby, ain't we, boys,' says Moonlight as he steps out of the stuttering darkness and into the white beam of a spotlight, mic in his hand, love in his heart.

'Yeah, we're fine, Mrs Gatsby,' dream lover George steps into another spotlight. 'And may I say, you're looking particularly attractive tonight.'

She laughs. 'You've obviously been drinking.' She sounds like a backing singer. And as her face becomes a multitude of colours she looks beautiful. Fuckable beautiful.

'Don't play silly buggers. Here, come in for a nice cup of tea before you go home.' It was the verse leading them into the chorus.

'No, that's all right, Mrs Gatsby,' says Paul the bass man, spinning in a third spotlight–deep throat, deep scars, deep shit.

'Sounds great,' I say, clicking my fingers and biding my time in the stuttering darkness.

And we all reach down and sing 'Will You Still Love Me Tomorrow' like it's a Motown song.

I think I see Mrs Gatsby dance a little as we follow her into the flat and Moonlight closes the door behind us.

There are ashtrays everywhere–huge, green glass ashtrays, ashtrays on stands that spin round and round sending fag ends into oblivion when you push down the knob in the middle, pub ashtrays, ashtrays with names of holiday camps emblazoned on the side. A huge marble table lighter in the shape of a gondola dominates the glass top of the teak coffee table on the fake tiger-skin rug languishing in front of a flame-effect electric fire.

Mrs Gatsby, thanks to her son, has the only colour TV on the estate and Callan is on. In the corner, a cocktail cabinet the size of a wardrobe is open, displaying its contents like Aladdin's Cave–Gordon's, Teachers, Courvoisier, Captain Morgan, Warninks Advocaat, De Kuyper cherry brandy; every conceivable alcoholic treasure.

'Tea, everyone?'

'I'd like an Advocaat with lemonade,' says Moonlight. 'A snowball. White and pure.'

'Snowballs are yellow,' says Mrs Gatsby, a snake tongue darting from her mouth.

Ready for it. Longing for it.

'I'll have a cup of tea, Mrs Gatsby,' says George. 'I'll help you make it in the kitchen.'

'Oh, there's no need.'

'It'll be my pleasure, Mrs Gatsby,' says George.

'You are a lovely boy.'

The room is all wrapped up in orange flock wallpaper laced with white Grecian urns that swim in infinity. I walk into the kitchen with George, carefully avoiding the swaying seaweed that litters her carpet. When Mrs Gatsby opens her fridge door, another Aladdin's Cave appears—a whole bread-crumbed gammon ham, a school of smoked salmon, a hundred bottles of Mackeson, clotted cream, gold top milk, a box of Fry's Turkish Delight, a freezer full of Cream of Cornish ice cream and strawberry splits.

George and I are transfixed by the gastronomic cornucopia. Everything is in caves. Aladdin's Caves.

From the living room, the incessant noise of a spinning ashtray that Paul keeps pressing and pressing, watching it go round and round.

'How many of you boys take sugar?'

Her voice is dungeon deep. Paul and Moonlight giggle uncontrollably. Everything starts getting creepy. She's going to lock us all up. We shouldn't be here. Something bad is gonna happen in these caves. Something really bad.

'That's Life' glides out of the stereogram into the kitchen and flies around like a huge bat. Bad. Sinatra is way too weird at this moment.

As Mrs Gatsby pours out the tea, George walks up behind her and lifts her dress.

'What are you doing? Silly boy.' And she laughs and she's so far away.

'Nothing Mrs Gatsby. I want to look at your knickers. What colour are they?'

'Now go and sit down and don't be so saucy. I'll tell your mother if you're not careful. You boys drink too much; my Gordon's the same. It'll do you no good in the long run, you mark my words.'

Her face is dazzling.

'They're golden,' says George. 'Your knickers are the colour of gold. You are so fucking beautiful Mrs Gatsby. I want to kiss you so much, Mrs Gatsby, so fucking hard.'

I watch George turn her face to his, watch his mouth press against hers. She drops the teapot and it smashes on the floor. I watch the tea slowly spread across the lino like a pool of blood. Paul and Moonlight are still giggling in the living room. I watch George put his hand over her mouth to stifle her screams and lift her dress again and pull down her knickers.

'Ouch! The fucking bitch bit me.' He punches her in the face, hard, and she would've gone down if he wasn't holding her.

'Sorry, Mrs Gatsby, but I must fuck you from behind. I hope you don't mind. It's only a bit of fun while Callan's on.'

I must do something, I must tell Paul and Moonlight. I must turn, slowly, and get out of this defiled, whirligig of a room. I must tell Paul and Moonlight.

'Quick, George is raping Mrs Gatsby.'

Paul and Moonlight haul themselves out of the leather sofa, still laughing, and go into the kitchen. I sit on the sofa, carefully avoiding sitting on the marks their arses made in the leather because they look like bottomless pits.

'Go on, my son!' yells Moonlight. 'I'm next. What a night. Is your hair on fire, Paul?

'Just been kissing the sky, Moonlight, just been kissing the sky. Oh yeah, and I wanna toss for who's next.'

I want to leave but this acid is like no other and the sofa has engulfed me. 'That's Life' is on an endless loop and it's different every time as my senses mingle and I can see, taste, smell and touch the music. The walls and the ceiling liquefy and I'm tripping through time, backwards, forwards, sideways; colliding with stars and flying over massive armies battling each other on giant fields of poppies. I have no time for poxy reality. There's life everywhere, even in the dead. How can anyone die when this is really what's all around?

'I think we'd better get out of here, quick.'

It's Paul. His words stop the room shaking, like an earthquake in reverse.

'What's up, Doc?' I start to laugh.

'We've done something bad. I think. But I know we have to go.'

I stand up, there's an aftershock and I totter for a moment. 'Where's George and Moonlight?'

'They're in the kitchen, cleaning up the mess, but they don't know what they're doing and I can't watch them anymore. I can't. Did you see that?' He pointed to the ceiling. Sinatra was still preaching.

'What?'

'A bird, a duck I think.'

'Mrs Gatsby has real flying ducks in her living room.' I started to laugh again.

'Mrs Gatsby. What mess, Paul? What fucking mess? What have you done?'

'I can't talk in this room, he says.' This is a dangerous room. This room will keep spoken words locked-up forever, suffocating everyone who lives here. We must leave this room. This flat. Mrs Gatsby.'

I walk into the kitchen and the scene before me I immediately attribute to the acid. It can't possibly be real. I'm still inside that sofa, still stepping on the words of 'That's Life' as they lead me to heaven. This is another battlefield.

Gordon Gatsby's mother is lying face down on the kitchen floor, a little old woman in a pool of tea stained blood. Her knickers encase one ankle and her M&S dress is ripped to shreds. Shards of heavy green ashtray glass pepper her blue rinse hair now caked with red. Her sad, wrinkled body is a wasteland for cigarette burns and gently setting semen. Her legs are wide apart, and an unopened bottle of Mackeson has been rammed into her anus. Gleaming slivers of bowels ripped out *by the bottle cap stick to her arse like leeches. A bread knife protrudes from the centre of her back and ancient blood trickles through the blue ridges of her skimpy flesh.*

The headless body of Astaire, her ginger tom, is nearby. Its head has been stuffed into Mrs Gatsby's mouth and I wonder, matter-of-factly, whether it was done while she was still alive, while the bottle of Mackeson plucked bits of bowels from her bum like dirt from a fingernail.

George and Moonlight are gorging on ham, smoked salmon and ice-cream, oblivious to the horror. Paul, anxious to leave a moment ago, joins them.

'Mrs Gatsby is 82, isn't she?' I ask George, matter-of-factly, as I place a whole slice of smoked salmon into my mouth.

'Shit, that's right, it's Gordon Gatsby's mum,' says Paul. 'Gordon fucking Gatsby.'

'Don't worry about him,' says George. 'I fancy a snowball, a yellow one, with a dollop of ice cream,' and he goes into the living room, stepping over Mrs Gatsby like she wasn't there. Moonlight and Paul follow him, and I'm left with a mouthful of smoked salmon, staring at this sweet old woman's mutilated body and wondering where this all fitted into my universe.

Bits of bowels from her bum. Lot of bs. GatsBy! I start to laugh uncontrollably and walk into the living room where George, Moonlight and Paul are sitting on my sofa, downing snowballs and watching TV. I laugh as I step into the hall and out the front door. I laugh in the rain all the way home. Bits of bowels from her bum. GatsBy!

Pitter-patter. Pitter-patter. Pitter-patter.

Adam closed the book. 'Phew! I haven't done that in a long, long time.'

'Please read me some more.'

'Maybe later.'

'It is pretty shocking,' she said.

'Thanks very much.'

'You know what I mean. It still shocks, even after all these years.'

'Can't put an age on shock, gorgeous.'

'I sincerely hope not. The thing is, do you still have the 's' factor, Adam? Do you still have the ability to shock?'

'Can I make love to you tonight?'

She looked shocked. Then she laughed.

'Nice one, Adam, you got me.'

In for a penny.

'I'm not trying to get you, Kate.' His legs trembled slightly as he spoke. 'Can I make love to you tonight? I don't know how else to put it.

'I've thought of nothing else since the second time we met. You're in my dreams when I sleep, you're in my thoughts when I'm awake, your face lights up my day. The night we danced and kissed was one of the truly great moments of my life. I've never been unfaithful to my wife even though my marriage is as dog-eared as that book; but with you, Miss Kate Lyle, I would, if you'd have me, make a wonderful exception. You are, without any doubt, the most beautiful woman I've met in precisely 35 years. That's straight from the heart.

'It's the most important question I've asked in a long, long time– can I make love to you tonight?'

There, it was done. He fooled himself into believing it squared things with Laura simply by implying she was the last 'most beautiful woman' he'd met. It helped ease the tremendous guilt that suddenly overcame him.

He now wanted Kate to say 'No.' He wanted her to be insulted and order him out. This was wrong. He was on the verge of making the biggest mistake of his life and could never forgive himself. Thank God, he'd seen the light now. Thank God, he could prevent it from happening. But no matter. She'll refuse anyway, and he'll never see her again and his life will go back to normal…

'Well, when you put it like that, how can a girl refuse?'

…and who the fuck wants normal?

'"You know, Norman, you really are the sweetest man in the world, but I'm the only one who knows it."'

'Katharine Hepburn, *On Golden Pond*. Can't remember the character name but that's what you call a quote.'

'Ah, caught you out at last. It was Ethel Thayer.'

'You don't Thayer.'

Without even realising it, Adam had leaned across the table and now their faces were almost touching. He gently kissed her lips but then, afraid of that swirling darkness, he pulled away.

'I don't bite.'

'In that case, I might as well go home.' God, he sounded cool. But would he be able to transfer that cool to the bedroom?

'Fancy a line, before you go?'

'Don't mind if I do. I'll nip to the loo while you slip those little white lumps into something more comfortable.'

'We are talking coke-cutting, right?'

'Who am I to say?'

The white packet in his top pocket skipped across his left nipple as he left the room. He wanted to get his tongue a date inside the pretty flamingo between her legs—if he just could, huh, if she just would...

In the toilet, Adam realised he needed an erection to apply the coke properly and there wasn't one available. He could probably get one going but by the time he returned to the kitchen, had a line, another drink, a chat, it would've long gone, and the coke would end up lining his boxers.

However, this was his only chance, so he put about half a gram on his flaccid penis and kept his fingers crossed. He figured the other half gram could be needed to come off the bench later in the game. But then he felt he ought to compensate for the powder that would fall off when he returned his penis to his pants, so he slapped on the other half gram. He felt like an old bald man donning a wig.

As he flushed the toilet it occurred to him that Kate might like oral sex. She'd be sure to taste the coke and how would he explain that one? Could be construed as verging on the pervy, but it was a chance he had to take.

Christ, why was sex such a minefield? He'd been dreaming of this moment for weeks but having to contend with all the minutiae of seduction because of his fear of coming first and coming quick was destroying the romance.

'Clap hands, here comes Charlie,' said Kate as Adam and his limp, coked-up dick, sat down at the kitchen table and hoovered up another inch and a half.

He wrapped his arms around her and held on tight. Her hands slid up and down his back and he was bewitched. They kissed, and he spun through time, like clockwork...

CHAPTER 13

Cock-a-Oops

The swirling darkness never lifted and his worst fears were confirmed.

It was shit coke–his, not hers.

He took the night bus and arrived home at 3am. He would've stayed the night, using his parents as an excuse. But it didn't happen.

He slid quietly into bed next to Laura who was sound asleep. The coke–Kate's– and an agonising feeling of incompleteness, kept his eyes open.

He could see Kate's bedroom. He could see them both on her bed from above like an out-of-body experience. He could see her taking off her jeans, her Bengal Tiger top, her bra, her knickers, laughing all the while. He could see her undressing him and how he held his stomach in and how white he looked in the darkness and how his shiny Thai-silk black boxers looked faintly ridiculous against his soft pale skin. He could see him playfully kiss her thighs and then move slowly upwards towards that long-lost club where he used to dance 'til dawn. He could see his tongue searching for that peg where he could hang his hat, and the noises coming out of her mouth rattled like diamonds in his head.

He could see how Kate seemed to be so much more experienced than him. She held his head while his tongue was twisting and turning inside her. She knew what she wanted, and she knew how to get it. After a few minutes she pushed his head away.

'Let me suck you now, before you come inside me.'

That's when it all started to go wrong.

See, did she mean he could come inside her? Or merely the physical act of inserting his penis into her vagina? What about contraception? What about AIDS? Either way, Don Giovanni hadn't bought a Durex. He did try. He went into a chemist but felt like a hopelessly-embarrassed teenager, too afraid to ask for a packet of Fetherlite. He also tried a machine in a pub toilet, but it took his money and failed to deliver, and he wasn't about to complain. Story of his life.

And he certainly didn't want her mouth around his penis. Well, he did, of course, but not tonight, Josephine. A whole gram plus in one go might kill her, for all he knew. Besides, he was already feeling pretty, uh, ticking time-bomb sensitive and she hadn't even touched him yet. If she put him in her mouth he'd come like a volcano, splattering her uvula with hot lava. Contraception would be irrelevant because he didn't think he could manage a second coming.

He wondered how long it would take for the coke to clock in on his cock, though he knew deep down it should've already done so by now. It wasn't late, it was off sick.

Shit coke.

He panicked. He could see himself panic.

Laura turned over and snored soft, girlie snores, the soundtrack to the tragedy still raging in his head.

'No, Kate, don't worry about me.'

'This is worry?' and she grabbed his cock and started licking the end and it was getting all too much and he desperately tried to rise above it, concentrate on something else, but he couldn't and pulled away.

'Relax, Adam. Hey, what's that taste in my mouth? Coke? Adam, no, you didn't put coke on your cock, did you?' She burst out laughing. 'That's fucking amazing.'

Now he felt like a bald man with his wig on his pillow. It was the most embarrassing moment of his embarrassment of a life. Until...

He came.

Just like that.

Ha ha ha ha!

'I'm so sorry,' he said, mopping up the semen on the sheet with his Thai-silk black boxers. 'Now you know why I tried the coke. I guess I'm not accustomed to these out-of-hours seductions. I'd love to say it's because you're so damned beautiful but that's probably the oldest excuse in the world.'

'But hey, it's not a bad one,' she said. 'Please don't worry, Adam– and that's probably the oldest reaction to the oldest excuse in the world. I knew a guy once who loved slapping Charlie on his dick during sex.'

'How do you always know what to say and when to say it? God, I've never met anyone like you before. You really are a one-off. A very special one-off.'

'Thank you, kind sir. Shit, is that the time? I have to be up at seven. I'll make us some tea before you go.'

She quickly dressed and left the room. Adam fell back on the bed and saw out-of-body Adam peering down from above.

'Who the fuck are you looking at?'

Throughout the night, Adam hovered above Kate's bed, watching that sad play on repeat and hoping beyond hope that the ending would change.

'Goodnight, Kate.' They were standing on her doorstep. 'Thank you for a truly memorable evening. If you ever want to do it again, without the sex, please just whistle. You know how to whistle, don't you?'

'What, you mean I put my lips together and blow?'

It was Kate, not Lauren Bacall.

'That's exactly what I mean.'

She put her lips together and blew, and slowly closed the door. No kiss.

Why did it always end like that?

And who the fuck are you still looking at?

CHAPTER 14

Slurps All Round

The next morning, after Laura had gone to work, Adam walked into the kitchen, bleary-eyed and heartbroken. He was shocked to see his son, Ben, eating a bowl of Coco Pops–which Laura obviously bought especially for his homecoming–and reading the paper. He'd completely forgotten Ben arrived last night.

'Hello Dad. Christ, you look like shit.'

He needed his smartass son at this moment like he needed a hole in the head the size of Bobby's.

'Why aren't you at work?'

'A spot of "compassionate" leave,' said Ben. 'Need it big time.'

'Oh, yes. Sorry to hear about you and Julia. What happened? You both seemed happy–on the few occasions I saw you.'

'Still hot with the barbs, I see. I can't be arsed to talk about it now. Too fucking early, in more ways than one.'

Adam felt uncomfortable whenever Ben swore. It didn't sound right coming from someone he once cradled in his arms.

Ben continued eating the cereal and slurped a little and Adam thought he couldn't live with a person who slurped a little. It was a miracle Julia stayed with him for as long as she did. Why was he here? What was the point? Why, on this day of all days, when his dreams crash-landed, killing everyone on board because of a sleepless night and premature ejaculation, why was this man slurping and reading his newspaper in his kitchen?

Go away. Piss off.

'I'll be out for most of the day, dad. Look, I appreciate you letting me stay here. It won't be for long–I have my eye on an apartment in Canary Wharf. Looks like the bachelor life for me again.'

'But what about Amy?'

'She'll be fine. Julia's a great mother. I intend to be a very hands-on parent.'

Ben Tate was fast approaching thirty with a failed marriage, a two-year old daughter, a precarious but richly-rewarding job and a red Porsche 911 cabriolet. They all went together nicely–it was a sign of the times. He was six-three, played football and cricket and looked a little like Christian Bale.

He loved his mum and accepted his dad, there was no other way. His dad always seemed to have an aura of gloom about him and that depressed the hell out of Ben from an early age. When he finally left home and went to university, he knew within days, he'd never go back. The freedom was too pure, too clean and simple, and Ben decided he wanted it to last forever. A first-class honours degree in accountancy from Warwick and the confidence of a man who never relied on his father for guidance, landed him a job in investor relations at a pukka hedge fund operation.

He spent his days, and nights, schmoozing with clients, talking new funds, explaining lock-up periods and how investments are protected from downturns in the market while enjoying the full benefits of upswings–hence hedging your bets–and arranging meetings for hedge fund managers.

Whenever he was in town entertaining a potential investor, which was at least three times a week, Ben would hook up with a few of the guys after the meeting and hit clubs like Funky Buddha in Mayfair or The Valmont in Chelsea where they'd drink Cristal 'til three.

Some years he made a million, others he lost a few hundred thousand.

The last few years hadn't been kind. After the Madoff scandal, a lot of hedge fund companies went to the wall. But there was growing evidence that the recession was receding. City slickers are notoriously optimistic, it comes with the territory.

He met Julia at Home House, a private members'-only club in Portman Square behind Oxford Street. She was a solicitor at a prestigious firm in the City and was dressed like a Liver bird out clubbing on a hot Saturday night in July.

She looked stunning, but Ben soon forgot that when they started talking on the balcony over a couple of cigarettes and a bottle of champagne.

He'd never been so interested in a woman. What she said and how she said it fascinated him. Unlike most of the people he knew, she could discuss anything from the most volatile shares on the New York Stock Exchange to Katie Price via Arsenal and the shifting sands of politics in the Middle East. She genuinely laughed at his quips and insisted on buying another bottle which they shared over a few more cigarettes.

They were married within a year and Amy came along ten months later. Julia wanted two children one after the other, so she could return to work without further interruption. After having Amy, she decided one was enough and informed Ben that it was contraception all the way from now on.

Ben was disappointed. He liked the idea of a big family after spending his childhood and teenage years with either no sibling or one too young to give a toss. But he knew that once Julia made a decision, she wasn't for turning.

Their respective careers kept them apart most of the time and Ben started to lose interest in sex. He rekindled it with a PA at his office and their two-month fling made him realise that his desire for marriage was at an end.

But it was Julia who confessed to an affair first, with another lawyer at her firm. Ben kicked himself for reacting as he did. What he should've done was look incredibly hurt, say, 'How could you do this to me?', wipe a tear from his eye and trudge out of the room.

Instead, he said, 'Well, I hope sex with him is as good as the sex I've been having with Emma at work! You remember Emma, the leggy blonde I danced with at the Christmas party.'

Julia slapped him and stormed out of the room giving the

impression, as lawyers do, that he was in the wrong. A far more effective reaction than Ben's lame 'yah boo sucks' jibe.

It was over. Ben was more hurt than Julia. He loved Amy deeply and it broke his heart to think she'd be brought up by another man. But Ben, unlike his dad, wore it well. It was the Christian Bale in him.

And now he was back home–a place where, he once vowed, he would never live again–watching his dad slurp his Oatibix and wondering where it all went wrong.

CHAPTER 15

Just That Kinda Guy

Two weeks had passed since his prodigal son's return and still no word from Kate. He tried hard to forget her, but it was impossible.

Adam could stand it no longer–he had to know if it really was the end of their relationship. Then it would be okay. Then he could get on with his life, or get off, or realise there is no life to get on or get off.

If only it hadn't ended so badly. He fetched her last email and clicked reply.

Hi Kate

How's tricks? You never call, you never write. Was it something I said/did/didn't say/didn't do? Was I just your plaything, someone to toy around with until the real thing came along? And I don't mean Coke!

Or are you truly, madly, deeply in love with me and terrified of confronting feelings you've never experienced before? That's it, isn't it?

Oh well, you've got a friend, y'know, whenever you're feeling blue.

Sweet dreams, Kate. Miss you.

Adam x

Two kisses would've been overkill.

Now, should it stay or should it go? His finger hovered over the send key. He could think of every reason in the world why he shouldn't launch the email into electric ladyland. So he sent it. Adam Tate was just that kinda guy.

He immediately wished he hadn't. 'Miss you?' That stinks. What a shit thing to say, 'Miss you.' Fuck. And would she get the real thing-Coca Cola allusion? The Carole King? Kate was cool and sharp but one thing she wasn't, was old. It all proved that the one thing he wasn't, was young.

He'd had a dusty grope with a woman young enough to be his daughter, granddaughter at a push, and he should be grateful. Guys his age would shake him by the hand and praise him for being a stud and envy the pants off him. He almost shagged a babe and the world was all right.

Except it wasn't.

Kate was his real thing. Anything else was tomfoolery. What was the point of it all if he couldn't see her again? A life with Kate in it was a life less ordinary. He wanted to live once more before he died, and he wanted to live it with Kate.

The email was his last chance.

Click.

Hey Adam, lovely to hear from you. I've been so busy you wouldn't believe. Why don't we meet for lunch next week? How does Thursday sound? There's a nice little Japanese place around the corner from my office, I think you said you'd eaten there once.

Shall we say 12.15?

K x

Lunch? And so early. Sex was out. She probably wanted a proper lunch date to see what he looked like in natural light. Or just talk without the aid of chemicals.

Okay, there was a kiss at the end, although the x wasn't snuggled up against her initial as usual. It was only a single space away, but it was as wide as an ocean.

Whatever, she wanted to see him again and that can't be bad.

Hi Kate

I know the one.

That should be fine. See you there.

He couldn't resist it.

You can't miss me – I'm the guy in the corner with a heart on his sleeve and a dagger in his soul.

Adam xx

He was just that kinda guy.

CHAPTER 16

Like a Virgin

S CENE 1
   The hand luggage X-ray area at Southampton Port. 2pm. Adam and Ben place their belongings into baskets that glide on a conveyor belt into the scanner. They are about to go on a two-night all-expenses-paid cruise for travel agents and the media to Amsterdam and back to celebrate the arrival of a brand-new ship. Forty hours of totally free fun. Adam thought Ben might appreciate it and Laura encouraged them to go when Adam received the invitation out of the blue.

S CENE 2
   Deck Nine. 2.20pm. Inside a stateroom. Adam and Ben reach it via a gangplank, some pretty impressive carpets and a glass elevator to the stars. The room has two single beds, a sofa, flat screen TV, en suite bathroom and, crucially, a balcony. Once the domain of the wealthy and the dying, cruising is the fastest growing sector of the UK travel industry and it costs the same as a good quality hotel in a land-based resort. However, round-the-clock eating (ships have more food in their holds than a small island republic in the Pacific), entertainment in lavish theatres, room service and a chance to drift through laughing seas on a ship that casts you ashore at the oldest and wisest cities in the world, are all included in the price.

   Ben has never set foot on a ship in his life. In cruise-speak that means he's a virgin. He and Adam stand in the middle of the room holding their bags.

   Adam–Which bed do you want?
   Ben–Not fussed, but I usually sleep nearest the window.
   Adam–Okay. I'll take the other one.
   Ben–Sure?

Adam–I hope you're not going to be like this for the next two days.

Ben–Like what?

Adam–Like Ben.

Ben–What's that supposed to mean?

Adam–It doesn't matter.

Ben–Of course it matters when you make a remark like that.

Adam–I just meant schmoozing me, y'know?

Ben–'Schmoozing' you?

Adam–Like saying you're not fussed when you are, and then rubbing it in with a subtle, 'Sure?' I'm not a client, Ben. I'm your dad.

Ben–Sorry, *dad*. I guess it was an easy mistake to make.

Adam–Sarcasm, huh? Jeez, this is a good start to a free piss-up to Amsterdam on a luxury cruise. Lighten up, son. Chill.

Ben–Says the dope smoker.

Adam–Can we unpack?

Adam hated it when his son alluded to his little habit. He felt embarrassed and self-indulgent and a poor excuse for a father. But it didn't stop him smoking. His dark life needed rainbows as much as it needed Kate's tongue. They both unpack in silence. Adam then checks out the press programme.

Adam–Tonight's dress code is informal–thank Christ for that. Shit, dickey bows tomorrow.

Ben–I like a dinner suit party. Creates a nice atmosphere.

Adam–I sometimes wonder if you're my son. Dinner jackets are coffins containing the undead.

Ben–Isn't that a line from *Like Clockwork*?

Adam–How would you know?

Ben–Just sounded like a preconceived line from a book.

Adam–Actually, it's from *Up In The Dumps*.

Ben–Never read it. Who's it by? I guess I'm not a well-read person.

Adam–Believe me, if you'd read my books you still wouldn't be a well-read person.

They both laugh.

Adam–C'mon, let's go and get a drink. The Beachcomber on the top deck appears to be serving cocktails. The sun is shining and we can have a cigarette.

Ben–Just have a quick slash first.

SCENE 3

The Beachcomber, Deck Twelve. Filipino bar staff in Hawaiian shirts serve banana daiquiris and Harvey Wallbangers to breast-blessed blondes in tight skirts who are busy eyeing up tall, young dudes with bizarre hairstyles.

They all answer to the name of Travel Agent and they all have uncertain futures, like every other fucker. 'Single Ladies' scoops out of the speakers. Adam and Ben feel good, Adam because Ben looks impressed and Ben because those two lines of coke in the stateroom bathroom hit the spot. He liked a line now and again and paid £150 a gram for the real deal that lasted a good hour longer than the fifty-quid variety.

Adam–What do you want to drink and don't say you're not fucking fussed.

Ben–Why, is the 'You're Not Fucking Fussed' off? In that case, I'll have a frozen strawberry daiquiri.

Adam–Do you want ice with that?

Ben–Do you want a punch in the gob?

Adam laughs and goes to the bar where he queues for ten minutes. When he returns with the drinks, Ben is chatting to a familiar face.

Kate–Hi, Adam.

Adam–Kate? What are you doing here?

Kate–It's my job, remember?

Ben–Almighty coincidence. We happened to be standing next to each other and started talking. Kate here asks me who I'm with, I mention your name and voila! She said you're old friends and actually having lunch next week.

Adam–We certainly are.

Kate–So this is your son. I can't believe it. Has anyone ever told you that you look a lot like Christian Bale?

Ben–Funnily enough...

Kate–Bruce, don't make me your one hope for a normal life.

Ben–Bruce? Oh yes. Jesus, you sound just like her.

Kate–Who?

Ben–Maggie Gyllenhaal. From *The Dark Knight*.

Kate–Character name?

Ben–Rachel.

Kate–Surname?

Ben–Oh, er, Smith?

Kate–Adam?

Adam–Dawes.

Kate–Correct.

Adam–She has a million of 'em.

Kate–Not that many. Anyway, must dash, I'm arranging all the press events and there's a meeting tonight over dinner. Let's get together tomorrow night when the heat's off. Why don't we have dinner? I'll text you the details.

Ben–Great. Look forward to it.

Adam–Me too.

Kate disappears into the crowd. Adam watches her walk away.

Ben–She's nice. On the ball. Runs her own PR company. She's the sort of girl who'd succeed in anything she did.

Adam–She does.

Ben–Plus, she's gorgeous.

Adam–She is. *(To himself)* She is.

SCENE 4

Deck Fourteen. 8pm. A lone figure smokes a joint in the darkness near the basketball court at the back of the ship. Adam left Ben in the cabin while he was getting ready and he made his way to the top deck where the air is cool and the smell of skunk vaporises high above the tall funnels. The North Sea is jumpy tonight. He wonders why Kate was washed up on his beach and wonders when she'll return to the sea. The mean sea. He always wonders when he's stoned.

SCENE 5

The Hispaniola Restaurant. Deck Six and decked out like Treasure Island. 8.30pm. Adam and Ben drink Long John Silver cocktails, rum-based, naturally, and share a table with Sean, a travel agent from Ireland who specialises in cruising, and his wife Patricia, who helps run the business. Sean is 45 and has cruised with every line from Silversea to Royal Caribbean via Star Clippers and Oceania. He says bookings are up twenty per cent on last year and appears to be a happy man. They have three children under ten, met in a Dublin bar on St Patrick's night and are members of a hiking club. Adam wonders why. The conversation runs dry over coffee, but the wine pleases and lightens the load. Seating plans are loose cannons and beggars can't be choosers, but Sean and Patricia turn out to be good company.

The rest of the evening is made up of small talk in various bars, a glimpse of the show in the theatre, another cocktail in the Ben Gunn disco on the top deck and then both back in bed at 1.30am watching 300 on the movie channel.

SCENE 6

11am. The Grey Area coffee shop in Amsterdam. It's one of Amsterdam's smallest but it's in a smart area away from the red-light district and Adam remembers from a previous visit that it sold great weed and played classic punk. Adam is relieved to discover it still does, on both counts.

Adam and Ben are seated at one of only two tables drinking jasmine-flavoured green tea. Adam begins to roll a joint of White Widow. The music kicks in...

'New Rose', The Damned...

Adam–So you've smoked before?

Ben–You are joking, right?

Adam–Well, I don't know.

Ben–You wouldn't. We never discussed it. We never discussed a lot of things. Funny, when someone handed me my first joint, I was a naïve 14-year-old. I never knew what it smelled like, but when I caught that first whiff I realised what my dad had been smoking for all those years.

Adam lights the joint, inhales long and hard and passes it to his son.

Adam–This is strong stuff. That's number twelve in the 'Book of Stoned Clichés'.

Ben draws equally long and hard but retains the spliff for another two lots of long and hard.

Adam–Do you realise this is the first time we've ever taken drugs together? Amazing.

Ben–Do you mean amazing as in how many dads would ever do such a thing or amazing as in it's taken 29 years for it to happen? You may have stopped smoking when I was ten, but it didn't stop you smoking, if you get my drift. Do I get my drift? Fuck, this is strong shit.

Adam–I'll plump for the first amazing, I think.

'Hanging Around', The Stranglers…

Ben rarely swears in his dad's company and Adam is a little discomfited, made worse by the fact that it makes Ben sound uncannily like Bobby, complete with that customary snarl and the intimidating emphasis on the 'ck' in 'fuck'. They finish the joint, sip their teas and lean back in their chairs.

Ben–So what's number one in the 'Book of Stoned Clichés'?

Adam–I guess it has to be, 'I'm never smoking this stuff again,' closely followed by, 'What the fuck have I done with my life?'

Ben–Chastening words. Do you often think that?

Adam–What, about never smoking dope again? Constantly.

Ben–Y'know what I mean. What you said. The other thing. The, er, what have you done with your life line.

Adam–And I've just thrown you one.

Ben–Thrown me a what?

Adam – A lifeline. Let me see your hand.

'Police & Thieves', The Clash...

He takes Ben's hand and looks at the palm.

Adam–I know nothing of palmistry, but I know a good lifeline when I see it. Twice in my life, someone has offered to read my palm. The first time I was 17. I'd come out of hospital after having an operation to pin together a shattered elbow. The guy in the next bed had also been discharged. He was admitted a few nights earlier as a suspected heart attack victim, but it turned out to be acute indigestion. He was a vagrant, about sixty, who spoke eloquently and sincerely and wove a tale of Hampstead mansions he owned and film sets he built which I thought were the ramblings of an alcoholic fantasist. Then he showed me a copy of The Sunday Times Magazine, dated two years earlier, with his picture on the cover and an eight-page article about his hugely successful movie-set designer company inside.

'The life I was living, it stopped feeling right,' David, the mystery vagrant told me as we walked to a pub around the corner from the hospital with granddad, a packet of Peter Stuyvesant and a sudden desire for a pint of Red Barrel. We'd both just been discharged.

'I was suffocating, cocooned from life, true, unadulterated life,' said David. We were sitting around a table in the saloon bar with the drinks granddad bought in front of us. 'I had no idea what this glorious country of ours looked like, smelled like, tasted like. I wanted to find out by becoming part of it, by immersing myself in all its dirt and glory. So, one fine, bright, May morning after that article was published, I closed the front door behind me and, without a penny in my pocket, I ne'er cast a clout until that fine month was out and kept on walking. Took me a year to get to Loch Ness, another year to get back and I still haven't a penny in my pocket. But I'm alive, and I've never felt more satisfied, more complete.'

Ben wondered whether this was an interesting tale or the Widow working wonders. It was like reading a book, his dad's book, a book he secretly admired. Adam paused and sucked like a Dyson.

Ben—So what happened then?

Adam—When?

Ben—Don't start that again. After he told you that.

Adam—Told me what? Who?

Ben—The bloke from Hampstead. Er, Daniel.

Adam—David?

Ben—Yes, David.

Adam—So, we're sitting round the table and David said he had the gift of palmistry and it somehow sounded more plausible now I knew his background. He smiled at me and took my right hand, turned it over and looked carefully at my palm. Without saying a word, he closed my hand.

'Let's have a look at your dad's palm.' He studied it for a while, and then he said he'd have a long, healthy life—make it to a century no less—and never die of cancer.'

Ben—Well, he was wrong about the cancer bit.

Adam—Not necessarily. He said he'd never die of cancer, not that he'd never get it. And he's not dead yet.

Ben—Didn't you ask him why he refused to read your palm?

Adam—Of course I did. He smiled and said nothing. Nothing at all. Freaked me out. Granddad wanted to chin him, but I laughed it off and we sat there for another two hours.

Ben—You said there were two.

Adam—Two what?

Ben—Too much. Too soon. Shit, two tales.

Adam—A pushmi-pullyu.

They both laugh uncontrollably and a couple of German guys at the other table join in, although they have absolutely no idea why. The hoots soon change to toots and Adam strolls back into the second tale of two readings.

'Exodus', Bob Marley & The Wailers...

Adam–Christmas night that same year. I was at a party at my mate's flat and talking to his grandmother, an Irish woman called Tessie who had a twinkle in her eye and a sparkle in her words. My mate's mum came over and asked Tessie if she'd go into the kitchen where several women were waiting for her to tell their fortunes. I helped her get out of her chair and the two women left the room. After ten minutes, I decided to check out the kitchen. Tessie was wrapping up a palm reading.

'And this blonde guy will become the most important person in your life. Whether you'll marry him remains to be seen but there is an accident of some sort that, though not fatal, is pretty serious and has repercussions, y'know. There's a lot of happiness ahead for you but you have to work harder at looking for it otherwise you're in danger of losing out altogether.'

Tessie saw me leaning by the door and beckoned me over. 'Adam, let me read your palm for a moment. I'm curious, y'know.' Without waiting for a reply, she grasped my hand and spun it round and gazed at my palm for ten seconds before closing it without saying a word, like David had done seven months earlier.

'What's wrong?' Outside I was asking politely but inside I was begging. She smiled and said nothing. Nothing at all.

Ben–Well, you're still here.

Adam–But for how long?

Ben–You're coming up to sixty, dad. I'd say you've had a result even if you never made it back to the boat today and dropped down dead right here, right now.

Adam–Never say 'boat', it's a cardinal sin. Always use the word 'ship'.

Ben–But what if I say to the captain he has a 'cracking boat'?

Adam–Then if he's a Londoner, he might think you're gay.

They both start laughing and the boys from Berlin on the next table join in again.

Adam–This is a little too surreal. Shall we go for a walk?

Ben–If I can stand up. That's cliché number eleven.

Adam–And it's cliché number one for me. At the moment.

SCENE 7

The Cafe Majestic in Dam Square. The square is a wonderland bathed in the delicate warmth of a northern sun and full of smiling faces and an honest-to-goodness dope-induced happiness so thick you could bite into it. Adam and Ben sit at a table in the sunshine drinking ice cold bottles of Amstel and watching the girls and boys go by. Smoking dope with a son he thought he'd lost is a magical moment for Adam. Smoking dope with a father he never had is delightfully strange for Ben and, strangely, reassuring.

Ben–This is one of the good days.

Adam–Amen.

Ben–You're not so bad, for a twat.

Adam–Takes one to know one. In fact, you're such a twat, you're not on Twitter, you're on Twatter.

Ben–Twatter be the day.

They start to laugh. The German guys from the coffee shop walk by and crease up.

Ben–This'll surprise you, I read *Like Clockwork* about five years ago.

Adam–And?

Ben–I thought it was brilliant.

Adam–Why did you never tell me?

Ben–I didn't want to give you the satisfaction. You were a peripheral figure in my life, more like a next-door neighbour than a dad. I guess my ambivalence knew no bounds.

Adam–I didn't know how to be a dad. Nobody showed me. I could handle you and Jack when you were kids but when you started getting minds of your own, I didn't have a strong enough personality to exert control, unlike your mother, and you both knew that. And as you've grown, I simply couldn't believe I was a father to another man who was faster, stronger, bigger and more successful than me. It's kinda unnerving.

Ben–So what you're telling me here is that you're basically a pussy. My dad's a pussy. I have a pussy for a dad.

Adam–Ain't that the truth. Have you read the others?

Ben–What, your books? I started *Up In The Dumps* but you lost me and I couldn't get past the first ten pages. I never attempted *Big Boys Don't Cry*. Sorry.

Adam–It's par for the course. But I'm so glad you read *Clockwork*. It means a lot to this pussy.

His son thinking Clockwork was 'brilliant' means the world to him, more than any glowing review, more than any award. Adam doesn't know why. How can he? It's father and son stuff, uncharted shit.

Adam–We'd better head back. Cliché number eleven again.

Ben–Which way do we go? Cliché number, what, six?

Adam–At this precise moment I haven't a clue. That's five.

SCENE 8

Deck Fourteen. 8.30pm. Two figures in dinner suits smoke a couple of joints in the darkness near the basketball court at the back of the ship. Adam sneaked half an ounce of Widow aboard in a dummy deodorant spray bought for the equivalent of twenty quid that neutralised the smell of the buds.

The temptation was too great; smoke like that was hard to come by back home.

It was worth the frisk. For the first time on a ship, Adam had a smoking partner.

Ben–I have some Charlie if you fancy a line later.

Adam–I can't believe my son is offering me drugs. Your mother would crucify me if she knew.

Ben–So, you don't want any?

Adam–Now, when did I say that? Just call me Jesus when we get home. I'll have a swift line after dinner, talking of which, we'd better head down.

(Exit)

SCENE 9
Deck Four. 9pm. The Santa Maria Restaurant.

Adam and Ben drink vodka-based Columbus cocktails and share a round table with three travel journalists.

Adam knows Phoebe, 49, who writes for the specialist cruise press, The Guardian and Cosmo. He's also familiar with Henry, 55, ex-travel editor of a national who spends half his life at sea reviewing cruises. It's the first time he's met Claire, 24, who works for a travel trade publication.

They've all been invited by the sixth diner, Kate. She insists Ben sits to her right, as he's the odd one out, and tells Henry to take the chair to her left, because he's just odd.

Adam sits in between Phoebe and Claire.

They gossip, exchange travel tales and hit the banter button now and again. They feel comfortable telling their wonderful stories because outside of such circles it would be mistaken for boasting.

Adam is wound up.

He's not sure if it's the Widow or the fact that everyone has taken to Ben, including Kate. In fact, Kate seems to be talking to Ben more than anyone else. In between quips and the jibes, the shadow of jealousy creeps over him like a slowly spreading wine stain on a crisp, white tablecloth.

Jealous? How is it possible? How did this happen? The woman he craves flirting with his son? My God, her tongue in Ben's mouth leading him through the swirling darkness, his swirling darkness, into that eternal light?

Henry–Funny how I've always found it impossible to write a story at any time but the night before deadline. It's the buccaneer in me.

Henry looks like a bald Richard Branson and is a sumptuous writer.

Adam tends to liken people to celebrities these days, it's easier to remember them.

Phoebe—In that case, a vast majority of journalists should brandish a cutlass and yell, 'me hearties!'

Phoebe has a Deirdre Barlow feel, without the vibrating throat and the manic eyes. It's the glasses and the sexycloggy voice of a lifelong smoker.

Claire—I'm the exact opposite. Sometimes I write a thousand words at seven in the morning weeks before it's due. It's the swot in me.

Claire is a definite Gwyneth Paltrow, peachy and perky and gorgeous, but far too straight.

Kate—Me too. I like a clear desk.

Phoebe—Ah, the young.

Henry—And exceedingly attractive.

Phoebe—Ah, the ignominy. I'm afraid under cover of the night works for me. I, too, am a buccaneer. What about you Adam? When do you like to write?

Adam—Me? I get stoned around midnight, write some words and read them the next night when I'm stoned again and either laugh out loud or cry. I then add some more stoned lines until it all becomes etched in stone. Writing is spontaneity, spontaneity is ingenuity and ingenuity buys time. Excuse me, it's the White Widow talking, I'm an innocent bystander.

Did he say that to impress Kate? Ben? Himself? Dumb.

Henry—Well, that seems like a capital way of writing, but it sounds like one article could take several months.

Phoebe—Or years even.

They both laugh. Adam joins in.

Claire—What's White Widow?

Kate—It's a type of skunk, I do believe. Ben, did you and your dad have a sneaky smoke in Amsterdam today?

Adam thought she said 'dad' in a condescending way, implying great age and senility. She swallowed coke off his senile cock, for fuck's sake.

Ben–There was nothing sneaky about it. The place is full of respectable tourists who treat coffee shops as must do's, like having breakfast at Tiffany's or watching the changing of the guard.

Phoebe–Tossing a coin into the Trevi fountain or sipping a Singapore Sling in Raffles.

Henry–Getting pissed at the carnival in Rio or getting pissed while sailing past the Sydney Opera House.

Kate–Or getting stoned in Amsterdam.

Ben–I'd never been to Amsterdam before, and I adored it. It's so relaxed, so friendly, so civilised. And if a spoonful of sugar helps the medicine go down then hit me with the Tate & Lyle.

Everyone laughs. Except Adam.

Ben–Hey, you're Lyle and I'm Tate. Wow!

Kate–Oh yes! I never thought of that.

Adam feels like Michael Corleone when he realised his brother Fredo had double-crossed him in Havana. The hurt is incalculable.

Phoebe–That's a coincidence. Are you sweet on each other?

Henry–She's caster spell on him. I'm sure you can throw one into the mix, Adam.

Adam–If they were caught in a fire would they turn to syrup?

Henry roars.

Phoebe–Bad taste Adam, and a little abstruse.

Ben–Absolutely. Everyone knows sugar would char in naked flames. You must keep stirring it in a pan to obtain syrup, duh.

Adam–Okay, would they turn to syrup if they were in a boiling hot pan and being stirred?

Kate – Well, they'd definitely be shaken.

Claire laughs and Adam wonders if Kate ever banged cocktail waitresses two at a time.

The dinner has drained him. He's been stoned by a Widow and the two lines of Ben's £150-a-gram coke he had after the meal in the Santa Maria toilet. He's been stoned by an endless free supply of exceedingly expensive red wine and Columbus cocktails. And he's been stoned by the Medusa eyes of Kate. He's heading for a tenth avenue freeze-out. His legs are starting to shake.

Adam—I have to pop back to the cabin for something. I'll catch up with you guys later.

Ben—Shall I come back with you?

Adam—No, that's all right. I'll see you in ten minutes.

(Exit)

SCENE 10

Deck Nine. 11pm, Inside Adam's stateroom. His mobile rings. He's puking in the toilet. He wipes his mouth and picks up the phone.

Ben—Hey dad, you've been a lot longer than ten minutes.

Adam—Sorry son, I dozed off.

Ben—Well, we're heading for the disco up on deck sixteen if you're game.

Adam—I think I'll pass.

Ben—You don't know what you're missing. Kate is a fireball. I gave her a line and she gave me one back. We're having a ball. Is cruising always like this?

Adam—Only when the drinks are free. Enjoy.

He starts to feel sick again...

SCENE 11

Deck Nine. 5am. Inside the same stateroom. The cabin door opens, and Ben enters quietly. He strips down to his Armani pants and slips into the bed nearest the window.

Ben—(in a loud whisper) Wow!

The sound of a tear falling onto the pillow in the next bed pierces the night in two.

CHAPTER 17

'D-l-r-o-w'

Bobby Tate was losing it. He'd ring Adam at 4am to ask him why he hadn't been round yet and remind him to bring a punnet of strawberries, a dozen mandarins and fifty lottery tickets. The only fruit his dad ever used to eat came out of a tin and was covered in syrup. Now he was eating fresh strawberries and mandarins with Birds custard like there was no tomorrow.

He'd weep for no apparent reason and plead with God to take him now, yet he truly believed he had a special brain that was 24 hours ahead of everyone else's. He was convinced that everything happening now had already happened and that could sometimes be mighty confusing. He could get so confused that he'd turn on all the gas cooker hobs to warm the place up when he came downstairs in the morning, and forget to light them, causing the newly-installed carbon monoxide alarm to kick in. 'I knew that was going to happen,' he'd tell Coral as she came downstairs and turned them off, yet again. 'Knew it.'

'Pity you could never do that when it came to the racing results, you senile old fucker.'

But it was when he started throwing himself down the stairs that the problems really began.

Bobby got it into his head that Adam and Coral were plotting to get him sectioned. It was the spiv inside. He believed they were after his money, his house, his life.

Right up until his eighties, Bobby liked nothing more than a good funeral. Watching his friends slide through the crematorium curtains on that *Generation Game* conveyor belt into the big heat as Sinatra sang 'My Way' gave him such a thrill. It was divine confirmation that he always knew what was best. None of these bastards would live longer than Bobby Tate because Bobby Tate always knew what was best. He was living proof that knowing what was best would keep you alive.

The funerals of people he knew dried up years ago, but he carried on living. He carried on living through the funerals of those people's sons and daughters and, occasionally, their sons and daughters, too.

He truly believed he would outlive his wife and son and those bastard grandsons that he never set eyes on and Laura, the shitty whore. Why would any son of his want to get cased up with a slag out of Walthamstow? It didn't make any sense.

He thought none of them deserved to live longer than him, especially Coral and his conniving son.

'I know things about your mother, things you wouldn't like to hear,' he'd say in front of them both, his eyes riddled with rancour of the most devout kind.

The first time Bobby launched himself backwards down five stairs, Adam caught him under each arm. He'd been threatening to kill himself all day and threw the front door keys out into the street before standing at the top of the stairs plucking up the courage to jump.

Adam dashed round when Coral rang him and managed to calm his dad down. He still thought it wise to ring the GP and a doctor in his late twenties popped in after the surgery closed. The moment he walked into the room, Bobby got out of his customary armchair and said he was going to the toilet upstairs. After a couple of minutes, Adam became suspicious and walked out to the staircase in time to catch his flying father who screamed, 'Fucking traitorous cunt!'

The visibly shocked GP made Bobby sit down and warned him he would have to take drastic action if he ever tried anything like that again.

Over the next week, Bobby received visits from the palliative care team, Crisis in Islington, a council social worker, the head of the district nurses and a mental health specialist attached to the council who asked him a series of questions to determine his mental capacity.

'What's your name?'

'Robert.' He rolled the 'r'. 'Edward James Tate.'

'What's your date of birth, Robert?'

'Er, thirteenth of the eleventh, 1916.'

'What day is it?'

'Thursday, no, wait a minute, Wednesday, or could it be Friday?'

Good, thought Adam who sat in the other room but could still hear the conversation. He messed that one up. His dad was a natural hoodwinker, but it looked like he may have winked his last hood.

'What month?'

'June, no, I tell a lie. May.'

'Where are you now, Bobby?'

'In my home. My home where I want to stay.' He could still really nail the Mr Pitiful look.

'And what's the address?'

'36 Marsley Crescent.'

'Good.'

The specialist asked a few simple arithmetic questions and then some about personal hygiene and eating habits. Then he threw a curve-ball:

'Can you spell the word "world" for me, Bobby?'

Tricky.

'W-o-r-l-d.'

'Can you spell it backwards?'

'D-l-r-o-w.'

Just like that. Hahahahaha!

'There's some senility but that's only to be expected,' the specialist told Adam on his way out.

'In fact, his mental state is surprisingly pretty good and I feel he's capable of making decisions. I'll write a report and recommend a further visit in a week.'

The second time Bobby launched himself backwards down five stairs, three days after that test, there was nobody around to catch the fallen star that had made a capable decision. Coral rang for an ambulance and then called Adam. By the time he arrived, three paramedics were carrying Bobby out on a stretcher.

'You fucker,' he screamed. 'You did this to me.'

'Did what, dad?'

'This.' Bobby pointed to himself.

Inside, Coral showed him a note Bobby had written before his backward flip.

To whom it may concern

I am taking my own life because my son, Adam, and my wife, Coral, have been plotting to get me out of my home so they can get their hands on my money and I cannot take it anymore. Robert Tate

'I showed it to the ambulance men and they said it was common for old people to turn on the people they love the most.'

'In that case,' said Coral, 'I certainly won't be turning on him when I lose my marbles.'

That last remark terrified Adam because it pre-supposed she would live long enough to become senile and, even worse, Bobby would still be around to witness it.

His dad wasn't his dad anymore. He was this strange bloke who didn't trust his son or his wife. A seven-stone, 95-year-old spiv who could only eat purees from Meals on Wheels and who recently started shitting the bed.

Why was he still alive? He had all the symptoms of a quick-change schizoid–smiling one minute, snarling the next. He inhabited a murky world of dead gangsters and indifference, constantly veering between hate and despair. It was demeaning whenever the hole in his face was exposed, revealing a bottomless cavern and an old faithful geyser that spouted blood and foul-smelling pus onto his shirt collar.

We really do stink. Our insides reek of decay from the moment we're born. Only skin prevents the stench and the swill from saturating the space around us. This was a train of thought Adam shouldn't have boarded but there's nothing more intoxicatingly painful than the smell of mortality.

It was a good job he jumped. He won't get over that. Not at his age. Adam felt an overwhelming sense of relief, immediately followed by an overwhelming sense of grief. His dad had sacrificed himself, for his son. He did the right thing in the end. He was made of the right stuff. Mr Right. My dad.

Bobby sprained his ankle. Lightly.

They kept him in hospital for a while because he was in no fit state to go home to be cared for by a sick wife and Adam. Always Adam. Old age and illness were up ahead a ways and he didn't want them seeping into his 56-year-old life now, like the witches' brew that left filthy brown stains on Bobby's shirt collars.

His dad had regressed into a hideous stroppy adolescent who demanded the world and detested his son for not letting him have it. Adam had gone from no fatherhood to four fatherhoods, having to be a different man to his 15-year-old son, his 29-year-old son and his mum and his dad, all at the same time. He should be on *Britain's Got Talent*. He'd piss it.

And then there was Coral. She was glad to see the back of Bobby but after two days of sleeping home alone she realised it wasn't all it was cracked up to be and yearned for the strength of her gangster husband who protected her from the world.

Adam now had two journeys each day; to see his dad in hospital and then drive round to check on his mum and invariably cook for her because she couldn't be bothered to prepare food for herself. He'd microwave 'ready steady go' meals perfect for the weak and the old and the infirm, full of dumplings and casseroles and cheddar mash potato.

It went on for a week, his dad ranting and raving at him every time he visited but laughing and joking with the nurses who laughed and joked back and told Adam his dad was wonderful and so charming. Hoodwinker extraordinaire. Coral looked more and more depressed and took prescribed sedatives that rendered her a zombie.

Then, one night, in her undead state, she broke her hip after falling down those accursed stairs and stayed there, home alone, for nine hours until Adam found her the next day on the floor surrounded by broken video tapes that she grabbed from the shelf nearby and threw at the wall desperately hoping someone would hear the noise.

The ambulance arrived with two paramedics. It took them an hour to get her out through the front window because the special stretcher that strapped her in like an astronaut was too wide to go through the front door.

Adam stayed at the hospital with her until four am. She won't get over that. A crumpled heap for all those hours? At her age? And in her condition? It was for the best. Adam felt an overwhelming sense of relief immediately followed by an overwhelming sense of grief. His mum had sacrificed herself. For her son. She did the right thing in the end. She was made of the right stuff. Mrs Right.

Coral underwent emergency surgery lasting four hours. She won't get over that. A four-hour operation? At her age? And in her condition? It was for the best.

Adam tentatively rang the hospital after the operation, expecting the worst.

'Your mum is conscious now and the operation was successful.'

When he saw Coral a few hours after surgery, she was sitting up and drinking tea. Her cheeks were bright but her eyes were yellow.

'All right, mum?'

'I'm fine. I'm so sorry.'

'There's nothing to be sorry about. It broke my heart to see you in that state, and for all that time. It's those pills. They knocked the stuffing out of you. What were they called? Began with an L.'

'Langoustine?'

'No, mum, not langoustine. I told you to stop taking them.'

'What, the langoustine?

'No. Oh, I can't remember now. You slept through 'til 5pm the first time you took one. Remember? I thought the same thing had happened but then I started to get worried.'

'I'm so sorry, Adam.'

'Don't keep saying you're sorry. There's nothing to be sorry about. Remember?'

Her ward was two floors below Bobby's and most days Adam wheeled his dad down to see her. At first, Bobby was sweetness and light. He kissed her cheek and held her hand and said how he couldn't wait to get home. But then Mr Hyde would stroll in from the wings.

'You're both conspiring to keep me in here. There's nothing wrong with me. I was dancing in the ward this morning in front of everyone. Why are you fuckers doing this to me? You're an evil pair of bastards. You're not my son, your mother whored herself out to anyone who would fuck her. I have plenty of money. I could be in the best nursing home in the country with the likes of Thatcher and Bruce Forsyth and Kirk Douglas. I could, but you fuckers won't let me. Why won't you let me? Why? I knew all this would happen. I watched it happen, before.'

It was the same rant most days, with the odd extra 'fuck' to break the monotony.

Coral, initially upset by these outbursts, now told him to piss off back to his ward because he was a silly old bastard. Then Bobby would weep and his ear would leak and his heart would break and Adam pitied him more than anyone else he'd ever known. He knew his dad didn't mean what he said–he never spoke like that before in front of him or his mum. In that pre-bonkers world, his dad had once respected him, and Adam couldn't forget.

Coral was discharged from hospital two weeks after her operation, far earlier than Adam expected. He'd hired a plumber to install a bathroom and new boiler in the small utility room downstairs and it was taking a lot longer than expected mainly because the plumber was in the middle of four other jobs.

Coral was confined to her bed upstairs so Adam had arranged at the last minute for an aerial socket to be installed in her bedroom and he nipped out and bought a 22-inch HD-ready special so she could watch David Dickinson and Noel Edmunds to her heart's content. He also bought a mini fridge which kept her Ensure food supplement shakes chilled in her bedside cabinet.

It was back to the old routine, two visits a day to cook for his mum and keep her company for a few hours and then a few more hours with his dad in the hospital. At least when they were both in hospital he didn't have to do the shopping, but now she was out, the ready meal section at Tesco's beckoned.

For the first six weeks after leaving hospital, Coral had a daily half-hour visit from a re-enablement carer. Adam requested that the carers arrive around midday so they could prepare ready meals. They gained access via a key safe on the wall by the front door that could only be opened with a 'secret' combination known, by Adam's reckoning, to at least a dozen people from occupational therapy to palliative care via social services and the district nurses. The days when Bobby refused the care offered by the council had long gone.

But Coral didn't like the idea of her food being microwaved by a stranger, especially one with an exotic name and an incoherent accent. The visits slowly became earlier and all that was provided was tea and a little sympathy. It fell upon Adam to become head chef. Every afternoon he'd nuke a cottage pie or a chicken korma and every afternoon he'd throw half of it away. The only thing Coral enjoyed was a slice of apple pie submerged in a bowl of hot Ambrosia Devon cream custard.

They'd sit and watch *Deal Or No Deal* and reminisce and he'd help her with her exercises. A funny thing, he always kissed her goodbye. Adam hardly ever kissed his mum, but she looked so vulnerable and he knew she wouldn't see a soul until the following morning. He wished he could take her with him and protect her from harm. And then there was the money. A lonely old woman in a house full of cash.

And a gun.

He remembered seeing it once, when he was eleven. He had a pet hamster that sometimes escaped from its cage and Adam would try and find it around the house. On this occasion, Bobby and Coral were both out so he went into their bedroom and saw that a drawer on the bedside table wasn't closed properly. There were bits of shredded tissue on the floor directly beneath it and he guessed the hamster was in there.

And it was, nestling up against a Luger pistol. He recognised the make because he had a toy one. That was the first time it dawned on Adam that his father was a villain.

He was too afraid to touch it and never mentioned he'd seen it and never saw it again.

Someone had won £250,000 on *Deal Or No Deal* for only the third time in five years.

'Think of winning all that money,' said Coral.

'But dad reckons he has loads more than that stashed away,' said Adam. 'Where does he keep all that money?'

'What money?'

'You know full well what money, mum. He's told us enough times. I hate to think it's lying around here when the whole world and its mother knows the combination of the key safe.'

'And you believed him? We live on our pensions and disablement benefits. That's all.'

Adam had turned the place upside down while they were both in hospital. He couldn't find a penny.'

'C'mon mum. You know.'

'Well, now you come to think of it, I do remember seeing the odd bag of money, every so often. But it soon went. I'm talking some years back now.'

'What do you mean, "it soon went"?'

'Well, I never saw it again.'

'So, you don't know where it went?'

'No, I suppose I don't. But if it's in the house, he's hidden it well. And do you honestly think he'd tell me about it? No, you're on your own there, son.'

'But what happened to all the money he made?'

'What money?'

'The money he mentioned in the, "suicide note." The money he made as a...' Adam lowered his voice even though they were the only people in the house, 'gangster.' It was the first time he'd said the 'g' word in front of his mum.

'Your father wasn't a gangster.'

'You do realise that I'm 56 now, mum. He was a gangster from the moment he could walk, we both know that.'

'He wasn't a gangster. He was more of a businessman. Most nights he was home by eight. He used to stroll through the door with a bunch of flowers and a smile and kiss me and tell me how lucky he was to be my husband. Then he'd chase you round the room, Adam, and sweep you up in those big arms of his and laugh like a child. He never once came home drunk and I know for a fact he never went with other women. You couldn't have wished for a better father, Adam. He always provided and provided well. You never wanted for anything. I miss him not being here.'

She started to cry.

'Pull yourself together, mum. What, you miss him threatening to kill himself and screaming at you and pissing the bed?' The unsympathetic approach usually pulled her round.

'I know. You're right. You're right.'

'Anyway, I have to go.'

'Thanks for coming. You're a good son.'

He bent down and pecked her on the lips.

'You never did answer my question.'

'What question?'

'What happened to all the money he made?'

'What money?'

He always knew when she was lying. As a kid, when she told him everything would be all right, he never believed her.

CHAPTER 18

Diamond Geezer

Bobby was coming home. After six weeks in hospital, this weeping man with the pernicious snarl and the gaping, leaky hole where half his face had been, was being discharged. Coral, though still bedbound, was as excited as a wartime bride. Her man was coming home.

Adam had explained to his dad in the hospital that the house was upside-down and he would have to live upstairs until the bathroom downstairs was operational. But Bobby was obviously too excited at the prospect of going home again to listen. He was about to be reunited with his wife after the longest time they'd ever been apart. Coral, the love of his life, the most beautiful woman he'd ever known.

By an almighty coincidence, that same day was their diamond wedding anniversary and, unbeknown to both, Adam had arranged for a telegram from the Queen (he only found out they were sent out to couples celebrating their diamond anniversaries during a recent pub quiz) which was due to arrive that morning.

The social services wanted Bobby to go into residential care, but he refused. Old people's homes were for old people, not for him. Not Bobby Tate. After all, wasn't he dancing in the ward only last night, and in front of everyone?

No, he had a lot more life in him. A lot more. Care homes were for losers, people who never looked after themselves the way he did. His wife was only 79. They could each have another ten years left. Easy. Besides, it was their wedding anniversary. He had to be with Coral to celebrate such a momentous occasion. He had to.

And Coral so wanted him to be there to share it.

Bobby was due to arrive home in an ambulance at around 10.30am and Adam figured he'd get there by ten. The plan was to usher his dad upstairs before he had time to take in the mess, and then hit them both with the telegram.

He took a leisurely drive down in his Mercedes 190E. It was black and felt hot to trot when he bought it nearly twenty years ago. Now he hadn't washed it in nine months. Outside–nicks and scratches and the occasional dent. Inside–dead matches, chewing gum wrappers, dog ends, screwed up bits of paper, more dog ends. The Slobmobile. Like driver like car.

He kept the car because his 36-year-old self and his 46-year-old self were his constant passengers, having once been the drivers, and they'd all trade tales and laugh and commiserate with each other. Adam often wondered if he'd be talking to his 66-year-old self as he sat in the back seat ten years from now.

He sauntered past the Edwardian facades that dominated the north London avenues, their elegance occasionally diminished by paper blinds and hotel signs and UPVC double glazing. For Sale notices, now more numerous than pigeons, festooned the streets. Nobody could sell, nobody could afford to buy, nobody could afford to pay for what they already owned.

'Life is fragile, handle it with prayer' was written on a placard outside a church.

His mobile rang. 'Hullo, Mr Tate?'

'Yes.'

'Oh, it's the ambulance HQ. We have a crew with your father outside 36, Marsley Crescent.'

'But you're not supposed to be there until 10.30, it's only 9.30. I'm on my way to the house now.'

'We never specify an exact time.'

'But that's a world away from exact.'

'Anyway, they are currently outside 36, Marsley Crescent, and unable to gain access.'

'There's a key safe outside the front door.'

'Where is the exact location of the key safe?'

'On the wall right by the door.' Jesus, it wasn't rocket science.

'Do you have the combination of the key safe?'

Oh well, there's another lot that know how to stroll into a house full of money with a gun in the mythical attic.

'3275H.'

'Thank you, Mr Tate.'

Adam had a bad feeling about this. He hoped the paramedics, having been made aware of Bobby's current situation and history, and knowing Adam was on his way, would help him upstairs to Coral's room and stay with them until they were settled.

When he arrived at the house there was no sign of an ambulance. As Adam got out of the car, a guy who lived down the road pulled up alongside on his motor bike and spoke through the open visor on his helmet.

'How's your dad?'

'Funnily enough, he's due out of hospital today. He's been in for six weeks.'

'Really? I didn't know it was that long. I saw the ambulance guys take him in, but they left almost immediately after I heard your dad telling them to go.'

Bobby appeared at the front door.

'You fuckpig!'

'Anyway,' said the neighbour, 'I'll catch you later.' He quickly pulled down his visor and zoomed off.

Adam didn't know if his dad was talking to him or the neighbour.

'Me?'

'Yes, you. You fucker.'

'Let's go inside, dad.'

'Look at the fucking state of this place.'

'It'll be all right in a few days.'

'A few days? A few fucking days?'

'Adam!'

It was his mum screaming and sobbing upstairs.

He ran up to her bedroom. She was in bed.

'He called me a shithouse. A shithouse! He said, "Look at you, snuggled up in bed watching Jeremy Kyle like a fucking lady of the manor stuffing food all day." Have him taken back, Adam. Ring for an ambulance and have him taken back again. I don't want him here.

'Get him out!'

'You ain't fucking getting me out.' Bobby shouted from downstairs. 'This is my home and I'm never leaving it again. You can count on that.'

Happy Anniversary.

CHAPTER 19

Alexei Sale

For Adam, the secret of a long marriage was seeing the girl you first met, every day.

Sometimes he would look at Laura and see that beautiful face in The Unicorn framed by long, straight, black-as-night hair almost touching the hem of her mini skirt.

But then a single word would add forty years to her face and conjure up the shadows of mortality that he tried so hard to avoid.

For Laura, there was no magic in marriage and if there was, it would be of the Tommy Cooper cock-up kind.

She envied her parents' happiness.

Her dad, Terry, was a black cab driver who played the piano and sang in pubs under the name, 'Terry Ray–The Entertainer'. He married Betty when they were both 19 in 1939 before Terry, bursting with optimism, went to Dunkirk where he was injured by a bullet that shattered his knee. He missed out on the rest of the war and worked as a builder with his dad.

But Terry was a night bird who couldn't cope with 6am alarms. So, he quit and started working as a receptionist in a West End night club before becoming a cabbie in the early fifties.

As The Entertainer, Terry was much sought after in those hi-fi free days. It was always a decent supplement to his earnings.

Terry knew all about Bobby Tate and his connection to the top dogs of the day–Jack Spot, the Whites, Billy Hill, Albert Dimes. He had a fearsome reputation and was known to everyone as 'The Enforcer'. Terry knew he was a dangerous bastard and steered well clear, although he did meet him on the rare occasions he visited the night club where Terry worked.

Bobby struck him as a sober, sombre kinda guy who looked like he could handle himself better than anyone he'd ever met. It came as a shock when Laura started going out with Bobby's son, compounded when she announced she was marrying him.

Terry took to Adam the moment he met him. He was mature for 19 and the fact that he eschewed a life of villainy and was training to be a journalist was impressive. His daughter could've done a lot worse.

He only met Bobby on three occasions as an in-law–the wedding and the two christenings. We'll never know if he saw him at his own funeral two years after Jack was born. But if Terry did, he would've heard Bobby say under his breath, 'Never did like the bastard. Bobby Tate always knows best. You won't catch me getting cancer. Fucking piano-playing ponce.'

Laura's mum knew she wouldn't be seeing much of Coral when they first met at the wedding. She thought it was odd they hadn't been introduced before. When Terry first clued her in about Bobby Tate, she feared for her daughter's safety. But when she got to know Adam, she was curious to find out what a real gangster looked like and, moreover, what a gangster's moll looked like, and she was bitterly disappointed at never being given the opportunity.

Betty took an instant dislike to Coral who appeared to look down her nose most of the time and make the odd snide remark that indicated she wasn't particularly happy about the marriage. She adopted the same attitude at both christenings and Betty avoided her, as much as common courtesy would allow, on both occasions, seeing as the Tates paid for everything.

Betty worked for the civil service at an employment exchange specialising in catering and had a decent salary. She read historical romances and sometimes cooked spaghetti to an authentic Italian recipe involving bacon, tomatoes, herbs and parmesan. She had a little gypsy in her soul and Terry Ray–The Entertainer, was different enough to love.

A brain tumour killed her a year after Terry's death. Suddenly, Laura was an orphan with two kids of her own and a husband who was an inch away from useless. She felt lonely for a few years, but life soon became tolerably predictable again. She had a good job, a successful son and a soon-to-be successful son. She was comfortable at home, she was comfortable with the odd wrinkle and she was comfortable with herself.

She looked good. In Adam's easy description mode, you would say she was a little like Geena Davis, only he never saw the resemblance, even though it had been pointed out to him on more than one occasion. She swam half a mile three mornings a week before going to work and she still had the look.

She could've done better than Adam, but Laura had a little gypsy in her soul and Adam Tate, Author, was different enough to love.

Laura, like her mother, had never been unfaithful, although she came close, once.

Terry had made enough money to buy a small retirement home in Cyprus. He and Betty had the holiday of their lives in Famagusta in 1973.

During their stay, they hired a couple of mopeds and one day chanced upon a deserted beach that was the closest thing to paradise they'd ever seen–blonde on blonde sand and a diaphanous shallow sea revealing curious fish that brushed purposely against their bodies as they swam.

After drying off, they strolled into a nearby fishing village devoid of people and traffic, devoured by the burning midday sun. The village was dominated by a 500-year-old sandstone monastery where monks meditated in cool cloister shadows. The only sound that greeted them as they wandered in through an open gate, unaware the monastery was still occupied, was conjured up by water dancing in a nearby fountain. They found themselves in a small courtyard. A monk was seated next to a well that appeared to be used as a font. He offered them some water and Betty never forgot his smile as he handed her a metal cup overflowing with cold, crisp nectar. He looked like Jesus. She'd never felt such peace, such tranquillity. She'd parachuted into paradise and wanted a slice. They decided there and then this was the place they would retire to and they bought a small villa on the side of a hill just outside the village on the opposite side to the monastery, commanding an impressive view of the sea beyond.

The village was called Ayia Napa and within ten years it got way too big for the Rays as it morphed into the party capital of the Med. They sold the villa and moved to Paralimni, a quiet village seven kilometres north-west of Napa, and bought a small house a stone's throw from the beach.

Laura used to take Ben and later, Jack, to the house for the entire summer holiday–she had an arrangement with her boss–while Adam stayed at home writing shit books for nobody.

Every year, her mum and dad and two brothers and their families would join them for a fortnight and Adam missed out on shiny days as broad as they were long, days overflowing with laughter and hope that went on forever. He thought the boys would be young forever too and that he'd always be able to catch up. But childhood withered and died and Adam's shot at ever being a father perished with it, daddio.

Laura learned how to speak Greek, or rather, Greek Cypriot, and became friendly with the locals. New languages came naturally to her. Adam went to Cyprus a few times in the early days when he was flush with a little success, but he found he could write so much more at home knowing everyone was away.

Laura always flew from Heathrow direct to Larnaca, which took over four hours. On one flight, the first without Ben who'd gone on holiday with some friends and was flying out to join her in two weeks, she started talking to the person in the next seat, a Greek guy, when three-year-old Jack had nodded off in the window seat. She usually avoided any interaction with fellow passengers, especially men, but Alexei was, well, pretty stunning. A laid-back, highly intelligent, supremely witty hunk of burnin' classic Greek love–dark hair, dark eyes, dark smile–who exuded wealth.

He was a thirty-year-old architect who worked for his father's large Nicosia-based firm that had offices in London, Zurich and Sydney.

'I've been in London for several weeks and received an urgent business call today summoning me back to Cyprus. First class was full.' He said the words 'first class' effortlessly and without a blemish of conceit and Laura was impressed. Alexei was more impressed when he discovered she spoke Greek and they conversed in both languages for the remainder of the flight.

His mother was English, he went to Eton and Oxford, and his manners were exquisite.

'It is so rare for an Englishwoman to know my language,' he told her. 'Many British people live in Cyprus, but only a tiny percentage speak Greek as well as you. And you say you only come here for a holiday?'

'A six-week holiday. Every year.'

'Six weeks, six months, six years, still no Englishwoman could comprehend the subtleties and then be able to express them as wonderfully as you. Laura, you have the key to my Greek soul.'

Laura Tate knew when she was being chatted up, and boy, was that a come-on.

'I was always good at languages at school,' she said, like a schoolgirl. How delightfully ludicrous, how sweetly embarrassing.

Alexei handed her his business card when Laura told him she was thinking of selling the house in Paralimni. Betty had passed away six months earlier and Laura and her two brothers were waiting for probate to be granted and then the house was to be sold and the proceeds split equally amongst the entire family. Adam was rubbing his hands at the prospect.

'I know every estate agent in Cyprus and I'm confident I could secure you the very best deal when you decide to go ahead,' he said.

'Give me your phone number.'

And she did.

He rang two days later.

They arranged to meet for dinner in Larnaca, a major tourist resort roughly halfway between Nicosia and Paralimni. Alexei initially suggested he'd drive to her place to pick her up, but she knew that wouldn't look good in front of the neighbours. She also wanted to avoid nearby holiday hotspots, Protoras and Ayia Napa, because it was always possible to bump into someone you didn't want to bump into when there's a young, handsome man at your side.

Laura left Jack with a friend on the other side of town.

She didn't know why she decided to drive the 65 kilometres to Larnaca for an assignation with an attractive man on the pretence of discussing a property sale. Obviously, he knew it was a pretence, so what was expected? She hadn't been on a date since she met Adam, so she was a little out of shape, experience-wise.

'Will he ask me to stay the night in his beachfront villa? Am I going to have sex? An affair? Will he still love me tomorrow? Will I leave Adam? How many times a week should I allow Adam access to Ben? WHAT ABOUT CONTRACEPTIVES? Say I got pregnant with Alexei's child which I pass off as Adam's and twenty years later Alexei turns up on my doorstep to tell me he's discovered by a freak coincidence that my third son is his and he wants to offer him a partnership in a billion-dollar architect company because, surprise, surprise, my son is studying to be a surveyor.

'And Adam finds out.

'And kills Alexei.

'And then kills me?

'Imagine.'

It was a forty-minute drive, the stereo was bust and her thoughts smashed into the windscreen on the inside like the big, fat, blinded-by-the-light insects on the outside. She was usually so calm, so reticent, so indistinguishable from the rest of the human race and it was all a little unnerving. But that splash of gypsy kept her foot on the gas and her eyes on the road. And she went all the way.

They had a fish meze on a candlelit balcony overlooking the sea and the waiter treated them like royalty. This handsome, successful man had the hots for her and Laura couldn't believe it. She knew she wasn't exactly unattractive, but why would a guy like Alexei, who could patently have anyone he desired, ask a 44-year-old mum out on a date?

It was way beyond her.

Was he a pervert with an Oedipus complex?

Or was he just plain bonkers?

But maybe she had a spark that eluded other women, a spark that never got the chance to flame because of a damp marriage and clammy maternity. Alexei may have seen that spark, wiped up the moisture, pressed the ignition button and watched her burn at gas mark nine.

After dinner they walked along the beach. It was 10.30pm.

'Do you know something...' said Laura, in Greek.

'I know a lot of things,' said Alexei, in English.

'We haven't talked about my house once this evening,' again, in Greek.

'No, we did. I'm sure we did,' Alexei–in English. And so it continued, Laura only speaking in English when the phrase she wanted alluded her. He thought it was cool.

'Well, if I remember correctly, you were supposed to recommend an estate agent.'

'Oh yes. I thought we could talk about that over an aperitif. I simply didn't want to discuss business and ruin the most delightful dinner I've had in a long time. Look, I know a fantastic bar along the beach. The perfect place for a nightcap. Quiet and private.'

'I must be home by midnight.'

'Yes Cinderella, but first you shall go to the ball.'

'Alas, I have no pumpkin or mice to turn into a gleaming coach and horses. Just an old Suzuki jeep. So, I can't drink any more. I've already had two glasses of wine.'

'They were tiny glasses and you ate lots.'

'Well, thank you so much for making me sound like an old sow.'

When he realised how inappropriate his last remark sounded, Alexei laughed like a schoolboy. Laura was caught in the laughter lines and joined in.

'I'm so, so sorry, Laura. I didn't mean it like that. You know what I meant. What an idiot I must appear. Let's have one for the road, as an apology. They do great non-alcoholic cocktails in this place plus I have some potentially good news for you.'

'Well, okay. Do they have a toilet at this bar?'

'But of course. Why on earth would you ask that?'

'Because this old sow wants to take a piss before that long drive home.'

'Your Greek is perfection,' laughed Alexei.

'Oh,' said Laura, 'and while I'm in there, could you get me half a dozen bags of smoky bacon crisps and a couple of packets of salted peanuts? That'll do for starters.

'By the way, can I talk in English now? It's starting to hurt my brain.'

'I could listen to you speak Greek all night, Laura, but I would hate to think I was in any way responsible for damaging your health.

'Ah, here we are.' They stopped outside a large bar on Palm Beach promenade. It was packed and loud and overflowing with House and completely unsuitable for even a semblance of coherent conversation.

'I thought you said it was quiet and private.'

'Follow me.'

He took her hand and edged through the crowd to the bar. The bartender smiled when he recognised Alexei and almost saluted as he raised the flap on the bar to let them both through.

'Good evening, sir. Everything is prepared.'

'Thank you, Bambos. It's good to see you.'

'Thank you, sir. And it's a pleasure to see you again.'

Alexei led her into a small hallway behind the bar area that was just big enough for an elevator door.

'There is a main entrance, but I thought you might like to go through the back.'

'It has been known,' said Laura desperately trying to keep it together under this bombardment of bewilderment. 'What did that guy, er, Bambos, mean, "Everything is prepared,"? What were you planning?'

'I just wanted to show you something.'

'As the bishop said to the actress.'

'What bishop?'

'Don't worry, Alexei.'

The lift door opened and they went in. There were only two buttons, one had 'G' inscribed on it and the other 'PS'.

'As this is 'G', I guess that means 'ground'. But what's with the 'PS'?'

'That stands for 'Penthouse Suite'.'

'Your Penthouse Suite?'

'Yes. My company owns this entire building, and the ones either side. There are around twelve apartments in each property and they're all rented out, along with the various restaurants and bars on the ground floors. We keep this apartment for company use. It stretches across all the buildings.'

The lift door opened and revealed the largest lounge Laura had ever seen outside of Dallas and Dynasty. One wall was made entirely of glass, affording a breath-taking view of the sea. A spiral staircase in the centre of the room looked like a vain attempt to break up the overall hugeness of everything.

'You're going to love this.' Alexei hadn't let go of her hand since he grabbed it in the bar.

He took her to the spiral staircase and they started to climb the stairs.

'Er, what exactly is it I'm going to love, Alexei?'

'This.'

They reached the top and Laura stepped out into an impeccably-manicured, floodlit roof garden, although she thought 'roof park' was a more appropriate description, which overlooked the whole of Larnaca to the north and the whole of the world to the south.

'There's the toilet,' said Alexei, indicating a light about thirty metres away, 'as I know how desperately you want to go. Meet me at the bar over there when you're through.'

'And what's over there, a fucking football pitch?' It was the first time Laura had uttered a profanity in a long time. This was all way out of her league.

'No, just a swimming pool,' said Alexei.

The toilet door opened automatically, the toilet flushed automatically, the tap turned itself on automatically and the individual towels were hand-pressed and as fluffy as a poodle. Laura looked at herself in the mirror–the vanity lights around it were activated by her reflection–and wondered how on earth she had wound up in a situation like this.

The fact she drove all the way here tonight was a signal to him that she was ready and willing. The fact she wore a clichéd black number with a nudge of cleavage was a signal to him that she was ready and willing.

The fact she was 44 and on holiday without a husband was a signal to him that she was ready and willing.

The fact that she was there, drying her hands on that fluffy poodle, was a signal to herself that she was ready and willing. She was determined to walk out of that toilet ready and willing, and in actual fact she did. But it was a long walk to the bar where Alexei was doing fancy Tom Cruise moves with a cocktail shaker, and by the time she reached it, her resolve had been vanquished by the languid lights of Larnaca and the reassuring sound of dying waves collapsing on moonlit beaches.

'Don't worry,' said Alexei, 'it's non-alcoholic. I've christened this little baby "Laura's Fantasy". There's freshly squeezed lemonade and orange, a dash of Galliano, a hint of mint and a secret ingredient that gives it some pizazz.'

'Matches my personality perfectly, but without the pizazz. Sorry to disappoint. So, Alexei, what's this potential good news?'

He explained that a client of his was looking for a property in Paralimni and if he liked her house he would offer the market price and pay all her costs. And not an estate agent fee in sight.

'Great,' said Laura. 'Well, let me know when he wants a viewing. By the way, your cocktail is divine. I adore ginger.' Where did they come from–'divine', 'adore'? This was a schoolgirl trying to impress.

'Wow, you guessed the secret ingredient. Glad you like it, Laura. I aim to please.'

She wanted to kiss him at that moment. He was so cute and so in command. Alexei homed in on the vibes and leaned across the bar and gently kissed her forehead. At that precise moment Bob Marley started singing 'Waiting In Vain'. It was automatic.

'Would you like to dance?'

God, would she.

'Oh no, it's 11.15. I must go.'

'One dance and I'll see you to your car. You'll be home before the witching hour.'

He vaulted over the bar like a gymnast and stood on the lawn with outstretched arms. She couldn't refuse. Of course, he danced like an angel, she knew that before he held her like nobody had held her before. They swayed as the music dived into her blood and she felt in perfect harmony with the waves and the gentle six-storey high breeze and the memories of other dance-floors, other dances.

He was going to kiss her. She felt his body tense. It was going to happen. She can't stop it now. She can't.

His tongue brushed hers and she tasted freedom. She put her hand around the back of his head and they kissed honeymoon kisses.

His hands caressed her back, his lips caressed her neck, his thighs caressed her thighs. She rubbed against him in search of an erection as he lifted her dress from behind and pulled her towards him. She was about to get laid on synthetic lawn fifty feet above sea level and it was the right thing to do. His mouth searched for her breast and his hand started to tug at her knickers...

It was like pulling the ripcord on a parachute when you're plummeting to earth at 150mph.

'No,' she said and pushed his hands away. 'I'm sorry. I don't know what came over me, only I do know it won't be you tonight, cowboy.' Laura Tate had a way with words when it suited her. And it sure suited her now. She backed away and straightened her dress.

'Laura, oh Laura. I'm terribly sorry. It was so ungallant. I couldn't help myself.'

'I'm flattered Alexei, but I'm married and have a family I love and that means more to me than a quick roll in the hay or, in this case, grass, of sorts. I'm a family gal and late-night loving on floodlit rooftops overlooking the sea is, alas, a thing of the past. Not that I ever made love on a floodlit rooftop, but you get my drift.'

'You are a very special woman, Laura.' She felt like Shirley Valentine without the bonk. 'Let me walk you to your car.'

'That's okay, Alexei. I'm only parked around the corner. It's been fun.'

'We must do it again.'

'Yes.' She knew 'must' was a euphemism for 'mustn't'.

'And I'll be in touch about the potential buyer.'

'Great. Thanks for that, Alexei.' She knew 'be in touch' was a euphemism for cutting her out of his life completely.

On the drive home she fell in love with the idea that Alexei thought she was an easy lay. It was oddly comforting. Maybe 44 wasn't as old as she thought. Maybe she should've let him screw her; it would've been something she could tell her grandchildren. Her thoughts may be wrinkled, thanks to Adam, but she still cut it. Cut it good.

And that was the only time Laura dipped her tongue into uncharted waters since the night she met Adam in The Unicorn, Stepney Green, all those years ago. The memory never faded, in fact, it grew more vivid, more alive and it got her through a lot of lonely nights. Occasional tears on her pillow, like rain finding its way through a loose tile on the roof, were evidence of despair. The hole grew bigger over the years and sometimes the pillow was a little damp in the morning, but the summers were getting longer and it didn't seem to rain much anymore.

The house in Paralimni was eventually sold and the proceeds split equally between her, the two brothers and all eight grandchildren. The family house in Walthamstow belonged to the council.

It wasn't much, but it was a lot more than Terry and Betty received from their parents, if you don't count a lifelong nicotine habit and osteoporosis.

'Should've been split equally three ways, between each family,' was Adam's first reaction when Laura told him about the eleven-way split. 'There's only two payments to us while the others get five and four each. Doesn't seem fair.'

'It's not about the money,' she said.

Oh, yes it is. But some things are better left unsaid.

CHAPTER 20

And Here's to You, Mr Robinson

Thursday. Lunch. Adam was 15 minutes early.

He wanted to make sure he arrived before Kate because he knew this chain of Japanese restaurants had tables that were sunk into the floor and required the dexterity of a 12-year-old to slide into. Lithe had checked out of his life years back and he didn't want to look a complete prick of an old bloke during the inevitable inscrutable struggle while Kate looked on.

He made the right decision. The restaurant was empty at that time, so nobody saw him make a pig's ear out of clambering into his seat. However, he tore a muscle in his calf during the inevitable inscrutable struggle but the skunk he'd smoked a little earlier numbed the pain and he didn't realise the extent of his injury until he tried to stand up to go to the toilet an hour later and yelled out in agony while Kate looked on.

Whenever he recalled that moment, Adam was convinced his cry of pain wasn't so much the torn muscle in his leg but the broken muscle in his chest. But let's not talk of love or change yet. There's a lunch ahead.

After he managed to sit down, Adam ordered a large JD and Coke and asked the waiter to plunge a bottle of sake in boiling water until it was hot, hot, hot. He knew Kate liked sake because he'd heard her mention it to Ben over dinner on the ship. He only caught snatches of their conversation while making out he was listening to the person talking directly at him and it made the night disjointed, White Widow disjointed.

Ben hadn't mentioned Kate since the drive back home from

Southampton when he said how entertaining she was and how she, 'brightened up the whole experience.'

His son's whispered 'wow' in the cabin continued to haunt him. Was it a reaction to a good night of partying? Or was it a kiss? Kate's kiss. Surely not more? The fact that her name hadn't cropped up in any conversation seemed to suggest his first hunch was the more likely.

Adam ordered another drink. It was 1.15 and she still hadn't shown. He'd convinced himself there was nothing going on between Ben and Kate. It was too absurd, too cruel. The fates had conspired to wreak a little havoc in his life, sure, but this would be a storm of biblical proportions in comparison.

Kate would never entertain the idea. She's not stupid. She'd know how much it would hurt him. Destroy him. No. She's incapable of inflicting such pain. She's the most beautiful girl in the world. No.

Then he laughed at the absurdity again and imagined a Mrs Robinson scenario with him banging on Kate's car window in the pouring rain, hair dye streaming down his face.

'Hi Adam. Sorry I'm late.

'With your period? Am I the father? Sorry, it's impossible to stand up.'

She was dressed simply in an immaculately-cut black two-piece skirt suit drenched in blonde over a glistening white silk blouse and laughed her way effortlessly into the seat. She leaned over and delivered a tongue-less kiss on the lips accompanied by a loud 'Mwah'.

Passionless. It wasn't the kiss of a lover.

His worst fears were confirmed by that kiss. This was a termination lunch and he won't be able to deal with it. She's gonna tell him it's over and he'll blub. The goodbye look was in her eyes.

'Don't worry, old man,' she said. 'That was very funny, by the way.'

Wait, he'll deal with it. He must. He got lucky. You win some, you lose some. Let's not talk about it yet, Kate. Please, not yet. Let's drink and have some fun before I walk that green mile to oblivion. Let's drink.

He called the waiter.

'Same again for me, please. I'm having a large JD and Coke, Kate. Care to join me?

'Just a San Pellegrino for me,' she said to the waiter.

'Water? Not like you.'

'I never drink at lunchtime. In fact, I've been too busy to drink full stop. I'm off to New York tomorrow.'

'You ol' jetsetter.'

'I've made some brilliant contacts recently and I'm actually thinking of opening an office in Manhattan. It's all very exciting.'

Water. Adam had already knocked back two doubles and was about to embark on a third. Water. That is not a word you want to hear coming out of the mouth of this most gorgeous of women, a mouth that tasted spit from his mouth and coke from his cock. Water.

'Oh dear. I've already had a few 'cos I thought I needed to catch up, what with you swigging all morning from that bottle of vodka secreted away in your desk at work. Screw it, I'll down the sake too.'

'You go for it, Adam. You look like you need it. How are your parents? Alive? Dead? Or still in between?'

Please don't do that, Kate. Don't remind me of what I'll miss. Nobody would make an inquiry like that. Nobody. And it was so on the money. She knew what to say and how to say it.

'In-between, as usual. Know any hit men?' He then remembered he'd made the same crack before at her dinner party.

'Funnily enough... But let's not go there. What are you having?'

'I thought I made that perfectly clear, another JD and Coke and a large, hot bottle of sake.'

'Oh, I love sake. Tell you what, I'll have a small cup to keep you company. There's nothing worse than drinking alcohol while the only other person at the table is on the water. But honestly, Adam, drinking at lunch went out with the ark. I haven't done it in years, and don't say, "But what about drinking at lunch?" I can read you like a book.'

You sure can, Kate. You sure can. But will you make it to the last page?

'I've even given up smoking.'

His world was changing fast. 'What about drugs? Does anyone do coke at lunch, for example?'

'Not in my company. They'd be out through the front door.'

'Isn't that a little hypocritical?'

'Not in the least,' said Kate. 'Oh, I like the odd line but only when I'm partying, which isn't often these days. It's all work and no play, I'm afraid. In fact, I haven't touched any since the last time we met up.'

'Neither have I.'

She started to laugh.

'I know what you're laughing at,' said Adam, a little uncomfortably, 'I guess it was pretty funny.'

'Funny? It was hilarious. You know when I said I had a boyfriend who used to do that?'

'Yeah.'

'I lied.'

'Thank you. I am now, officially, a nervous wreck.'

'I'm having my usual, vegetable tempura and zaru soba. What's the nervous wreck having?'

'The s-s-scallop and s-s-salmon teppanyaki meal.'

'Seems like you have the hippy, hippy shakes. I think it's a side effect of spreading cocaine on your penis.'

Number one, is she taking the piss? Number two, is she being cruel to be kind? And number three, how on earth did she know about the hippy, hippy shake?

'Impress me, Kate. Who had a hit with 'Hippy, Hippy Shake'?'

'That would be the Swinging Blue Jeans. What a wonderful name for a band.'

Please don't do that, Kate. Don't remind me of what I'll miss. Before he met her the only interesting conversations he had were with women over fifty. Although many of them were attractive, none could hold a candle to the sparkling girl with stars in her eyes sitting a snog away, over 25 years younger but who knew 25 times more.

'Jaw drops in amazement. How does a mere slip of a girl know that?'

'My dad loved his sixties and seventies music and kept every record he ever bought, the first of which was, 'Hippy, Hippy Shake' way back in '63. Up until he died, my life was filled with The Beatles, Pink Floyd, Dylan, The Doors, Bowie, Ten Years After, Eagles, Steely Dan, you name it. Sometimes he'd have a real nostalgia attack and play records like 'Shakes', 'House Of The Rising Sun', 'Keep On Runnin'' or go heavy on the Motown with the Isley Brothers and Marvin Gaye or sixties soul from Otis to Sam & Dave. He told me all their names and pointed out the real creamy bits in their music.

'My dad has had the biggest impact on my life and whatever I am, I am because of him.'

'For a CEO of an engineering firm, your dad sounds kinda cool.'

'Well remembered, Adam.'

'Hey, it's my job.'

The waiter brought the JD refill and Pellegrino and took their order. Adam hadn't eaten a thing, not even breakfast, and, for the moment, the booze and skunk weren't dancing well together. His innate pessimism was leading him into dark places and he prayed to God he wouldn't have a white out. From Kate's cool, now dead fifty-year-old dad to a distinctly uncool 56-year-old grey haired bloke who faints in public and tries to screw women with coke on his cock. He had to ride it out. Let her talk.

'So, what's with New York?' Good. He managed to say it coherently. Now hold it together. Hide the whitey. How he'd love that water, that cold, crystal-clear water. Hide the whitey.

'An opportunity has come up and I'm checking it out.'

Oh, no, don't stop there. Tell me more. Don't make me speak again. Please don't make me speak again. I just can't. Please Kate. Please don't.

'Opportunity?'

'An American friend of mine has opened a PR agency in Greenwich Village. She deals with a lot of travel companies too and reckons we should pool our resources and go global, at least two cities. These days there's a lot of crossover in the industry and a UK client can be represented in the US under the same aegis. It makes a lot of sense.'

'If she's as lovely as you, it'll be some hot tail of two cities.' The white had gone, replaced by a sub-standard pun machine; a man with six shots of Jack Daniels partying in his empty stomach. The goodbye look wasn't in her eyes anymore. Maybe there was hope. Maybe she'd missed him. Maybe, just maybe, she'd let him in again. But wasn't it Roger Whittaker who once said he didn't believe in 'if' anymore?

'Picked up any new accounts recently?' Adam decided to step out of old Durham town and into the arms of chance.

'Three, actually, all in the last fortnight. Two cruise companies and a small chain of boutique hotels with branches in London and...'

'New York.'

'But of course. You know me so well. Too well, sometimes. I guess a lot of writers read people like books and store them in the library, y'know, that huge building next-door to the soul.'

'So, a poet too, huh? You're a renaissance woman, Kate. Tell me, do you play a musical instrument?'

'The piano. Pretty well, too.'

'How many languages do you speak?

'Three, including English.'

'And they would be...?'

'French, naturally.'

'Naturally,' said Adam, who could never harness the dexterity required for playing an instrument or learning a language at school.

In other words, he was crap at music, French and German.

'And German. I spent six months in Berlin once and it was the craziest of my life. A lot of acid and a load of new-fangled tango.'

'So, you like Lena Horne.'

'Only when it's stormy weather.'

Please don't do that, Kate. Don't remind me of what I'll miss.

The food was great and the sake was hot. Kate did most of the talking because there was infinitely more going on in her life than his stagnant wheeze of an excuse for existence. He envied Kate her youth and joy and constant excitement. She was Noddy–young, gifted and enthusiastic with a bell on her head that was always ringing, and nifty red spats on her itchy feet. He was PC Plod–an obese loser going nowhere and destined to remain on the beat until the torrents of fat cavorting through his blood would finally drown his heart in a tsunami of grease before he hit 65.

Kate stuck to her guns and only had one small cup of sake. She ordered a pot of green tea as the waiter cleared the table.

'Adam.'

The goodbye look was back. This was it. This was really it. How wrong can you be? Roger Whittaker knew the score. Ifs were just that, ifs. Only the chosen few make their ifs real, the rest of us cling on and cower.

And here he was, clinging on and cowering.

'Adam, I want to talk to you.'

'Sorry, but haven't you been doing that for the last hour?'

'No, really talk to you.'

'"Really" is a big word, Kate. I'm not good at handling reallys.' Or ifs.

'Don't underestimate yourself, Adam. It's so annoying. You're a lovely, sweet, sharp man and I hope we'll always be friends.'

'That's a hell of a kiss-off, Kate. Where did you find it, in that library next door to your soul?'

'Don't make this more difficult than it already is.'

'And that's straight out of Mills & Boon.'

'Please, Adam.'

'Hold on, I know who that is, that's, er. Katherine Hepburn, er Meryl Streep, er Kate Winslet, er...'

'You're behaving like a fool.'

I'm sorry, Kate. It's that I wasn't expecting this. I really do care for you.'

'And I care for you. But it got too serious, too quickly. Besides, could you imagine if we married–I'd be Kate Tate for Chrissake! Nobody would ever take me seriously again.'

Please don't do that, Kate.

'Well,' he said, 'as this is the official termination of the physical interlude in our, hopefully, on-going relationship, I can now say, hand on heart, that during that sweet interlude I loved you more than words can say. The night we danced was the most romantic night of my life. You flattered me with your presence.' He knew he was repeating himself, but he couldn't help it.

'Hey, I'm not a flatter fuck y'know. And unlike the first cut, the first fuck is never the deepest. Let's put it down to an abundance of coke that melts on your dick, not up your nose.'

Adam's head was swimming. The more she said, the more it hurt.

'Adam, you are, without a doubt, a fantastic writer. A good friend of mine is an editor for a large book publisher; in fact, he was due to come around the evening of the dinner party but cancelled at the last minute. I've talked about you to him and he's a *Clockwork* fan, would you believe? He'd like to meet you and he'd be pleased to have a look at anything you've written since *Big Boys Don't Cry*.'

Please don't.

'Well remembered, Kate, well remembered.'

'God, Adam, you are such a lovely man.'

Don't.

He needed to use the toilet. He hadn't reckoned on that, but then again, he hadn't reckoned on drinking almost a bottle of sake on top of a sea of Jack Daniels-flavoured Coke. His bladder was bursting; he would have to face the inevitable inscrutable struggle like a man when he returned, while Kate looked on.

Getting out was a lot easier than getting in, but as Adam lifted his legs to slide out, an inferno of pain surged through his whole body. The inevitable inscrutable scream smothered the conversations at every table in the packed restaurant.

The waiter came rushing over, convinced Adam was either having a heart attack or the tasty blonde he was with had stabbed him with a chopstick. When he saw Adam clutching his leg, he thought he was simply an old git with cramp.

'Are you all right, sir?'

'Yes, I'm so sorry. I think I've torn something in my leg,' said Adam, through an acre of grimaces. 'It's very painful.'

'God, Adam, I thought you were dying,' said Kate, with more than a hint of a smile.

I am, Kate. I am.

On the whole, this was shaping up to be a shit day. And it wasn't over yet, not by a country mile.

CHAPTER 21

'Here's Bobby!'

Bobby was dying, fading fast. He could still walk, just; he could still have a row when he was frustrated by pain and inevitability and he could still muster up an appetite. But to Adam, he still looked like he was losing a pound a day and he still stank like a cesspit.

Bobby grew the first beard of his life–thin, white and fragile–as shaving was impossible. He also wore an eye patch because the tumour paralysed a nerve that meant he couldn't close his eye. He looked like Long John Silver after he'd been dead for a month.

He wore pyjamas all day and only left the armchair to go to bed or the toilet, although he was often too late for the latter and had to wear incontinence pads. Since he had been discharged from hospital, the council provided a carer for free under the continuing care scheme because the nature of his illness was so severe. His name was Zachariah, a Watusi-tall guy from Burundi with a heart of gold who visited twice daily.

Coral was making rapid progress. She'd gone from Zimmer to crutches to walking stick within a month of the operation. Her brain was as sharp as a pin and when she smiled, she meant it. She'd started to come downstairs every day and eventually got the hang of the microwave so they could feed themselves on the odd–very odd–day Adam wasn't around. They argued a lot, Coral often couldn't bear to be under the same roof as her chamber-of-horrors husband. It was all part of a routine that used to make life manageable for both when Bobby was well. But now they seemed to really mean the nasty, spiteful jibes.

Bobby could no longer trust Coral, or Adam, no matter how hard he tried. Recently, he reluctantly started wearing a morphine patch again because the pain was so bad. It released forty mgs into his blood every day and was replaced every week. While Coral watched Emmerdale and Corrie, Bobby stared into space and saw faces from the past, faces that warned him to beware his family.

This time, the morphine made him feel young again, made him feel like he would have stayed young if he hadn't married Coral and if that fucker of a son hadn't come along.

One night, while he was gliding through the morph zone, *The Shining* was on TV. He started watching it with his good eye and it all made sense. In Bobby's one-eyed, morphine-soaked brain, Jack Torrance was the good guy and he shed a tear at the end when Jack froze to death in the snow. Bobby wept a lot these days and Coral ignored him.

He wanted Jack's wife and kid to die. They were holding the poor bastard back, telling lies to get him shackled, put away, left to rot in his own shit and piss. All he wanted was the freedom to roam with people long gone who meant so much to him, who could show him a better, truer way.

No, Bobby wasn't ready to die yet.

But he knew someone who was...

'Adam? Adam? Can you hear me?'

'Yes, mum.' It was Wednesday morning, the day before his disastrous lunch with Kate.

'Adam, is that you, Adam?'

'Yes, mum. Put the receiver right up to your ear. Can you hear me now?'

'Oh, that's better. I can hear you now.'

'What's wrong?' What would ever be right?

'It's your dad.' Who else would it be?

'What?'

'He's walking about the house in the middle of the night, stark naked.'

'Maybe he's horny.'

'Don't be so disgusting. He's been doing it for the last three nights and I can't sleep. He goes downstairs and I can hear him wandering around getting up to God knows what.'

'He's harmless, mum. There's nothing he can get up to except lose weight by the minute. Let him do what he wants.'

'You don't have to live with him. I can't go on like this much longer. I'll be dead before him at this rate.'

'Okay, mum, I'll be round in a few hours. Everything will be all right. Honest.'

An hour later, the phone rang again.

'Hullo, is that Mr Adam?'

'Yes.'

'Oh, it's Zachariah. Your mum is looking very pale this morning and seems to be depressed. She tells me she's not sleeping at night. I wanted to let you know that I've asked her GP to pop round and see her today.'

By the time Adam arrived at the house, the doctor had already called.

'What did she say?'

'Oh no, it was a man,' said Coral. 'He was a new doctor I've never seen him before. He could only have been in his late twenties. Nice young man. He prescribed these tablets and said he'd fax the prescription to the chemist and they only delivered them just this minute.'

'What are they?'

'Oh, I don't know. Something ending in 'an' or 'am'?'

Adam looked at the bottle.

'I hope it's nothing like the pills you had before, when you fell down the stairs.'

'No, nothing like that. He assured me that 1mg was a small dose and said it was okay for me to take one before I go to bed.'

'Well, you be careful.'

'I'll be all right, son. Don't worry.'

Adam knew his mother loved him unreservedly, and he loved her for it.

Bobby may have been pretty vacant in his armchair time machine, but he was still sharp when he wanted to be. This was his opportunity.

As Coral and Adam continued to talk, while they plotted and schemed, he smiled. As the *Countdown* clock on the TV wound down, he smiled. As the morphine tumbled through his veins, he smiled. He was heading for a new world, and it wasn't fucking Respite.

After Adam left, Bobby and Coral went up around 10.30pm.

'Did you take the tablet the doctor gave you?' asked Bobby. They slept in separate bedrooms and still kissed each other goodnight on the landing.

'Yes,' said Coral. 'Stop fussing.'

'Goodnight, darlin'.'

'Goodnight, Bobby.'

They both sighed and went to their rooms. Bobby slipped into an incontinence pad and sat on the bed in the darkness. He was prepared to wait all night. He knew that, at some point, sleeping pill or no sleeping pill, Coral would get up to go to the toilet.

She was frail, she wasn't eating, and she took a whole cocktail of other medication. She won't know what hit her. Take my money, would she?

'Nobody will suspect. Nobody. An old, depressed woman with a gammy leg who never ate and had more drugs than Boots? A fucking recipe for disaster. A fucking accident waiting to happen. A fucking result.'

It was 2am when Bobby heard Coral's bedroom door open. He gingerly put his ulcerated legs onto the floor, stood up and made delicate shuffling steps, like a geisha, across the room. He opened the door slightly and saw a light from the toilet. He heard her pull the chain and wash her hands. He saw the light go out and Coral emerge, and he watched as she slowly limped past his door. He came out and walked behind her. Coral's room was near the top of the stairs and she was a foot away when she heard the last words she would ever hear...

'Take my money, would you, you fucking whore!'

Bobby gathered every ounce of strength his now six-stone frame could muster and pushed her in the back. She fell down all 15 stairs, smashing her head open on the wall where the staircase turned at a ninety-degree angle.

'That'll be one for Zachariah to see in the morning,' he laughed. 'I can have a good sleep now.'

Coral's blood beamed in the black at the bottom of the stairs. Her murdering husband had finally murdered her, and he slept like a log.

CHAPTER 22

Something Bad on the Other Side of Town

When Adam realised he couldn't walk properly, Kate called the cab firm her company used. Together with the waiter, she helped him first to the toilet, then out of the restaurant past a mass of confused diners with chopsticks in their hands, and into the back seat of the cab parked right outside.

'I hope you'll be okay,' said Kate through the car window. 'Don't worry about the bill, I've taken care of it. And the taxi is on my account. You owe me one, and then we'll have lunch.'

Please don't do that, Kate.

She laughed and kissed him gently on the forehead.

'I should avoid Japanese food in future if I was you. It obviously doesn't agree with you. Let me know what the hospital says.'

She laughed again and waved goodbye as the cab pulled away.

'Nice looking girl, your daughter,' said the cab driver, a Somali with a master's degree in technical engineering. 'You must be very proud.'

'Very proud. Yes.' Adam felt old and tired and useless. He reeked of booze and mediocrity.

'Had a few too many, eh boss?' The driver smiled.

'No. I pulled a muscle in my leg.'

'Sorry, boss. Is it painful?'

'Yes.'

'Well, you sit back and relax and I'll get you to casualty in no time.'

Adam was desperate for a cab driver fix. His leg was aching and his heart was breaking; he needed something, anything, to take his mind off the hurt.

He knew he would never see Kate again. He knew he would never feel that way about anybody again. His road to perdition was fully mapped out and if he grew weary of walking, the buses were pretty regular and ran right through the night.

He liked talking to minicab drivers. They were exotic denizens of the night, armed with harrowing tales of killing fields and families ripped apart by war and promising careers lost forever. You can find out a lot about someone in three-and-a-half London miles, if you ask.

Turned out this driver had a simpler story to tell. He'd lived in Holland for nearly eight years after leaving Somalia, where he gained his degree, and worked with his brother in an export company before coming to London, falling in love with a cute Somali girl and working marathon minicab shifts to provide a home for her and, later, their two children. He was a supremely intelligent guy who spoke perfect English and only knew London as an intoxicating multicultural cinemascope of a city.

Adam thought they were through talking.

'What about you?' the driver asked. 'Where are you from?' It was the first time a driver had ducked out of the spotlight just to drag Adam into it. He looked genuinely interested.

'London.'

'London!' He was shocked. 'What, you were actually *born* in London?'

'Yes.'

'Where?'

'Halfway between Kings Cross and The Angel, off Pentonville Road. I was born in the same house as my dad and his dad before him.'

'Wow, that's years back, man.'

These days, most native Londoners were under 25. At Jack's primary school, nearly all of the parents were either born and raised in the provinces or abroad while their offspring were born and raised in London. Dig the new breed.

Everyone he was brought up with quit the city years ago, turning their backs on Babylon in search of hanging gardens in Essex and Hertfordshire.

'And the same house? What sort of house?'

'It had five-stories, including the basement, and on each floor there were two rooms shared by a family of up to ten and they all had to share one toilet at the top of the house. There were no bathrooms.'

'No bathrooms?'

'No bathrooms.'

'No?'

'And you know what?' Talking dulled the pain but not as much as the booze and dope. 'That street turned into Nicosia almost overnight back in the fifties and on hot summer Sundays, bouzouki music from old gramophones crept out of open windows and strange food aromas plundered your senses. It was intoxicating.

'Growing up with people from different worlds has enriched my life.

'We were all brought up in shitholes. Row after row of streets full of these houses were demolished right up until the seventies and replaced by council blocks of flats that seemed like paradise.

'My mum and dad moved out of the shithole two years after I was born and entered paradise. Thankfully, they took me with them.'

The driver laughed. This guy was odd, but good odd. Cool. Kinda.

'Where did you go?'

'We moved into an estate around the corner. Two moves later we ended up in a council house in Highbury. My mum and dad still live there.'

'Arsenal, eh?'

Cue inevitable football chat...

Adam felt the mobile phone in his jacket pocket.

He realised he hadn't checked it since turning it off when he got on the tube, to preserve the battery he'd forgotten to charge. He was horrified to see twenty missed calls and four new messages. He didn't get that many calls in a week. Most of the calls were from his dad's carer and then there was a whole bunch of numbers he didn't recognise plus several blocked ones. Something had obviously happened. Something urgent and bad.

He rang the carer. 'Hi, Zachariah?'

'Yes, is that Mr Adam?'

'Yes. What's the problem? Is dad all right?'

He could hear someone sobbing in the background.

'It's your mother, Mr Adam.'

'What's happened?'

'She's dead, Mr Adam.'

'Dead? My mother's dead?'

'Yes, Mr Adam.'

'How? What happened?'

'The stairs, Mr Adam. She fell down the stairs. I found her this morning. I could not reach you at home or your mobile. Other people have been trying, too. Your dad is very upset. He's crying a lot. Can you come?'

'Yes. What's happened to my mum?'

'The ambulance took her away, Mr Adam. Please hurry. Your dad is begging for you to come.'

'I'll be there soon.'

'Hey,' said the driver. 'I couldn't help overhearing. I'm so sorry. Do you want me to take you there now?'

'Yes.'

Adam told him the address. His leg was aching and his heart was breaking as the cab headed to north London where an old gangster was crying his heart out, but laughing like a child inside...

CHAPTER 23

Four Complicated Syllables

Adam was the only person at his mum's funeral. Bobby was too sick and too 'distraught' to attend and Adam's wife and sons couldn't give a toss.

Any friends or relatives Coral or Bobby managed to acquire were either dead, catatonic or five-thousand miles away. The crematorium minister was clearly disappointed by such a low turnout and that was reflected by the perfunctory sermon during which Adam was convinced he once referred to his mother as 'Coral Kate'. Judy Garland sang Coral's favourite song, 'I'm Always Chasing Rainbows', as the coffin bobbled through the sliding doors like a *Stars In Their Eyes* contestant.

A crowd of about a hundred had gathered outside for the next service. A huge wreath that spelt out the words 'To A Darling Mum' adorned the nearside window of the hearse like an advert on the side of a bus. It was raining heavily and Adam had to dodge through the waterfalls that cascaded from a mass of umbrellas to get to his old black Merc.

He watched through the car window as the undertakers laid the 'Darling Mum' wreath on top of the coffin. Six black guys in black suits carried the coffin into the church. Over a hundred people followed and another hundred stood outside in the rain.

A popular woman, thought Adam, but obviously a bit on the heavy side–the six guys were visibly struggling. Okay, so he was a little jealous. After nearly eighty years on this earth, Coral Tate had one person at her funeral, her only child. A sad, lonely end, bereft of grief and flowers. Sure, Adam was upset, it was his mum after all. But an overpowering feeling of relief coursed through his veins as a dark voice inside dared whisper, 'One down, one to go.'

Coral's life had been unrewarding but comfortable. She hadn't worked a day since she married, accepting her husband's villainy without question and enjoying its not inconsiderable rewards. Adam knew she was capable of more, but she went for the soft option and drifted through the years before falling so ignominiously from the sky.

The post mortem revealed multiple fractures to the body, including the skull, coupled with a massive heart attack.

When Adam reached the house on the day of her death, his leg was beginning to swell.

'Oh, Mr Adam, I'm so glad you're here.' Zachariah, big, smiley Zachariah, greeted him in the passage with a tear in his eye and a tremor in his voice that smacked of goodness.

'I'm worried about Mr Bobby. He won't stop crying.'

'Who's that?' Bobby called from the living room. 'Who's that at the door? Is that you, Adam?'

Adam went into the room. Bobby was sitting in the usual place. 'Do you know what's happened?' he said. 'My darling, lovely wife has gone. They've taken her away. She'll be all right, won't she? She hurt herself, but I don't think it's serious. Zachariah helped her. Thank you, Zachariah. Thank you.

'She's gone,' he wailed.

'He's been like this all the time,' said Zachariah. 'I'm afraid something might happen to him. I've called the doctor.'

'You've called the doctor?' said Bobby in disbelief. 'It was the fucking doctor dishing out drugs that caused all this in the first place. If he comes in this house, I'll fucking kill him.'

He said it with such vindictiveness that he almost believed it himself.

It was easy for an old villain to utter threats no matter how hollow, and it scared the hell out of Zachariah. 'I should ring the doctor and tell him not to come,' he said.

'No, Zack.' Adam was fed up with repeating four complicated syllables in nearly every sentence. 'He needs sorting out.'

'Who needs fucking sorting out? I'll fucking sort you out, you conniving little bastard.'

'Don't talk to me like that or I'll have you put away. I'll tell them you pushed mum down the stairs–for all I know, you probably did, you mad bastard. They'll lock you up and throw away the key.'

Bobby was genuinely concerned by his son's outburst and his demeanour changed.

'Why are you having a go at me, Adam? Can't you see how I feel? My darling Coral is suffering in hospital. You must go to her. You have to make sure she's all right.'

'I've told him many times that Mrs Coral is dead, but he ignores me. He won't accept it,' said Zachariah, who was a little shocked by Adam's aggression.

Adam sensed it and acted swiftly. 'I'm sorry, Zack–you don't mind me calling you that?'

'No, that's fine, Mr Adam.'

'Just call me Adam, Zack.'

'Yes, Adam.'

'I'm sorry I reacted as I did. But you must understand, I'm at breaking point here. My mother is dead, my father is like a fucking zombie and I've given up my life for them, yet still he insults me.'

'I understand, Adam,' said Zachariah, though Adam wasn't entirely convinced. But his words smacked of goodness.

The front door bell rang.

'That'll be the doctor,' said Zachariah and he went to open it. Adam wished the doctor were for him. His leg was throbbing.

'I'll tell you something,' said Bobby, who heard every word, every syllable, 'if it's that fucker who gave your mother the heavy-duty sedatives, I'll put an 'ammer over his 'ed, mark my words. Over his fucking 'ed.' When Bobby Tate started dropping aitches there was usually trouble ahead.

Even at 95, he sounded fearsome—and if he had had a hammer and if it didn't take him five minutes to get out of the chair, Adam was convinced he would've seen it through.

'I fucking mean it. I'll fucking kill 'im.'

'Hullo Bobby. My name is Doctor Emma Wallace.'

She was a stunner. Twisty red hair like Rebekah Brooks, early thirties, tall, shot through with love. Even though she wore jeans and a tee shirt, it still seemed like a uniform to Adam.

'Hullo, doctor,' said Bobby, who was now no longer inclined to reach for his 'ammer. 'How is my poor wife? When is she coming home? I don't want her in the hospital. She'll never come out, I know it. Please bring her home. Please.'

It dawned on Adam how distinctive his dad's voice had become. When half his face was first paralyzed, Bobby was incomprehensible to everyone but himself which really frustrated him. But he managed to master the art of communicating with half a mouth because he couldn't bear not being centre stage or hearing the sound of his own voice.

She turned to Adam. 'I take it you're the son?'

'Yes, I'm Adam, their only child,' he said, like a martyr.

'Has he been a little delusional since Mrs Tate had the accident?'

'Yes,' said Zachariah.'

'Bobby,' said Doctor Wallace as she took hold of both his hands. 'I'm afraid I've got some bad news.

'What?'

'Beryl has died.'

'Beryl, who the fuck's Beryl?' said Bobby.

'It's Coral, doctor,' said Adam.

'Oh, I'm so sorry. Your wife, Coral, has passed away, I'm afraid.'

'No. Why are you lying to me? Do you want to have me put away? Has my son put you up to this? Just bring her back. She belongs here.

I can care for her, look after her. We don't need no carers. We'll be all right, me and Coral. We'll be all right.'

'No Bobby. She can't come back. The fall down the stairs killed her. I can assure you, by the nature of her injuries, she didn't suffer too much. Death was instantaneous, almost.'

Adam figured she hadn't done too much in the way of breaking bad news before.

'My wife's dead, you say? Dead?' It was time to accept it. It was all about the timing with Bobby—and this one he timed to perfection. It came wet and windy. It had to.

'Dead? Dead! No! Not my Coral. No. No!' He sobbed long and loudly.

'I'm very sorry, Mr Tate.'

'I apologise for crying, doctor. You must think I'm a fool.'

'Don't be silly. It won't hurt you to cry a little.'

'You know we just celebrated our diamond wedding anniversary.'

'No, I didn't.'

'Yes. We got a telegram from the Queen.'

'Really? I never knew you received a telegram for a wedding anniversary. Well, congratulations.'

'And we had our photo in the local paper.'

'So, you're a celebrity?'

'Not many people celebrate sixty years of marriage. It's remarkable, really.'

'It certainly is, Bobby. Anyway, you look after yourself. I'll prescribe you something that will help a little.'

'No, thank you, doctor. I'll be all right. You do know that I'm consulting a lawyer to look into why my wife was prescribed powerful sedatives on two occasions which caused her falls? I mean, that's tantamount to murder.'

Adam looked at his father in amazement. Tantamount to murder! Where did that come from? A few weeks ago, he was a vegetable with a beard and now he was fucking Perry Mason.

'I'm afraid I don't know anything about that, Mr Tate, but I'm sure the doctor was certain that anything prescribed was in the patient's best interests. Now, don't you fret about that and concentrate on getting better.'

'I'm never going to get better, doctor, we both know that. I want to die. Can't you give me something that will kill me, painlessly? I've outstayed my welcome and even my son wants me locked away.'

Adam refused to take the bait.

'I'll fax the prescription through to the chemist anyway. Well, cheerio, Bobby–and you, Mr Tate. I'll probably look in again tomorrow.'

Adam knew 'probably' meant 'won't' but Bobby didn't need a doctor. He didn't even need a helping hand. What he needed was to be alone with his phantom friends, free of interference.

'I don't think there's any need to have your father put away somewhere,' said the woman with the twisty hair as she stood at the front door with Adam. Music to his ears–no care home fees. 'He's now beginning to accept the fact that your mother has actually died and that will help. Old people are made of sturdy stuff, that's why they're old.

'Your father seems more than capable of making rational decisions, remarkable in the circumstances. I would like him to take the pills I've prescribed because they will help, but I understand from his notes that he can be a bit stubborn when it comes to taking medication of any kind, so I'll leave that for you to sort out.

'Don't hesitate to ring the surgery if there are any more problems and I'm terribly sorry for your loss.'

He watched Doctor Wallace walk away and wondered what it would be like to dance with her in the dark to Marvin Gaye.

And from his armchair, Bobby looked at Zachariah and smiled. He could get away with anything. He always could.

As Adam drove out of the crematorium, he glimpsed in the rear-view mirror a finger of smoke drifting out of the chapel chimney and wondered if that was his mum. It was alarmingly comforting. 'She needs to be buried, not burnt,' Bobby told him. 'They nick the fucking coffins and burn the bodies in batches. You end up with the ashes of some old wino's prick.'

A burial was so much more expensive and Coral, a confirmed atheist, wanted to be cremated anyway, so he paid for the ashes to be buried in the earth beneath a sapling rose plant in the crematorium garden. It was like leaving your kid at school for the first time and never seeing them again.

He hoped it was a good batch of corpses that accompanied her in the holy smoke as it floated through the universe for a trillion years before being sucked into a gigantic star that conjured life from emptiness and winos' pricks.

In the days that followed, his mother's death gnawed him to the bone. There were moments when he was dragged down beneath icy waters by a ton of memories–kisses goodnight dripping with love and reassurance, smiles of pride, the sheer joy she derived at his very existence. Gone. A mother's love, gone forever.

For the first time in his life, Adam understood what loss was, and it hurt more than anything he'd ever known. He hoped and prayed that her kisses and smiles would be preserved for centuries to come.

Mummified, even.

And then he'd smile and swim up to the surface like a sleek dolphin on heat and leap into the air, and hang, and hang, before plunging back into that deathly-cold sea.

Adam had cared for his mother for a long time and, after several weeks, he started to spend a lot more time hanging in the air, thanks to hefty amounts of skunk and a renewed interest in writing. Okay, he knew she loved him more than anything on earth and he appreciated that love, but she stole years from him and he wanted them back.

He told his dad he buried her, but Bobby knew he was lying. It would have mattered to him once, not any more. Like her favourite film, she was gone with the wind.

And Bobby Tate didn't give a damn.

END OF PART ONE

It was dark outside when DC Tom Evans realised he was hungry. He made himself a sardine and tomato sandwich on wholemeal with plain crisps on the side and washed it all down with a mug of green tea.

Adam Tate was a name he'd never Googled, and he couldn't now because he wasn't yet connected to Wi-Fi and had a cheap, shit mobile phone that took a lifetime to load on 3G because of a one-bar reception. He was due a Blackberry from work but there'd been a mix-up and he was still waiting for it. But he wouldn't have checked even if he had been connected.

He was eavesdropping on the lives of others and it was a unique reading experience. He didn't want to know anything, any snippet of information, that might explain why Adam shot his father and son because the more he read, the more he realised *Fuck The Sheds* was no work of fiction–and that made him feel like an intruder.

He was as gripped as a weightlifter's hand, as his dad used to say.

But when does an intruder become a voyeur?

When he can't taste the sardines.

Or the tomato…

PART TWO

At the end of the rainbow there's happiness
And to find it how often I've tried.
But my life is a race, just a wild goose chase
And my dreams have all been denied.
Why have I always been a failure?
What can the reason be?
I wonder if the world's to blame,
I wonder if it could be me.
I'm always chasing rainbows
Watching clouds drifting by,
My schemes are just like all of my dreams, ending in the sky.
Some fellows look and find the sunshine
I always look and find the rain.
Some fellows make a winning sometime,
I never even make a gain.
Believe me ...
I'm always chasing rainbows
Waiting to find a little blue bird in vain.

('I'm Always Chasing Rainbows'
by Harry Carroll & Joseph McCarthy)

CHAPTER 1

Bespoke Bandages and Broken Hearts

A dam reckoned his dad had no more than six months, a year at best, then everything would be his. All the shopping and cleaning and cooking and driving would've been worth it.

In a way, it was good his mother went first. She could easily have carried on for another ten years–probably in a nursing home for most of them, costing hundreds a week. Eating up his time and the money and then him having to sell the house to pay for her care until he was too old to care. Whereas his dad, well, he could die at any moment.

Adam had gone past the 'give a toss' stage and was now praying to God for his dad's death every night of the week, including Sundays. He'd had enough, he'd paid his dues. They'd never have looked after their parents the way he did. Bobby's mum went straight into a council-run home when his dad died, and Coral's parents were both well until they copped it.

Zachariah was now in attendance for 45 minutes, four times a day and prepared Bobby's food. He also washed Bobby three times a week and hoovered and dusted once a week.

Bobby could no longer face the meals-on-wheels pureed menu and now managed on a diet of porridge, mashed potatoes, cod in parsley sauce, corned beef hash, the occasional plate of jellied eels, mandarins in custard and coconut biscuits saturated with sweet tea. Adam still did the shopping twice a week, paid for by Bobby's debit card.

The district nurse still came every day to change the bandage on his face, but the wound had grown far too big for conventional dressings. They had to order bespoke bandages and the dining table was covered with boxes of them, delivered almost daily by the local chemist.

Adam popped in several times a week, usually when he did the shopping, and they'd sit in virtual silence watching *Countdown* with just the odd chuckle from Bobby when he spotted an obscenity in the nine letters on display. There had to be someone else in the room before they could talk to each other. It had been that way since Adam started shaving.

Now the daily visits were no longer required, Adam was almost as free as a bird. He could start working again, earn money again.

Kate had emailed him several times, inquiring after the state of his leg, passing on her condolences and giving him the details of the publisher she mentioned over lunch. Adam sent him an email but received an out of office reply set for the next two weeks and with no emergency contact number. When he tried three weeks later, the email address was no longer recognised.

He didn't bother telling Kate. What was the point? She'd made it clear that it–short, sweet, unforgettable it–was over. He could never be just friends, the temptation to kiss her would be far too painful to bear. He thought it best to sever all connections and didn't respond to her last email. It was over.

But he couldn't get her out of his dreams where she'd call out to him from a passing car and he'd chase after it, following the sound of his own name down wide, empty avenues before waking himself up by repeating 'Adam' again and again.

His heart was broken and it would take a lifetime to heal, which he didn't have.

His career as a travel writer had also taken a pounding. He'd been out of the game long enough for faces to change and memories to fade and now the only commissions in town involved nil pounds. The kudos of being published with a free holiday to boot was deemed sufficient reward.

But Adam needed the money. He had a lot of spare time but no spare cash, his savings were shot to pieces and the re-mortgage payment was not getting any lower anytime soon. As long as he paid the bills at home, he could still hold his head fairly high. If Laura discovered the truth, any vestige of affection for him would leap from her heart like a Twin Towers jumper.

He needed a sharp intake of cash and his dad held the key to his salvation–the key to the stash. He would have to woo him.

Adam knew little of his father's past. He realised what his dad was, but not what he did or why he did it. Bobby never spoke about his job outside of office hours. He'd rather sit at home in front of the TV than hang out with the boys. But what did he do during those working hours? Steal, kill, deal? Adam never knew because they never discussed it. He lost sight of his father at puberty when he'd rather be with The Beatles in his bedroom

Adam couldn't complain that he never saw his father as he was growing up, he just didn't particularly want to know him. He was too entangled in his own pubic hairs and vagrant semen to care about anything else. When he eventually cut himself free, he scurried off to Gloucester for three years and when he returned home, he spent most of his time with Laura.

He and Bobby had never shared any adult time together. It was all a bit uncomfortable. They'd grown too far apart and the words that passed between them were brittle and soulless and unbinding. There was still a love there, but its pulse was weak.

Adam knew he had to forget the father and find the man if he wanted to get his hands on the money.

It would also help with the new book he was writing.

CHAPTER 2

A Great Addition to the Tate gallery

'You want to what?' Bobby looked shocked.

'I want to talk to you about your life and record it,' said Adam.

'Why?'

'It's for a book I'm writing.'

'About what?'

'It's an idea, nothing concrete.'

'So where do I come into it?'

'I want some background information about your era, that's all. Look dad, no more questions, please. Do you want to do it or not?'

'Well, as long as nobody can identify me.'

'It's a novel, dad. And everyone who could identify you died of old age years ago.'

'That's right,' said Bobby. 'They all fucking did, didn't they? I knew they would. Knew it all along.'

'How did you know?' Adam casually put the tiny digital recorder on the table next to Bobby's armchair and switched it on.

'How did I know? I just did. I knew when I was a kid I'd outlive everybody in my school. It gave me the confidence to do things other people didn't want to do. Dangerous things.'

Sometimes his words slipped out the side of his mouth on the back of a spit dribble, but he was focussed with a world full of memories at his fingertips.

He was articulate and sharp and there was an unmistakable mean streak that pervaded every word.

Morphine can be a wonderful thing.

On this form, Adam thought his dad would outlive him as well.

'What sort of dangerous things, dad?'

'I thought you said you only wanted background information.'

'Okay, so tell me a little about your childhood.' Adam knew he would eventually get to the dangerous things with a bit of oil and a lot of patience.

'Like what?'

'Anything, your family.'

'Well there were five of us and mum and dad…'

'Five?' interrupted Adam.

'Three boys and two girls.'

'But I thought you only had one brother. Uncle Steve the cab driver.'

'Been dead 25 years, your uncle Steve. Lung cancer. He was seven years younger than me. And both sisters, Mary and Katherine, were also younger than me yet they died long ago, too.'

'I know that. So, what happened to the other brother? And why was he never mentioned?'

'You mean Michael. He was five years older than me and the only person I ever looked up to. The old man, your granddad, was tough but he sometimes laid into mum when he got pissed. Your uncle Michael knocked him out one night after he punched mum in the stomach. Michael was as hard as nails and had a left hook that was better than, than, Henry Cooper's. Nobody messed with him, so nobody messed with me.

'He got in with a big family who lived in Kings Cross. The father, Bill, was a hard-nut bookie in the days when off-course betting was illegal. He had a pitch at every racecourse in the country after taking them from an Italian family in a gang fight. His six sons were gangsters and he'd hold court at a snooker hall in Kings Cross.

'It was a serious set-up. They fucking meant business.

'Michael went to Catholic school with the youngest brother, Teddy, and they became great friends. When they left at 14, Michael was invited to join the family business—extortion, robbery, fraud, torture, murder, you name it. He discovered he was good at four out of five. Fraud wasn't his forte.'

Adam couldn't believe he was hearing these well-crafted words from such a misshapen mouth.

'Your uncle had one weakness, burglary. He loved to burgle the wealthy and would shimmy up some toff's thirty-foot drainpipe in search of a string of pearls. He was like Raffles. He used to work alone and sell the proceeds to a local fence. He didn't do it just for the money, he did it for the thrill. He knew, like me, he'd outlive everyone.

'Then one night, the drainpipe snapped and he fell to his death. He was 22.'

'So why hasn't anyone ever talked about him? Sounds like a great addition to the Tate gallery.'

'I've never repeated this to a living soul and you must swear not to either.'

'Like anyone would care, dad.'

'Swear,' said fiercely but not angrily. It was all too familiar to Adam's ears. It had to be obeyed.

'Swear.'

'No, say "I swear".'

'Shit, dad. I swear, all right.'

'That I will not repeat one word of what I'm about to hear to a living soul.'

'That I will not repeat one word of what I'm about to hear to a living soul.'

'So help me God.'

'So help me God.'

And the digital recorder spun noiselessly in the shadows cast by an afternoon sun.

'It turned out your uncle Michael had another weakness–his youngest sister Katherine. After his death, she let the cat out of the bag–he'd been abusing her regularly since she was five years old.

It started when he was 16 and continued up until the day he died. None of us knew.

'We all swore her to secrecy, she was only eleven for fuck's sake, and it was never mentioned again. It would've brought a ton of shame on us if it ever got out. For all these years, I've been the only one carrying that secret, until today. None of your cousins know he even existed. Poor Katherine died a spinster. He scarred her for life. Remember, this is fucking confidential.'

'There's only three cousins left, and I haven't seen them in years,' said Adam. 'They certainly didn't come to mum's funeral, so I don't think I'll be blurting all this out to them anytime soon.

'An incestuous paedophile in the family. My uncle. Nice to know.'

'His funeral was massive. The biggest wreath came from the Kings Cross bookie and all his sons brought one each. It was at the funeral that Michael's mate, Teddy, told me I should follow in my brother's footsteps and get involved with the family. He'd heard I could look after myself and said I reminded him of Michael.

'I was 15 and navvying on building sites for pennies. Teddy slipped me a fiver, a fucking fortune in 1932, and said there was plenty more where that came from. So, I became a villain. There didn't seem much point in doing anything else.

'I want to sleep now. Close the door as you go out.'

CHAPTER 3

I'm All Wrong, Jack

Jack Tate was a precocious, funny, handsome young man with rings on his fingers and bells on his toes and he'd completely passed Adam by. He'd done it all with Ben who also happened to pass him by. He knew that sweet babies bite back, eventually. He knew that Laura would take the boy to Cyprus every summer as big Ben grew up and found his own way and he knew he'd be left home alone again with only a Word document for company that told him things he didn't want to hear.

He knew, from the start, what to expect. And he knew he didn't like it.

He didn't like the guilt trips and the worry, the bills and the responsibility, the rows and the tears. As far as he was concerned, a kid was for life, two kids were for death–his, early.

Jack wasn't far away from that watershed year, 16, and Adam knew little about him. He could play the guitar–the lessons cost a small fortune–and speak French, which Adam found strange. He was also good at maths which Adam found even stranger. This was his antithesis, his own son. How was this guy going to comfort him in his dotage?

Adam knew Ben and Jack would never care for him in his old age in the way he cared for his father. It was all down to respect. He never 'bonded' with Bobby, never got past the Iron Man force field, but he respected him. That was the way with most of the families he knew back then. Mothers were loved, fathers were respected.

But Laura received all the love and respect and Adam was left with the odd acknowledgement of his existence. Neither Ben nor Jack had seen their father go to work each morning–he was usually still in bed when they left for school.

Laura was always up first, making breakfast before leaving for the office at 8am.

She spent weeks with them every year under a toasting Cypriot sun, igniting their imaginations and fuelling their curiosities. She cooked for them, cleaned for them; Adam never stood a chance. He was too busy trying to ignite his own imagination to care about anyone else's.

He saw the signs in Jack early on. The occasional contemptuous word staining a sentence, the dollops of incertitude that peppered his breaking voice during even the inanest conversations. To Jack, Adam was a man about the house who held the TV remote control tightly when he wasn't locked away in the dining room writing some old shit that was never published.

It didn't matter. Jack spent most of his time in his room, multi-tasking–playing *Call of Duty* on line and speaking through headphones to adversaries around the world while checking out Facebook on his Apple laptop and doing pure maths homework.

When Jack was through with everything for the night, he'd pick up his guitar and sing a few tunes, anything from 'Great Balls Of Fire' to 'Lately' via 'Smells Like Teen Spirit' and 'Wonderwall'. The adolescent creak in his voice lent the songs character. Adam always meant to tell Jack that he loved to listen to him play, but he never did.

It was a far cry from 15-year-old Adam's room where the only multi-tasking he did was put a stylus on a record and scratch his arse.

One night, around 11.30, Adam was in the spare room working on a novel. He'd started six in the last three years and ran out of patience with all of them. But this one, this one felt right, and he was already half way through. He told nobody about it, not even himself, because the words appeared on the screen by themselves. Like clockwork.

He didn't know how it would end or how he'd get there, but he'd get there. He knew that much.

As the words flowed, Adam heard the opening lines to 'Vincent' with the sweetest guitar accompaniment. He stood up and walked into the hallway. The music was coming from Jack's room. He needed to hear it.

Jack was more remote than Ben, if that was possible. Adam and his teenage son never clicked. He wondered how many teenage boys clicked with their dads and imagined Bruce Forsyth on *Play Your Cards Right*–'We asked a hundred fathers if they clicked with their teenage sons. How many said they *didn't* click with their teenage sons?'

'Ninety-five, Bruce.'

Higher or lower?

It was the attitude he hated; the monosyllabic answers to his questions; the impatience; the invisible sneers of utter contempt. Adam was convinced his son disliked him.

Jack hated his dad's attitude. He hated the monosyllabic answers to his questions; the impatience; the invisible sneers of utter contempt. He was convinced his father disliked him.

But when Adam heard 'Vincent' that starry night, his heart skipped a beat. He climbed the stairs and stood outside Jack's bedroom. The sounds were pure and true. This was his son and it was a thing of beauty.

The song ended and Adam turned away, fearful he would be caught lurking. But Jack segued perfectly into 'Wild Is The Wind'. It was mesmerising. As he caressed the final words, Jack tumbled into 'God Only Knows' and that drifted into 'The Dock Of The Bay', which magically became Patsy Cline's 'Crazy' and it all seemed the most natural thing in the world.

Adam had heard his son sing before, but not like this. He wanted to congratulate him, to tell him how wonderful he was. He tried to knock on the door, he really did, but he'd had enough attitude and invisible sneers to last a lifetime and headed for the stairs.

'Dad.' Jack opened the door before Adam took two steps. 'I thought you were downstairs.'

'I was. But then I heard you sing.'

'I presume it was too loud.'

'No. No. Far from it. It was, well, great.'

'Oh.'

'Honestly Jack, I've never heard you sing like that before. What happened?'

'My voice got a bit deeper, I guess, and it kinda beefed it up a bit.'

'A bit? And where did you dig up those songs? 'Crazy'?'

'Trawling through YouTube.'

'What, they have all those on there?'

'Don't you ever go on YouTube?'

'Only when someone sends me a link in an email.'

'You should check it out. I know you love your music and it has everything on it that you could possibly imagine.'

'Even Patsy Cline?'

'Even Patsy Cline.'

'Well, Jack, I loved your song choices and I loved what you did with them. It was magical. Your voice overflows with emotion and depth.'

'Overflows with emotion and depth?' Where did that come from? But he couldn't help himself because it was true. His son sang like an angel and he wanted him to know it.

'Thanks.'

'My pleasure, Jack. My pleasure. Why don't you sing something else before I go back downstairs?' Wow, he wasn't expecting to say that.

'Sure. What about your favourite song?'

'What favourite song?'

'Y'know.'

'What?' Adam did have a favourite song, a cheesy, wheezy classic that still touched his soul for some strange reason. Muse had even done a version. Kate told him.

Kate.

But he didn't remember ever telling his son what it was.

Jack picked up his guitar and started to sing 'Can't Take My Eyes Off You', but slowly, each word drenched with soul.

He was so right, and it was so good. Adam had to fight back the tears that always flowed when he was genuinely moved by music.

He suddenly felt younger than Jack as that honeydew voice manipulated his senses, making him vulnerable and indistinct and it was the sweetest feeling.

Lauryn Hill was never like this, or rather she was, until this came along.

'That was brilliant, Jack. Utterly brilliant. Honestly, I've never heard a better version.'

'Really? Not even the Boys Town Gang?'

'Not even the Boys Town Gang.'

They laughed, and Adam couldn't recall ever having laughed in his son's bedroom before. In fact, he couldn't recall the last time they did laugh together. Adam laughed with Ben everywhere, until his son started shooting up some germ-free adolescence. The purity and the dosage determine its duration–the stronger the hit, the more you shoot, the longer the adolescence. And for some losers, it lasts way too long.

Thankfully, Ben's adolescence was like March, it came in like a lion and went out like a lamb. Thirteen was far worse than sixteen and by eighteen he was out of emotional rehab and totally clean.

'Thanks, dad.' Jack honestly didn't realise how good he was and that impressed Adam even more. He never knew his son was so disarming.

'No Jack. Thank you. Goodnight.'

'He obviously got his talent from his grandfather, The Entertainer,' Laura said the next morning after Jack left for school.

'I guess so, 'cos he certainly didn't get it from my side,' said Adam. They were sitting at the kitchen table breakfasting on Lapsang souchong and Best of Both toast. Laura had a dentist's appointment and took the morning off.

'Jack is seriously good. He should be doing something about it.'

'He's too young. Plus, he doesn't want to get distracted from his GCSEs. This is an important year.'

'He's not too young,' said Adam. 'He'll be 16 when the next *X Factor* auditions are held. They love 'em at that age on there.'

'You can't be serious. *The X Factor*? I hope you haven't mentioned this to him. Don't start filling his head with all kinds of shit; keep them in your own head where they belong. Jack wants to be a doctor, you know that. Don't distract him. These next two years are important.'

'I'm simply telling you that what I heard last night was something special. His voice is unique, Laura. When he sang 'Can't Take My Eyes Off You', every pubic hair on my body straightened out.'

She also heard Jack last night and she knew Adam was right about his voice. There was a clarity, a resonance she hadn't noticed before. And the guitar break in the middle of 'God Only Knows' shivered her timbers.

'Okay, on your head be it, Adam. You want him on *X Factor*, you take him on *X Factor*, if he wants to go. I hope for both your sakes that he won't get affected by the inevitable rejection.'

'Why inevitable?'

'God, have you seen how many people turn up for the auditions? You have to be either very talented or absolute shit to get through to the judges.'

'I'm confident he'll at least get that far,' said Adam. 'Trust me on this.'

'Why should I?'

'Because you love me.'

'Ha! I don't think so.'

'Yes, you do. Furthermore, you want to go to bed with me right now.'

'Why? Are you tired, you poor old sod? You've only just got up.'

'Who said anything about sleep? I'm talking about having some wide-awake dreams.'

'I know exactly what you're talking about and the only dreams you're getting have the prefix "in your".'

'C'mon Laura. When was the last time we made love during daylight hours? Was John Lennon still alive?'

'My body is shot to pieces,' said Laura in semi-jest. 'That's why I like the dark.'

'So's mine. Who cares? These days I can't see a thing anyway. Light, dark, it's all the same to me. My eyes are as bad as my ears.'

'That's what happens at your age.'

'What?'

'That's what happens at your age.'

'What?'

'I said, that's what happens...' She laughed when she twigged it. She always did.

'C'mon Laura, let me grab a granny, just this once. I promise I won't ask you again for another thirty years.' Adam couldn't believe his audacity. He hadn't been this forward in a long time. Then again, they hadn't been home alone on a weekday morning in a long time. His erection was doing all the talking.

He wanted to kiss her, to feel her tongue in his mouth, but he'd tried a hundred times before and a hundred times she declined, and he was all out of trying. Instead, in the bedroom a few minutes later, he felt his tongue in her vagina, which was the next best thing.

Laura was a cunnilingus fan because it was more pleasurable than intercourse, yet no amount of flicking and licking could make her come. Orgasms were a distant memory.

However, on this fine, finger-licking, fuck-fest morning, Laura came. Twice. Once with his tongue and once with his penis. She'd never come twice like that in her life. It was a miracle.

But a bigger miracle was the fact that Adam didn't come until her second orgasm, a full twenty minutes after uttering the words, 'grab a granny' in the kitchen. It was the first time Adam had made love since the Kate debacle–maybe the coke was only just starting to take effect.

Maybe the shame and embarrassment of that night finally enabled him to apply the brakes. Maybe he was just getting old. Whatever it was, it certainly put the look of love back into Laura's eyes. She almost felt like kissing him, it was that good.

'Adam, what just happened? Whatever it was, it was amazing.'

'I aim to please,' said Adam, a little worse for wear after having entered uncharted territory. He'd never lasted that long in his life.

Kate's face suddenly flashed in front of him.

It was so real he could smell her.

He wondered how it might've turned out if he'd made her come twice, and he was overcome by a great sadness. Death, money and a mentally itinerant father had taken centre stage in his life since that last meeting and Adam had to be content with catching glimpses of Kate in those passing cars of his dreams. He was now just going through the motions in a motionless life. It was no way to live but it was all he had. He wondered how much longer he could take it.

'Adam,' said Laura as she lay next to him and looked up at the ceiling, 'there's something I've always wanted to tell you. Promise you won't be angry.'

You couldn't get angry with Laura. She just wasn't that kinda gal, especially when she was naked. On the rare occasions Adam did lose his temper, he was angrier with himself for getting angry with her.

'I won't be angry.'

'Because nothing happened. Not really.'

'I promise I won't be angry.'

'Well, it happened a long time ago.'

'You said nothing happened.'

'You know what I mean.'

'How long ago are we talking?'

'Twelve years? A long time.'

'Not such a long time.'

'It could've been more. Anyway, I met a man on a plane going to Cyprus.'

'My God, Laura, don't tell me you had an affair.' It was the last thing Adam expected to hear. It had never once crossed his mind that his wife would ever cheat on him. Him.

'No. Not even close. It was a kiss, one kiss.'

She told him what happened that night in Larnaca with Alexei under a sky full of stars.

'I guess the real reason it didn't go any further was you,' said Laura.

'Well, I should hope so,' he said and forgave her immediately.

'I knew you could never be unfaithful, Adam. I know you've always loved me. How could I repay that kind of devotion with a rooftop shag? Besides, I bet Alexei wasn't capable of inducing dual orgasms. Want to try for the triple crown?'

Adam didn't know whether to laugh, cry or be physically sick, so he fell asleep instead.

Laura was still beautiful, still sexy, still reliable, but she wasn't Kate. She knew what he liked but she wasn't Kate. She smiled in all the right places, but she wasn't Kate.

And there's that itch again, the one he couldn't reach because it was deep inside.

And getting deeper every day.

CHAPTER 4

Little Man Tate

Adam and Jack were sitting on the sofa watching *American Idol* and talking about the possibility of auditioning for *X Factor*.

'You think I'm that good?' Jack asked, seeking reassurance.

'Certainly do,' said Adam. 'We'll find out where they're holding it in London and apply.'

'I think it's at the O2. But there'll be thousands.'

'Let's go to Liverpool or Newcastle, might not be so many. We could drive up the night before, check into a hotel, have a nice meal and you could rehearse in your room before getting an early night. We'd head for the auditions first thing, after a hearty breakfast, naturally.'

'Sounds good, dad. I'd be up for that.'

'Just keep practising, it makes perfect.'

'I practise a lot.'

'And you're perfect. What song will you sing?'

'"Vincent', 'cos I've never heard it on *X Factor*. I won't use any backtrack, I'll just play the guitar.'

'Like I said, perfect.'

Adam was more excited than his son. He felt like a parent for the first time in years and it was a feeling he could get seriously used to. He hoped none of Uncle Michael's genes were surfing on his son's blood and thanked God Jack didn't have a younger sister. Wouldn't look good on the front page of a red top.

X FACTOR WINNER 'RAPED' KID SISTER

Inventing headlines was a hard habit to break. He often thought in headlines and, like the real thing, they often promised more than they delivered.

Jack picked up his iPad and became engrossed.

'What are you looking at?'

'Facebook. You're not on it, are you, dad?'

'Never appealed to me. Not my age group.'

'There's thousands of old gits like you on it.'

'Yeah, probably trying to groom young kids.' He was sounding more like Booby every day. It was unnerving.

Adam thought of Uncle Michael and wondered if he'd ever had his photo taken. He was curious to know what a serial baby-sister-shagger looked like, especially one who happened to be his dad's brother.

'That only happens in chat rooms,' said Jack. 'Facebook is completely different. Here, have a look.' Adam snuggled up to him. He could feel his heartbeat.

'This is my wall.'

'Your what?'

'My wall. It's like my crib, innit.'

'Your what?'

'Crib. House, bruv. You get me?'

Adam laughed. 'Don't talk like that on *X Factor*. Oh, I don't know, though…'

As Jack explained the Facebook process, Adam's eyes wandered to the screen.

Ben T–Don't forget the big one. Tomorrow night. Sasha in Camden.

He saw the top four of 37 responses.

Jason Rowland–Wouldn't miss it for the world, mate.

Duncan Thomas–Count me in.

Elizabeth Hall–Me too.

Lyle Associates–I'll be there, Sonja. Looking forward to it, Ben xxxxx

'Who's Ben T, Jack?'

'There's his picture.'

'Ben? Our Ben?'

Jack clicked on the profile pic and Ben's face flashed up on the screen.

'Who do you think?'

No. It can't be.

'You okay, dad? You look a bit pale.'

Wait. It just says 'Lyle Associates'. It could be anyone from there. How many girls did Kate say worked for her? Fifteen? Twenty? Yes. That's what it is.

Wait, Kate wouldn't allow them to use her company's name on Facebook. It must be her. Her and her five kisses. Five! She was practically raping him.

He scrolled down to the previous message that sealed it with a kiss.

Sonja Kowlowski–Are you going, Kate?

'Oi, don't read my messages.'

'Sorry, Jack. Force of habit. I am a journalist. Looks like Ben's having a big night out.'

'It is his birthday.'

Of course! His birthday. That explains it. Kate's just an acquaintance. Someone he met on a cruise ship. There's absolutely nothing in it.

But acquaintances don't send five kisses. The most she ever sent him was two. Two. And after they had sex, the kisses dried up completely.

Ben was obviously a five-star lover. His son had entered the body of the woman he adored, the woman he craved, the woman who haunted his dreams, and those five kisses were a message to the whole world how wonderful it was, how infinitely better than his pathetic attempt.

He was part of an incestuous triangle. Uncle Michael would be proud. It was the closest he'd ever been to disgusted in his life.

'Dad, you don't look well.'

'Says the doctor-in-waiting. I'll be fine.' But the hurt was bad, and he couldn't disguise it. 'Thanks for showing me some of the tricks of the trade, Jack. I think I took most of it in.'

The following evening at 7.30, Adam found himself smoking a joint in a dark recess opposite Sasha's near Camden Market. The sign outside the restaurant said, 'Private Function'. Adam had the entrance in his sights and his mind was racing.

What if she turns up? It doesn't mean anything. Just that they've been in contact since the ship. Since the night he heard his son say, 'Wow.' She ended their relationship a week after she met Ben. Was that it? Did she ditch him for his son? My God, no! Did she tell Ben about him? Did they laugh at him? After they made love, did they laugh at him?

But it might not even be his Kate. The PR world is full of Kates. How many people worked for her, 15, twenty? Five per cent of them could be called Kate, shit, ten per cent. Lyle Associates was the generic email address open to everyone. Five kisses. No. It's too absurd. Kate Lyle wasn't a five kisses kinda girl. No way.

He'd had enough. It was now 9pm and about sixty people had gone into the restaurant, including Ben, and not one face belonged to Kate Lyle. Adam discarded his second joint and turned to leave. He stepped out of the shadows and stepped right back in when he saw her.

The hair was a little shorter, but the walk was unmistakable. She wore a simple black suit over a white blouse. The skirt was short, the elegance, breath-taking. It was the Pretty Flamingo that haunted his dreams and called out his name a million times. It was the woman he needed, the woman he loved more than life itself.

Kate walked within ten feet of Adam without noticing him and went into the restaurant. Adam lit another joint and waited.

CHAPTER 5

Pigs in Shit

'So, what exactly did a 15-year-old gangster do in 1932?'

Adam switched on the recorder. He was as white as a ghost, left reeling from the events of last night when he shat his heart out onto the pavement and left it steaming in those chilly Camden Market shadows.

Ben and Kate were the last to leave. Arm in arm. And from the shadows, Adam watched them kiss. They kissed blatantly and passionately. Then they walked away, arm in arm, and he could hear their laughter. Adam stunk of skunk, but his eyes and his ears weren't deceiving him.

He couldn't get that laughter out of his head; that insidious, mocking laughter that revealed their treachery.

Focus.

Listen.

'Oh, it took me a few years to develop the art–and it is an art, make no mistake,' said Bobby. His wound was leaking badly. He'd refused to let the district nurse change his dressing because it was too painful, and the smell of decaying flesh and stale blood permeated the room.

'There's only a handful of people in the world that are capable of becoming successful villains, just as there are only a handful of people capable of becoming great painters or writers or singers or actors.'

'It's all in the wrist action, eh?'

'You may mock, but a great gangster is a fucking rare thing.'

'Were you a great gangster?'

'Of course. I'm fucking still here, ain't I?'

'So, your only criteria for greatness is longevity?'

'Oh, posh words, son, posh words. Well, in answer to your question and using your fucking vernacular, in the criminal sense, yes. It's the yardstick.'

'What about the accumulation of wealth?'

'I had my fair share.'

'I haven't seen any evidence of that.'

'You will, son, you will. Don't dance on my grave just yet.' He spoke like a 40-year-old. This man could live forever.

Bobby knew Adam was after his money. He would kill for his son, but money was a little more sacred. He liked to keep it close by, it made him sleep easier at night. Adam would never find the cash, it was hidden too well. Bobby always vowed he'd spend his money and leave not a penny behind. Trouble was, he couldn't think of a single thing he wanted. And that hurt.

'So,' said Adam, 'let's start at the very beginning.'

'That's a fucking good place to start,' said Bobby.

'Where were you born?'

'You know where I was fucking born,' said Bobby. 'Is this a fucking joke or what? We had all this the other day.'

'Tell me more about the conditions. How many people lived in the house?'

'How many people? How many people?' Bobby snarled the words, his disdain as apparent as the scar on his face.

'It was a five-storey tenement block. Aunt Liza and her husband Bill shared the two basement rooms with their daughter and son. They had a toilet in the yard. Granny Mead, an old Irish lady, lived in one room on the ground floor with her son Ronnie Sharp who used to have fits. They all shared the same outside toilet.

Mr and Mrs Buckingham had the two rooms on the first floor with their three kids. They also had a little anteroom with a sink and shared the toilet on the next floor with Mr and Mrs Brown who lived in two rooms with five kids. We were in the top two rooms, seven of us too. So how many people is that?'

'Twenty-five.'

'That's right. Twenty-five people in a house with one toilet inside and one outside and no bathroom. The rows over the toilets could get fucking violent. There was always a bucket in the corner of the front room where we all slept, in case of emergency. We shared the same bug-ridden bed which was folded up during the day. We used to have a bath in the tin tub by the fire every other Friday night with water heated on the range in the backroom.

'People in this country don't know what poverty is. We lived in shit, but we were as happy as fucking pigs.'

'But you wanted out.'

'Who fucking wouldn't? You can't be a pig all your fucking life. The only way you could make good money was by being crooked. And the only way you could make really good money was by being crooked and violent. And I wanted to make *really* good money.'

'You ever killed anyone, dad?

'Committed my first murder when I was 16. Stuck a screwdriver right up his big fat arse and watched the geezer bleed to death. Always had good upper arm strength.'

Against his better judgement, Adam was a little impressed.

'And you got away with it?'

'The ol' bill wanted him dead as much as the geezer who paid me to kill him. He was a local villain who raped kids. I was only too happy to fucking oblige. I followed him home from the pub one night and fucking disembowelled him on the corner of Richmond Avenue and Caledonian Road. He cried like a fucking girl.'

'You said your first victim. How many were there?'

'Six, seven. I lost count.'

Seven! His dad had murdered seven people. Seven! In cold blood. He knew Bobby was a villain but he never in his wildest dreams… seven! Maybe more!

'You're joking me. Right?'

'No. It's the truth. And every one of the fuckers deserved it, believe you me.'

'But, seven!'

'Seven less cunts. The world's full of them. I don't want to talk anymore. I'm tired.' With that, Bobby drifted instantly into a deep blue sleep.

'Seven!' shouted Adam. 'Or more!'

But it didn't disturb his father, who slept like a pig.

In shit.

CHAPTER 6

Sweet and Sour

They never made it to Liverpool or Newcastle. They did, however, make it to the O2 in Docklands.

The X Factor auditions were like Adam imagined them to be, with a little help from the Internet. Jack spent hours being filtered through several levels of anonymous judges where contestants were considered either talented enough or absurd enough to face the celebrity panel.

Jack sailed through them all. One producer told Adam that if his son performed like that in front of the cameras, the judges would 'adore' him.

'He's a shade nervous.'

'That's what makes him so good,' said Adam.

An hour later he was standing side-stage with Jack who was about to face the judges.

'Nervous?'

'A bit.'

'That's what makes you so good.'

Jack sang 'Vincent' like Adam first heard it and the panel was ecstatic.

'One hundred per cent, yes!'

'One thousand per cent, yes!'

'One million per cent, yes!'

'You've got four very big yesses. I predict a great future for you, young man.'

Jack came bounding down the stairs and straight into the arms of, Ben.

'That *was* fucking brilliant.'

'Watch your tongue, Ben,' said Laura. 'Oh, what the fuck, it was fucking brilliant.'

'What are you two doing here?' said Adam, a little crestfallen.

'When you rang me and said Jack made it through to the judges, I contacted Ben and we drove down immediately,' said Laura. 'We saw it all. You were fantastic.'

Adam hadn't seen Ben since the night he watched his tongue slide into Kate's mouth. He prayed that tonight Ben would say something to him, something like, 'I snogged that Kate Lyle the other night. I invited her to my birthday party at a restaurant in Camden as a thank you for entertaining us on the ship. We both got a little pissed and well, one thing led to another and we kissed in the middle of the street. I took her home in a cab but she didn't invite me in, thank goodness.'

Or, at a push: 'You know your mate Kate we met on the ship? Well, we're a bit of an item now and it's all thanks to you. She's fantastic. I've never met a girl like her.'

His prayers would be in vain.

'Not bad, eh?' said Jack.

'Not bad?' said Adam. 'It was one million, one thousand and one hundred per cent genius. Am I right or am I right? I should've been a pop music manager.'

'You should've been a lot of things,' said Laura before showering Jack with kisses.

He looked at Ben. Their eyes met. Ben smiled. It was an inky smile blotted with treachery. The smile of a clown in a three-ringed circus. His own son was cheating on him with the only girl he'd ever truly loved. His own son. His own, treacherous son.

You can still be hanged for treason.

'Let's go to the Shanghai Palace to celebrate,' said Ben. 'I've booked us a table for 8.30 and it's on me.'

It was around the corner from home and it was Jack's favourite restaurant.

'No! My treat,' said Adam.

'If you insist.'

'I insist.'

In the Shanghai Palace, Laura dumped a chunk of Singapore noodles onto Jack's plate. She was a little tipsy. Adam wondered if she was this drunk when she nearly shagged Alexei up on the roof.

'So, how's the job?' she asked Ben. 'Still making millions?'

'It has its ups and downs.'

'I'm not talking about your sex life, Ben.'

Jack rolled up laughing and Adam couldn't resist a smile.

'Mum, you are so pissed,' said Jack.

'No, I'm not. I'm so deliriously happy that my son became famous for singing like an angel. I can't believe it. Adam, our little boys, one a successful businessman and the other a superstar.'

'Steady on, mum,' said Jack.

'You are so going to win this competition,' she said. 'I know it. And, talking about sex lives, how is yours, Ben?'

Jack laughed again while Adam baited (sic) his breath with a fat, juicy maggot.

He was hoping to catch a big one.

He looked for a flicker, a minuscule sign of treachery.

Nothing.

'Nothing to report there, I'm afraid.'

The king prawn slid down Ben's throat like Kate's tongue.

'No sign,' Adam paused but covered it with a cough, 'of you and,' he momentarily forgot his daughter-in-law's name and coughed again.

'That's quite a cough you have there, dad,' said Ben. 'You should get it checked out.'

'...of you and Julia getting back together. You wouldn't even know we had a grandchild.'

'Like you care,' said Ben.

'What's that supposed to mean?'

'You're not exactly Mother Theresa when it comes to kids, as I recall,' said Ben.

Not exactly Mother fucking Theresa? You obnoxious little conniving bastard. 'Well you didn't turn out too badly.'

'Mainly thanks to mum.'

He could feel his hands on Ben's neck. 'I can't argue with that. But I was always around.'

'Round what, exactly? Let's try the bend for starters and work upwards.'

Squeezing.

'He's all right, really,' said Jack, defusing and defrosting. 'A little flaky maybe but his heart's in the right place. And I wouldn't have done this today without him.'

'Well, that's one thing you got right, dad,' said Ben, laughing.

Kate had spilled the beans. It was obvious. But so what? So what if he knows his dad cheated on his mum? Ben can't say a thing because it was worse to admit he was shagging the woman his dad almost shagged.

'I married your mum, surely that's two things.'

'I'll give you that. But fuck all else.'

'Ben, that's enough. Why are you insulting your dad like this? Stop swearing.' Laura never remained tipsy for long.

'I'm only pulling his leg. Dad knows, don't you dad?'

'I know, Ben. I know.'

'See,' said Ben. 'Okay, let's eat; we have some celebrating to do.' He raised his glass. 'To my kid brother, TV celebrity. Nice one, bruv. Nice one.'

They all said, 'Jack,' even Jack, who had knocked back four cups of hot sake and was smiling a lot.

'You know you won't be able to sit like this again, in public, once the audition is aired,' said Laura as she carefully rolled her crispy duck pancake as tight as a spliff.

'The girls will be queuing up for a cute guy like Jack, won't they, dad?' said Ben.

Oh, how he knows. 'They have to like his voice first. The right song choices are crucial. So often…' Adam was distracted by a gorgeous blonde aged about 25 who walked past the table, glanced at Ben, continued walking, then back-tracked.

'Excuse me, you must get this all time, but you look like…'

'Christian Bale. Yes. It's an occupational hazard.'

'What do you mean, you really are Christian Bale?'

'Yes, as a matter of fact, I am.'

'No. Really? What on earth are you doing in here?'

'At this moment, talking to a beautiful blonde with a hint of soy sauce on her upper lip which is rather sexy.'

She laughed and wiped away the sauce with the side of her finger.

'Well, it was lovely meeting you, Mr Bale. Enjoy the rest of your evening.' She looked at Adam. 'And my apologies for interrupting your conversation. One thing. Can I have your autograph?

'Of course.'

'Hold on. I'll get a pen and paper.' She walked back to her table.

'Ben, how could you?' said Laura with a smile. 'That poor girl.'

'Don't worry, I'll let her down gently. Watch this, it never fails.'

When she returned, she handed him a napkin and a biro.

'Can you put, "To Melinda, love Christian Bale"?'

'Of course.'

Adam watched Ben write, 'Actually, I'm not Christian Bale, but I'd love to spend a dark night with you. I'm Ben. Here's my number. x'

Melinda took the napkin, read the words, turned and walked away.

'Give it a few minutes,' said Ben. Jack was entranced.

His mobile broke into song. It was John Lennon delivering a text message while pleading not be let down.

Ben read it out.

'It's me, Melinda. Checking in. And now you have my number. So dial. I just might be your Robin. Turn around.'

Melinda was in the corner of the packed restaurant with two other girls. She waved. Adam was stunned. Ben was prepared to cheat on Kate. Kate! It was inconceivable. This man was a wretch of Dickensian proportions. He was toying with a dream, his dream.

'See.'

'Girls are so stupid these days,' said Laura. 'I mean, you could be anyone.'

'Yeah, Christian Bale,' said Jack, still smiling. He downed another sake.

'Stop that,' said Laura. 'You'll be sick.'

'That's what rock stars do,' he said and laughed hard and loud.

'You're not a rock star yet,' said Adam. 'I'm sure your liver can wait. Besides, they'll throw us out of here if they catch you drinking.'

'Don't worry, dad. I'm being very discreet.'

'I don't think so. Oh well, get pissed if you want. I guess every cloud has a silver lining.'

'I know that one,' said Jack and started to sing.

Look for the silver lining
When e'er a cloud appears in the blue.
Remember, somewhere the sun is shining,
And so the right thing to do,
Is make it shine for you.
A heart full of joy and gladness,
Will always banish sadness and strife.
So always look for the silver lining,
And try to find the sunny side of life.

The other diners stopped talking and drank in the honey, even though Jack had his back to many of them and remained seated throughout the song. When he finished, the whole restaurant applauded, and there were even a few whoops and whistles. Jack turned around in utter amazement and went bright red.

When Adam explained to the waiter that they'd come straight from the *X Factor* where Jack had made it through to boot-camp, word got around and there was a buzz in the air.

'How do you know these songs?' asked Adam, a little stunned by his son's performance. 'That's a Jerome Kern tune written a hundred years ago.'

'It's the first time I've ever sung it. Sorry, I guess I am a little pissed.'

'In that case,' a wag on the next table said to Adam, 'get your grandson another bottle. Well done son. That was fantastic.'

'Thank you. By the way he's not my granddad, he's my dad.'

'Oh, sorry mate, I didn't mean...'

'Don't worry,' interrupted Adam, 'it could've been a lot worse. You could've said that to the wife.'

He always did have a way of defusing awkward situations, thought Laura as she laughed along with Ben, Jack and the whole of the next table who insisted on buying them a bottle of champagne.

'You can only have one sip of this,' said the guy to Jack. 'You want to be fit for boot-camp. With that voice, I think you'll walk it.'

After the waiter cleared the table, Laura and Jack ordered desserts.

'I'm going for a cigarette,' said Adam. 'Can someone get me a coffee?'

'I'll join you,' said Ben. 'I'll have an Irish coffee and make sure it's Jameson's.'

Adam wasn't expecting this. 'I thought you didn't smoke.'

'I don't, except marijuana of course.' Jack crowed with delight. 'But I fancy a fag now. It's all this excitement.'

It was drizzling. Adam and Ben stood in a shop doorway adjacent to the Shanghai Palace. The street was deserted. The silence was golden. Something had to give.

'Look dad, I know about you and Kate.'

'And I know about you and Kate.'

'How?'

'Don't you worry how. I just know.'

'Okay,' said Ben, 'here's the deal. I love Kate and I know she loves me and I don't want anything, and I do mean anything, to jeopardise it.'

'How can you say that when you've just given some random girl your telephone number?'

'That's a bit of fun. I'll never call her and she won't call me. It's a game. Look dad, I really do love her. She wanted to be completely honest and tell me everything before our relationship developed. I've forgiven her, but I'll never forgive you.'

'I won't breathe a word of what happened and not because of any misplaced loyalty. I don't see why mum should have to suffer any more than she already has with you.'

'But I'm disappointed. Bitterly disappointed. You were a bastard in a million different ways but never that much of a bastard, until now.'

Who the hell does he think he is? He's 'disappointed', is he? A 'bastard in a million different ways'? You don't know your dad, son. He can be a bastard in a billion different ways. A fucking billion.

'Sorry to hear you think that way, Ben. But you don't know the whole story.'

'I know it has a happy ending, for Kate and me. That's all I want to know. The rest is tomfoolery as far as I'm concerned. Tomfoolery. And I don't want to speak about it ever again. Is that clear?'

'As clear as crystal, Ben. As clear as crystal.' And crystal can be smashed into a billion pieces. A fucking billion.

So, will you be moving in together or is marriage all the rage these days?'

'She already lives with me.'

Adam was stunned

'That was quick.'

'Not quick enough. I now feel I have to make up for so much lost time, time lost looking for her. I've never met anyone like Kate and never will again. Look, I said I didn't want to discuss it. I'm going back inside.'

Adam watched his son dart between raindrops back to the restaurant and lit a half-finished joint. He had four big puffs and flicked it into the road.

His heart was pounding.

They live together. He sleeps with Kate every night. She wraps her lips around his son's cock Sunday through Sunday and when she removes it she tells him her dreams in a million voices.

The thought was too much to bear.

His son was pissing on him from a great height. This couldn't go on.

When he walked back into the restaurant, the owner was sitting in his chair.

'Hullo, Mr Tate. I was congratulating your son on his wonderful voice. You must come here on the night the show is aired. My treat, of course. Now, let me buy you all a drink.'

He watched Ben pissing on him. And the height was getting greater by the minute.

CHAPTER 7

Decapitated the Fucker

'So, name names. Name the people you murdered.'

'Oh, I can't remember them now. I'm too fucking old.'

'You must remember some. When was the last bloke you killed?'

'The last? Oh, that's gotta be well over sixty years ago. Before you were born. After you came along I stopped and got other people to do it for me. See, what you have to remember is back then I had no enemies. That was my secret. I knew everyone I needed to know and murdered anyone that I and a lot of other people didn't want to know. It was all sweet and the money was fucking great.'

'So, what came first with you, principle or money?'

'Money, definitely. I wouldn't have done it without the dough. But it helped that every one of my victims, and I mean every fucking one of them without exception, was a scumbag who didn't deserve to walk this good Earth. A fucking scumbag.'

'In what way?'

'In lots of fucking ways.'

'What ways?'

'Mainly hard-core spivs who were paedophiles. See, gangsterism is like the church, it has its fair share of perverts, I mean real perverts, not shagging some 15-year-old bird dressed up like a twenty-year-old.

'I'm talking sixty-year-old blokes banging five-year-olds.'

'How did you kill them?'

'With vengeance, son. With vengeance.'

'No, I mean what weapons did you use?'

'Butcher's knives, an axe.'

'An axe?'

'Yeah. Decapitated the fucker in a 24-hour public toilet. Jacky, Jacky Jefferies. Yeah, that was the last of the fuckers. 1951, January. Fucking freezing. Yeah.'

'An axe? In a public toilet? This is my dad talking, y'know, the dad who used to tuck me up in bed when I was a kid.'

'But I told you I'd stopped murdering people when you came along. I was happy to earn what I needed to without too much violence.'

'Hold on, you said you killed, "mainly hard-core spivs." Who were the exceptions?'

'Who *was* the exception. It was the only one I never got paid for. The third.'

'So, you do remember them.'

'I remember this one because it was during the war, 1943, and Kings Cross was crawling alive with Canadian soldiers. I was standing at a coffee stall one night near the Lucania billiard hall at the bottom of Pentonville Road. The snooker tables were upstairs, and downstairs was a bar called the Witness Box. Aptly, that's where old Bill, the bookmaker I told you about, would hold court. He and his six sons ran the on-course betting circuit by then. You could only bet legally at the course in those days. If I remember rightly, one of the sisters may have been married to Billy Hill.

'Anyway, I was there chatting with a few mates when this bunch of Canadians came along. They could be flash bastards after they'd had a drink and one of the geezers ran true to form.

'He pulls out a pistol, a Luger, and starts giving it loud, saying how he took it from a German soldier he killed. Then he started really giving it–how the London birds shagged like rabbits, how the Limeys weren't up to it, how our women needed men, real men. Canadian men.

'So, I'm listening to this for a few minutes and it's getting right up my fucking nose. And then he looks directly at me and asks why I ain't in uniform. "Are you a coward or something, bub?"

'He was a big guy and I'll never forget, he had a scar on his left cheek, only his ran horizontally. I walked slowly up to him, threw my scalding hot cup of tea in his face and then stuck a fork deep into his fucking forehead. He went down like a sack of potatoes and fell onto his forehead, embedding the fork even deeper.

'I took the gun out of his hand, ripped his ID tag from his throat - his name was Marvin Casey - lifted his wallet from his back pocket and snatched the garrison cap from his head.'

'What happened to the soldier?' asked Adam.

'We did a runner and so did the other Canadians. The next day, the bloke behind the coffee stall told me he'd heard the soldier died. Like I said, always did have good upper arm strength.'

'You murdered someone for calling you a coward? This is surreal.'

'It wasn't just for that. It was also because he was an obnoxious bastard and a bully who might've killed some innocent bloke in a fight in the future. I probably saved a life.'

'But he might have had too much to drink because he was about to be shipped out somewhere the next day to fight the good fight. And maybe he had a wife and kids at home and was a stand-up bloke who ran the local Boy Scout club.'

'Yeah, so he could fuck young boys up the arse,' said Bobby, who started to look tired. 'Stand on me, the geezer was a 24-carat melt and I did the world a favour.'

'How on earth did you get away with it?'

'Nobody would dare grass your ol' dad up, son. Nobody.'

'What happened to the gun?' asked Adam.

'It's still around.'

'What, in the house?'

'Could be.'

Adam knew it. And wherever that gun is, he'd bet his life there was a stack of money nearby. A stack.

'Where?'

'Like I'm fucking gonna tell you. I want to go to sleep now.'

He closed his eyes and drifted into no-one-is-innocent dreams. A look of utter content shone over that shattered face, like the sun on a bombsite, as he slept the sleep of the righteous.

CHAPTER 8

Third Set of Batteries

Adam wasn't sleeping much.

He didn't want to see Kate's face in a car anymore because he now knew where the car was going. It was heading to a place where she and Ben would make love 'til dawn. He didn't want to peer through the steamed-up bedroom window watching them; watching her hold him, watching her love him.

His son had a wife and kid. He had no right to possess the one thing in the world Adam wanted, needed. Ben had no right to be young, to flaunt those years in his face.

He couldn't see a future if his son ended up with Kate. It was unthinkable.

Unbearable.

He had to have her. He realised that now. Nothing else mattered. Nothing at all. Ben wasn't his son anymore. He was a man who stole his life the moment he was born. A man who ruined his love affair with Laura, who made him feel inadequate and hopeless.

And now this? This obscenity? This absurd tragedy? This, this insult of insults?

This man was not his son. What son would carry away his father's dream and turn it into a nightmare? No, this man was not his son.

Ben was the worst enemy he'd ever known. If Adam had his father's genes, he'd probably kill him with no compunction and an axe. Alas, that was something else Bobby failed to pass on.

But Adam knew a man who did have his father's genes and who, coincidentally, was a serial murderer.

He had the tools.

He needed a plan.

It was the eighth victim that Bobby now regretted.

Coral.

But that regret, mixed with copious amounts of Oramorph, enabled him to see life a little clearer, to slowly regain his sanity, his murderous sanity. He started to think straight, but it was Bobby Tate-straight. He got his mojo working again and it was little short of miraculous.

In the interviews with his son, he sparkled like a sane diamond. But it was his sane, his insane sane, a sane that would make him do just about anything. All he needed was a spark.

Adam's spark.

Adam's spark would light up his dad's life and make him yearn for the old days when a breadknife in the stomach meant a cool grand in the pocket and a pat on the back.

'Those blokes you killed were mainly perverts?'

Adam was onto his third set of batteries. He had compiled a rough dossier on his dad's life; how he became The Enforcer and how nobody messed with him; how he made money through a protection racket and the occasional post office job; how he never went to prison; how he met Coral and how beautiful she was; how the family came first, always first; how life was just a bowl of cherries as long as you ate them before anyone else; how liars ruled the world; how to live forever.

The interviews had the desired effect. Bobby called him 'son' a lot more, not the common or garden 'son' tag so often cheaply bestowed on friends and acquaintances and usually preceded by 'me', but in a genuine filial way.

'And it was a fucking pleasure.'

'Uncle Michael was a pervert, dad, worse than any of the blokes you took out. I mean, his own little sister. Would you have murdered him?'

'With my bare hands.'

'But you idolised him. He was your brother.'

'Listen, I would've strangled my own fucking mother if I found out she interfered with her kids. He was a wrong 'un,' said Bobby, suddenly feeling a little uncomfortable. 'The world is full of 'em.'

'Listen dad. I'm worried about Jack.'

'Who the fuck is Jack?'

'Your grandson, dad. Remember?

'Oh, Jack. Whaddya mean, you're worried about him?'

'He's not been himself. He's withdrawn. He has this *X Factor* thing coming up but his mind's not on it.'

'He's probably on drugs.'

'They all are. I was at his age. What do you expect? No, it's not that.'

'I'd never taken one drug in my life until I got this fucking thing on my face.'

'Different times, dad. Different times.'

'What do you think it is?' asked Bobby, still nursing an uneasy feeling.

'I don't know. But I do know he's been like it since Ben moved out.'

'He'll be all right,' said Bobby. 'I'm tired now. Let yourself out.'

He closed his eyes but opened them when Adam left the room. He wasn't tired. Bobby didn't need much sleep these days. He'd taken so much morphine that it started to act like coke. He had chemical overload of the bloodstream, his heart was beating fast and his five senses were working overtime, digging deep and hauling memories to the surface like rescued miners.

They were memories he didn't want, the kind that kept him awake through long, lonely nights when he sometimes forgot he was alive.

Memories of his brother Michael showing him his cock when he was barely five, of Michael sucking his limp little cock and then getting Bobby to do the same to him; of Michael sticking his erect cock into his tight, bloody bottom.

The worst memory of all was the jealousy he felt when he found out his brother had also stuck his erect cock into his kid sister. It was a shameful jealousy that confused and terrified him, one that he thought had been banished to a land that time forgot. It was the one memory he didn't want to take with him to the grave because it was the one that made his whole life a big, fat lie. He had to make some atonement for it now before it was too late, like he had to make some atonement for killing his dear, sweet wife of sixty diamond years.

He daren't close his eyes in the darkness for fear of dying in the deep, unable to be hauled to the surface, of becoming his own dead memory. And the night would be falling forever as he prayed for the morning and Zachariah.

On his way home in the car, Adam smoked a joint and smiled.

He was feeling smug. His creative juices were whisked into a smoothie of smug. The skunk was getting more and more expensive, and expansive, but it was worth every penny because it was The Whisk, and its smoothies were so sweet.

Adam wasn't an evil man. He often cried over sad movies and his writing possessed a sentimentality laced with an irascible morality in which no sin goes unpunished. He lived in an orderly universe with a lot of skunk and little money. Planet Earth was blue all right and there wasn't a thing he could do about it. Until now. Now he wanted to paint it red. Blood red.

Nobody steals the only thing that made him want to stay alive and then openly mocks him. Nobody does that. But Ben, his own flesh and blood, flouted that sacred law, breaking at least half the Ten Commandments from honouring your father through stealing to coveting your neighbour's ass.

Thou shalt not kill.

But Bobby can.

He has previous, so it doesn't count if he does it, he's already damned.

So, it's his grandson, so what? He said he would've murdered his own brother given half the chance. With his bare hands. Well, here's a whole chance. Ben must become Michael in Bobby's eyes and be killed with impunity in a grand act of grandson-slaying, because there's no fool like an old fool.

Especially an old fool with no reason to live. An old fool with a gun. And wherever that gun was, he'd bet his life there was a stack of money nearby. A stack.

The Luger with the lolly.

CHAPTER 9

Invisible Grandson Alert

Adam let himself into his dad's house around 12.30pm most days, after Zachariah left, and would sit with Bobby for an hour or two. He always smoked a joint in the car on the way round and then another in the car on the way home. In between, he floated like a butterfly and stung like one too.

'One thing I don't understand about Uncle Michael is...'

'I don't want to fucking talk about him anymore.'

Even at 95, Bobby Tate sounded hard. But Adam could afford to be persistent.

These days his dad was only hard in the head, and half of that was nearly gone.

'...how he got the opportunity to rape his sister. You all lived on top of each other.'

'He didn't fuck her in the house, he took her down alleyways, over the park, in shop fucking doorways. Nobody ever suspected - he was her fucking brother, for fuck's sake. He said he liked taking her out for their "little walks" and how he was proud to be seen with his "beautiful princess." I can hear him say those words like it was yesterday.

'If only I'd known.'

'What would you have done?'

'I told you, I would've killed him.'

'With your bare hands.'

'With my bare fucking hands. But I would've cut his bollocks off with a pair of blunt garden shears first.'

'Naturally,' said Adam who thought that procedure wouldn't

be necessary in the current circumstances, although it had its attractions. He smiled.

Bobby smiled back.

It was time.

'Listen, dad, you know I said I was worried about Jack?'

'Jack, yeah, my fucking invisible grandson. And as for that other long streak of piss, Ben, I haven't seen him in years. What a fucking pair your dear wife shat out.'

'You're wrong about Jack, dad. He's a decent, sensitive boy.'

'Well, why's he never fucking decent and sensitive round here?'

'Last time he was here you called him a little poof. Like he's gonna come back after that.'

'He must be a poof if he was offended by that. I was only having a fucking laugh.'

'Many a true word is said in jest.'

'What's that supposed to mean?'

'It means, I think there's something going on between Ben and Jack.'

'What do you mean, "something going on"?'

'I mean, I think there's something going on. Something not right. That's why I was asking about Uncle Michael. It's just that Ben takes Jack out a lot in his Porsche.'

'So pissy Ben's not short of a bob or two then?'

'He says he likes taking his young brother out because he's "cool," and "great company". Sometimes they're away for hours and when Jack gets home I can smell alcohol on his breath and weed on his clothes.'

'So pissy Ben is taking pissy Jack out for a few drinks and drugs. So what? You told me all 16-year-olds smoke that shit.'

'But there's more. The other evening when he came home, Jack wasn't wearing any underpants. I knew because every night without fail he leaves his dirty pants and socks on the bathroom floor even though the dirty linen basket is in the corner. But that night he left only his socks. There was no sign of any pants, not even in the linen basket.'

'Sounds like pissy Jack pissed himself.'

'Then there's...'

'I don't want to hear any more. I'm tired. I want to sleep before Zack comes back. I think he's washing me today. Close the door after you, son.'

Bobby closed his eyes and opened them when he heard the front door shut.

Could Ben have that rogue Michael gene? They certainly resembled each other physically—both were tall and slim, blue eyes, dark brown hair, both had a slight Burt Lancaster chin cleft and both fucked boys.

Okay, the proof against Ben wasn't irrefutable, but it didn't look good.

Bobby's morphine-laden dreams that night always ended in him falling down stairs, endlessly rolling over with Coral and then grabbing her hand and leaping into the light.

The next day, Adam sucked hard on a small, badly-rolled joint as he made his way to see Bobby. Skunk was 190 quid an ounce and he was fast running out. He hadn't written a word for money in nearly two years, but he was hoping the diary on the passenger seat would change all that.

He deserved something. Anything.

'Dad, I don't know what to do.'

'About what?' Bobby was sitting in his customary armchair like an ancient, hideous Marty Crane. His bandage was hanging off because he wouldn't let the district nurse dress the wound again that morning. It hurt too much. It wasn't a pretty sight.

'About Ben and Jack.'

'I don't wanna hear about it.'

'I have proof. I found Jack's diary. I can't believe it. How could this happen? It's the most disgusting thing I've ever heard. Listen to this.'

Adam produced the diary from a Tesco's carrier bag. He'd been up all night making entries, printing the words on the off-chance Bobby recognised his handwriting.

He thought of the night he read to Kate when love was in the air and life had taken shape again. He thought of the nights ahead when he would read the rest of *Like Clockwork* to her. And he'd read his other books because they were good too. And Kate would love them and love him and the world would be a better place and he'd spend the rest of his life cocooned by love and desire.

He was doing the right thing because Ben was a bastard. No question. A bastard who stole his reason for living. A bastard who pissed on the sanctity of the father-and-son bond. A bastard who wouldn't give a damn if Adam collapsed and died in front of him.

Bobby had a way of dealing with bastards. Adam had every faith in this frail old man with the blood-soaked bandage dangling from his head who still knew the way to San Jose. Adam was confident his dad would come good, when it mattered.

There was no turning back now. He read…

1st June: Went to Hyde Park with Ben. We'd been there a few times since he came to live back at home. He used to insist on taking me out and called me his 'handsome little brother' and we'd walk through the park and stop for a coffee on the way to the tube.

It was a warm evening and Ben said he fancied a cigarette. We sat down on a bench and he lit up. He blew smoke circles through his pursed lips and we watched them drift into the sky on smoky tails.

'D'you remember the old days, Jack?'

I knew what he meant. 'No, not really.' I didn't want to remember. That first time, I told mum the blood on my sheets was the result of a nosebleed.

'How old were you? Five, six?' The lord of the smoke rings blew his last. Perfection. I followed it and it was an excuse not to answer.

'It was before I went to uni,' Ben continued, and he moved a little closer. 'I'm sure of that. They were great times, weren't they.'

It wasn't a question.

'Yeah.' I felt uncomfortable. He did it to me seven times before he went to uni. I know. I counted them. I've never written about this before and tried to shut it out. Sometimes I go weeks without thinking about it and other times I can't stop. But what makes it doubly complicated is the fact that I missed him when he went to uni and I didn't want that guilt trip to be reawakened, I really didn't. It would be too horrific...

'Stop!' Unbeknown to Adam, this was far too close to home for Bobby. 'I don't want to hear anymore.'

'But dad, he actually tried to seduce Jack again.' Adam had no idea of the pain he was inflicting. He unwittingly touched the nerve that hurt the most.

'I don't want to hear it.'

'Listen!' He could see Bobby's discomfort and feel his rage. He was determined to ram it home.

Bobby tried to close his eyes to feign sleep, but Jack's words lit up the dark like fireworks, each one fizzing and banging and colliding off his malignant head. When he opened his eyes again it was a blessing. Almost.

Ben touched my thigh. 'I often dream of those few nights we spent together,' he said, his face up against my shoulder. 'You were amazing. When you told mum you had a nosebleed, I thought that was brilliant.'

He leaned over, and I swear he was going to kiss me. I stood up. 'Ben, that's never gonna happen again. I should call the police and tell them what you did to me.'

'Okay, bruv, but I think you've gotten hold of the wrong end of the stick. What you don't seem to recall is that it was you who came on to me.'

'Me? I was only five, for God's sake.'

'Five-year-olds are very sexual creatures,' he said. 'They have an innate sexuality that needs to be quenched. I simply helped you along the way to a greater understanding of who you are and what you're capable of. You owe me at least a hand job for that valuable education. I thought that's why you came out tonight.'

'*You're a fucking pervert, Ben. I'm too old for your bullshit, now. Talk to me like that again or try anything on and I'll spill the beans. I mean it.*'

I turned and walked away. I hope he's got the message.

'What has this fiend done to my son, dad? What has he done?'

Okay, so he played it like a Victorian melodrama, but Bobby was almost Victorian himself. He'd appreciate it.

He'd written more, but he figured his dad had heard enough for one day. Let it all sink in, and fester.

'I have to go. I can't do any taping today. I'll see you tomorrow.'

Adam wiped a tear from his eye as he left the room.

And in Bobby's head it was all sinking in.

And festering.

CHAPTER 10

Twenty Questions

It was a 9mm Luger P08 and it still sparkled in his hand. It was still alive.

Bobby always appreciated its engineering, its uniformed beauty, its dazzling feel. He loved the straight lines because straight lines meant reliability, and old Fritz was nothing if not reliable. It became an official military sidearm for the German army in 1900 and was finally 'dropped' in 1938, replaced by the Walther P38.

But it was too lovely to let go and over the next seven years it killed thousands with precision and uniformed beauty. For Bobby, it was the caviar of pistols, or 'Beluger' he would say to himself when there was no one around. It was one of the few jokes Bobby made up and he still laughed at it but never in front of anyone. He wasn't a laughing man in company and it was a demeanour that had served him well.

He remembered the moment he first used his precious–8th May 1945, VE Day. Bobby always thought 'VD Day' would've been more appropriate, another joke, what with the amount of shagging the GIs did in London. He used to watch them every morning at a government office near Leicester Square, queuing up for free prophylactics. Hundreds of the fuckers, their putrid disease-ridden cocks festering in their trousers, in their brittle, spunky pants. Fucking our women. Our fucking women.

He was in the bar downstairs from the snooker hall. A geezer from over the water, Alfie Peters, was down with a bunch of his mates and giving it large. Bobby hated him. The place was packed and they hadn't exchanged words all night but as Alfie left, he deliberately bumped into Bobby and didn't apologise.

'Oi, haven't you forgot something?'

'Oh, look guys, it's Bobby Tate,' said Alfie. ''ow's it going, Bobby me ol' mucker?'

'I asked if you forgot something.'

'Not that I know of, pal. What do you think it is?'

'An apology.'

'You can stick your apology right up your fat fucking arse.'

Bobby pulled out the Luger P08, Alfie shit his pants and Bobby shot him across the face.

Alfie Peters never died, but he couldn't see anymore, or smell, or hear, or speak. That's how good a Luger was.

Nobody ever messed with Bobby Tate again.

He'd hidden the gun well. Even Coral never knew, and she made it her business to know everything.

Bobby Tate was a new old man. An old man with a plan.

Why? Oh yeah, that's right, his son's boy, Jack. No, Ben. The older one. The fucking perv. The fucking reincarnation of his brother. It's a Tate gene. A spiteful, insidious creep of a gene that infected Tate blood, tarnished Tate veins, twisted Tate minds, made fools of them all. It had to be put out of its misery. It had to be destroyed. He was too old now to kill with his bare hands, but a Luger would do.

Would do nicely.

It took him an age to load the gun, but he finally snapped the magazine into the casing. He paused to get his breath back before attempting to raise the Luger into an aiming position. But it was too heavy and fell from his hand to the floor.

'Fuck!'

He reached down with both hands and scooped it up. Where did all his strength go? He lifted it again, but his emaciated arm shook like a wet dog and it fell. Where was that bloke who could beat the shit out of two blokes at the same time? He tried again. It fell. He tried again. Where was that bloke who could lift an upright piano single-handed? He held it a little longer because his arm shook a little slower, like a raft on a bad night in the Bay of Biscay.

He kept asking himself question after question and each time he managed to hold the gun a little longer.

By the time he hit question twenty, where was the bloke who was the heaviest of the heavies and who fucking outlived them all? - he could hold that Luger P08 long enough to pull the trigger.

He was ready.

He was doing it for his son. He knew that's what Coral would've wanted because she loved Adam more than life itself.

The guilt engulfed him. He loved Coral more than life itself, but he killed her. He blamed the morphine and all the other shit they kept dosing him up with. It ruined his mind. He had to atone, and this was the only way.

Besides, it'd be like killing Michael. And he'd wanted to do that all his life. This was the murder he'd been waiting for, the one that would square all the others, the one he was put on this earth to do.

Do it and Coral would forgive him. Do it and he could die a happy man.

He put the Luger back into the garrison cap…

'It's Ben.'

Adam wished he hadn't picked up the phone. It was the first time they'd spoken since the night at the Chinese restaurant.

Ben's voice reeked of Kate.

It spoke to her in the dark.

It shaped those dirty cock words that entered her ears and touched her soul. Words that stole her away.

'Yes, Ben.' It wasn't a question, it was an acknowledgement. That's all he could manage.

'I had a strange phone call from granddad. '

'What did he want?'

'He said he wanted to see me. He said he didn't have much longer to live and he wanted to give me something. Something special.'

'So why are you ringing me?'

'Do you think I ought to go around and see him?'

'That's up to you.'

'But I haven't seen him in ages. What could be so special?

'I have absolutely no idea.'

'But don't you still see him regularly?'

'Yes.'

'And he hasn't mentioned anything to you?'

'No. Not a word. Maybe he wants to award you a medal for being the world's best grandson.'

'He never wanted me there, dad. You know that. And when he deigned to speak to me he'd always take the piss.'

Dad? Dad? You dare call me fucking dad? You'll have a lot more than the fucking piss taken out of you, son. A lot fucking more. Adam was conveniently turning into Bobby. It was necessary. But he knew he could turn out of it at the end, when it mattered.

'He was like that with everyone, and you know that. It was his way.'

'Let's not get into all that again,' Ben replied. 'Face it, he's not a nice guy.'

'Like I said, it's up to you. But if you do decide to go, let me know because I don't want to be around. He obviously doesn't want me to know anything. Oh yeah, and you'd better take a map.'

'It's okay, I have sat-nav.'

Neither laughed. They would've done, once. But that was long ago and far away, when Kate was a speck on their horizons.

'Is mum there?'

'She's out.'

'It's late. It's nine o'clock.'

'She goes out walking three times a week.'

'Surely she doesn't go on her own?'

'No, with Maria from around the corner.' Please, enough. Adam was convinced Ben was doing it on purpose, like he knew it offended him, like he was rubbing his nose in shit, making him inhale it.

But your dad knows someone who made a lot of people eat shit, every last morsel.

'Okay Ben, must go. Don't forget, let me know if you go round. I don't want to be there.'

Oh, yes he does. There was nothing better than a good shit-eating session.

He put the phone down just before Laura came in.

'How was your walk?'

'Like the road to nowhere.'

'Talking Heads. Haven't heard that song in a long time. He started to sing.

'What's got into you?'

'It's a once in a lifetime thing, I guess.'

Laura laughed.

She laughed a lot more these days. For the first time in a long time, she remembered why she married Adam Tate.

They were in the kitchen, Laura was standing at the sink drinking a glass of water and Adam sat at the table.

'Where's Jack?' she asked.

'He's at Leo's. Said he'll be home by midnight. Oh yeah, Ben called.'

'That's a first. What did he want?'

'Apparently, my dad rang him to say that he was going to die and he wanted to give him something special while he was still alive.'

'Hopefully, he'll give him some money, the tight git. Not that Ben needs it, but it's the principle. He's 95 and could drop dead at any moment. He can't spend it and, knowing Bobby, he must have a few bob tucked away. What's the point of getting it out and just looking at it?'

'Because at his age, nobody else will.' Kate would've laughed at that.

Laura laughed. Sometimes, when he hadn't been smoking, something, a word, a touch, a spinning coin, a chestnut tree, something, in the spark of a moment, would dive deep, creating a splash and Adam would remember everything in one wonderfully chaotic mess of a vision.

Or was it the smoke? He was sure he wasn't stoned now and Laura's laugh cartwheeled across the room

'He should give whatever he has to the boys.'

'The boys? The boys? You must be joking. Ben is what, thirty? Hardly a boy, Laura. And he's got more money than Croesus.'

'And what about the house?'

'That's ours. Sell that and we're laughing.'

'But we don't need the money.'

Don't need the money? My God, if she only knew. The cash from the house sale would get him out of debt and leave him with a cool fifty grand. Not ideal but should keep them going for a while.

'We always need money. Everyone does. Can we stop talking about it? Please.' He felt like saying, 'I want to go to sleep now,' and close his eyes.

'But you brought it up.'

'All I said was that dad wanted to see him.'

'But isn't that odd? He never liked Ben. The miserable sod never liked anyone. All he ever did was take the piss. Let's face it, Adam, your dad isn't a nice bloke. He doesn't want to know me or the kids, and he hated the sight of my parents. They never had grandparents after my mum and dad died.'

'That's right, let's slag off my family. Mum used to love having the boys round when they were younger.'

'No, she didn't. Stop fooling yourself. She used to make excuses all the time, ring up and say she was feeling ill when you were about to take the boys to see them. You know I'm right, Adam. I'm ALWAYS right.'

He hadn't heard those capital letters in a while and it scared him.

'So that means I'm always wrong.'

'EXACTLY.'

'Thank you and good night.'

'You know what I mean.'

'I know what you mean, all right. What you've ALWAYS meant.'

Laura laughed. She was still wearing her jogging outfit, black leggings and a tee shirt. She still looked good, and she was still immensely screwable. She was facing him and the delicate contours of the bulge between her legs pressing against the sweaty viscose gave him the semblance of a hard-on.

They hadn't made love for a few weeks but when they did, he kissed her. He couldn't believe it. He actually put his tongue in her mouth and they exchanged saliva. He hoped it might lead to something else, but he was mistaken. It was only straight sex on the menu at Chez Laura.

But still, a kiss.

'I must have a shower,' she said. There was a sweat stain on her tee shirt and her face glowed.

'Give me a kiss first.'

'Don't be silly.'

'Just a quick one. Come and sit on my lap.'

'What's gotten into you?'

'This sweaty version of you. It's got right into me. Come and sit on my lap and feel how that sweaty fanny between your legs is making me rock hard.'

Laura was partial to dirty talk as long as she wasn't the one doing it. She moved towards Adam and gently rubbed her crotch in his face before sitting in his lap with her legs either side of him and her lips close to his.

Last time he kissed her but now she kissed him. And as their tongues collided he felt her hand on his jeans, searching for his bulge.

'I want to fuck you across the table.'

'You'll have to clear it first,' she said and they both laughed.

Then she did it. The unimaginable.

She went down on her knees, undid the zip on his flies and pulled out his cock. She started licking the tip of it with her tongue before sliding it into her mouth. She hadn't done that since their honeymoon.

'Never mind me, what the hell has got into YOU?'

She laughed with a mouthful of cock, but she kept on slip slidin' away.

'I think I'm gonna come.' Adam thought it polite to tell her, but he was hoping she'd keep him in her mouth and swallow those old salty sea dogs that could still dance to a tune, or part of one.

But she took it out immediately and he dribbled over her sweaty tee shirt, mingling with the sweat stains and a few psoriasis flakes that fell from his scalp when his head shook as he ejaculated. Never mind, he'd get her next time. He won't say when he's ready and let her finally find out what the taste of sperm was like.

Kate knew. She weighed him up and she knew he was one of the good guys who didn't put it about. She would've swallowed if he hadn't covered his cock with shit coke. Definitely. She knew him so well.

'Oh well, bang goes the fuck across the table,' said Laura, a little disappointed but not fussed.

'Sorry. But I do have another organ in full working order.'

Adam lifted her onto the table and peeled off her leggings and knickers. He put his tongue between her legs and danced in the old-fashioned way, danced in and out of those soft, creamy folds until she shuddered and came in the old-fashioned way, again. It was becoming a habit. She'd quit acting, there was no future in it. He was exciting her again and she was back on track.

But for Adam it was nothing new. She always came whether it was with his tongue, his cock or his fingers. Always. She was quick and always came the moment he came inside her. Always. And it was obvious she wasn't faking.

He knew her so well.

'Thank you, kind sir. That was terrific.'

Strange. He never recalled her saying, 'terrific,' before. Or, 'Thank you, kind sir,' come to that.

'Now I'm going to have that shower. You can join me if you like.'

'Jesus! You haven't suggested that since the honeymoon, either,' he said.

'Sorry?'

'I said you haven't suggested that since the honeymoon.'

'You said, "either."'

'Did I?'

'You're implying there's something else I haven't done since the honeymoon.'

'I guess I am.'

'And what is it?'

'What's what?'

'Come on, Adam. What is it?'

'Surely you know.'

'You don't mean a blowjob?'

'Well, yes.'

'I can't believe you could've forgotten that night,' she said

'What night?'

'You really don't remember?'

'No, I don't. I think I would.'

'That dope has completely frazzled your brain. Your memory banks are bankrupt.'

'A good turn of phrase. I taught you well. So, when was this memorable moment?'

'About 25 years ago, at your cousin's wedding. We were both totally pissed, sneaked out of the reception to the car and I, well, sucked you off.'

'That's right! You did! Shit. Who was looking after Ben?'

'Your mum. She held him nearly all day, in the church, at the wedding breakfast, the reception. So, I thought, screw it, I'll suck Adam's cock. And you didn't even remember. My one act of wantonness and you forgot all about it.'

'But I do remember. I do. It was great. Really.'

'Good job I didn't put that cock of yours into my mouth more often, your brain would be shot to pieces. You wouldn't remember a single thing. You do know I just gave you one. As you sat on that chair? Right?'

'What chair?'

They both laughed.

'Anyway, you have to admit that the sex is pretty good now.'

She's never said that before either. Strange.

'And it's ever since your mum died. Coincidence? Or is post-death sex hot?'

'Well, let me stick this knife in you and then I'll find out.'

'Don't worry,' said Laura, 'you'll only forget.'

'Forget what?'

'You old git.'

'You're older.'

'In years, but not looks. That's because I look after myself. I haven't smoked dope non-stop since I've been married. You'd better not get old, Adam. You've always been too young to be old. Don't age on me. I could cope with anything but that. The thought of living with an old man is terrifying. Don't be that old man.'

'And all because I couldn't remember a 25-year-old blowjob,' said Adam. 'I still knew where to put my tongue, didn't I?'

'What tongue?'

'What shower?'

'The one upstairs.'

'Let's go.'

'I still think your dad should give his money to the boys. I hope he's come to his senses at last.'

I hope not, thought Adam.

This is madness...

CHAPTER 11

This is Madness

It was Tuesday around 8am. The sky was leaden and heavy downpours were forecast.

Adam woke up in an empty house. Laura had gone to work and Jack had already left for school where his music teacher was helping him prepare for the upcoming *X Factor* Boot Camp before morning lessons. Jack had already been featured in the local paper and the school was showing its 'full support'.

Adam did what he did every morning when he opened his eyes and let Kate out for the day. He eased out of bed, fondly remembering the days when he leapt, and retrieved a large joint from the bedside table.

'Here's one I rolled earlier,' he said out loud and then thought that sounded like a feature in a juiced-up *Blue Peter* for the ghetto kids. Or you could call it *White Peter* with an old John Noakes in shades showing kids how to cut coke with baby powder.

'Wait a minute,' he said out loud again. 'Didn't I think the same thing yesterday?'

Yes, he did. And the day before that. And the day before that. It was a nightmare *Groundhog* D-Day–he was thinking the same thoughts and performing the same actions over and over, day after day. But unlike Phil Connors, he was also growing old. He consoled himself with the thought that most people's days are groundhogs anyway that chase us to the grave.

'Shit, I thought that yesterday too. Didn't I?'

Yes, he did. And the day before that. And the day before that. It was a nightmare *Groundhog* D-Day–he was thinking the same thoughts and performing the same actions over and over, day after day, but unlike Phil Connors, he was also growing old. He consoled himself with the thought that most people's days are groundhogs anyway that chase us to the grave.

'Shit, I thought that yesterday too. Didn't I?'

Yes, he did. And the day before that. And the day before that. It was a nightmare *Groundhog* D-*Day*–he was thinking the same thoughts and performing the same actions over and over, day after day, but unlike Phil Connors, he was also growing old. He consoled himself with the thought that most people's days are groundhogs anyway that chase us to the grave.

'Shit, I thought that yesterday too. Didn't I?'

Yes, he did. And the day before that. And the day before that.

Adam put on a tee shirt and jeans and went downstairs to the living room. He sat in front of the fireplace and lit a joint, blowing the smoke up the chimney, the smoke caressing every brick before drifting to the stars.

He was smoking about twenty joints of skunk a day, mainly in the morning and afternoon but always a couple in the garden after dinner, when Laura fell asleep in front of the television and Jack shut his bedroom door and did whatever 16-year-old boys did these days.

The fireplace was Adam's great escape and he always had a few joints when everyone else had gone to bed.

Laura may not have been able to smell it in the house, but she could smell it on his breath. He told her he only smoked one joint a day to help him finish writing the new book and she believed him because Adam wore it well on the outside. Inside, he was as stoned as an Old Testament blasphemer.

Jack had been smoking weed occasionally since he was 13. Like Ben, he never knew what it smelled like, but when he caught that first whiff he realised what his dad had been smoking all those years. He took it for granted that lots of people smoked in moderation and it all seemed perfectly natural.

Adam was one good session away from completing the book he'd been working on since he met Kate. He now knew how it would end and he thought it was the best thing he'd ever written because it was true, every word of it. Well, nearly every word. There was an element of fiction, of course, to oil the creative engine.

He blew some more smoke up the chimney.

But overall, it was a true account of his life in the last year. That's why he always carried a copy on a USB stick in the small front pocket of his jeans. The truth was too precious to lose.

Because he smoked a lot of dope while writing, Adam now couldn't get through the day without it. Plus, he was developing a paranoid fear of running out. He always had an emergency stash of two ounces which he kept in the loft like untaxed cash. He also made sure he never had less than half an ounce on the go. But it was getting more and more expensive, and recently he'd had to break into the emergency stash.

The habit was starting to hit his pocket hard but the idea of running out was too terrifying to contemplate.

Adam slowly lifted himself up from the hearth and heard every one of his 206 bones crack before heading for the kitchen to make a coffee. How he hated growing old. Laura may not have wanted to live with an old man but he sure as hell didn't want to live with an old woman who had hipster tits and a colostomy bag.

He wanted Kate. She was firm and young and open.

In the shower with Laura after that oral feast in the kitchen, he saw varicose veins and loose flesh and laughter lines, and it chilled every one of his 206 creaking, cracking bones.

He drank the coffee and went back into the living room for another chimney smoke.

Adam hadn't seen Bobby for a couple of days. He was letting it all sink in, fester. He congratulated himself on the kind of plan that only a celebrated author could come up with. Who else would have reached, with an outstretched, uncovered hand, into that dank pond of a past and grabbed a rotting, sordid memory that could be restored by expert hands, that could be reborn? And who else would rework that reborn memory into a ravishing deception that could hoodwink an old hood?

If it works he gets the girl, the cash and the house. Kate will be so upset that she'll fling herself into his arms and he'll whisk her off to Bora Bora, Business Class, and they'll walk across white sand and tell each other how much they miss Ben and make passionate love all night in their thatched-roof bungalow on the beach. And she'll swallow every last drop of his semen as the moonlight bounces off the Pacific.

It will work. It was too simple to fail. And it was a phone call away.

His mobile phone rang. Why did that always happen?

'It's Ben.'

This was lift off.

'Just to let you know that I'm seeing granddad around two tomorrow, so you can make sure you're not around.'

Perfect. That was the time he usually went. 'Thanks for letting me know. Give your mother a ring after and tell her why he wanted to see you. I don't want to know.'

'Will do. He also told me to ask you for the key code number, so I can get in.'

'3275H.'

'Thanks. Bye, Dad.'

Dad, dad. Fuck you. I'm not your dad. Not anymore.

'Bye, Ben.' He was tempted to ask after Kate but thought better of it. Besides, he'd find out for himself after today and then he'd never need to ask another living soul ever again because they'd be together in eternity.

Adam looked at the time on his phone–10.22am. He had the day ahead. He would finish the book. He rolled another joint. It was all about the timing. The wheels were in motion and they had to be steered in the right way.

And oiled.

Adam finished smoking the joint and went upstairs to Ben's old room where he slapped his laptop on top of Ben's old desk, closed Ben's old blinds and switched on Ben's old desk lamp. Adam could never write a word in daylight, which had its limitations.

It felt right to be there.

He opened the file marked 'Sheds4' and read what he'd written yesterday...

It was Wednesday around 8am. The sky was leaden and heavy downpours were forecast.

Adam woke up in an empty house. Laura had gone to work and Jack had already left for school–his music teacher was helping him prepare for the upcoming X Factor Boot Camp before morning lessons. Jack had already been featured in the local paper and the school was showing its 'full support.'

Adam did what he did every morning when he opened his eyes and let Kate out for the day. He eased out of bed, fondly remembering the days when he leapt, and fished out a large joint from the bedside table.

'Shit, was that all I wrote?' said Adam out loud as he scrolled down through blank pages in Ben's old room. 'I could've sworn I did more than that.'

He unwrapped a packet of cherry menthol Airwaves and slipped on some headphones. Steely Dan blew away the cobwebs and he started to oil.

'Right, let's take this baby home.'

'Here's one I rolled earlier,' he said out loud and then thought that sounded like a feature in a juiced-up Blue Peter for the ghetto kids. Or you could call it White Peter with an old John Noakes in shades showing kids how to cut coke with baby powder.

He went into the bathroom, opened the window and smoked half the joint. The smell would be gone by the time Jack reached home; a combination of steam, coal tar shampoo and perfumed shower gel would see to that.

Adam went downstairs to the kitchen. He switched on the TV, kettle and toaster in that order. Laura had started to leave bread in the toaster before she went to work along with a kettle full of water. He made a mental note of asking her to switch on the TV too which would mean one less job for him every morning.

It had turned 8.30am when the house phone rang.

'It's Ben.'

This was lift off.

'Just to let you know that I'm seeing granddad at two this afternoon, so you can make sure you're not around.'

Perfect. That was the time he usually went. 'Thanks for letting me know. Give your mother a ring after you've seen him and tell her what he said. I don't want to know.'

'Will do. He also told me to ask you for the key code number, so I can get in.'

'8653B.'

'Thanks. Bye, dad.'

Dad, dad? Fuck you. I'm not your dad. Not anymore.

'Bye, Ben.' He was tempted to ask after Kate but thought better of it. Besides, he'd find out for himself after today and then he'd never need to ask another living soul because they'd be together in eternity.

He would need to get there no later than five past two–Adam knew Ben was a punctual man. That's how long he figured it would take his dad to shoot Ben. Shoot him dead. Bobby wouldn't muck around. He'd have the gun in his hand as Ben let himself in and he'd fire off a round the moment he walked into the room. He wouldn't have the strength to hold it any longer.

Adam would listen for the shot. Most people who lived nearby were either out, ancient or not particularly law-abiding, so he knew the noise wouldn't be reported. There was an old woman who lived four doors down and she always popped her head round the curtain from an upstairs window when he parked the car. Adam would wave at her and she'd smile and wave back.

That's when he'd start oiling.

If, by some chance, Bobby had no intention of killing his grandson, then he was in the shit. He was banking on his dad's inveterate hatred of all things perverted–he'd never seen his father react the way he did when Adam read the fabricated diary entries. Like a half-blind, half-baked demon with a flicker in his one good eye where there once were flames. Adam was convinced there was a gun and he was convinced Bobby would use it.

Five past two seemed like light years away. He wanted it over so he could start his life anew. He wanted to be reborn like his dad's memory and become a ravishing deception. He lit another joint and hoped and prayed that everything would come together as he planned. It was all about the timing. It was all about his son's sense of punctuality.

Adam could barely repeat Ben's name now. He was afraid to even think of him because Kate would be there too, oozing with wit and sex and getting Ben's jokes and laughing and sucking that pulsating cock and making his life joyous.

If he didn't kill him, he'd kill himself. For the first time in his life, Adam had time for the pain and it hurt like hell.

The work had dried up completely and he had a grand left in the bank. Caring for his parents had cost him big time. Newspapers were awash with new faces, young, keen and despairing of anyone over forty. The journalists' graveyard is bigger than the elephant's and harder to find. His old travel press contacts were long gone, living the well-connected freelance vida loca, cruising the world for free on impressive retainers. He was Adam Tate from Broken Dream Boulevard, Palookaville, on the road to nowhere.

Kate showed him the way. She made him believe in himself again. He started writing again. He saw the sense of life again. He was reborn. She was the sunshine of his life. The smoke often made him think in song titles–they all seemed so relevant.

He didn't want to go back to Palookaville. He didn't want that life anymore. But to change it he needed two things–Kate and money.

With Ben out of the way, Kate would be his, of that he was rock-solid sure.

'She loves me, I know that.' Ben was an aberration, a flashback of him without the grey.

No, she'd get over that conniving bastard in a heartbeat and fall straight into Adam's arms because she knew Ben wasn't him and never would be.

The money was the problem. But now he'd solved that, provided his son was punctual and his dad could shoot straight. He was on a wing and a prayer, but he figured, as long as he said, 'Amen,' at the end, he'd be okay. And if the Luger doesn't work, no harm done.

He took a shower and sang 'Do It Again' as he waited for the T/Gel shampoo to take effect. He got dressed and went downstairs. It was pouring outside. It was 12.45 and Adam wondered where the time went. He made another coffee and then remembered he had a good line's worth of coke stashed away that he'd been saving for a rainy day.

Tooted and booted, Adam climbed into his dirty black Merc 190E at precisely 1.30, lit up a joint and headed to a lost horizon.

Adam arrived at 2.04, saw a gleaming red Porsche 911 cabriolet parked outside and pulled up two cars behind it, in front of the old woman's house. He got out of the Merc and, sure enough, there she was, in the upstairs window.

He waved.

As she waved back a shot rang out and she was visibly startled.

Perfect.

He indicated for her to open her window. 'Did you hear that?'

'Yes,' she replied. Her voice was surprisingly strong. 'It sounded like a gun going off.'

'Yes, it did. I'd better go and check to see if it frightened dad. Don't worry, if I find out it was a gunshot, I'll ring the police.'

'Okay. But I did see someone earlier, getting out of that sports car right outside your dad's house and letting himself in. I've not seen him *before. Is he a social worker?'* Prurience is a comfort when you're old and alone and have the time to lead a vicarious life.

'I wouldn't think so. It looks like my son's car. I'd better go.'

'Let me know, won't you?'

'Of course.' Adam walked swiftly but confidently to the house. There wasn't a soul around.

'Perfect.'

He closed the front door quietly behind him. The silence dripped with sweat as he approached the living room.

Ben was sitting on the floor with his back to the wall. His eyes were wide open, his mouth was wide open, his chest was wide open. Bobby's aim was true. The bullet passed clean through Ben's heart and was lodged in the wall behind him. The blood smears that stained the wall around the bullet hole and continued to the floor indicated that Ben had fallen backwards against it and slowly slid down like a ham actor in a fifties cowboy movie.

The carpet was blood red and Ben's face was an icy white.

'There you go, son,' said Bobby. 'He went down easy, I done him like a kipper. Fucking never knew what hit him.'

'My God! Dad, what have you done?' That was a line he prepared earlier. This was coming together like the London Olympics.

'Whaddya mean, "What have I done?" It's what you wanted.'

'It's what I wanted? What I wanted? What the fuck do you mean, you stupid old man? You think I wanted my son dead?'

'Yes. And after what you told me, I wanted him dead too.'

'Oh no! I don't believe it!' He'd rehearsed the exclamation marks and they came off nicely; not a hint of Victor Meldrew.

'I found out that the entries in his diary related to a short story Jack was writing for the school magazine. He used the names Ben and Jack because he couldn't be bothered to think of any others! He would've changed the names once he'd put it on his computer.

'Ben had done nothing wrong. Do you hear me? NOTHING!'

The tears came easy. He only had to think of his mum and the fact

*that he'd never set eyes upon her loving face again and he could cry like
a baby.*

'So, you're telling me that I've shot your son for nothing?'

'Yes,' sobbed Adam. 'Fuck you, YES!'

'Oh well, shit happens. Now get rid of the body before Zachariah gets
here.'

'You really have lost it, you crazy old fool. I have to ring the police.'

'You fucking what? Ring the fucking ol' bill? Over my dead body.'

'Look, dad, I must ring them, you know that. People would've heard
the shot and seen me rush in. There's probably a crowd outside already.
They won't lock you up. You're old, your mental powers are diminished.'

'No, they're fucking not.'

'That's my son over there, your grandson, and you shot him in cold
blood. For no reason.'

'But there was a reason.'

'No! There wasn't. And now it'll be all over the papers. Ben was a
wealthy man, dad. His lawyers will take you to the cleaners. They'll have
a field day. And the police will swarm all over the house. Do you know
they have sniffer dogs now that can locate cash?'

Adam had completely forgotten about Ben, the big, beautiful corpse
that looked a little like Christian Bale on the living room floor. He wanted
this over, but he had to be careful. Bobby still had a brain but, happily,
it was only full of memories. Common sense didn't live there anymore.

'If you have any cash lying around you'd better get it out of the way.
Now.'

'Well, there is some.' Bobby's reluctance in uttering that sentence was
wildly apparent. Undaunted, Adam persevered.

'You'd better get it then.'

'You'll have to get it. I'm too weak to move.'

They were the words Adam had been longing to hear.

'Where is it?'

'The fitted wardrobe in mum's bedroom has a false base. The cash is
in there.'

'How do I open it?'

'Just unscrew it.

'Okay. I'll put it in a bag and take it to the car before I ring the police. I'll hide it in the loft at home.'

'Son?'

'What, dad?'

'Don't ring the police. I've never been to prison in my life.'

'I have to. I'll tell them that you told me you showed Ben the gun because he wanted to see it and you didn't know it was loaded and it went off, accidently. You're 95 for fuck's sake. What can they do?'

'Thanks, son. I thought I was helping you and I thought I was avenging my sister. It's what your mother would've wanted.'

'Don't bring her into it.'

'I tell you what, son. You keep that money. I was going to leave it to you anyway, but why wait 'til I'm dead?'

'Look dad, I don't care about the money, I care that my wonderful son is lying over there with a hole in his chest. Look at him.'

'He wasn't so fucking wonderful when you thought he was sticking his cock up Jack's arse.' There was life in the old dog yet.

'I mean, how could they think a dying old man would deliberately kill his grandson? No, they'll see I'm too sick to be moved.'

'They'll have to take you to the station for questioning, but they won't press charges. Have you a licence for the gun?'

'No.'

'Well that'll complicate matters. Look, let me get this money before the police come.'

Adam could hardly restrain himself from laughing as he bounded up the stairs to cash heaven carrying a trusty Philips screwdriver and a heartful of soul.

He hadn't been in his mother's room since she died. Nothing had been moved. The blue and white energy once emitted by a host of cheap Lladro imitations that still bedecked the room had lost its potency under the weight of dust. Her smell was all around, in the furniture, the clothes, the sheets, the pillows, the shoes. The floor was covered with dead words six inches deep that had fallen from her mouth over the years and when he trod on them they crunched like fresh snow.

He opened the wardrobe and located the screws. Two minutes later, a million pounds was staring him in the face, all in twenty-pound notes.

'Are you babies a sight for sore eyes!'

This was it. First class tickets to the Maldives with Kate. Two weeks of sun, sex and spontaneity. Then back to her place where they'd live together and he'd pay the mortgage and write wonderful books again. It was meant to be.

There was a suitcase under Coral's bed and Adam moved the cash into it like a Million Pound Drop contestant. He replaced the wardrobe base and picked up the case. He could hardly lift it.

'So that's what a million pounds feels like, a good seven, eight stone.' So, a million pounds weighs about the same as an average 16-year-old girl. He would've carried Robbie Coltrane down the stairs on this fantastic day.

He put the cash into the boot of his car and as he closed it, the old woman appeared at the window.

'Hullo,' said Adam. 'There's been a terrible accident.'

'Oh dear. What's happened?'

'My son has been shot dead, accidently.'

'Oh dear. What happened?'

'I can't talk about it now. I'm about to ring the police. I'll speak to you later.'

Perfect.

'I'm so sorry for your loss.'

'Thank you.'

As he walked back to the house, Adam called the police on his mobile. Two cars pulled up within five minutes. He started to panic about the money. Say the police decided to search the car. Say the woman down the road said she heard the boot shut. How would he explain the money? He hadn't thought that one through properly and he kicked himself.

An hour later, the old woman four doors down whose name was unknown to Adam even though she'd lived there for forty years, watched Bobby Tate being carried out on a stretcher into an ambulance. She'd already corroborated Adam's statement after a WPC knocked on her door, and she never once mentioned the boot.

The murder squad detective that came to investigate looked a little disappointed when he told Adam that it did, indeed, bear all the hallmarks of a tragic accident.

The old woman, who spent the rest of the day at her window, watched Adam get into his car and drive away as the ambulance left. She didn't like to call out to him. He looked so deep in thought. Poor man. What a terrible day he'd had.

'Perfect,' said Adam as he cruised home in his trusty, rusty Merc, listening to Steely Dan and feeling that extra weight in the boot.

'Perfect.'

'That'll do nicely.'

Adam checked the time on his mobile, 4.20pm. He'd been writing for five hours, with the occasional skunk break, and it came easy. It was easy because that's exactly what was going to happen.

He left Ben's room after saving 'Sheds4' on his ever-present USB stick, and went downstairs for a coffee. He hadn't eaten anything since toast at breakfast, but the munchies' days were long gone. Twenty joints a day was a whole new vibe.

He drove round to his dad's later that evening to make sure he was okay and waved to the elderly woman as he climbed out of the car.

That night, Adam was too excited to eat. He was too excited to sleep and went downstairs several times in the night smoking that shit up the chimney and thinking of a million pounds lying like a 16-year-old girl in the boot of his car in the garage.

It had to be... perfect.

CHAPTER 12

It Don't Come Easy

It was Wednesday around 9am. The sky was leaden and heavy downpours were forecast. Adam woke up in an empty house. Laura had gone to work and Jack had already left for school where his music teacher was helping him prepare for the upcoming *X Factor* Boot Camp before morning lessons. Jack had already been featured in the local paper and the school was showing its 'full support'.

Adam did what he did every morning when he opened his eyes and let Kate out for the day. He eased out of bed, fondly remembering the days when he leapt, and fished out a large joint from the bedside table.

'Here's one I rolled earlier,' he said out loud and then thought that sounded like a feature in a juiced-up *Blue Peter* for the ghetto kids. Or you could call it *White Peter* with an old John Noakes in shades showing kids how to cut coke with baby powder.

'Wait a minute,' he said out loud again. 'Didn't I think exactly the same thing yesterday?'

Yes, he did. And the day before that. And the day before that. It was a nightmare *Groundhog* D-Day–he was thinking the same thoughts and performing the same actions over and over, day after day. But unlike Phil Connors, he was also growing old. He consoled himself with the thought that most people's days are groundhogs anyway that chase us to the grave.

'Shit, I thought that yesterday too. Didn't I?'

Yes, he did. And the day before that. And the day before that.

'Today, my dreams will come true.'

He didn't think that yesterday. He'd never thought that in his life.

Adam put on a tee shirt and jeans and went downstairs to the living room. He sat in front of the fireplace and lit a joint, blowing the smoke up the chimney, blessing his house, caressing every brick before drifting to the stars.

Like an actor who had memorized a script, he remembered everything he wrote yesterday. There was no reason why it shouldn't run like clockwork. Even if the old woman wasn't in, although he couldn't recall a day she didn't look out when he parked his car, it would still be easy to prove it was an accident.

Adam slowly lifted himself up from the hearth and heard every one of his 206 bones crack before he headed for the kitchen to make a coffee. Oh, how he hated growing old.

After he drank the coffee, he went back into the living room but, unlike the fictional Adam, he decided against having another smoke. He'd be dealing with the law this fine day and thought it prudent to see it through as straight as he could be.

But twenty joints a day can rightly be called a serious habit. Within half an hour, Adam was starting to get anxious.

He looked at the time on his phone–11am. Over two hours to kill. He desperately wanted a smoke but if the police got a whiff it would jeopardise everything.

He took a shower and sang 'Once In a Lifetime' as he waited for the T/Gel shampoo to take effect. But he couldn't wash away the anxiety. He hadn't felt like this before, it had all been so perfect.

Adam got dressed and went downstairs. It was pouring outside. He looked at the time, 11.30. He made another coffee and then remembered he had a good line's worth of coke stashed away that he'd been saving for a rainy day. He thought it might clear the anxiety from his muddled head. Two large snorts later he still couldn't banish the disquiet.

Was he guilty of murder? Of murdering his own son? He'd lied to his father because he knew all along that his dad would use the Luger if he took the bait. He'd seen the unresolved hatred in Bobby's eyes when he talked of his brother and this was his opportunity to make amends.

Adam had no idea what the real reason was behind his father's desire for vengeance.

Once Bobby decided to walk back down that familiar path, the gun was the only option.

It was unfinished business as far as Bobby was concerned. Ben and Michael were one and the same.

But they weren't. Michael was a pervert, Ben a pillar of society. He'd been a bright little boy with big dreams that all came true. And he was his son, his flesh. Okay, so he shagged the girl at the centre of his universe but how was Ben to know that? And when he found out it was too late because he, too, was captivated. He was right to be disparaging of Adam. His father had been cheating on his mother, how else was a son supposed to react?

But he never told Laura. Never breathed a word. He did the right thing.

Was this madness? Did he really want his son dead? Was he deluding himself? Kate didn't split up with him because she met Ben, no, she split up with him because he was an old bloke who smeared coke on his cock to prevent premature ejaculation, because his body was soft and white and because the gap was way too wide to be bridged.

But then, was there anything to split up from? He'd seen her six times in total, that's all. Hardly a relationship.

Adam regretted taking the coke. In fact, at that precise moment, Adam regretted every drug he had ever taken. Never again–number one in the 'Book of Stoned Clichés'.

He'd plotted the whole thing and he was writing it as it happened like a bard on the run. But it should have stayed in his head. It was too perfect.

He wanted his son dead because he fell in love with Kate. He wanted him dead because Ben knew his dad, who'd been married to his mum for 35 years, had loved her also.

This was ludicrous, even to a coked-up wreck like him. What, not smoking dope for two hours during the day and he sees the light? It was time to get off the Yellowbrick Road and head back to Kansas.

This wasn't fiction. This was real.

He had to stop it.

He checked the time on the microwave. 12.05. The journey to his dad's took twenty to thirty minutes in the car. Perfect. He'd nip this in the bud now, before Ben got anywhere near the place.

Tooted and booted, Adam climbed into his dirty black Merc 190E at precisely 12.10 and headed to a lost horizon.

The house phone rang as he pulled away. A minute later, his mobile phone, in the kitchen next to the microwave, rang, followed by a beep indicating a message had been received.

Adam never realised he'd forgotten his mobile phone until it was too late.

CHAPTER 13

Time, Gentlemen, Please

B en had to be somewhere at 2.15pm sharp.

He checked the time on the dashboard of his Porsche, 12.10. He didn't want to let his grandfather down, so he thought he'd turn up early. He figured Bobby wasn't going anywhere. The only worry was the possibility of bumping into his dad. He hadn't seen him since the night at the Shanghai Palace and he didn't want to see him again.

There were times when he wanted to spill the beans to Laura, tell her that she was married to a cheating bastard. Kate said she was certain it was Adam's first 'minor' dalliance (without going into the coke on the cock story). But how could she know? His dad might've been sleeping around for years. That's what happens when you smoke that shit.

Ben hadn't bought any coke in months. He never forgot a line from *Like Clockwork* that was possibly the only decent piece of advice Adam had ever imparted. He had to share that intelligence with all the other people who read it when it should've been between father and son, like a secret handed down through the Tate generations.

And the main lesson I've learnt in life is, only snort other people's coke.

Sure, if he was offered a no-strings-attached line at a party, he'd joyfully accept it and gleefully enjoy it. But there it would end. He knew he had a problem when he started snorting home alone with the lights down low and he blamed his father for his addictive personality. But when he met Kate, co-incidentally over a few lines on the ship, he realised it wasn't addiction, it was lack of inspiration.

She was more stimulating than Grade-A Charlie and he was a

helluva bloke to beat. And because he didn't need it anymore, Kate didn't either, although it was questionable whether she ever actually 'needed' it or simply snorted because it made cigarettes taste better. She gave up smoking too, but they drank a lotta wine to make them feel fine, though not enough to launch hangovers.

Ben and Kate were happy, convinced they'd found the loves of their lives. The shadow of Adam had slowly receded, replaced by a world of light where they would dance together in eternity.

No, Ben didn't want to bump into his dad. And he believed the feeling was mutual. He rang the house phone but there was no answer. He rang Adam's mobile and left a voice message saying he'd be at granddad's around 12.40pm.

He could do no more.

He pulled up outside the house at 12.39pm and after retrieving the key from the key safe, he let himself in.

Bobby pulled out the Luger from under the armchair cushion when Zachariah left at 12.15 and kept it under the blanket. He could lift it without too much effort now.

He was excited at the prospect of killing again, especially a descendant of Michael, the devil incarnate. He was duty-bound to rid the world of evil, that's why God had given him The Gun. He was ready and willing and he could barely stand the thought of waiting another hour and a half. He had itchy fingers and they oh-so wanted to dance around a trigger.

It's what Coral would've wanted. Anything to please Adam, the apple of her eye. This was justified, more so than any murder he'd ever committed and fittingly, it would be his last.

He was prepared. He lifted that gun every day like a geriatric Rocky until it felt as heavy as a mug of tea with four sugars. He'd shoot Ben the moment he entered the room and he'd shoot him cleanly and professionally. After all, that's what he was, a professional. They couldn't nick him. He was too old. He'd tell them that the gun went off accidently in his hand. They'd believe that from a 95-year-old who was far too frail to pick up a gun properly. Who wouldn't?

Bobby could still make out the clock on the wall–nearly 12.35.

He was prepared. On the stereogram turntable was a record, one of Coral's favourites, and he planned to play it at full blast before Jack, no, Ben, walked in. It would drown out the shot. Then he'd wait for Adam before they contacted the police to report a terrible accident.

Perfect.

He could have a snooze, he slept in bouts of twenty minutes. Three snoozes! He closed his eyes.

'Granddad.'

Bobby woke up and saw Ben peering over him. Had he slept that long? He squinted his good eye at the clock–12.40.

'Hope I didn't startle you,' said Ben. 'Something cropped up and I had to come earlier. Is that okay?' He said the words slowly and precisely, like he was talking to an old deaf mute who couldn't speak English.

Bobby felt his finger on the trigger. 'Hullo, er…'

'Ben, granddad, Ben.'

'Ben. Haven't seen you in a while, Ben. How's your mum?'

'She's fine, granddad.' Shit, how could the question, 'How's your mum,' sound so menacing? Now he remembered why he didn't like visiting.

'You said you wanted to see me.'

'Did I?'

Ben concluded he was on a wild goose chase and felt a little pissed-off.

'That's right, I did. Could you be a good boy and turn the record player on?'

'Sorry?'

'There's a record I want you to hear.'

'Why?'

He's a bit of a pushy bastard, thought Bobby. The fucking pleasure will be all mine. 'Because it has a bearing on why I asked you to come. It'll only take a minute.'

Ben turned around disconsolately. Bobby didn't want to shoot him in the back, he wanted Ben to turn and face him so he could see those two old friends again, shock and terror. He never murdered any of his previous victims from behind, although it would've been much easier. He was hooked on the looks and he never realised how hooked until this moment.

Fats Waller's corrosive honey filled the room.

Somebody stole my gal,
Somebody stole my pal,

'Louder.'

'Louder? It's pretty loud now.'

'It's my ear, son. I've only got the one now and that's nearly fucked. Just a bit louder.'

Neither of them heard the key in the lock.

Adam arrived at his dad's house at 12.43 and was shocked to see a gleaming red Porsche 911 cabriolet parked outside. He pulled up two cars behind it, in front of the old woman's house. He got out of the car and the woman appeared in the upstairs window. He waved. She smiled and waved back.

He walked swiftly to the house. There wasn't a soul around, but the silence dripped with sweat. Why was Ben here at this time? The elderly lady smiled, so nothing had happened, but with every step he feared the worst.

As he turned the key in the lock, Fats Waller greeted him:

Somebody came and took her away,
She didn't even say she was leavin',

He walked down the hall and when he stepped into the living room the first thing he saw was Ben. He was standing by the record player, wide-eyed and open-mouthed. Adam turned and saw Bobby sitting in his armchair. He was pointing the Luger directly at Ben.

'Hullo, son. Nice fucking timing.'

Her kisses I love so,
He's gettin' now I know...

Adam leapt in front of his son as Bobby pulled the trigger...

And gee, I know that she,
Would come to me
If she could see,
Her broken-hearted lonesome pal,
Somebody stole my gal.

Bobby fired again and again. Nothing.

Adam stood up, gingerly, lifted the stylus from the album, and walked towards his father.

'Dad, it's okay. It's all a misunderstanding. Ben hasn't done anything wrong. Give me the gun.'

The loudest noise Adam ever heard threw him backwards across the room and momentarily sent him into Captain Miller mode on Omaha beach in *Saving Private Ryan*–deaf, dumb and surrounded by mutilation.

The gun had gone off in Bobby's face and the left side now bore a distinct resemblance to the disease-ridden right side–it wasn't there anymore. His whole, weak, half a head had been completely blown off, the bloody brain-splattered wall behind the armchair bore testament to that, but his right hand kept a firm grip on the Luger and his legs were moving in a desperate attempt to stay alive.

In his dazed state, Adam saw his grandmother chopping up live eels she brought home in a shopping bag from the market and saw the bloody black bits still wriggling as they plopped into the sink taking an interminable time to die.

But Bobby was dead. Dead as a fucking doornail, as he would've described himself.

And Ben was alive!

'Are you okay, dad?'

The voice came from over the hills and far away. But it was recognisable.

'Yes.' He could barely hear his own voice above the ringing. 'You?'

'Fine. My God, it's blown his head clean off. I think I'm about to be sick.' Ben vomited over the well-worn shag pile, a remnant of sixties' gangster kitsch.

'Give me a moment and I'll ring the police,' said Adam. 'Although I'm sure everyone within a mile radius heard that.'

'Wh-what was he thinking?' Ben was a picture of incredulity as he wiped a smear of vomit from his chin with the back of his hand.

'God knows what went on in that head of his,' said Adam. 'What he had left of it.'

'And where did he get the gun?'

'God knows. It's a Luger, isn't it? Bet he's had that since the war.'

'I can't believe what's happened,' said Ben. 'It's beyond words. I-I think I'm gonna be sick again.' And he was. 'I'm sorry, I should go to the bathroom but it's like I'm nailed to this spot.'

'Don't worry. I'd better ring the police now.' He searched his pockets for the mobile then looked on the floor where he fell.

'I must've left it in the car. You ring.'

Ben was visibly shaking as he reached into his pocket and pulled out a phone. 'I don't think I can talk to anybody at this moment. You ring.'

Adam walked back to Ben, took the phone, walked backed again and rang 999 to report a 'terrible accident.'

'They'll be here soon.'

'You tried to save my life,' said Ben. 'You actually threw yourself in front of me. You could've been killed.' He darted across the room to hug his dad, treading in his vomit on the way and leaving a trail of sick.

Adam closed his eyes as Ben wrapped his arms around him. They embraced for over a minute, squeezing out all those impurities, all those disingenuous feelings that clung to them like leeches. It was a cathartic moment and they both wept.

'I'm so sorry, dad.'

'For what?'

'For everything. For ever doubting you, for ever underestimating you.'

'Just because I saved your life, there's no need to get all gooey. Besides, it didn't go off.'

'But you weren't to know that.'

'It didn't go off six times. I counted every one like it was my last. Shit, I feel like being sick now.' And he was. The room reeked of vomit and old blood. They stood in silence for a few moments, still not fully comprehending the situation.

'Why did you say that, dad?'

'Say what?'

'When you asked granddad to give you the gun you said, "It's all a misunderstanding."'

'Did I?'

'And then you said, "Ben hasn't done anything wrong." What had he said to you? What did he think I'd done wrong?'

They heard the police sirens in the distance. It gave Adam a moment to think. He hadn't prepared for anything like this.

'Your granddad was basically coked up on morphine, if that makes any sense. He was becoming increasingly delusional, thinking all kinds of weird and wonderful things. After you told me he wanted to see you, I started to think about it and decided that even though he was frail and virtually helpless, it would be advisable if I was there when you arrived. That's why I came early, or so I thought. Good job I did.' He hoped that did the trick.

'Absolutely! But why, "misunderstanding,"? What was being misunderstood?'

'Well, if you must know, it was you, for me.' He didn't know what else to say. He was cornered.

The sirens blasted outside.

'What?'

'It's a long story. Let's get this over with first and we'll talk about it over a pint. Just remember to tell the truth, the whole truth, exactly as it happened, because the truth is the best alibi of them all.'

Ben thought that was nearly as good as, 'only snort other people's coke.' And it was just between them this time. Adam actually used it in *Up In The Dumps* but nobody read it so no harm done.

'We have absolutely nothing to hide, remember that too. You won't go far wrong.'

He had a cool dad. He saved his life, at least that's what he thought he was doing. Cool. That's all he could think. Cool.

There was a bang on the front door.

'Police! Open up now, please!'

Ben threw up again.

CHAPTER 14

Number One in the Book of Stoned Clichés

'So, you were going to tell me about this misunderstanding.'

'Yes, I was,' said Adam.

Adam and Ben were sitting in a pub, over a pint. They'd been released from the local police station on unconditional bail after seven hours of, 'helping police with their inquiries.'

Ben called some hotshot lawyer and when their stories corroborated perfectly, and their characters were found to be impeccable, it became obvious that there was no foul play involved. The crazy old bastard lost it for the final time.

'I don't expect any charges to be made,' the lawyer told them on the steps of the police station as they left.

'Sorry for your loss.'

'Thanks for organising the lawyer, Ben.' Adam sipped his lager shandy and took a deep breath. 'Look, it's like I told the police, when I saw him yesterday for a moment he thought I was you. He was agitated and called me, "Ben". He asked why I hadn't been to see him recently and accused me, thinking I was you, of pushing Coral down the stairs on my last visit.

'I was pretty shocked at the time and all I could think of saying was, "It's all a misunderstanding, dad." Whether it was my voice that brought him back down to earth or whether the words made him realise he was heading for the funny farm and nobody was laughing, whatever, it seemed to do the trick. He was fine afterwards. That's why I said it again. It was like a reflex action.'

He waited for Ben to say something, and when nothing was forthcoming, Adam continued to lie.

'But it was a little worrying, so rather than cancel your visit I thought I'd be there when you came around. I'd no idea he had something like that planned. I actually thought he was going to give you the money he's supposed to have stashed away somewhere in the house.'

'How much?'

'Enough.'

'If you find it, save some for me and I'll treat you to a weekend in Amsterdam. We'll give our grey matters the once over in the Grey Area once again.'

'Shit,' said Adam. 'I suddenly thought of something. If dad thought I was you again back there, he'd have shot you and then shot me!'

They both laughed. It was the first time since Amsterdam. It felt good. A relief. It was a Kateless laugh, a Bobbyless laugh, a drug-free, fancy-free, duty-free laugh.

'But I barely set eyes on him, or them,' said Ben. 'How could He think I pushed nan down the stairs when I hadn't been round for what, five years before she died? At least. In fact, I think I stopped coming around when granddad gave me that generous cash gift on my twenty-first. Shit, that's nine years ago.'

'I told you, the morphine finally got to him. Mind you, I must admit, I knew he was capable of murder. There's something I didn't tell the police but now he's dead I'll tell you, but you mustn't breathe a word because you don't know who's out there, lurking in the shadows.'

'I won't.'

'Well, for several months I've been kinda interviewing granddad about his life and it turns out he was a pretty big-time villain.'

'I sort of gathered that.'

'But on his way to becoming a big-time villain he murdered seven people, at least.'

'No way! How did he murder them?'

'You name it. He decapitated one bloke, disembowelled another and stuck a fork in the head of a Canadian soldier during the war.'

'Jesus. He told you all this?'

'Yes. In graphic detail.'

'Seven? Jesus. Why did he kill them? Were they some kind of contract killings?'

'Something like that. I think they were mainly paedophiles, too. Gangster paedophiles.'

'This gets better by the minute. So, he was a sort of vigilante? An anti-paedo superhero? What a heritage I have. Don't tell me, Ronnie and Reg are second cousins and the Richardsons are my great uncles. How come you never turned out like that?'

'Pure luck. Plus, I'm a complete coward and hate pain. It was your nan who was determined to keep me on the straight and narrow. She encouraged me to follow my nose, which I did. I wanted to be a writer and she said if that was the case, I'd be the best damn writer in the world.

'I nearly got it right first time out but got it wrong ever since. I achieved far more than I ever dreamed, far too early.'

'That's because you had a killer for a dad,' said Ben, as light-heartedly as he could, in the circumstances.

'Same again?'

'Yes, lager shandy.' He'd be pissing eternally tonight.

'Don't know how you can drink that.'

'You will when you get to my age.'

When Ben returned, he put the drinks on the table, sat down and said, rather sheepishly, 'I've spoken to Kate. She sends her condolences.'

Adam wondered when the elephant in the room would stir. He hoped it wouldn't run around like a *Blue Peter* Lulu.

'How is she?'

'Fine. She's getting new contracts all the time. I swear that girl could achieve anything she wants.'

'Without a doubt. You're a lucky man, Ben.'

'I know. This has been such an awkward situation. Just when I thought we were getting back on track after that cruise to Amsterdam, this is the last thing I expected. You cheated on mum.'

'I cheated on her with a girl that you couldn't resist, Ben. Kate is unique, and I was infatuated. She loved my book and for someone of her age to say that was pretty wonderful. I was flattered to get the attention of someone so attractive and so young. I'd never been unfaithful in all the years I was married to your mother, I swear on my grave. But Kate brought some sunshine into my life and you don't get much of that when you're knocking sixty. You'll never know how it feels until you reach my age, Ben.

'I must admit, I still have feelings for Kate, I defy any man not to, but I acknowledge those feelings are wrong, insane even. I still love your mother and I always will. That's all you'll ever need to know.'

Adam thought the whole 'misunderstanding' question had been successfully sidestepped. He was now resigned to a life of sex with a 60-year-old who would be seventy in the blink of an eye. Ten years of groping sagging breasts while his belly exploded, his hair blew away in the wind and his arteries clogged like an M25 jam. After that? Who gives a toss?

His novel would be turned down by every agent with a semblance of common sense and he'd die with a soupçon of recognition and a belly full of half laughs.

'What happens now?' he asked.

'I have to tell you, dad, I've asked Kate to marry me and she said yes. We plan to get hitched when my divorce comes through. Are you comfortable with that?'

'I'll have to be, if only for your mother's sake.'

Adam knew he could never be comfortable in Kate's presence and he didn't think he was strong enough to see this whole thing through. He started to think of alternatives but there was only one. His dad's house was worth half a million at least. He'd clear over 400 grand after inheritance tax. The bastard never did agree to the tenants-in-common idea.

Plus, there was the hidden cash and that could easily be a good few hundred grand. A mill even.

Adam knew it was there all right, even though his earlier search had been unsuccessful, and he knew he'd find it. He'd sell the house, give all the proceeds to Laura, and leave.

He'd rent a flat in Amsterdam and watch the world go by from a coffee shop while a MacBook Air purred away under his deft touches. He'd publish the books himself, say five thousand, and distribute them for free to strangers that interested him. A million quid would last him a lifetime.

'Look, dad, I can't begin to tell you what a great thing you did today. It doesn't change the way I feel about what happened with Kate, but it has helped me realise that you are my father and that blood is thicker than water.'

'Your granddad's wasn't, that's for sure.' Adam was getting a little embarrassed and thought a jibe would make it easier for both of them.

Ben smiled. 'I'll never mention a word to mum. I don't want to lose sight of you, dad. I still want you in my life.'

Adam thought he saw a tear in his son's eye and it broke his heart. He vowed he'd never smoke weed again.

CHAPTER 15

Stairway to Heaven

Adam lit a joint. He was almost out of dope and cash. The world was an empty place.

He stood in his dad's bedroom surveying the chaos. He'd spent the last two days ransacking the house–ripping up chairs, sofas, mattresses; cutting all the carpets into strips with a Stanley knife and lifting every floorboard; emptying every drawer; searching every pocket in all the clothes belonging to both his parents that filled five large wardrobes–each of which were checked for false bottoms; stripping the TV, fridge, washing machine, cooker and, more desperately, vacuum cleaner and microwave. So far, he'd found a few pound coins, a 20p piece, six 2ps and 15 1ps.

While he was contemplating opening up the water-tank in the bedroom cupboard, he heard the post.

It was 4pm. Adam remembered the times when there were three deliveries a day as he carved out a route between the mess that littered every room.

It was an official-looking envelope addressed to the Executor of the Estate of Robert Tate. Adam was still in ripping mode and nearly tore the letter inside when he slit open the envelope with the Stanley knife.

This is to inform you that as of 25th March when Robert Tate sadly passed away, the freehold of 36, Marsley Crescent is now assumed by Grant Holdings as set out in the notice attached. We also enclose a copy of the record of payments made to Robert Tate since he signed the equity release lifetime mortgage agreement. A copy of said agreement is further enclosed in this communication

We hereby give notice that Grant Holdings will become legal owners

*of 36, Marsley Crescent, seven days from the date of this letter. Please
arrange for all valuables, furniture and electrical items to be removed
from the said premises by that day.*

Adam looked at the enclosed documents.

'You fucking cunt!' It was almost as loud as the gunshot.

He tore the letter to shreds.

Bobby had drawn down a legitimate four hundred grand over
twenty years and blew the lot on cruises and five-star restaurants.
He obviously wasn't concerned about spending it all because he
knew he had the stash to fall back on. Adam figured time ran out on
his dad before he could break into it. Or he just forgot where he'd
hidden it.

He had to find the money and he had less than a week. Okay, his
million pounds had been cut in half because he had to leave enough
for Laura and Jack, but he could live with that. He'd still flee to
Amsterdam, but it wouldn't be a MacBook Air and he'd only print
500 copies and he'd grow his own because he read somewhere that
every Dutch household was allowed to for their own consumption.
But what the hell, it was only about the escape from Coldtits anyway.

The next morning, bright and early, Adam came armed with a
spade and proceeded to dig up the tiny, overgrown garden, including
the grave of their dead pet Yorkie, Sandy. He was now convinced
Bobby must've buried the loot with the dog but all he found, after
nearly two hours of toil, was a bunch of bones in a black plastic bag
and the whiff of decay.

It started to rain.

Well, that was it. Short of dismantling the house brick by brick,
there was nothing else he could do. There was obviously no money.
It was all a myth. Even his own mother had given him a bum steer.

Adam threw the spade onto the floor in disgust and walked
dejectedly back into the house through the French windows. He sat
on the stairs, head in hands.

The account would be empty in a week; paid work was a thing

of the past; he still had a big mortgage; he'd never be able to smoke again; the woman of his dreams was marrying his son...

Wait! What about Jack? *The X Factor*?

He'd see it in Amsterdam.

But there's no money. He can't go.

Say Jack went all the way? He'd have to stay and join the audience to cheer him on live TV every week and they'd probably make him wear a white 'Jack on the box' tee shirt and look suitably excited alongside Laura, Ben and even, God no, Kate.

Could he cope with another son becoming far more successful than he'd ever been? Had he become that self-obsessed?

That sad?

Forget *The X Factor*, Adam wanted the X, Y and Z Factor but he only got as far as G before slipping back to a sore C.

He was a fuck-up.

Laura knew. She always knew. But she went along for the ride and never got off. Why? It certainly wasn't in his kiss.

Laura may have known he was a fuck-up, but she had no idea how much of a fuck-up he was. How could he possibly face her and tell her about the re-mortgages and unpaid credit card bills when she was about to lose her job? They'd only have her pension to live on. They'd have to sell the house, pay off the debts, move miles away to a small ex-council two-bedroom flat and try and bank a few grand to live on until death. And there was no way Jack could go to university.

The longer they lived, the poorer they'd become.

But Ben was wealthy. He'd look after them.

No...

First Ben steals his girl and then becomes his landlord?

No...

There'd be family get-togethers and he'd grow old and fat in front of Kate and feel so terribly ashamed. He'd always wonder what his life would've been like if he'd found his dad's stash.

No...

He wouldn't be able to bear being around Kate, to see her with Ben, to watch them hold each other and laugh together, to see her pregnant with his child. He couldn't live that lie. Surely Kate must see that. Why did she choose to hurt him so much? Did she have no idea of his feelings?

She must adore Ben, and that was the unkindest cut of all. He wanted to feel her sweet, sweet tongue in his mouth again, coiling itself around him like a snake on heat and pulling them both down through that swirling darkness into a world of light where he would dance with her in eternity.

He was willing to kill his own son to get that feeling back and his soul would be forever tainted. How could he live with the torment of wanting his son dead? How?

And he knew that one day, Laura would find out about the brief affair because, like in soap operas, dark secrets always slip out eventually and it would destroy her. How could he live with the guilt of being responsible for that? How?

He couldn't take it anymore. There wasn't any point. He didn't want to grow old and bitter and broken-hearted. It'd be best for everybody if he wasn't around. He'd write a letter, addressed to Laura, explaining his reasons—omitting the affair—then take a shitload of the prescribed morphine he found while clearing out the kitchen cabinets.

He was exhausted and there was nowhere to sit downstairs. The only space was a couple of treads at the foot of the staircase.

He pulled a joint from a cigarette pack. He was down to his last two and the one left in the pack would be his last. Forever. He knew that now.

Adam flicked a shiny blue lighter inscribed with the words Bada Bing and inhaled deeply. He would savour this one.

He needed a drink. A drink would be good. Yes, that's what he needed. Last smokes, last drink. Something to take with him into oblivion, send him out on a high. Something hard. He could drink as much as he liked. He wouldn't wake up with a hangover because he wouldn't wake up. A drink. Yes. There was a litre of brandy in one of the kitchen cupboards. His dad always kept a bottle, 'for emergencies'. He hobbled to the kitchen and returned to that one vacant spot on the stairs.

The stair started to feel comfortable. He inhaled again and swigged from the bottle of brandy. He was knackered–he wasn't used to digging up gardens. Should've dug his own grave while he was about it. Should've done a lot of things. He needed to close his eyes, just for a moment. He inhaled again, in his sleep...

A minute went by, Adam inhaled again and coughed his heart out. He opened his eyes and saw a plume of black smoke floating past his face. When he looked down he saw the flames. Even in his dazed state he realised he'd dropped the joint onto the stair below when he nodded off, and the carpet runner had caught alight.

He ran to the kitchen, filled a saucepan with water and threw it over the blaze that had already spread to the next stair. Three saucepan runs later he sent the flames back down to hell.

Adam opened all the windows and checked the damage. It looked like the treads on the two stairs had trod their last and the riser separating them would rise no more.

But what was that sparkling in the ashes in the burnt-out stair? It was a box. A large, sturdy, metal box. Adam tried to pull it through the burnt riser, but it appeared to be screwed down.

Bobby always kept a well-equipped toolbox and Adam knew exactly where it was, despite being pissed and stoned, although he was feeling straighter by the moment. He found a heavy-duty screwdriver and used it to prise open the metal box. He lifted the lid and was confronted by a mountain of twenty-pound notes. But it wasn't a million.

Unless.

With the help of a hammer and crowbar, he proceeded to work on the tread of another stair. After several minutes, he managed to lift it up and–sure enough–there was an identical large, sturdy, metal box and that too was stuffed with twenty-pound notes. It turned out there was a large, sturdy, metal box encased in every stair and when he opened the final one, Adam felt like the fucking Count of Monte Cristo.

In one of the boxes, along with the money, was a Smith & Wesson Victory, an old British Army service pistol, wrapped up in a polythene bag. In another was an A4 envelope containing three expired passports bearing three different names but with the same photo in each–Bobby when he was about sixty. In another were three First World War medals belonging to Bobby's dad, with the original ribbons still attached, and an ID tag bearing the name 'Marvin Casey'.

'Shit,' said Adam. 'The Canadian who was forked to death.'

Underneath the medals was an old black-and-white photo of two boys dressed in rags standing in front of some railings outside a sepia-tinted slum. The older of the two had his arm around the shoulders of the smaller boy and both were smiling at the camera. Adam recognised the younger boy, he'd seen photos of his dad as a child before. He turned the photo over. In pencil was the inscription, 'Me and my brother Mike.'

'So that's the keep-it-in-the family paedo, Uncle Michael.' He thought it a little odd that his dad kept the photo with all his valuables, but who cared?

He was rich. He'd won the lottery–you had to be in it to win it.

The dropped joint had turned into the Burning Bush and the bad times were finally behind him. He was about to embrace a brave new world, to kick out the jams, and live the rest of his Kate-free life in a skunk haze with a MacBook Air and a lot of Indonesian food.

Everybody likes cash. It makes a refreshing change.

Adam had no idea how much money there was, but each box seemed to have roughly the same amount. He counted the contents of one–the notes were pristine and appeared to be packed in bundles of one hundred. There were around 75 bundles in each box and there were 14 stairs. He did the calculation on his mobile. Two-point one million!

Two-point one million. He'd give Laura 750 grand, pay off the debts and pocket the rest. It was the right thing to do.

He wanted a smoke. He knew it wouldn't be his last one now. Besides, he wanted to celebrate. It wasn't every day you became a millionaire, twice over. He lit up the joint and laughed when he thought how he nearly lit up the joint. On this occasion, smoking weed had saved his life.

'Thank you, God. And I haven't said that in a long time.'

After just one deep drag, Adam picked up a bundle of the twenties and waved them like a fan in front of his face. William Shakespeare smiled.

Shakespeare?

How long had the boxes been in the staircase?

He Googled 'Shakespeare twenty-pound notes' on his mobile and the bankofengland.co.uk told him that notes bearing the image of the playwright were introduced on 9th July 1970 and withdrawn 19th March 1993.

Withdrawn.

The 3G connection was weak. It took an age to search the site for information about exchanging old banknotes. He read it and wept.

'Genuine Bank of England banknotes that have been withdrawn from circulation retain their face value for all time and can be exchanged at the Bank of England in London. There is no fee for this service. Banknotes of this type can be exchanged either by post or in person.

'If the total value you wish to exchange is £1,000 or more, please send photocopy evidence of identity (ID) verification and proof of address.

'If the value of the exchange is £10,000 or more (or if you have previously exchanged banknotes with a cumulative value of £10,000 or more) these may not be exchanged the same day. If this is the case, you will be issued with a receipt and the Bank will send a BACS payment crediting your account within ten working days. If you require cash, we will make an appointment for you to collect the cash. This is because the Bank needs to complete anti-money laundering checks and other administrative procedures associated with large banknote exchanges.'

Not only was the money well past its sell-by date, it was obviously as bent as a nine-bob note. Laundering checks? This whole stash had probably been cleaned and pressed a hundred times. For all he knew, some might even have been counterfeit. If he tried to exchange any of it he'd probably be arrested, and it wasn't worth it for the sake of ten grand.

The dejection ran deep.

It was back to Plan A.

It was the least he could do.

Words. He needed to say some words to some people. Explain so they'll understand. Understand everything.

Thank God he still had most of what had again become his final joint. He decided to keep it until after he'd poured his heart out.

He remembered seeing a Basildon Bond letter writing set in a leather case in a drawer somewhere...

Laura. Dear Laura

I'm so, so sorry. Your fuck-up of a husband has fucked-up for the last time. With a bit of luck, as you read this, I'll be prancing around with all the other fuck-ups in fuck-up heaven getting more fucked-up than ever.

Enough of me. Literally.

I'm afraid I've left you in the shit, but then, you never expected anything less. You see, all those years I told you the royalties from Like Clockwork *and the Channel Four deal paid the bills, well, that wasn't strictly true. In the early days they did, but when that all dried up, I re-mortgaged the house a couple of times. In effect, I was using one mortgage to pay off another. You'll soon find out how much I owe, or, as of one hour hence, owed, to the bank and they will probably try and force you to sell. After the mortgage and the credit card bills, sorry again, are settled, you should clear enough for a deposit on a two-bedroom flat, admittedly, a fair way from home.*

But I'm sure Ben will step in and do something. He could buy the house from the bank at a knockdown price. He can afford it.

In my defence, I was counting on dad dying and me inheriting the lot, but he did an Adam on me. He'd been in an equity release scheme for twenty years and spent everything.

I was right about one thing, make that two things. I was right about the money. He'd stashed away an absolute fortune. And I found it. The police will no doubt tell you all about it.

My defence stinks. I'm guilty as sin and demand the death penalty.

It's all become too much, Laura. The words didn't work anymore. Caring for mum and dad brought me down and I can't get back up. And seeing dad die like that, well, camel's back well and truly broken. For good.

I tripped over success and fell flat on my face. It was all too brief and now too painful to recall.

I was turning into a junkie, smoking twenty spliffs a day. Twenty! Can you believe it? And the cost! God, you are so much better off without me.

My darling, you've been the love of my life. I'm sorry I never lived up to expectations, but cookies crumble and worlds collide, whatever that means. We were meant to be together and I firmly believe we will be in eternity. Kiss the boys for me.

Tell them I was a good man who meant well. Or tell them I was cunt. I'll leave that up to you.

And now I'm about to succumb to the ultimate blowjob, apart from the one you gave me in the kitchen the other day, that is.

Oh yeah, and the one in the car at my cousin's wedding on 23rd May 1987. The dashboard clock said precisely 8.17 as I slid into your mouth and 8.18 when I slid out and came all over your face and dress by accident. Too embarrassing to repeat I guess. Still, something to remember me by.

Goodbye, Laura.

Adam xxxx

It was the first letter he'd written to his wife in over thirty years. There wouldn't be another.

Next, Jack:

Hey Jack

Look mate, I'm sorry about all this. The last thing I wanted to do was hurt you, that's why I killed myself. What a cracking sentence, wish I'd used it before. But really, by me not being around, you can't get hurt and believe me, you would get hurt.

Y'see, your old man is, was, a bit of a fuck-up—mum will fill you in on the details. Fact is, financially, I messed up big time. And on top of that, I developed an almost insatiable desire for weed so, mentally, I've messed up big time, too. If you're smoking it regularly, stop. This is what it can do to you. Just smoke dope socially, never your own. And only ever snort other people's coke. You won't go far wrong if you remember that advice. I know I haven't exactly been the world's greatest dad, but I took a shot.

You have a great talent, Jack, and I have a feeling you'll win The X Factor. My death alone should get you the sympathy vote. Make sure you have a tear in your eye when you tell them your old dad killed himself. Sing straight and true and see the meaning in your head. Don't fake it and never be too afraid to close your eyes when a note ricochets off your soul.

Look after yourself, son, and look after your mother. If, as you grow older, you ever feel the need to find out more about your dad, read his books. It's all there.

Goodnight, sweet prince.

Dad xx

That was the first letter he'd ever written to Jack. And he called himself a writer.

The third and most difficult–Ben. Adam had written to him once before, when Ben was at scout camp, to tell him he had a new brother.

Hi Ben

I'm sorry it had to end like this but I'm so happy we clicked in the end. Mind you, when it comes to happy, granddad's gun clicking was just about the happiest moment of my life. I never wanted to live so much when he pulled that trigger. Now I wish the bullet had gone straight through my head. At least I'm prepared this time.

Nan and granddad's deaths, and the way they died, had a profound effect on me and I'm afraid I refuse to continue with my joke of a life, waiting for the inevitable on the railway line with my eyes closed and my hands in my pockets. It just ain't worth it, mate. Too many sacrifices. For what? A life like granddad's for the last twenty-odd years? No thanks.

You know, I'm convinced he pushed nan down the stairs. After she died, he came back down to earth and became almost normal again. In fact, I never knew he was so erudite. If you're interested, the tapes of the interviews I told you about are on a digital recorder in a drawer in my bedroom. Who knows, you might be able to do something with them.

I hope you and Kate live long, happy lives and I bless your marriage and your children. Look after her, son. Never let her go.

Look after mum and Jack. I'm afraid I've left them in the shit. Never did have your business acumen. I was rather hoping you might be able to help them out. Mum will tell you the situation and if she doesn't, ask her.

I've taken the liberty of enclosing a note to Kate. Don't let your mother know and please never tell her what happened. It would serve no purpose and just make her miserable.

Look me up sixty years from now, Ben. I'll be smoking on some cloud and we can hang out and strengthen that click.

Tell Laura I Love Her.

Be lucky, Ben.
Dad xx

It was getting dark outside. Adam had one more letter to complete. He switched on the light and started to cry. These were the last words he would write in eternity.

Dearest Kate

My one and only letter to you, of the non-electronic variety.

I guess I kinda fell in love with you when we met for the second time at the cruise reception. But I really fell in love with you at your place when you came straight back at my lame Bill Murray impression with an unmistakable Andie McDowell. Magic. Magic I thought I'd never find again.

Alas, the years have cheated me. To paraphrase Bruce Banner, 'They're making me old. You wouldn't like me when I'm old.' By the way, I'm doing a perfect impression of him as I write!

I'll see you in my dreams.

I wanted to end this note with a line from 'Vincent'. Y'know, the one about being too beautiful for this world, meaning me, of course.

But no. That line is my farewell gift to you. You are too beautiful for this world, Kate, and you always will be. God Bless you, Kate Lyle. It's been a privilege and a brief-encounter pleasure. I wish only the best for you and Ben. Have a glorious life.

I'll finish with the only poem I know off by heart. I figure Byron can put it a mite better than what I can, know what I mean?

Take a look at it once in a while and think of me.

So, we'll go no more a roving
So late into the night,
Though the heart be still as loving,
And the moon be still as bright.

For the sword outwears its sheath,
And the soul wears out the breast,
And the heart must pause to breathe,
And love itself have rest.

Though the night was made for loving,
And the day returns too soon,
Yet, we'll go no more a roving
By the light of the moon.

Goodbye, Kate
Adamxxx

Too cheesy? Who gives a fuck.

Adam put the letters in separate envelopes and kept his fingers crossed that the gum was still sticky when he licked it. But with a name like 'Bond' he shouldn't have worried. Then he thought he'd better write something for the police. So, these were now the last words he would write in eternity.

To whom it may concern

I, Adam Robert Tate, being of sound mind and body, do solemnly declare that I am about to kill myself. Not sure how I'm going to do it yet, it's a toss-up between my dad's morphine or the gun I've just found. But, rest assured, I do this entirely under my own volition. There's absolutely nobody else involved in my decision to commit suicide. I swear that's the truth, the whole truth and nothing but the truth, so help me God.

I'm simply another bloke who found it all a bit much.

You'll find letters addressed to my wife and two sons on the mantelpiece. Please don't open them, they concern private family matters.

Also, in the small front pocket of my jeans you'll find a USB stick that contains a novel I've written called Fuck The Sheds–A Gangster's

Revenge. *It's around 80,000 words. If there's anyone at the station who'd like to read it, be my guest.*

Well, T-T-T-That's all, folks.

Adam Tate

The key to everything was the USB stick. That was now his only hope, his only salvation. It was his one chance to burn in that eternal fame. He had wiped all the documents from his laptop–lot of private shit. Didn't need it anymore. The only document he copied onto the USB was *Fuck The Sheds*.

Adam was convinced the story surrounding the discovery of the disk would get a lot of publicity, providing the perfect launch-pad for *Fuck The Sheds*. He hoped a sharp cop with a vivacious vocabulary who might remember *Like Clockwork* would do something with it. Or know a man who could. A sharp cop with a streak of audacity who might see the potential. Or know a man who did.

He went into the bathroom upstairs and located a small Tupperware container marked 'morphine' in mum's unmistakable hand. But instead of the expected Oramorph, he found 36 morphine patches.

Undaunted, Adam went into his dad's bedroom, took off his shirt and slapped the patches on his chest, shoulders, back and arms and then dropped his trousers and put the rest on his thighs and backside. He knew he would look a faintly ridiculous corpse, but what the hell. He'd be dead.

Then he lit the final joint and kept it in his mouth, constantly inhaling.

He picked up the gun from one of the large, sturdy, metal boxes, kicked a load of shit off the bed and sank back, clutching the brandy, the joint still in his mouth. Waiting for the inevitable on the railway line.

Within minutes he started throwing up, his heart rate plummeted, and his flesh ran cold. When his fingernails turned blue, he'd had enough. He picked up the gun and pointed the barrel to the side of his head–after all, he didn't want to mutilate his kissing Casanovian tongue by poking it in his mouth where the joint still danced.

In the time it took to pull the trigger, two thoughts flashed through his head–'Shit, I forgot to change the names on the disk,' and, 'It probably isn't even loaded.'

It was.

The blood gushed down his body and the brandy bottle slipped out of his hand. It fell onto Adam's discarded clothes by the side of the bed and emptied its contents onto his jeans, followed by a steady flow of blood and brains. The USB stick was ruined. Adam didn't have a backup.

That was always his problem.

'That's *the sheds* well and truly fucked, then,' quipped one forensics wag while retrieving the ruined stick from Adam's bloody, brandy-soaked jeans.

CHAPTER 16

Loose Ends

In the Land of the Living, Jack Tate won *The X Factor*.

The publicity generated by his dad's suicide was huge. Adam couldn't have timed it better. A week later, Jack sang 'Vincent'–'One of my dad's favourite songs'–in a judge's home in The Bahamas and brought tears to the eyes of everyone who saw it.

In the live shows, Jack received a record number of votes every week–his version of Green Day's 'Wake Me Up When September Ends' topped the download chart for three weeks. He reached the final where he declared 'Can't Take My Eyes Off You' to be his dad's all-time favourite song before singing it in front of a giant screen in perfect sync with videos of all the artists that had covered it–Muse, Lauryn Hill, Gloria Gaynor, the Four Seasons, the Boys Town Gang and Frank Sinatra. Near the end, in a heart-tugging finale, Andy Williams strolled onto the stage on the arm of a young, blonde nurse, and joined Jack in the final chorus. It was to be Andy's final appearance.

Jack's second performance of the night, a duet with Don McLean and their version of 'Vincent', nailed it. It was mesmerising and later voted the best *X Factor* performance of all time.

He had the Christmas number one with 'Vincent' and his next single, the self-penned 'Ode', released nearly a year later, also briefly topped the charts. Alas, he never had another hit and was dropped by the record label a further year down the line.

Jack re-invented himself, thanks to an astute agent, and went on to become the youngest ever presenter of *Blue Peter*. After a surprise appearance on *Have I Got News For You*, he impressed the right people and was offered various stints as a stand-in presenter on *This Morning* and *The One Show*.

He even landed his own teatime quiz show, *Out For The Count*, which ran for two series.

Jack made a lot of contacts along the way and, with the backing of his brother, he started an immensely successful production company that was sold five years later for £95 million.

He married three times and had six children, but everyone was deliriously happy, the money saw to that. He died in Los Angeles, a delighted 81-year-old.

And he only ever snorted other people's coke.

Adam's suicide was too great a burden on Ben and Kate. Their relationship fell apart under the dead weights of self-reproach and utter guilt and the more they fought against it, the more it hurt. Kate eventually moved out and returned to her flat. They never saw each other again.

Ben and Julia patched up their marriage and stayed together for the rest of their lives. He decided to jack in his career at forty and bought a huge farm in Devon. They had two more children and lived long, contented lives.

But every night, when he closed his eyes, he said a little prayer for Kate and her face would appear out of the darkness and she'd smile and the dark would become light. Then he'd fall asleep next to his plump, sultry wife and the world was good.

After her break-up with Ben, Kate decided she'd had enough of PR. She sold the company to another agency and used some of the money, and some of her contacts, to go on a world cruise. To escape her sadness, she read dozens of books in her stateroom on long, leisurely days at sea. The large on-board library was stuffed with classics she'd always meant to get around to reading, along with contemporary hits, Mills & Boon, thrillers and detective stories.

She picked up the writing bug again and sketched out an idea for a novel while sipping Manhattans in sun-drenched bars. When she returned to London, Kate wrote her book and sent it to a literary agent acquaintance.

A year later, *Lust In Space* hit the bookshelves. The story of sex in a far-flung future caught the zeitgeist and catapulted her to the top of the bestseller lists. Two years later, the movie version won an Oscar for best picture and Kate received one for best screenplay.

Her acceptance speech, in which she mimicked Keira Knightly, Madonna, Michelle Obama, Oprah Winfrey, Adele and Tom Cruise, captured the imagination of Hollywood. She was a hot babe in hot demand for chat shows and when she told David Letterman that *Like Clockwork* was the book that inspired her to write, sales on Amazon went through the roof. It topped the New York Times bestseller list and Adam's other books, *Big Boys Don't Cry* and *Up In The Dumps*, were republished as a result and also made the list. All royalties were paid to Laura.

Like Clockwork became a celebrated novel and is now included in university curricula around the world.

Kate never wrote another book, but she did become a movie actress and made eight films playing opposite such luminaries as Christian Bale, who reminded her of Ben, Leonardo Di Caprio and Tom Cruise—yes, there was a scene where she impersonated him.

She married a US senator when she was 41 and they had two children. He went on to become President and America found itself with a British First Lady.

Kate was killed in a car crash in Monaco when she was 63 and the world mourned. When her handbag was searched at the scene, they found an old dog-eared copy of *Like Clockwork* with Adam's lone letter to her inside.

She only ever snorted her own coke.

Ben bought his mum's house and sorted the debts. Laura took a redundancy package at her job and her life had never been easier. She thought Jack had taken Adam's death pretty well. *The X Factor* success was storming, and it wouldn't have happened if Adam hadn't encouraged him.

Laura never knew what grief was until her husband died. She never realised how much she loved him, how his smile was so genuine, so full of feeling. She wanted to feel him next to her in that big old bed again when she woke up in the middle of the night afraid of time and looking for an escape.

She missed him like crazy and the gap he left was too wide to cross. So, she stayed where she was and built her life on the edge of that gap because that's where she was meant to be.

She'd never felt so alone. She blamed the dope for his untimely death–he was probably out of his skull when he did it and now his skull was out of him. She couldn't stand the pain.

But she still had the Geena Davis look. And that gypsy in her soul.

She was 61 when she went on her first date in nearly forty years. And his name was Adam. They met at the *X Factor* season finale party two years previously, he was the divorced father of one of the other contestants, and they kept in touch by email. It took Adam all that time to ask Laura out on a date. But she liked the way he asked.

'Do you consider two years to be a respectable amount of time to wait before asking a bereaved wife if she would care to have dinner one evening?'

And she liked the fact his name was Adam. She tried to remember his face, she was good at that, and seemed to recall salt and pepper stubble, sharp, short, grey hair and eyes without a trace of vanity. She didn't think he was as old as her, but then, who was these days?

She accepted, and he was exactly as she remembered, a great relief.

They met in an Italian restaurant in Southgate where he told Laura about his job–he had his own accountancy firm–his defunct marriage, his kids, his favourite film, song, food, TV show, and how he'd thought about her a lot since they'd first met.

Laura told him about Adam; how he died, how he wrote, how he talked, how he cared for his parents, how he tried to save his son's life. And she said her favourite song was 'Nights In White Satin' because that was the first one she and Adam danced to.

Adam didn't mind. He liked hearing her say Adam, even if it wasn't him. He was that kinda guy.

A few months of dating later, when she finally ran out of things to say about Adam, he proposed.

They were happily married for eleven years until Adam died of cancer. He left Laura two million pounds and not one of them had Shakespeare's face. She was already well-heeled from the sales of *Like Clockwork* and the other two books. She never could remember their names.

Laura spent the rest of her capable days, of which there were many, seeing the wonders of the world on organised trips. She'd never been happier, or richer. And some nights she'd look at the night sky from a cruise ship balcony, or a piazza in Florence, or a beach bar in St Lucia, and thank her lucky stars she met Adam Tate.

The gap had long gone. He'd taken his life, as lovers often do.

Baby, you're a rich man.

THE END

© 2013 Adam Tate

Epilogue

It was light outside when Tom realised he was starving.

He made another sardine and tomato sandwich washed down with green tea.

'This doesn't make any sense,' he said, finding comfort in the first words he'd heard in a day. 'That's not how it's supposed to end. The three of them were found together. All of them dead.

'And why was it called *Fuck The Sheds–A Gangster's Revenge*?'

Tom felt incredibly cheated.

He didn't get it. He didn't get it at all. But he wanted to, badly. He knew these people intimately now and needed to find out the truth. The ending was pure fantasy–Kate becomes the First Lady? Laura marries another Adam? It was a Dickensian device but it wasn't what he wanted.

Ben is dead, yet in the book he lives long and prospers.

And why were his last words, 'Shit, I forgot to change the names on the disk'?

And then there was *that* passage, near the end. Tom noted the page when he read it.

The key to everything was the USB stick in the small front pocket of his jeans. That was now his only hope, his only salvation. It was his one chance to burn in that eternal fame.

Adam was convinced the story surrounding the discovery of the disk would get a lot of publicity, providing the perfect launch-pad for Fuck The Sheds. A sharp cop with a vivacious vocabulary who might remember Like Clockwork could do something with it. Or know a man who could. A sharp cop with a streak of audacity who might just see the potential. Or know a man who did.

Was he talking to him?

He hadn't slept and the whole of Sunday stretched before him like a sleepy cat, but Tom got dressed, took the USB stick out of his laptop, put it carefully into the small front pocket of his jeans and headed for the office. The roads were quiet and it took 15 minutes to get there in the Audi A3 sports number he bought for five grand from his Uncle Huw, a second-hand car dealer who had his own showroom, the tortuously-titled Huwsed Cars, in Rhyl. 'You'll look the bollocks in that, up in the smoke,' he told Tom. 'Just like *The Sweeney*.'

'What are you doing here?' asked DC Michael Chambers as Tom walked into the office. 'It's your day off, dickhead.' Then he said, in a Welsh accent that bordered on the Bangladeshi, 'Oh Toto, I don't think we're in Taff Town anymore.'

Tom didn't like DC Michael Chambers, but he had considered the possibility that his behaviour was deliberately inflammatory, an inverted 'bad cop' routine, like Mark Wahlberg as staff sergeant Sean Dignam in *The Departed*. But then he thought, nah, DC Michael Chambers was simply an obnoxious fuckpig. There were a lot of them about.

'I need to check something on the computer.'

'Why didn't you do it at home?' DC Chambers was six-foot four, an imposing mass of cockney flash who could easily have been a villain. Tom was glad he was on his side, even if he was an obnoxious fuckpig. When Tom came in, he was playing solitaire on the computer. It was a lazy Sunday.

'I'm not connected to Wi-Fi yet. It's a pain in the arse,' said Tom.

'Don't see what can be so urgent. But, it's your life. Sad. Very sad.' DC Chambers shook his head mournfully and returned to the solitaire on his screen. It appeared to be the only game in town this morning.

Tom Googled 'Adam Tate' and saw 32,400 entries.

He Googled '*Like Clockwork*' and saw 3,240,000.

He Googled '*Like Clockwork* by Adam Tate', and saw 48. They were mostly booksellers that didn't stock it anymore, including Amazon. Trusty Wikipedia came across with the goods.

And what goods.

Filed under *Like Clockwork*, Tom clicked 'Adam Tate' and read the following:

Adam Tate was born on January 16, 1955 on a council housing estate in Islington, London, the only child of Coral and Bobby Tate. He left Dame Alice Owen's School in 1972 and worked as a reporter on several local newspapers. His first book–Like Clockwork–was published in 1985 and became a cult classic. It was subsequently turned into a three-part drama on Channel 4. He wrote two further books–Up In The Dumps and Big Boys Don't Cry–but both titles sold poorly and Tate was dropped by his publisher. Like Clockwork is now largely forgotten.

Tate married Laura Ray, a local government officer, in 1976, and they had two children, Ben and Jack. In 1994, Laura and Jack, who was two at the time, were both killed in a car crash in Bounds Green, London. Adam Tate was driving the car and was uninjured, but he failed a drug test and was sentenced to four years for causing death by dangerous driving. While in prison, his son Ben, who was 14, moved in with Tate's parents. Since his release, Tate has remained in obscurity. He was last believed to be living with his parents and son in Islington.

Wide-eyed and legless, Tom pushed his chair back from the desk.

How could it be?

Laura and Jack both dead for years? Ben living with Coral and Bobby? Adam in prison?

So, the whole book was a lie.

But Adam did write *Like Clockwork*, he did marry Laura, they had Ben, they had Jack. Coral and Bobby were his parents.

So, what were the lies?

He pulled himself back to his desk on the chair's castors and Googled 'Lyle Associates'. There were 9000 entries.

He Googled 'Kate Lyle of Lyle Associates'. Zilch.

He Googled her name every which way but loose, but nothing matched.

She didn't exist. Why should she? She was only of use if he was married. Right?

Ben existed, his corpse was a testament to that. But how could he have had an affair with the fictional Kate Lyle?

So why was he dead?

And why was Bobby dead? He was just an old bloke who took on his grandson when his son went off the rails. He obviously hadn't committed any murders.

He was entrenched in thought, oblivious to the world around him, like he was wearing headphones and listening to his thoughts with the volume pumped up real high.

When DS Choudhury tapped him on the shoulder he leapt a couple of inches.

'Sorry, Evans. Did I startle you?'

Tom heard DC Chambers sniggering.

'DC Chambers,' said DS Choudhury with some authority, 'I need to speak to DC Evans regarding a private matter. Could you make yourself scarce for five minutes, there's a good chap?'

DC Chambers shuffled out of the office.

'Bet he's calling me a bastard under his breath,' said DS Choudhury. 'Once, when he didn't know I was nearby, I heard him do an imitation of me. It was awful, he sounded like a fucking Welshman. No offence.'

'None taken, sir.'

'What are you doing in the office on your day off?'

'What are you doing, sir? I thought you were supposed to be playing golf.'

'I was, but those wretched shootings have had to be dealt with swiftly to save a lot more work further down the line. It's all over the Sunday papers. Early reports from forensics suggest there was nobody else involved. The reports do throw up a convincing scenario, backed by gossip garnered from the local gypsies, tramps and thieves.

'There were two guns at the scene, a second world war Luger...'

'9mm P08?' said Tom, cautiously.

'Er, yes, and an old British Army service pistol.'

'Not a Smith & Wesson Victory by any chance?'

'Yes, it was. How did you know that?'

'It was a common army issue, sir. I know a little about guns.' Tom knew nothing about guns. He knew more about Persian carpets than guns and he knew absolutely nothing about Persian carpets. He was just that kinda guy.

'The Smith & Wesson was found in the trouser pocket of the youngest victim, Ben Tate, aged 29,' continued a slightly irritated DS Choudhury. 'It hadn't been fired. Ben had been shot three times, two bullets in the chest and one through the head. The eldest victim, Bobby Tate, aged 95, had been shot once to the body. Another bullet was found lodged in the wall behind the chair where Bobby was seated indicating a miss, obviously.'

'Obviously. Sir.' Tom was lost in France and regretted his comment. It wasn't meant to be sarcastic, but it sounded like it. Sure enough.

'If I wanted sarcasm, DC Evans, I'd call my mother-in-law.'

'Sorry, sir. Just got carried away with the story.'

'It's hardly Henry James.'

'Oh no, I assure you, I never got carried away by Henry James. Your report is far more interesting, sir.'

'I like your style of grovelling, Evans. Keep it up and you'll go far. Now, where was I? Ah yes. The body of Adam Tate, that's Bobby's son and Ben's father if you're a bit confused, was found slumped against the wall. Half his head was missing but he gripped the Luger so tightly that it had to be prised out of his hand.

'The bullets found in Ben and Bobby Tate were fired by the Luger that Adam held onto for dear life. It's obvious, Adam Tate shot his son and father and then put the barrel in his mouth and pulled the trigger. There were no other fingerprints on the Luger but Adam's.

'Ben Tate was a crazy junkie dealer known to us. Word on the street was he liked young girls, the younger the better, and had recently been questioned by officers about the rape of an eight-year-old.

'Bobby Tate was a gangster back in the day involved with several north London heavy mobs, but he was well past his sell-by date.

'Adam Tate was the enigma. He was an ex-journalist and author who killed his wife and two-year-old son in a car crash.'

'I read on Google that he went down for four years.'

'That's right.'

'I also read his book, *Like Clockwork*, when I was a young blade. It became a bit of a cult.'

'Quite a coincidence. Guess you've read a lot of books, huh?'

'Not nearly enough. But definitely no Henry James, sir.'

'Adam obviously met a few bad influences inside because when he came out it appears he became involved in dealing, mainly coke, operating out of his parents' house where he also lived with Ben.

'When Adam was sent down, Ben was 14. He went to live with his grandparents, but they couldn't control him and he ran wild. He was busted a few times for possession, weed and ecstasy, and was put on probation first time around then received community service. He was too young, they didn't know what to do with him.

'Adam's mum, Coral Tate, died in an accident at home a couple of years back.'

'What happened?' asked Tom.

'She fell down the stairs, apparently. It happened while Adam was in prison.'

'I thought you said she died a couple of years ago?'

'That's right,' said DS Choudhury.

'What, you mean Adam went to prison again?'

'Yes, in fact he only came out a couple of weeks ago and was living back at the ranch with the brothers grim, Bobby and Ben.'

'No!'

'Yes. You look a little shocked, Evans.'

'Wasn't expecting that, sir. What did he go inside for?'

'A little birdie tells me that the son and grandfather grassed up Adam when the heat got too much and it looked like all three would be nicked, even the old man. Adam ended up getting nine years for dealing.

'So, it's pretty much an open and shut case. Adam Tate shot his father and son and then made a holy ghost out of himself. You might like to have a look at this, if you can handle any more reading. It was handed to the police last night.'

DS Choudhury slid a file across Tom's desk. He opened it and found a printed document, simply entitled, 'Suicide Note.'

My name is Adam Robert Tate and I'm of sound mind but not so sound body. What you saw before you that day was a triple death–father, son and grandson. I, that's Adam Robert Tate, shot my son, Ben Tate and my father, Robert Tate, before blowing my own brains out.

Cut and dried.

I have three perfectly valid reasons why I carried out these, on the face of it, heinous, murders.

1.   My son, Ben, was a paedophile junkie who carried out some despicable acts and was known to the police.

2.   My father, Bobby, was a vicious killer who I suspected of murdering my mother while I was busy inside, dying.

3.   Whilst detained at Her Majesty's pleasure, I was diagnosed with stomach cancer and given six months to live. I still had another year to serve and I made sure I served it. I survived because I didn't see why those two fuckers should outlive me. I survived because I wanted to gain my freedom simply to kill them. I survived because I knew I was going to die.

As you are now probably aware, the USB disk in my jeans pocket contained a novel I wrote in prison after I found out I had cancer. I hope somebody there had the foresight to pass it on to someone who might actually read it as it just might help with your inquiries.

Thank you and goodnight.

Adam Robert Tate

'Oh yes,' said DS Choudhury. Tom looked up.

'We also have an eye witness.'

Tom immediately thought of the old woman in the window. 'Who's that, sir?'

'Bobby Tate.'

'Bobby Tate? But you said he was dead.'

'I was misinformed.'

'You mean he survived the shooting?'

'Sure did. Unbelievable. The bullet that didn't miss passed clean through the only bit of flesh left on him, around his hip bone, leaving everything else intact. He's in hospital recovering but he managed to tell us exactly what happened. And it's pretty much how I described it. Straightforward murder and suicide. Nice and neat.

'All we had to go on was the USB disk and Adam's mobile phone that was also found on the body. As it turned out, we didn't need anything. Bobby was our main man. It's incredible, he's 95, yet talks coherently. He's more on the ball than half of the people that work here, and that includes DC Chambers.'

'You've met him? You've met Bobby Tate?'

'Yes, this morning. Incredible old chap. He has a hole in his head the size of Japan,'–last time it was a melon, Tom recalled–'but he's still the complete spiv. They certainly don't make them like that anymore. You look a little shocked again, Evans.'

'Well, in the novel that Adam Tate wrote...'

'I don't want to hear about it, Evans. This case needs no embellishment. Keep the disk as a souvenir. There doesn't appear to be any immediate family, or distant. The file is now officially closed. Nice and clean.'

'In that case, sir, would it be at all possible to get hold of the contact list on Adam's mobile phone?'

'That's a highly irregular request, Evans. Why would you want such a thing?'

'I know it's irregular, sir, but I'm a little intrigued by this, probably because I was such a big fan of him as a kid. And who knows, it might throw up a few leads, if he was such a prolific dealer. It'll give me something to do in this cold, lonely city when I'm not working. And I did sacrifice my weekend in your best interests, sir.'

DS Choudhury smiled. 'I'll make a few discreet enquiries, but I'm not promising anything. Can't see as it'll do much harm, though. It seems all the loose ends have been tied.'

Not if Bobby Tate is still alive, thought Tom.

He had to see him. He was desperate to find out which Bobby Tate was still breathing.

Fact or fiction?

'Robert Tate, Robert Tate, Robert, ah yes, here he is. Yes, he's in the second room on the left. I don't think he's supposed to be receiving any visitors, ah yes, here it is. Yes, the police have told us that in no circumstances must Mr Tate receive any visitors.'

She was cute, Filipino, about 24.

'Oh, that's okay, nurse. I am the police.' He flashed his card for the first time in public. It felt good.

'Oh yes. Of course. Please go ahead. Let me know if you need anything.'

Flashing his card was more than enough for one day.

A simple phone call had confirmed the name of the hospital Bobby had been taken to after the shooting and Tom couldn't wait. He was desperate to see this wet dream villain of Adam's imagination. As he walked down the corridor, Tom couldn't help thinking he was about to enter the room of a fictitious character, a storybook gangster who put a fork through the head of a soldier, chopped another man's head off, was buggered by his brother and kept bundles of useless money under the stairs.

It was almost hypnotic.

'Mr Tate?'

'What's that?'

'Mr Tate?'

'Yeah. Who the fuck is that?'

'DC Tom Evans, sir.'

'Not another fucking copper. I've said everything I can. Please, do me a favour and fuck off.' His words were old and broken but Tom could understand everything.

Half his face was heavily bandaged, and the wound wasn't visible. The other half was dominated by a scar that had healed untidily and looked like the fossilised remains of some large, prehistoric exotic insect. He was sitting up in bed, a bony bundle of woe weighed down by a saucerful of secrets.

'It's okay sir, I'm just checking that you're comfortable and feeling all right. I'm not here to ask any questions.'

The use of the word 'sir' had a calming effect on Bobby–like Adam's, 'It's all a misunderstanding.' Tom was a natural.

'I'm all right but I want to get out of here. I want to go home. Can you sort it? I don't like being away from my home. I'm never away from it. Never. There's squatters and all sorts of fuckers out there. I'd have 'em all publicly pissed upon and then set alight.'

'You're not well enough to leave, Mr Tate. You'll need to stay here for a few days until you feel better.'

'But I am all right. I am.' He was almost pleading.

'Don't worry about the house. It'll be safe. It was a crime scene, so the police will be watching it for a while.'

'Well make sure they don't touch anything or start digging around and lifting up floorboards and stuff.'

'I assure you, nothing like that will happen.' What was he worried they would find? The stash?

'It'd better fucking not.'

'I'm sorry to hear you lost your son and grandson, especially in that shocking way. Why on earth would Adam want to kill Ben?' Tom remembered he promised not to ask any questions, so he quickly added a makeshift answer–'It doesn't make any sense.'

'It's those fucking drugs that don't make any sense,' said Bobby. 'They were both addicted. Fucking pathetic. To be honest, Tom, that is your name? Right? Well, Tom, between you, me and the gatepost, I'm glad to see the fucking back of 'em. Waste of fucking space. I tell you something, if I'd have had a gun, I'd have shot the fucking pair of 'em. Waste of fucking space. The pair of 'em. If I'd have had a gun…'

'What, you'd actually be able to kill someone?' Tom felt he could ask him anything now.

'Too fucking right. Easy as pie.'

'But you don't know what it's like to kill someone, Mr Tate. You'll probably find you wouldn't be able to do it, given the chance.'

'Don't you worry about me, mate. I know I'd be able to do it.'

'How do you know?'

'I know.'

'But how?'

'Because I've done…,' Bobby hesitated. He forgot he was a spiv for a moment and eased back in the groove. 'I want you to go now. I'm tired. I want to sleep. Please go.'

Bobby closed his good eye. Tom knew he wasn't asleep. Adam told him. He also knew this decaying old man sounded like a thug whose broken words had dangerously sharp ends. Adam told him that also. He was beginning to believe in Adam again.

But it was still the weirdest moment of his life. As he walked past the cute Filipino nurse, he felt he'd just left the room of a fictitious character, a storybook gangster who'd put a fork through the head of a soldier, chopped another man's head off, been buggered by his brother and kept bundles of useless money under the stairs.

It was almost hypnotic.

The following morning, Tom saw a new file on his desktop when he logged on, simply titled, *sheds.docx*. He wondered how it got there, then remembered he worked in a police station. Note to self: don't store private files at work.

When he opened it, he found about five hundred names and telephone numbers taken from Adam Tate's mobile. He started to work through them, though he didn't have a clue what he was looking for. He hoped something might click.

Many of the entries were first names followed by the occasional initial when they clashed. There was no Kate. Some were companies. There was no Lyle Associates.

Tom refused to believe there wasn't a Kate Lyle out there. Everyone else in the novel existed, in one form or other, so why not Kate? It was only natural Adam wouldn't reveal her real name. He didn't know who would read it. All the other players were dead, except Bobby, so using their identities didn't matter. Kate existed all right. She had to. And he was determined, no, needed to find her. It was a yearning he couldn't explain.

He rang Katherine Leverton, Karen Lee, Ken Last and Kev Lowe and asked to speak to Kate Lyle and they all said, 'Sorry, wrong number.' Then he rang Les King, Lonnie Kane and Luke Love and asked to speak to Kate Lyle and they all said, 'Sorry, wrong number.'

Real work got in the way and for the next few days Tom found himself staking out a suspected brothel, attending the scene of a robbery at an all-night corner shop and filling out a million forms relating to both matters. But whenever he had a free moment, he'd check the contact list searching for clues.

He must've seen the entry–'Yell–teak company'–fifty times and ignored it, assuming it was straight out of Yellow Pages. But the fifty-first time he saw it, his brain slipped into code-breaking mode and he saw the words 'Lyle–Kate company' appear like a hidden name in a word search box.

He dialled the mobile number next to it.

'Hullo, can I speak to Kate Lyle please?'

There was a silence. 'There's nobody here of that name.' It was a female voice. Soft. Tender. 'How did you get this number?'

'I found it in *Like Clockwork*.'

Another silence.

'Are you a policeman?'

'Let's just say I'm intrigued. Can we meet?'

'Why?'

'Because you know something about Kate Lyle.'

'Who's Kate Lyle?'

'A character in a novel.'

'What novel?'

'I think you know. Look, I'll make a deal with you. If you say the first two words of the title and I can say the next ones, we meet tomorrow at six at the Pizza Express near Islington Green.' He figured she was a north London girl. Adam told him.

'I don't know what you're talking about.'

'Then why haven't you hung up? In answer to all your questions, I'm Detective Constable Tom Evans, although this isn't strictly a police matter. As far as I know, I'm the only person to have read Adam Tate's novel that was on the USB stick found in his pocket at the scene of the shooting. I read *Like Clockwork* when I was a kid and loved it. I'm curious.

'I found your number on Adam's mobile phone. I guess you know you were filed under 'Yell-Teak,' an anagram for Kate Lyle.'

'You mean Lyle Kate.'

'And you're all yellow.'

Another silence. Then her voice came out of the swirling darkness where all dreams end.

'*Fuck The...*'

   '*Sheds.*'

It was one of the precious few balmy evenings during a long, wet summer. Tom managed to secure a table outside the restaurant and watched the Upper Street hipsters' parade.

This was even more bizarre than meeting Bobby Tate.

Kate Lyle was about to step into his world like Tom Baxter in *The*

Purple Rose of Cairo. Would she be able to impersonate Mia Farrow? Would she have that sexycloggy body? Would her face shine like a crazy diamond when she laughed? Would she have snorted any coke? Would he fall in love with this piece of work?

Piece of work. He kept repeating it. It made him feel safe.

He took a swig from a bottle of Peroni and lit a Marlboro Light. He rarely smoked but he knew Kate did because Adam told him. She was 15 minutes late and he started to bite a fingernail, something he hadn't done in twenty years.

A striking blonde in a yellow dress walked past his table and entered the restaurant. A minute later she came outside again, looked up and down the tables, and then went over to where Tom was sitting.

'Detective Constable Evans?'

'Please call me Tom, Miss Lyle.'

'No, the name's not Lyle.'

'Yes, but I didn't know what else to call you.'

'Linda.'

'Linda…?' He was searching for a surname.

'Just Linda.' She laughed.

Linda didn't sound as sexycloggy as Kate. She was in her mid-thirties, long, dyed blonde hair and too much make-up. She was blatantly attractive, in a Botox, soap-opera kinda way, and when she laughed it was more crazy zircon. For a moment, Tom thought he was on a dodgy blind date.

'He said you'd come.' Her voice was tender, vulnerable. It was the voice he heard in his head when he read Kate Lyle's words.

'Who, Adam?'

'Yes. He said it would be a policeman but not on duty. He even got your age about right. 26?'

'Next birthday.'

'He was quite a man. I thought he was talking shit, of course. Who wouldn't? I thought he'd gone stir crazy.'

'How long had you known him?'

'Do you think I could get something to drink?'

'Yes, of course. How remiss of me, Linda.' It was a tough name for him to say after days of Kate.

She ordered a large gin and tonic and lit up a super slim menthol cigarette.

'So, you were going to tell me how long you'd known Adam.'

'I was, what, twenty when we met. I worked behind the bar at a pub in the City. He breezed in one afternoon with a couple of mates and spent a small fortune on champagne. He chatted me up like nobody else had ever done and I think I fell for him there and then.

'Are we ordering any food?'

'Yes, of course.'

Linda plumped for the Calabrese pizza and Tom had his usual, pomodoro pesto Romana.

'Shall we get some wine.' It wasn't a request.

'Yes,' said Tom.

'White.'

'Yes,' said Tom. Her voice was so tender.

'So,' he said, 'you were saying it was love at first sight.'

'Did I? Yes, I guess it was. He swept me off my feet. I knew he'd been in prison and I knew he was dealing–I can say that now, can't I?'

'Don't worry, this is all strictly off the record. Besides, there's nobody left to charge except a dying 95-year-old bloke and it's not worth the hassle. The case has been effectively closed.'

'I take it the 95-year-old bloke is Adam's dad, Bobby.'

He loved hearing her voice. Even though her words were soft, they drowned out the traffic and the conversations and the high-heeled footsteps and he caught every syllable.

'Yes.'

'Have you met him?'

'Yes.'

'Fucking prick. Right?'

Tom was taken aback.

'I'm sorry if that shocks you, Tom, but he is. Anyway, I tried to get Adam to stop dealing but he was making a lot of money and his son, Ben, was involved. Nasty little bastard who was smacked out of it most of the time and had a bit of a paedo reputation.

'Look, I could tell you more, but I think you'll find everything you need to know on this.' She handed him a USB stick.

'Not another novel?'

'No. Just something he wanted you, who had come this far, to read and hopefully act upon. I have the necessary papers if you want to proceed after reading it. It could be an interesting ride and I'm game.'

Wow! Tom wasn't expecting anything like this.

'But why me?' The words squirted out like a follow-through fart.

'There's a smell of kismet in the air, don't you think?' said Linda. 'I believe this was meant to be. Anybody could've read that disk, Tom. But it was you, and you're here. Now. That's proof enough for me. Like I said, Adam knew you would come because you cared. And you also like white wine.'

Linda liked white wine. Over a couple of bottles, she told him about her job as a beautician–she ran her own salon–and her dreams of being a singer. Her guilty secret was passing an audition on the X Factor in one of its early shows.

'What do you think of Adam's novel?'

'Fuck The Sheds?'

'Er, yes.'

'Oh, I haven't read it. I can honestly say, hand on heart, I've read about, what, six books, in my entire life, all by Martina Cole and all read on beaches in Spain and Barbados. I've tried to read his books, but I can't get past the first few chapters. Life's too short to delve too long.

'You knew about Kate Lyle.'

'That's only because Adam said you, or mythical you as you were then, would ask for someone by that name after calling me on my mobile phone,' said Linda. 'You knew he wrote it all in prison?'

'I do now. I read the suicide note that was handed to the police the day after the shootings.'

'Oh yes, I forgot you were a detective,' she was being facetious, tenderly. 'Anyway, I've said too much. I won't ask anything about you this evening because, frankly, I'd rather not know. You may decide not to see me again after you've read the contents of that disk, so what's the point? But I guarantee that will all change if you're prepared to "hitch a ride to Adventureland" as Adam often said.'

Tom asked for the bill.

'I must go now,' she said, soberly, tenderly. 'Do I owe you anything for the meal?' she shook her head as she said the words.

It was hypnotic.

'No, it's on me.

'Thank you. If I don't see you again, it's been nice. And by the way, the contents of the disk are strictly confidential, whatever you decide to do.'

'You have my word.'

'I know. That's why you have the disk now. I'm good at judging people.'

She turned and walked down Upper Street towards The Angel, hugging the last remnants of sunshine that lit up the pavement and bounced off a few shop windows.

All yellow.

Tom put the disk in the small front pocket of his jeans and kept checking it was there all the way home.

He put it in the laptop. There was only one file on the disk and it was called *For You*.

He had the taste for a drink and fixed himself a very large JD and Coke. He even lit another cigarette. He was about to have a one-way conversation with Adam Tate and he wanted it to be special.

Tom had a good feeling about this.

For You

So, I'm dead then. Wonder what it feels like.

Dead.

Can I see you?

Can you see me?

Anyway, Plod, as I assume you are, I gather you've read my book. Can I also assume that you've read my previous works–Like Clockwork, Up In The Dumps *or* Big Boys Don't Cry? *If not, I strongly recommend them. Essential reading.*

Apologies for the blatant ad but some books will last an eternity and it's comforting to know there's a miniscule possibility one of them could be mine, simply because it's out there, somewhere. I once thought Like Clockwork *would be the one, but it's faded away because it was a book about a generation that perished long ago. This generation is only interested in this generation and history is a thing of the past. It's no longer of use. Shit, yesterday is no longer of use. Today's headlines will be dead and buried under a ton of new stuff within a week. Not even time to knock up a coffin.*

You've got to go with the flow. Pull out all the stops and let fate take a hand. Or should that be Kate? I had a hunch the police would've wanted someone to read it through quickly and take it all in, and that someone would be you. And it is, if you're reading this. It is you.

Linda would've given it to you and I trust her judgement implicitly. She's made me happy for a while and this is as much for her benefit as mine.

She would've received a suicide note by guaranteed next day delivery after the killing, saying exactly what the police wanted to hear, that I executed my son and my father and then shot myself, and the reasons why. End of. File under S for Some junkie ex-con shoots dodgy family and then himself. Three generations slain, The Father, Son & Holy Ghost. Amen. Fancy a pint?

I suspect you've already read the note, but if you haven't, I've taken the liberty of enclosing a copy.

What that letter doesn't say is that Ben raped Linda while I was inside and then beat her so badly she was in hospital for a week. He hated me that much. Guess he never forgave me for the death of his mother. I tried so hard to understand him, to solicit his love, to embrace his pain, to try and forge a relationship, all to no avail. His depravity knew no bounds— he was a menace to himself and everyone around him. That rogue Tate gene had to be extinguished and I was the only one who could do it. I didn't even pity him anymore.

Linda is letting you read this and that means she trusts you. She obviously thinks, like Neo in The Matrix, you're the one—bet Kate could've done a mean Trinity. I told Linda to keep quiet about the rape and not tell the police. I didn't want him to go down for a few years, I wouldn't survive that long. I wanted him to die.

The reason I was sent down was because he grassed me up, with the backing of my father. The police were leaning on Ben and he turned me in. He told them where I was picking up a shipment of two kilos of coke—around eighty grand's worth wholesale—and I got busted. Nine years they gave me after taking into account the druggie car-crash conviction. Nine years.

When I was told inside that I only had six months to live, the idea of not writing another book terrified me. After Big Boys Don't Cry, I gave up and sunk into depression as the dope took hold. That's when I lost Laura and Jack.

I figured I'd have a better chance of completing a book if I stayed put. Besides, the medical attention was probably better than I'd get on the outside, and no waiting time.

The authorities were sympathetic and let me have a laptop, peace, even marijuana. I wanted to beat the six-month deadline, complete Fuck The Sheds and kill my father and son. They were scum, the pair of them. My father was a murdering gangster who probably did push my mother down the stairs. When he wasn't beating her up in his drunken rages, he'd lay into me. I still bear the scars, at least, I did. That's why I wanted him buggered at an early age. Very therapeutic writing.

Not only did my son rape Linda, he also raped an eight-year girl and God knows how many others. He was gone with the wind and tomorrow would never be another day.

Only with both of them dead could I die a happy man, knowing I had a disk in my pocket and those two bastards bleeding to death close by. Anyway, it's not like I hadn't killed before, and served time for it. Keep it in the family when it comes to killing, that's what I say.

I completed the novel and I'm due to be released tomorrow. This is the last thing I will ever write. Strange, a suicide note should be the last thing. Always did get things arse upwards.

I hope you liked the book. I suppose you probably wouldn't be reading this if you didn't.

The truth is, I wanted to salvage something noble from this sordid, sleazy little squabble between a coke dealer, a junkie, and a malicious old gangster, and I wanted that to be Fuck The Sheds. *I apologise if you thought you were reading a true romance when it turned out to be, in the main, a work of fiction. The people existed but only in the way I wanted them to exist. I'm a novelist. It's what I do, did, apart from dealing Charlie. Using their real names is more of a gimmick than anything else. Kate Lyle is the only character who is totally fabricated.*

The suicide note was a good story and I guarantee that'll grab the public's attention for a day or so. A few weeks later, the book can go out on Kindle and that should get some national coverage because it's another good story—a novel in which all the characters are real but playing different roles. A novel written in prison by a man dying of cancer. A novel written by someone who murdered his dad and his son.

Well, can you think of a better way to get published? Kill yourself and your immediate family—a trio of bodies pumping out the same blood. Is that cool, or what? A USP on a USB. I guarantee the big boys will come running with open cheque books when they see sales take off online, which they will.

Some people will do anything to get published, eh?

So, if we're about to become partners, I should tell you a little bit more about myself than you already know, especially how a guy like me–ex-journalist, ex-author–got involved in all this.

When I went inside after the car crash, you can't imagine how bad I felt. If they'd passed a death sentence I would've embraced it. I tried to kill myself twice in prison by slashing my wrists with a sharpened plastic knife when I worked in the kitchen and by making a noose out of my bed sheet.

Obviously, suicide wasn't my forte.

A couple of the older inmates knew my father and I was treated with a little respect, like I was a made man or something.

It was strange. I'd never realised my dad carried such a name amongst high-end villains. One of the inmates got nicked on purpose just to sell drugs to other cons on the inside at inflated prices via credit card payments on the outside.

They told me of a sure-fire way of making money with little risk–coke dealing. Not a gram here or there but substantial amounts. If I wanted it, I could be part of a little chain and pulling in a regular two or three grand a week. It was a bit rich for me but out of politeness I took their mobile numbers.

When I came out, the house had been repossessed and sold on and I still owed the bank money. I had to move in with my parents and they were both unwell. Ben was 17 and running wild. I started doing everything for them. It was a nightmare.

I figured I had nothing to lose. I'd killed my wife and son; how much worse could it get? I followed up the leads I was given inside and became heavily involved in drug dealing the moment I started seeing bundles of fifty-pound notes. I think my one gangster gene beat the shit out of the other twenty-odd thousand and became the Boss. I even ran a few cannabis farms with some tricky Vietnamese guys. Amazing what you can do with a legendary villain for a father and a couldn't-give-a-fuck attitude to life.

The old man knew I was up to no good, but he was happy with the money I was bunging him. My father was an extremely violent man with a vile temper and was always screwing other women while he was married. He'd often go missing for days on end. It was an absolute pleasure to kill him.

The financial rewards from the dealing were fast and furious and the network appeared to be foolproof. Predictably, it didn't last. One guy got busted and the whole lot collapsed like a pack of cards. I was okay, but it was unexpected and I hadn't put much aside. I'd blown most of the money I had on drugs, booze, meals and exotic holidays. That's the only time Linda ever read a book, on holiday. Always the same author, too—Martina Cole.

When the money ran out, I was desperate and had to start dealing again. I'd become a man of little sense, as you can see. I left it behind in my books. I knew it would end in tears, the old man was panicking all the time and Ben was up to God knows what, but always smack-induced and dangerous.

I got involved in another chain through an Albanian guy I met in prison and managed to stash about fifty grand in two months. That's when my flesh and blood grassed me up and pocketed the money. Life kinda lost its resonance for me from that moment, or maybe it was the cancer knocking on the door.

Who knows?

Who cares?

I'm dead.

Oh, that reminds me. Do you know why I called it Fuck The Sheds? Well...

Several workmen were digging a hole in the pavement when a brand-new chauffeur-driven Bentley passed by, stopped, and reversed. The blacked-out passenger window slid open and a head popped out.

'Terry?' One of the builders looked up.

'It is you, isn't it? Terry Nolan.'

'Pete?' said Terry as he walked over to the car. 'Blow me, Pete Morris. It's been years.'

'It certainly has,' said Pete, as he turned down the Eagles, who were singing 'Take It Easy' on the car music system, with a tiny remote control. 'So, how long have you been in the building game?'

'Since I left school. There wasn't much else for blokes like us. But it looks like you've done well for yourself. How did you end up with all this?'

'Well, it's a simple story really. We all left school at 16, didn't we, Tel? No futures, no careers. The only thing I was good at in school was woodwork.'

'Yeah, I remember that, Pete. Dab hand with the old plane and saw, I recall.'

Pete laughed.

'When I was 14 I had a pet hamster and I built a wooden extension to its cage. When it died, I put it in a coffin I'd made and buried it over the park. Later, we bought a dog and I made a kennel for it. I had time on my hands 'cos there was no work about.

'Anyway, a mate of my dad's came around one day and liked the kennel. When dad said I'd made it, he asked me to make one for him. He'd pay for all the materials and give me twenty quid. I knocked it up in a day. The bloke loved it and pretty soon I was making about five of them a month.

'Then one day a bloke asked me if I could make him a garden shed. I had a go and did it in three days. I was paid £150 for it and received loads of recommendations. After a year, I had too much work and had to take on an assistant. I rented a small studio where I could live and run the business.

'I started making all kinds of sheds—for garden furniture, tools, even cars. My turnover was about £100,000 after two years and I had to take on two more staff. It all looked promising.

'Then I won fifty million quid on the lottery and said, "Fuck The Sheds".

'Home, James.'

When opportunity knocks, Plod, take it. This is a genuine opportunity and you have nothing to lose. All the necessary papers are ready for you to sign. You'll be a director of a limited company in which you have *a forty per cent interest. Linda will own the rest. The company has the rights to my book, the title of which I suggest you change to Wet Dreams Dry Lives. No need to risk unnecessary controversy.*

In return, all you have to do is sort out the eBook. I'm sure an intelligent man like you, probably university-educated, will have contacts that can help. Graphic designers, PRs, that sort of thing. Also, Linda's name is never to be mentioned. She represents my interest and authorises all payments. You will run the company, but that'll be a doddle. Just get that eBook out, backed up with a bit of publicity.

Linda will fill you in on all the details and you'll find she'll be of great assistance. I think she's going to surprise you.

Go on, give it a go.

Fuck the sheds.

Regards,

Adam Tate

TWO YEARS LATER

The ocean sounds good at seven in the morning. Tom doesn't need an alarm to wake him; the waves always know when it's time and push a little harder for a few moments until he opens his eyes.

He walks onto the balcony from the bedroom of his beachfront condo in Santa Monica and breathes in air turned blue by the big sky and the warm, greeting sea.

'Come back to bed, birthday boy.'

'You remembered?'

'Of course.'

'It's so beautiful. I could stand here all day.'

'You can afford to, now.'

'I suppose I can. So can you.'

'Yes, but I don't want to. There's places to go, people to see. But not this early. Come back to bed and I'll give you your first present.' Her voice is so tender.

'Okay, Kate, if you insist.'

'If you call me that again,' says Linda, 'I swear I'll swing for you.'

Tom laughs. 'They don't execute people in California anymore.'

'I think you'll find 53 per cent of the population recently voted for capital punishment to be retained. That's why I'm staying put because if I murdered you, I wouldn't want to live anymore but I'd be too afraid to kill myself. Here, that can still be done for you.'

'Adam wasn't,' says Tom.

'Wasn't what?'

'Too afraid to kill himself.'

'He was dying.'

'We all are.'

'Yes, but to varying degrees.'

'So, you're saying you couldn't live without me.'

'I suppose I am,' says Linda.

'But you have to kill me first.'

'Oh, that's the easy bit.'

'I am an ex-policeman.'

'I am an ex-beautician.'

'Okay, Linda, I tell you what, let's stay here and you don't kill me. Deal?'

'Let me think about it while you make love to me.'

'Let me think about that while you give me a blowjob first. Deal?'

'You drive a hard bargain.'

'I rather hope so.'

The sex is easy and substantial and new, and all wrapped up in blue.

Life is easy and substantial. *Wet Dreams Dry Lives* has done well, very well, but under another title.

Tom had decided it was worth a punt and signed up for the ride to Adventureland. The first thing he did was change the title. He really liked the phrase but thought it was a little ambiguous. Linda agreed, and he told her he wanted to call it *The Tapes Of Wrath* and Linda agreed to that too, even though she thought that title was even more obscure. Tom had used the line while at university in a paper about Dylan Thomas and he was always quite proud of it.

One of his London-based Welsh gang (they called themselves the Toff Taffs) was a computer nerd and put the book on Kindle within a few days. *The Daily Mail*, that had previously run a story on the shootings–*Family Feud Killings*–with a follow-up piece in the *Mail On Sunday*–*95-Year-Old Cheats Death*–picked up on a lead passed to them by a PR who also happened to be a member of the TTs.

Under the headline–*Family Feud Killer's Novel Touch*–was a heartrending story of a once-successful author and scriptwriter who turned to drug-dealing after his wife and child were tragically killed in a car he was driving. His final novel, *The Tapes Of Wrath*, was written in prison where he was dying of cancer.

The book went to number one on the Amazon eBook fiction chart overnight and the big boys did come running with open cheque books. Then the movie offers came flooding in. That's when Tom decided a career in the police force was not an option anymore.

At first, Linda remained in the background, not wishing to be associated with the company. But as Adam's comet soared, she wanted to become more hands-on. In every way.

She and Tom became lovers. It took him a while to make a move, even though he was besotted from the moment he saw her. She was Kate in disguise and all that was missing was the coke and the impressions.

A movie of *Like Clockwork* was in pre-production phase and *Up In The Dumps* and *Big Boys Don't Cry* had both been republished and were selling well. Tom and Linda had recently decided to relocate to Los Angeles, where the celluloid action is, and life had become a big cut-glass bowl of cherries.

Adam told her this would happen. He said the man who asked for Kate Lyle would be the right man for her and if she ever bothered to read the book, she'd understand why. But she still hadn't read it.

'You should definitely consider changing your name to Kate, Linda,' says Tom.

The easy sex is over and now it's cigarette time. They vowed they would only smoke after having sex and now Tom wasn't sure whether it was all the screwing or all the smoking that was making him tired and wheezy.

'Why would I want to call myself Kate Linda?'

Tom ignores her.

'I said, why would I want to call myself Kate Linda?'

He continues to ignore her.

'I said,' she shouts, 'why would I want to call myself Kate Linda?'

'Oh, you're still here?' says Tom.

'That line reminds me of the scene in *Groundhog Day*,' says Linda, and Tom's ears twist like a lizard's, 'when Bill Murray said something like that and Andie McDowell said, "How are you doing this? I thought you were supposed to disappear, or I was or something."'

She sounds exactly like Andie McDowell. Tom is shocked. 'I never knew you could do impressions.'

'I can't, well, I can, but only Andie McDowell and only a few lines from that film. Talking of lines, I scored some coke off that producer yesterday. Haven't had any in ages. Fancy a livener, Plod? I guarantee the sex will be even better, if that's possible.'

Ex-Detective Constable Tom Evans considers rubbing some onto his cock, then thinks better of it.

'Hey,' he says. 'I've just remembered. You said, "first present."'

'Well?'

'The blowjob was the first present, right?'

'You make me sound like a whore.'

'But you are. That's why I love you.'

'And you're a prick. That's why I love you.'

'So, come on. What's my second present?'

'I was going to give it to you later.'

'Forget that, what about my present?'

Linda laughs that sexycloggy laugh of the smoker that Tom always finds so attractive.

'Okay.'

She reaches under the bed and drags out a hefty, gift-wrapped package.

'Give me a hand, Tom. It's heavy.'

He rolls over her and lifts it onto the bed.

'Shit, that's heavy. I like presents that weigh a lot.'

'Well, open it.'

'Patience, patience. I'm admiring the presentation.'

He slowly and meticulously begins to unwrap the present by carefully unpeeling the Sellotape.

'Oh, for God's sake, open the damn thing,' says Linda and she rips the remaining paper off with a single flourish, revealing a large, sturdy, metal box.

He looks at her, he looks at the box, he looks at her again.

'Do I know what's in here?'

'Maybe. Maybe not. Open it.'

He lifts the lid and is confronted by endless bundles of twenty-pound notes. He looks at one of them and William Shakespeare looks back.

Amongst the notes, he finds an A4 envelope containing three expired passports bearing three different names but with the same photo in each, three First World War medals with the original ribbons still attached, and an ID tag bearing the name 'Marvin Casey'.

'Shit,' says Tom, 'the Canadian who was forked to death.'

Underneath the medals is an old black-and-white photo of two boys dressed in rags standing in front of some railings outside a sepia-tinted slum. The older of the two has his arm around the shoulders of the smaller boy and both are smiling at the camera. Ben turns the photo over. In pencil is the inscription, 'Me and my brother Mike.'

There's also an envelope addressed to, 'Plod'.

'Open it,' says Linda.

Inside is a USB stick and a letter.

Hi again, Plod

A quick one, as Pete Townshend once said to Roger Daltrey.

So, you did fuck the sheds.

Congratulations. And it seems to have worked too, 'cos you're still around, celebrating your birthday with Linda. My Linda. Isn't she fabulous? Isn't she the stuff of dreams, the warmth in the dark, the glow in the flame? Isn't she a piece of work? A real piece of work.

You're in love with her. Right? Of course you are. I miss her more than life itself. That's the one thing I hate about death. Apart from that, it's all good.

Okay.

I thought you might like this box of goodies. Recognised a few things, eh? But I thought you might like the USB stick more. It contains the original recordings of my dad, Bobby—all twenty hours of them, some of which I used in the book. I taped him years ago. Thought it might come in handy one day but I never did get around to transcribing it.

Might I suggest getting one of your mates to transcribe and edit them? Then might I suggest turning this into a follow-up, or rather, prequel, to Wet Dreams Dry Lives?

Might I also suggest that you call the new book The Tapes Of Wrath? *I came up with that phrase while in the nick. Pretty neat, huh? Knew immediately it was the perfect title.*

I told Linda to give you this box when, and only when, she knew she either loved you, or, if you're an ugly git, trusted you with her life. Hopefully, it's both, plus you're a handsome devil.

Oh, and tell the guy who edits them to make my dad look like the fuckpig he really was. I'm so glad he's dead.

That's me done. I swear there'll be no more USB sticks.

Enjoy.

Adam

For the first time in two years, Tom Evans feels like a character in an Adam Tate novel.

5456 miles away at a house in Islington, Bobby Tate, in a morphine state of mind, tells Zachariah the story of his life, again, minus the murders of course.

After all, he doesn't want to come across as a complete villain...

THE END

About the Author

Barry Cain was born in Kings Cross, went to school in The Angel and started his journalistic career as a trainee court reporter at Marlborough Street magistrates' court opposite Carnaby Street, working in the same office as Charles Dickens, who was dead at the time. He completed his indentures on the *Evening Citizen* newspaper in Gloucester.

Barry became the entertainments editor on the *South-East London Mercury* in Deptford, where he interviewed the Bay City Rollers and Status Quo, before joining *Record Mirror* at the start of the punk explosion. He toured with The Clash, The Jam and Johnny Thunder, accompanied The Damned on their first trip to New York, saw The Pistols play in America and travelled around Japan with The Stranglers.

After a brief stint as PR for Blondie, The Buzzcocks, Generation X and The Stranglers, Barry wrote the pop columns for the *Daily Record*, *Daily Star* and *London Evening News* and went on the road with, amongst others, Bruce Springsteen, Paul McCartney, The Stones, Bob Marley and The Beach Boys. His experiences are recorded in the book '77 *Sulphate Strip*, which was recently republished, and the sequel, *57 Varieties Of Talk Soup* (a phrase John Lydon used to describe *Sulphate Strip*). But he was still hopelessly devoted to punk. Malcolm McLaren asked him to ghost-write his autobiography, which he did but, due to various legal reasons, it has yet to see the light of day.

In 1980, Barry launched *Flexipop!* magazine which featured an exclusive flexi disc on the cover of each issue by artists like The Jam, Blondie, Madness, Boomtown Rats, The Cure and Motörhead. Alas, it was banned three years later after the police seized copies from WH Smith in Blackpool (long story). He also started *Pop Shop* magazine in 1988 (which ended up in the hands of Robert Maxwell) and *18-Rated* magazine in 1992, again banned by WH Smith for showing a man's bare arse made up to look like Elvis Presley on the cover. He continued to publish a string of official, and unofficial, pop magazines throughout the eighties and nineties before publishing a magazine about (ship!) cruising and becoming a travel writer.

He has recently resurrected *Flexipop!* online, accompanied by a *Best Of* book.

The Tapes Of Wrath is his first novel.

Barry is married, has three sons and lives in North London.

Hornet Books
www.hornetbooks.com
info@hornetbooks.com

Follow us on Facebook
www.Facebook.com/HornetBooksPublishing/